A LOVING THREAT

Justin led Christina to one of the shelters and laid her on the thick cushion of sweet-smelling moss. He lay down next to her, careful to keep her partially beneath him. He stared down at her and unmasked tenderness showed in his eyes, confusing her almost as much as the sweeping warmth that sprang so quickly between them.

"Christina," he whispered, gently brushing his hand over her forehead, then through her hair. "This fear of yours, is it just a maiden's fear, or is there something more?"

She could not answer him through all she felt and she tried to turn from him, but he stopped the movement. "No, don't turn from me, sweetheart. Close your eyes and pretend we're back on ship. I want to know."

"But that's just it," she cried in a whisper. "We're not on the ship and you're not the . . . the Justin that I . . . I—" She stopped, for to finish would be a confession that she was not willing to make.

"Fell in love with?" He smiled. "Christina, I assure you the man you fell in love with is the same man lying with you now."

"No." She denied it adamantly. "He would never . . . never force me."

He ran a hand along her side, stopping once a small shiver swept over her body. "Christina, the only thing I will force is your desire . . ."

CRIMSON RAPTURE

JENNIFER HORSMAN

ZEBRA BOOKS
KENSINGTON PUBLISHING CORP.

ZEBRA BOOKS

are published by

Kensington Publishing Corp.
475 Park Avenue South
New York, NY 10016

First printing: April 1986

Printed in the United States of America

Chapter One

Justin Phillips's unconventional height allowed him
to stare out a rectangular hole in his prison cell to
observe a pair of worn black boots belonging to a
young lady strolling on deck. A hemline of heavy
black bombazine material brushed the tips of the
small boots and told him she was in mourning,
wearing widow's weeds. She stopped in front of his
only opening to the outside world and she turned
toward the sea to stare at the expansive blue space
there, and for this seemingly insignificant freedom, he
envied her.

Unlike the other twenty-three civilian passengers
aboard the HMS *Defiant* traveling to Australia,
Christina Ann Marks had not been able to nap during
this the hottest part of the day, and, always inclined
toward optimism, she stepped out on deck in hopes of
finding a breeze. She knew it was probably ill-advised
to stroll on deck unescorted, without benefit of chap-
eron or companion—the act could in fact incite comment—and had the air in her tiny cabin not been so

insufferably stifling, she would have remained below deck, content with her solitude and a cherished copy of Marvel.

Unfortunately, it was as stifling above as below and not a breeze stirred. The proud British naval ship stood motionless on the smooth blanket of blue ocean beneath a cloudless azure sky and the air remained unnaturally still, exactly as it had been for the past four days. A weather condition the crew called the doldrums. The ship's normally ceaseless rocking motion was gone too and the great ship's sails hung lifeless from its three tall masts. Like a ghost ship, she thought.

The quiet was also complete. Small waves gently lapped against the side of the ship and she could hear her own soft breaths, somewhat labored in the oppressive heat and the cruel tightness of her stays. The sudden sound of a small mouse scurrying along the deck startled her, and she turned, washed in a hot wave of brief panic.

Never in all her seventeen years had she been so hot! The heavy black dress, weighted with a cumbersome petticoat of thick crinoline, absorbed the relentless sun like a magnifying glass. Small beads of perspiration tickled her unmercifully. Her boots felt like braces and she was acutely aware of her feet swelling in protest, crying for freedom. She untied the black ribbon of her bonnet, stole the hat from her head, and began to fan her flushed face, thinking with a sad longing of the carefree windy days roaming the green hills, meadows, and woods of her home, Hollingsborne, in Kent.

Abruptly seized with an irresistible idea, she bit her

lip and anxiously looked in both directions for passersby. The ship seemed deserted and not even a crew
member was in sight. With no further hesitation, she
plopped down on the deck and began removing her
boots and stockings.

Justin knew he had reached the limit of human
deprivation when the highlight of his day was watching the young lady unlace and slip off her boots, then
her stockings. He was shown a brief glimpse of two
slender legs and pale white feet, pinched red where
they had rubbed against the boots. He watched her
toes wiggle with their new freedom, heard a sigh of
contentment, and he chuckled.

"I would say . . . oh, perhaps seventeen or eighteen
years old, much too slender and small for my taste
and from the looks of your hands, I suspect you have
fair features—which some might find pleasing to look
at, if it only weren't for your mousy brown hair.
Unfortunately—and I'm hardly surprised considering
how my luck's been running—I prefer my women tall,
dark, and exotic."

With a sudden pounding of her heart, Christina
looked down both sides of the deserted deck, then
toward the heavens and, not finding anyone or anything, she concluded her mind had finally collapsed
under the burden of her grief. She was about to run
off for the ship's surgeon when the sound of his
amusement forced her eyes to the small hole at her
feet. A pair of dark blue eyes laughed back at her.

"You!" she accused and rather breathlessly. "You
spoke to me!"

"Slow wits to boot," he observed. "Too bad, I was
hoping you might make up in conversation what you

7

lack in appearance."

So stunned that the prisoner dared speak to her, Christina took a full minute to grasp the nature of his insults. "Why . . . why, I never—"

Justin chuckled again, shaking his head. "Close your mouth, sweetheart, it's unladylike."

Her hand flew to her open mouth, her large gray eyes widened enormously. She glanced around the deck in search of the quickest escape route, but spotted a wooden bucket of water instead. She wasted neither a thought nor a second.

Justin howled his surprise as the blessed relief of cool water splashed over his face, down the wide expanse of his bare chest. Nothing could have felt better to him. Nothing with the possible exception of turning the young lady over his knee.

Tension marked Captain Forester's tanned, weathered face and showed in his rigid carriage, as, with telescope to eye, he straightened to his full height and began a routine search of the horizon.

Colonel Carrington, the first officer, stood next to him, gathering all his small patience not to show a certain bemusement. Bemusement resting on the border of scorn. Which in itself was unusual, for his captain rarely solicited any unfavorable judgments from his men, much less scorn.

Captain Forester's long career had been illustrious; he was considered one of the finest officers in His Majesty's royal navy and this despite rumors of Irish ancestry. Not only had he been decorated for valorous conduct numerous times, most noteworthy during the great Admirals Jervis and Nelson's campaign against

France and Spain in the battle of Saint Vincent, but his men considered him exceptionally fair and worthy of respect; few would willingly sail with anyone else.

The captain lowered his glass, though kept his narrowed gaze on the distance. "Nothing but empty ocean, vast and endless and barren."

"I daresay, it shall remain that way," Carrington added with but a bare hint of exasperation.

The captain turned to his subordinate and stared unkindly, seeing the tall lean man's reckless confidence, the sentiments he was trying to hide.

The colonel in turn shifted uncomfortably under such scrutiny. "With all due respect, sir," he sought to explain, "I can't help but believe your fears are unfounded."

"A fool's wish," the captain replied bluntly. "Believe me, young man, it is just a matter of time. Justin Phillips's ships—two, maybe three, of the boldest sailing ships known—are out there and, at this very moment, held motionless by the exact same weather. And we shall see them at first wind."

"Perhaps the swine had abandoned their leader," he suggested. "After all, one hardly expects a virtue such as loyalty from such disreputable creatures."

"That's precisely what my superiors thought when I tried to warn them. But no, the collective concern from the king down to the magistrates officiating at Mr. Phillips's trial was expedience. Get the wretched matter over as quickly as possible before popular opinion turned completely to make Mr. Phillips into a hero, some kind of modern-day Robin Hood."

"A hero?" Carrington questioned incredulously. "That bastard is the basest of criminals, a notorious

9

traitor to both his country and his heritage, operating from the lowest principle of self-interest. He's made a fine fortune pirating anything with a British or French flag, playing both sides against the other; playing us for fools!" And the worst crime as far as he was concerned, "Profiting off the war!"

"And getting away with it." Captain Forester pointed out. Justin Phillips indeed had played both countries for a pack of bloody fools, amassing a fortune doing it. England was at war with France and both countries desperately depended on American shipping for supplies. There were demands in both countries for anything an American ship could hold, especially munitions. Each country, in turn, had outlawed American shipping to the other country. Besides outraging the citizens of the young republic, all this had done was create ideal conditions for any man bold enough to risk smuggling. Justin Phillips was such a man. He had started off as a smuggler, quickly making a fortune and quadrupling the number of his ships.

It wasn't enough for the young man. He started one of the most cunning pirating operations the world ever had the misfortune to bear. Typically he would smuggle munitions to the French. No sooner would the transfer of goods and money be done when another of his ships would pirate the goods back. Then the same munitions would be sold to England, thereby leaving Justin Phillips with twice what was already an outrageous profit. If it only went this one way, the situation would not have been so bad, but just as many times France ended up owning the goods and if the results weren't so devastating for England, the story might have been humorous.

Carrington was using the pause in their conversation to contemplate the amount of money lost to Justin Phillips's deviousness. "Does he really own thirteen ships?" he asked no one in particular. "And how could he have gotten away with it for so long? What an unscrupulous bastard. Even in his own country, mind you! Why, there are rumors Phillips takes American ships, traitor to his new country as well as the old."

"Only American slavers," the captain said in defense of Phillips, explaining. "And having personally smelled the stench of death on those ships—that is one offense any decent man would forgive, nay even commend Phillips for."

"Hmmm." Carrington dismissed this without consideration. "Slavers or not, the man deserves hanging and had he not been the bastard son of the high and mighty Lord Winston Phillips, that is exactly what he would have got."

Stroking his neat gray beard, Captain Forester hardly listened to his first officer's tirade, sentiments he had heard so many times before. It hardly mattered. What mattered was that at some point the HMS *Defiant* would battle Justin Phillips's ships. Not only would the *Defiant* lose such a battle but the safety of the civilian passengers would be at grave risk. Passengers that included a lord and two ladies, as well as half a dozen innocent women.

"England should have turned Mr. Phillips over to France for French justice." Carrington continued to muse out loud. "As much as any decent Englishmen loathes the French, one does have to admire how

11

quickly they sever a traitor's head." The idea of Phillips meeting this demise pleased him, and a wry smile lifted on his thin lips. Only to disappear when he encountered the captain's irritated, rather displeased look.

"Colonel Carrington, in the future you will spare me your speculations, unless by some unprecedented happenstance, they provide something I might find useful. I'll have the work schedule on my desk in the hour. Dismissed."

"Yes, sir," Carrington replied icily with a reddening face as he straightened formally and turned about-face to walk away.

Watching him go, the captain sighed and then, ignoring the heat shimmering in waves around him, he turned back to the sea and was soon lost in contemplation.

"Captain?" a small voice beckoned minutes later.

"What?" the captain nearly yelled, swinging abruptly around, unpleasant thoughts having raised his dander.

Startled visibly, Christina flushed and froze, and quickly lowered her eyes. She tried to speak but no sound was forthcoming.

"Oh lord, Miss Marks, forgive me, please," the captain quickly apologized, "I had no idea it was you." He watched Christina struggle still and thought again how the lovely young lady was the shyest creature he had ever had chance to meet. She had not spoken two words the entire voyage and now, the first time she tried to address him, he snaps at her like she was a young green ensign, scaring her senseless no doubt. "Come now, young lady, I swear I didn't mean

12

to scare you like that." His voice softened. "Do forgive me now."

It was all Christina could do not to run away; she barely managed a nod. How could she have thought to bother the captain over such a petty incident? He had infinitely more important things on his mind: managing the ship and crew, concerns over the severe weather and all . . .

"Did you want something, miss?" the captain asked encouragingly.

"Yes," she whispered in the small voice, keeping her head lowered, her eyes fastened to the deck. "I'm sorry for interrupting you, sir . . . but I—" A hand reached to her mouth as she attempted to clear her throat, always striving for a louder voice that was forever out of reach. "I was strolling by on deck and the prisoner spoke to me as I passed. He made rather rude comments and . . . and, thinking of other passengers, I thought you might want to know," she finished in a whispered rush and turned quickly to leave.

"Ah, Miss Marks." The captain stopped her retreat, hoping to pull her into a conversation. Her struggle quite easily broke his heart. All his officers had tried to pay her court, each man lured by a delicate beauty, large translucent gray eyes, the promise hidden under her dark mourning clothes. Each in turn had given up. So shy, she sometimes even lacked the courage to reply to addresses made to her. "What was it Mr. Phillips said to you?"

Christina waved her hand in dismissal of the remarks. "Oh . . . it was really nothing."

"Well, perhaps I ought to speak to him. You be on

your guard now, walking that way. Might even avoid that area altogether. Mr. Phillips is a notorious devil, you know."

Christina shifted with sudden alarm. Would the captain punish the prisoner for the slight impertinence? She had just wanted to warn the captain, thinking only of other passengers. Concerned, she overcame her temerity and raised her gaze. "You're . . . you're not going to punish him, are you?"

"Heavens no, lass. Mr. Phillips will receive his due, this life and the next. The young man's headed to a prison in Queensboro to serve a life sentence for high treason. Didn't any of you people in Kent hear of Mr. Justin Phillips?"

Relieved, Christina shook her head. She apologized again for interrupting him, curtsied, and left. Watching the gentle swish of her skirts, the captain wondered how such innocence would fare in the new and untamed world. Her father, the Reverend Marks, had recently passed on, leaving his daughter no other choice than to journey to Australia to take up residence with her only living connections, an uncle and his family.

An elderly woman—apparently the Reverend Marks's housekeeper—had seen Miss Marks off, and the old woman had confided the girl's unfortunate circumstances to him. Miss Marks's uncle was a farmer in a relatively isolated area of Australia and not very successful. While Chancey Marks agreed to accept his Christian duty by taking his niece into his home, Christina would have to work as a common field hand. The idea seemed at once absurd and cruel; she had been raised a lady, educated and well bred.

14

Why, her hands had probably never lifted anything heavier than a tea pot, or toiled with anything more arduous than embroidery! He could not imagine such a gentle creature working from sunup to sundown, pulling potatoes from an unyielding soil.

Lord have mercy, he shook his head.

One glance down and a shocking realization clamored into Christina's mind. She had addressed the good captain in bare feet! Had he noticed her imprudence? No, he surely would have said something, especially considering the indiscretion came from a young lady in her period of mourning.

She glanced quickly around, thankfully found the deck still empty, and with a rush of skirts, she raced back to find her boots. She stopped dead in her tracks. They were gone!

"Looking for something, Miss Marks?" Justin asked unseen, after having overheard her conversation with the captain.

Christina bit her lip in vexation, immediately perceiving the problem. He had taken her boots. She could hardly solicit help in retrieving them, for that would mean admitting to having taken them off in the first place.

"You have my total sympathy, Miss Marks. You do seem to face a monumental problem. God knows what people will think of you after learning of such wanton, careless behavior. Imagine! A young lady removing her shoes and permitting a man—a hardened criminal no less—a glimpse of her bare feet. And furthermore, from the looks of these boots I'm holding, I'd wager they're your only pair, which in turn brings me to yet

15

another unfavorable conclusion. In addition to poor looks and slow wits, you have little enough fortune to recommend you to the state of matrimony—"

"Please," she whispered, frightened and unable to hear his cruel comments, comments she could easily believe about herself. "Please give them over."

"Not a chance."

"Ohhh . . . Mr. . . . Mr.—"

"Justin."

"Whatever could you want with my shoes?"

"Tell me your Christian name," he demanded.

She cast an anxious glance in both directions, then replied, "Christina."

"Well, Christina, permit me to explain my situation and the favor I'd ask for the return of your boots. I have never in all my twenty-eight years been so bored . . ."

He proceeded to list the ways in which he had coped with imprisonment so far; twice daily he completed two hundred pull-ups on an overhanging beam, two hundred push-ups, stood on his hands for over an hour, and then, being intimately familiar with Indian religions, he meditated for hours on end, "Though unfortunately," he added, "I rarely find the peace that most other people practicing what is called yoga seem to do. And so I turn to mathematics, both mundane types of figuring and difficult equations . . ."

The list seemed endless and Christina listened avidly to this monologue, confused and quite anxious, not at all understanding what this had to do with her boots. Though his remarkable ingenuity and cleverness was noted, especially considering his circumstances. He was obviously an uncommonly intelligent man. Her father had read many reports from India, some on Indian mysticism and she might have inquired about the subject had she been able to think with her heart pounding so.

"So you see, Christina," he finally concluded, "I'm forced to blackmail you into doing me a favor."

"What would you have me do?"

"Bring me a few books. I'm dying for something to read."

"Oh, goodness." She smiled, the first smile in long months. "You certainly asked the right person. I've brought half a trunk full of books. It was the only thing I permitted myself to take of my father's because . . . well, I'm told that there are no books in Australia, that the sin of illiteracy abounds—" She stopped and blushed, realizing abruptly she had quite forgotten herself. Perhaps owing to the fact that she couldn't see him or that he couldn't see her, she had—without a thought—overcome her shyness! She had just spoken to him like other people speak to each other, like . . . like how she had always wanted to speak . . .

Justin grinned. "Well, I can hardly believe my luck finding a young lady with a trunk of books. I had thought you'd have to beg, borrow, or steal. Do I have a selection?"

"Oh yes. I'm sure I might find something you like—"

"I prefer philosophy, especially political philosophy and history."

"I'll see what I might find." She started to rise but remembered her bare feet, looked in both directions, and knelt again. "Might I have my boots back," she

17

whispered. "I promise not to let you down."

Justin reached a hand through the hole to touch a long braided rope of hair that had fallen when she knelt, coiling neatly in front of him. He had never seen hair like that. It seemed there was no end to it, at least two feet of thick braided hair. The color struck him most though, a blondish red flame like gold on fire. "Christina," he asked suddenly, "what do you look like?"

Christina hardly heard his question. She stared at the hand stroking her hair, bronze-colored, lean and calloused, his hand spoke at once of strength, while the intimacy of his gesture brought a flush rising from the tips of her toes to the very roots of her hair.

"Hmmm?" He smiled unseen. "Might I have been mistaken about your looks?"

"I'm . . . I'm afraid not," she assured him softly. "I truly don't have very much to recommend me, as you had guessed." Being plain of face was not the worst of it, she knew. Her social awkwardness and ineptitude, what others thought of as shyness, was by far her worst and most debilitating fault. A fault strangely missing with Justin Phillips.

"Every woman has something—at least one thing— to recommend her and you, Christina," his voice softened, "have this hair. It's beautiful. Like silk through my fingers." He withdrew his hand reluctantly, ignorant of the warm blush his compliment caused. "Back to your question. I'm afraid I can't return your boots yet. These boots are worth their weight in gold. It's my only guarantee you'll return."

"Yes, of course, I quite understand," she replied, recovering somewhat and standing up. She would just have to hope no one would see her. "I'll return soon."

Christina never saw the lift of his brow, the smile that followed, as Justin suddenly realized he had just met a most sympathetic and sweet young lady, all plainness aside.

Christina sat in Lady Everett's more spacious cabin after the midday meal, reading out loud at the lady's request. The lady lay reclined on the divan, a cloth dipped in salt water cooling her face, while Hanna, her maid, methodically waved a large ostrich feather over the bed. Lady Knolls lounged in a nearby chair, while her maid, Elsie, knelt in front to work on the lady's nails. All pretended to listen to Christina's soft voice as she read to them.

The HMS *Defiant* had remained motionless on a glasslike blanket of windless sea for another long week and the situation had soon become dangerous. Supplies dwindled; apparently less than two weeks worth of food and water remained. Supplies were rationed daily and the captain warned that even if the wind picked up immediately, it would be at least another two weeks before the ship reached the shores of Australia.

Tension soared among the passengers and crew alike. Christina, who had just endured a meager—though she thought certainly adequate—meal with the other passengers, was beginning to be embarrassed by their incessant complaining. How could people fail to grasp the necessity of food and water rationing? How could the good captain be held culpable for a situation orchestrated by fate, one that might only be changed by the hand of God?

19

Christina read as best she could, thankful for the peacefulness that settled on the room. The ladies would soon indulge in an afternoon nap; Hanna and Elsie would also retire, as would most of the crew, and then she would be free to visit Justin.

Lady Carolyn Knolls leaned back in a miserably uncomfortable chair as Elsie finished her nails and she stared at the small gathering and thought—not for the first time—what a pathetic lot they were. Lady Everett, in a ridiculously absurd state of undress, looked old and haggard, her normally stout, solid frame sagging wearily in the severe heat. At least the old hag was silent and for this she was glad. God knew how that high shrill voice could shatter nerves.

She gasped suddenly and then glared at Elsie for scraping her fingers. Even the wretched servants were becoming infuriatingly indolent with the unpleasant conditions on board ship. It was bad enough to have to endure this voyage in the first place, leaving every small comfort behind, but to have to endure such insufferable society—Lady Everett of all women, this awkward little Miss Marks, old boring men like Lord Henry and Captain Forester—well, it was nearly intolerable. Should anyone—anyone!—ever know exactly how bad it was, she would surely be ruined socially.

She sighed, leaned back, and closed her eyes, cursing fortune and fate, this miserable world, cursing most of all the tiresome journey. How had she ever gotten to this point. In the beginning the plan had seemed perfectly flawless. It would have succeeded, too, had not the barest hint of scandal crept through the gossip monger's mouths. Scandal enough to force

20

her to accept Lady Everett's invitation to Australia—
of all ungodly places—until the odious speculations
on Lord Knolls's untimely death subsided somewhat.
Those stupid idiots! Of course she had married the
old lord for his money. Why else would a beautiful
young lady marry anyone? And she had had everything then: wealth, position, a whole string of adoring
lovers, and if only . . .

It had started when, to her shock, Lord Knolls
insisted on his marriage rites. She had assumed from
the start that he was simply too old, never imagining
the old gizzard could perform, not even in his wildest
dreams. She had laughed at him then, the mere
thought of his crooked old hands on her flesh was as
absurd as it was disgusting.

She shivered slightly, remembering his face torn
with pained humiliation—as well it might—but then
his anger, threats and the ultimatum. She had had no
choice. No, no, not really. Once Charles, her current
lover, suggested the obvious solution to the problem,
she had not been able to get it out of her mind. She
had tried—oh how she tried—but the thought persisted and persisted and persisted, until it became an
obsession.

After all the lord had been terribly old . . .

"Miss Marks," Lady Everett abruptly interrupted
in a tired voice and without condescending to look up,
"do read with a bit more inflection."

The lady's reprimand visibly shook Christina and it
took a moment to recover. The lady insisted on
finding fault with her every movement and manner.
Hanna had sworn her lady's criticisms only meant to
instruct, given without malicious intent and "do for-

give the Lady 'er trumps. She don't know 'ow she sounds and really, she does it to everyone, she does." Christina had her doubts and, owing to her nature, she could not help but take each criticism to heart.

Hanna shrugged her plump shoulders, winked, and smiled sweetly. Christina returned the smile, gained some courage back, and began reading again. But she continued to steal quick glances up, waiting for the lady to drift to sleep. This with an impatience she had never before known.

In the total of seventeen years, Christina had had only one friend and that had been her father. She had loved him tremendously and she considered him the wisest of men; worthy of respect, admiration, and her complete devotion. Since his death, her mind, body, and soul ached with the debilitating pain of his loss. She would miss him the rest of her life.

She never expected her heart's void to be filled by Justin Phillips.

Three times each day, before anyone rose in the morning, during everyone's naps in the afternoon heat and after everyone retired, she stole a visit to Justin's small opening to the world. She brought him books daily. He read voraciously; his appetite was insatiable. Though he had already read most of the books she brought—his education seemed to have been the finest—he found it worthwhile to reread them.

After each book they shared their thoughts and the discussion at night often lasted well past the midnight hour. She hung on his every word, compelled and intrigued by his thoughts. His ideas seemed iconoclastic in the extreme. Ideas her father would disown her

22

for even listening to, yet alone sometimes agreeing with. She did not often think of what her father would have done to her had he ever lived to learn of her liaison with Justin.

While at first their secret talks were limited to the intellectual, they soon transcended into the personal. She could hardly believe the life he had lived, a life vastly different from hers and ever so adventurous. She loved listening to his descriptions of the many different people and lands he had known, and at times she felt she relived the adventures and experiences to find enchantment, intrigues, and mysteries in his telling. She especially loved his stories of the young republic of America, a country he called home.

She forgave Justin his crimes, and while for the most part she lacked the necessary presumptive authority to judge another, the matter had been completely settled once she had asked if he had any regrets in his heart. Justin had laughed and had assured her that any thinking man has regrets, though as far as his crimes against the crown, "No, sweetheart, I have no regrets and, given the opportunity to do it all over again, I'd not hesitate." He scorned England's imperialistic colonial practices, her callous disregard and stealing of wealth and riches of the conquered lands, especially England's attempt to control America's future. "I could have no regrets about stirring up all the trouble. And," he smiled unseen, "I'm only too glad to make a fortune doing it."

Each passing day Justin became more special to her and each passing day her anxiety increased. It was not the thought of her liaison being discovered—an event that spelled certain disaster—but rather, she could not bear the thought of Justin spending the rest of his life behind bars. This concern grew to a point that at night she lay in her small bunk shedding tears for Justin, praying for God or even fortune to find a way to free him. And secretly—she could not even tell him this—she greeted each windless day with thanks and relief, for it meant yet another stall, another day to share with him.

Lady Everett finally dropped off and, with a heavy sigh, Lady Knolls rose, interrupting Christina's reading. Christina watched the lovely woman smooth her pretty pink silk day dress—so incongruent with the oppressive air of the ship—and leave the cabin without so much as a nod in her direction. Elsie followed obediently, silently. Christina set down the book and lifted her reticule. Her purse was filled with bread and cheese from her midday meal for Justin. She grasped her ever-present sketchbook and, with a soft rustle of skirts, followed Hanna from the cabin.

Hanna whispered in the dark hall, "I half thought she'd never drop off and oh me aching back." She stretched like a cat and then sighed, "Kin 'ardly wait to loosin' me stays—don't know 'ow I kin be gettin' thinner what with not eatin' proper and all, and yet my corset feels like 'tis gettin' tighter."

Another lady might have found the reference to undergarments vulgar but Christina thought such boldness remarkable, wonderfully remarkable, that was all. "The flesh swells to heat," she quietly suggested.

"Aye, that it does and I'm near swelling to burst. Are you comin' to rest?"

"No." She glanced nervously down the empty hall.

24

"I think I shall remain about, reading or sketching."

"I 'aven't a clue as to where you get your stamina but, Christy," Hanna kissed her cheek sweetly, "I 'ave to thank you. You're a regular angel of mercy, you are—w'at with all your kindness to me and the misses."

"Oh," Christina waved her hand in dismissal, whispered, "it's nothing, really."

"It 'tis to me." Hanna smiled. "Well, see ya later."

Christina watched Hanna disappear down the hall to their cabin, and oblivious to the climbing temperature, she nearly ran to the stairs leading on deck, leading to a small hole of happiness.

Two more days passed uneventfully, except for smaller rations, which predictably led to increasing distress among the passengers. Most of the passengers, the captain, and the ship's surgeon began to notice Christina's quiet fortitude, thoughtfulness, and kindness, the way she was always willing to administer to everyone's needs first. She never complained, and those rare times she spoke out loud it was to voice optimism and hope. Not the least of the people considering Christina an angel of mercy was Justin.

The afternoon sun had just began to sink slowly toward the horizon and Christina, sitting on an overturned bucket, listened to Justin's heated argument concerning Hobbes's *Leviathan*. He spoke passionately and she smiled to herself, thinking how much he sounded like her father on the pulpit.

Justin was enjoying himself too and at times the very fact amazed him, for never in all his imaginings had had he thought to find such an unexpected friendship with a young lady of her restricted background. Her fondness for him was returned twofold: He felt the affection an older brother might feel for a younger sister toward her. He was also incredibly grateful for her books, the extra food she brought, as well as their conversation. She was unquestionably the kindest and most gentle young lady he had ever known. And then, too, he had never enjoyed a woman's intellectual facilities as much and, while her naïveté and irrational idealism constantly amused him, he admired her brightness, the breadth of her education through books.

As soon as his men rescued him from this hellhole, he would offer Christina passage to anywhere she wanted to go in the world. He certainly had enough connections to set her up in any position she might want, as a governess, shopkeeper, lady of leisure— whatever. If she still wanted to journey to Australia to stay with her uncle's family, then he'd give her a trust fund with enough money so that she'd never be in want of anything. He'd also make certain she could always reach him in the event she needed something.

Lost to his pontifications, Justin launched into an attack of man's greatest crime against humanity— that of slavery—and Christina could hardly believe she was hearing her father's exact sentiments voiced again, though even more astutely. So taken by what she perceived as a growing, even uncanny similarity between Justin and her father, she almost failed to stop Justin in time.

Lady Everett and Lady Knolls strolled toward her, out for an unprecedented stroll before supper and followed as always by Elsie and Hanna. The ladies' gaily colored day dresses, the fashionable hats, and colorful parasols looked bizarrely ostentatious against the lifeless air of the ship and somehow accentuated rather than hid the two pale and tired faces of the owners.

Christina quickly tapped her boot against the wall, warning of people approaching. Justin immediately fell silent. Elsie winked conspiratorially but Christina quickly lowered her eyes, bracing for the inevitable. Sure enough, as the party reached speaking distance, Lady Everett cast a disapproving look toward Christina and wasted no time in voicing her complaint.

"Why, Miss Marks!" she exclaimed at once. "What in heaven's name are you doing in this sun without a proper bonnet?"

Christina stole a furtive look up to confront Lady Everett's stern face, then Lady Knolls's condescending nod. She dared not reply and she swallowed, feeling her cheeks flush.

"Well, my word," the lady continued. "Have you no wits, child? You will surely catch a sun rash, my dear, to say nothing of ruining your complexion. Run along now and fetch a bonnet, then join us for tea. You spend far too much time alone, my dear, and if I say so, it's most unnatural for a young lady of your age and circumstances."

Justin swung down to his small cot, waiting to hear Christina politely, though nonetheless curtly, tell the lady to mind her own concerns. He was intimately familiar with the woman's tone of condescension and he loathed it perhaps more than all other banalities common to his class.

But he heard only silence.

A pained expression crossed Christina's features,

she nodded, and then quickly left. Once beneath the deck she leaned against the wall, trying to stop the hot sting of tears. How she hated herself at those moments! Hated her childish inability to make proper addresses, indeed any address! Hated the way her body flushed, then froze, the way her tongue became as immobile as an inert block of wood!

Why couldn't she be like others, like Elsie or Hanna? She shared quarters with Elsie and Hanna, along with two other young ladies, Marianna and Katie. At first she had been amazed, but then envious of their easy manners, the gay and carefree way they had of just being. How she envied the buxom young Hanna, her plump and smiling face, a head crowned with untamed red curls and Elsie, Hanna's opposite in appearance—small and dark and cute, the way they always had fun with their mistresses's shenangians, making others laugh and chatting so easily. How she wanted to be like them! To be like she was with Justin . . .

Justin had been a bit taken aback by Christina's wordless departure, but was surprised even more by the ladies' comments that followed.

"Such a shy young lady," Lady Everett mused. "God knows how the unfortunate creature will survive in the New World, having to fend for herself in a family she knows nothing about—people she's never even met before."

"Undoubtedly of the lowest society," Lady Knolls bothered to add.

"Undoubtedly. It's a shame her late father failed to arrange a marriage for her before he departed— Hanna!" she nearly shrieked in the same breath. "Do keep the parasol over my person!"

"Yes, ma'am."

"The captain has assured me," she resumed quickly, "that most all of the young men on board have had an interest in Miss Marks—one is forced to see she'd be quite a lovely thing if she'd do something with that hair—but he says her social awkwardness turns each man away."

"That is a shame," Lady Knolls smiled cruelly, "for if the chit is suited to any one thing, it's bearing some man a string of brats."

"Hmmm." Lady Everett seemed to agree. "Well, I daresay, one can't blame the young men. Why, I can hardly get a word from her myself except when she reads out loud, and my! Her terror whenever anyone tries to address her."

Hanna was unable to stand another word. "Aye, Miss Marks be a shy creature for sure but she is lovely and you know, my ladies," she felt suddenly bold, "Elsie and myself, we share quarters with 'er and 'tis true, she 'ardly ever says a word, but she's very thoughtful and sweet like. Just think of all she does for everyone! A real angel of mercy, she is and, why, we've taken quite a fancy to 'er, we 'ave."

"Exactly what one might expect," Lady Knolls commented dryly, her meaning implied.

"Oh, me lady, you're being unkind now." Elsie too felt compelled to scold. "Miss Marks be a lady for sure, she just 'asn't any airs is all—"

"Elsie." Lady Everett's shrill voice rose. "I do hope your impertinence is due to this tiresome journey. You're quite forgetting your manners . . ."

The ladies' voices drifted off as they resumed their

stroll. Somewhat confused, Justin had never known this side of Christina, a side that never manifested when with him. He knew her as a most gentle young lady, intelligent and sweet, incapable of harboring a harsh sentiment toward anyone or thing, but shy? Socially awkward, unable to stand up to anyone? Nor had he imagined others found Christina pretty. She had said she was plain and so he had always thought of her as homely, probably as homely as they come . . .

Christina returned that night and, as always, she brought Justin food. Tonight a roll, a hard egg, a potato, and a small container of stew. He received only a daily bowl of mush and he often thought he'd starve if it were not for Christina's supplements. Tonight, however, before she had even taken her seat on the overturned bucket, he began questioning her.

"Christina, why didn't you speak up to that woman today?"

She swallowed hard, whispered, "What do you mean?"

"Well, sweetheart, pardon the expression, but that lady needed a swift kick in the ass. I didn't like the tone she used with you, the condescension she implied and I especially didn't like the way you ran off so quickly to do her bidding."

"Oh . . . well . . ."

"Surely you found her offensive, ordering you about like a child?"

"No . . . well, yes. Yes I do sometimes. Though I'm told by Hanna she doesn't really mean anything by it."

"Why didn't you say something?"

30

"I . . . I have difficulty speaking to others," she whispered still.

"You don't seem to have any difficulty speaking to me."

"No I don't but I'm not like this with other people. I don't know why, but well, with you it's just so easy for me. Maybe because we've never seen each other before, but there's something about you—the way you are—it's like I know you're not judging me unkindly." She struggled to say the next words, "I've never had a friend like you before."

And then it began to dawn on him how special he was to her, and after a thoughtful pause, he replied honestly, "I've known literally hundreds of women and, Christina, you're by far one of the brightest and certainly the most pleasant company. And I know you're capable of making friends and passing social pleasantries. So what seems to be the trouble?"

"I . . . I don't really know," she managed, always affected to the core by his smallest compliment. She squeezed her handkerchief, and then suddenly rushed forward with words. "Oh Justin, I've tried to be like others so many times! How I envy others like Elsie and Hanna their easy manners, idle chatter and all. My father used to think the characteristic admirable in a girl, I mean being quiet and all, but as I grow older even he began to see there was something wrong with me."

"I don't understand," he said hesitantly, for needless to say the problem was alien to his experience. "Is it that you don't know what to say to people?"

"That's the odd thing. I always know what I should or might say to others, but somehow—as soon as I see

31

them—the words choke inside, and I become all flustered, embarrassed, my heart races so, and oh, Justin, I'm really just . . . so inept and . . . clumsy."

Justin hated her self-deprecation and he felt a sudden urge to draw her into his arms for comfort while gently scolding her for speaking of herself like that. He was just about to suggest something when her boot kicked the wall and hard.

Colonel Carrington and one of his mates, Stephens, had stepped on deck to enjoy the only slightly cooler, still night air and a bottle of whiskey. They strolled leisurely toward her spot and Christina, wearing black and hidden in dark shadows, pressed herself against the wall in hopes they would pass without noticing her.

Carrington abruptly spotted her hidden against the wall. "Why, Miss Marks." He bowed politely. "A pleasant good evening to you."

Christina cast a quick glance up to the two gazes appraising her through the darkness and she nodded slightly. Without a word, she rose and disappeared quickly down the deck.

Carrington shook his head in frustration, then pushed his hands through his thick dark curls. "That one would drive a sober man to drink—haven't got a damn word from that pretty mouth yet."

"Aye, you're not the only one striking out. I don't know anyone who's gotten anywhere with her. And from the looks of what's beneath that skirt," Stephens chuckled, "it's a darn shame too."

"She is most definitely ripe for the picking. One of the loveliest little creatures I think I've ever seen—even in those appalling rags of hers."

"If she wasn't such a scared mouse, I'd be the first one up those skirts."

"The second," Carrington assured him.

Justin had certainly heard baser comments in his lifetime but because Christina was the subject, he felt his muscles tense and his blood rise to a quick boil. Given any freedom, he would not hesitate to make any man regret the mere thought of her in that way. And this surprised him, for he had never felt especially protective toward any woman. He supposed the feeling was due as much to Christina's femininity and gentleness as it was to the nature of their relationship.

"What was that?" Justin asked Christina the next night, hearing a faint grumbling sound.

Christina swallowed her panic. "I didn't hear anything. Justin, I was wondering—"

"Be still a moment," he ordered, suddenly suspicious and wanting his suspicions confirmed. To Christina's horror the sound came again and he exploded, "Damn you, Christina! You've been lying to me about this food, haven't you? This isn't food left over from the others!"

"Justin, no . . . I—"

"You've been giving me your rations! Starving yourself for me—"

"Oh, but Justin, I don't need very much, honestly—"

"I assure you, young lady," he began harshly, furious at himself, "I am perfectly capable of fending for myself. I don't need some slip of a girl to—"

"Please don't be angry at me! I just can't bear it—" And demonstrating the truth of this, she ran

33

quickly away.

Captain Forester stormed into his cabin and, before anyone could rush in with another catastrophe, he shut and locked his door. He went immediately to the large oak desk and withdrew a silver flask of rum. He pressed it to his lips, swallowed several times without tasting, and then felt the hot burst of fire in his stomach.

He was afraid. Everyone lived in fear, a tightening knot of dread in their stomach. Fights broke out hourly among the crew. He had already confined nine men to their quarters for insubordination. Left exhausted, worn and listless from the meager rations and the severe heat, passengers remained in their quarters, moaning their fate. Stretching food and water to minimum, they had a mere handful of days left.

A mere handful of days. What to do? What to do?

Owing to Christina's nature, she wasn't suffering as much as the others, or if she was no one ever heard about it. She busied herself helping others from dawn to midnight, pulling and transporting bucket after bucket of cool salt water for the brief comfort of a bath, serving the meager rations personally to those who could no longer rise from bed. She became the right arm of the overburdened, exhausted ship surgeon, Dr. Michaels. She surprised everyone, for no one had suspected that such a delicate young lady possessed such a strong constitution. She even managed to overcome her temerity to promise everyone the wind would rise any time now to feed the sails before a real tragedy could happen.

Even she became alarmed the next morning. A vicious fight broke out in her small quarters. She barely understood the initial outburst of words between Elsie and Hanna and Marianna and Katie—something about a chamber pot—but suddenly the women were all screaming at each other, cursing like any group of hardened sailors and then, then Marianna flung the full pot in Elsie's face and Hanna flung herself on Marianna. Like four crazed cats—all claws and teeth—arms and legs flew wildly, hair pulled, bodies knocked against the wall. Stunned, horrified, Christina had never seen anything like it in her life, and finally managed to mobilize her dazed wits to run for help.

She wanted to speak with Justin, always finding comfort with him. But the day rushed forward with one crisis after another. Dr. Michaels himself fell faint in the early afternoon, leaving Christina with the burden of a growing number of patients. She never stopped.

Late in the afternoon, Carrington opted for the short-term relief from both tension and thirst in a bottle of potent rum. He knew well that ultimately, even within a few hours, the rum would make his thirst a raging monster, especially considering the meager substance he, like everyone else, was forced to subsist on. He didn't care. Nor did it matter that the captain had banned all spirits, or that he had stolen the rum from a mate. He was a desperate man, one who had just faced the unbearable reality that he was doomed.

And he was so young! His career, his great ambitions, indeed his whole life had stretched before him.

All was lost, stolen by a dark unpleasant death lying in wait around the corner.

For the better part of an hour the rum fueled an impotent rage as he lay on his bunk staring blankly at the four walls, in futile search of some hope, any hope. There was none, though his senses heightened insidiously until it seemed as though death hovered directly overhead. Shadows darkened and the air grew thick and stifling.

He had to escape . . .

The sun had just disappeared on the horizon and the air was a breath cooler when Christina finally managed to steal a few precious moments to talk with Justin. She felt disturbed, a vague restlessness put her on the edge of her seat, despite the hectic and exhausting day. And Justin could hear the strain in her voice as she related the events.

"I've never been more scared in my life." She related the fight that had occurred in her cabin. Like most men, he found physical fights among females at best amusing, at worst disgusting. "And goodness but Marianna needed Dr. Michaels's services and it took Elsie nearly an hour to calm poor Hanna down and my, but it was awful, just awful. I don't know what's happening to everyone. Everyone's behaving so cruelly, so . . . uncivilized."

Justin smiled, for it was exactly what he would expect Christina to think in such a situation.

"Even the ladies are behaving poorly. Do you know what Lady Everett said to Hanna yesterday?"

"No, what?" he asked, not really concerned until he heard it.

"She asked Hanna to give up her water ration to

her, practically making it an order! Can you imagine— Oh no—" she stopped abruptly, looking up to see Mr. Carrington standing just feet away.

"Well, well," Carrington said with a slight slur as he stepped toward her. "It seems the lovely Miss Marks does favor at least one man with her company."

Something was terrible wrong and Christina recognized the trouble. Smiling wryly at having caught her in the act, the man had a crazed look. His hair and uniform were disheveled, perspiration lined his brow, and he seemed at once like a madman. She never hesitated or bothered to reply. She immediately rose to leave but as she stood up, Carrington grabbed her in a painful grasp and jerked her hard around.

"Please . . . let me go!"

"Scream, Christina!" Justin yelled.

A scream rose in her throat, but Carrington clamped his hand hard over her mouth. He shoved her against the wall, knocking the wind from her, and then stopping her struggle by pressing his body into her.

"You bastard! Take your hands off her!"

She squirmed desperately and terrified, she could not catch her breath. She thought for a blessed moment she would faint.

Carrington loosened his hold on her mouth and she gulped in breath. He looked down at the hole, amused by Justin's outrage, his helplessness to do anything about it. "Ah, have no fear, Mister High and Mighty Phillips," he laughed, returning his gaze to Christina's terrified eyes. "I will give you the pleasure of listening as I have this treat."

Carrington's mistake was in thinking Justin was

helpless, for anyone who knew him knew that he was never but never helpless. Justin reached his arm through the hole, managed to find Carrington's booted foot and, like the jaws of a shark, he grabbed the man's ankle and pulled with frightening strength. Caught off guard, Carrington was thrown off balance and fell with a loud thud against the deck.

"Run, sweetheart!" Justin shouted and then, with one merciless strong hand still on Carrington's ankle, he pulled the leg, twisted it through the hole, and pressed down until he heard a sickening crack of bone.

Christina swung open the door of her quarters and burst inside. The door slammed shut. She collapsed to the floor and pulled her knees up into a tight ball, trying first to quiet the pounding of her heart and then to make sense of the furious noises on deck.

Hanna lifted herself onto her elbows and looked curiously at Christina. "Christy! W'at's 'appened to you?"

Christina's eyes lifted to the lower bunk and instantly she flew to Hanna's side. "Oh Hanna—" The story gushed out in a rush of whispered words, all of it—her friendship with Justin, the horrid Mister Carrington's attack, and Justin's rescue.

Hanna's soft brown eyes widened in stages. Christina and Mr. Justin Phillips! She had heard, oh just the most wickedly delicious stories of Mister Justin Phillips and it had been a great thrill just knowing Elsie and she were voyaging on the very ship that carried the man to Australia. But to discover that shy Christina had been talking with him the whole trip long—so that's what she was always doing on deck!—

was about the most exciting, juicy bit of news.

Hanna kicked Elsie's bunk, waking Elsie from a deep sleep. The whole story was quickly repeated. Elsie, who shared Hanna's exact sentiments, looked down at Christina first with incredulity and then respect.

"Why Christina! You and Mister Justin Phillips! Oh goodness, I kin 'ardly believe it!" She clamped her hands together. "Ere we be doomed for sure and you've been 'aving an affair with the very devil 'imself! W'at's 'e like," she asked breathlessly. "W'at's 'e really like?"

Confusion lifted through Christina's distress. They had completely missed the point. "You don't understand! Justin hurt Mister Carrington! He'll be in trouble with the captain! I—" A furious banging sounded on deck interrupting her. There was shouting, running and orders. "What's happening?" Christina cried.

"I'll go find out," Hanna said, climbing down.

"Oh would you?"

"Sure I will," she whispered, grabbing only a flimsy shawl to put over her nightdress and tiptoeing through the door.

In other circumstances even Hanna would never dare venture out among men dressed in flimsy nightclothes. Predictably however, as each windless day passed and added ever increasing increments of desperation to the situation, one by one manners and formalities dropped. Few passengers even rose from bed, yet alone bothered to attend to pretenses, propriety, or appearances.

Elsie took Christina's hand and squeezed it reassuringly, but they remained in anxious silence, waiting and listening to what was now sounding like a furious battle above. Christina kept glancing at the opposite bunks, wondering how in the world Marianna and Katie could sleep through the noise? At one point she thought she heard laughter, Justin's laughter, but surely that couldn't be.

It seemed well over half an hour had passed before Hanna finally slipped back through the door, her dark eyes wide as saucers.

"What happened?" Christina asked, jumping to her feet.

"You won't believe it! I swear you won't! Seems your Mister Phillips broke the bloody bastard's leg. No one kin figure 'ow 'e did it, locked up like that. But oh my, the captain's in a rage, 'e is! 'E ordered Mister Phillips whipped—"

"Oh no!"

"Yes! 'E did! 'E did! But seems it can't be done. That's the ruckus we've been over'earing. Mister Phillips is a fightin' like a wild animal, 'e is and so far 'e's knocked out four of the crew, knocked 'em out cold. The captain orders 'is men in, then Mister Phillips throws 'em out, until now there's not a bloody soul left willin' ta go in!"

"Justin?" She didn't believe Justin was capable of this, of such violence. There was a mistake—

"Yes!" Hanna answered excitedly. "The captain, well, 'e's furious, 'e is. 'E's standin' on deck screamin' 'tis mutiny and that if'n we reach Aussie, 'e'll see 'em all court-martialed and that 'e's a gonna starve Mister Phillips out if 'e don't shoot 'im first—"

"Shoot him!" Christina cried, and hearing the

40

unthinkable, she raced from the cabin. She ran down the dark hall, up the steps, and out on deck. She spotted Captain Forester on the quarterdeck, still shouting orders at his men. In a swift rush of skirts, she climbed the ladder, ran, and fell to her knees before the captain.

"Please Captain Forester," she begged with all the drama her youth afforded, "please don't shoot him! It was all my fault . . ."

Captain Forester interrupted his orders and looked down at Miss Christina Marks's lovely upturned face. Tears streamed down flushed cheeks, making her eyes so misty, so translucent, and, for a brief moment, he could only stare in stupefaction.

My God, what was the girl going on about? Here he was in the middle of an emergency that could cost his ship. He had hardly the time and even less inclination or energy to listen to Miss Marks's trouble, whatever it was, though her sudden rush of words was noted. Like every other passenger and crew member, Miss Marks had finally lost her wits under the strain of events and small wonder too, considering how arduously the young lady worked alongside Dr. Michaels to help others.

"Secure these men to quarters!" the captain shouted, interrupting her lamenting and lifting her to her feet. She seemed most distraught though, her tone of desperation touched his heart even through his far weightier concerns. He was just about to order her off to the overburdened ship's surgeon, or perhaps those women with whom she shared quarters, when, suddenly—by some miraculous intervention—the barest whisper of a breeze blew across the deck.

41

For the response it solicited, the breeze might have been the trumpets of heaven signaling an opening of the gates. Everyone, the twenty or so men standing on deck, the captain, and Christina, stopped and then froze, waiting for senses to confirm the long-awaited phenomenon. Each half feared their dazed and desperate minds might have just played a cruel trick.

But no, it was real. It was real!

Cheers sounded loud and long, mixed with cries of hallelujah, as men jumped up and down hugging and slapping each other on the back. The captain cried too and having lifted Christina to her feet, he embraced her as though she was a long-lost daughter. "We're saved! The Lord has saved us!" and in the same breath, the captain turned to the welcomed labor of starting his ship sailing.

Left suddenly alone, Christina stared first at the captain shouting orders to his excited crew and the abrupt bustling of activity. She stepped quietly to the side of the ship and looked out into the ink-black night. A thousand blinking lights and the cloudy ribbon of the Milky Way laced the vast black night, separating sea and sky. Lanterns on the ship cast long ribbons of light into the water. Ribbons of light that began to move with this wisp of a breeze.

The breeze grew stronger as she stood there. It tickled her skin and blew stray wisps of hair from her face. A chill ran up her spine and she knew, she knew as surely as she drew breath that something tragic waited for her. Waited for everyone.

"Justin!"

She experienced the premonition of a feeling rather than a conscious level and the feeling was one of fear, a panic of startling intensity. She attributed it immediately to a turn of events that would bring Justin to a life in prison. Without a thought that the decks swarmed with men and even other passengers now, she raced to Justin's small hole and flung herself on her hands and knees.

"Justin! Justin," she could barely manage to whisper through her tears.

Justin rose swiftly to his feet. Her voice was just what he wanted to hear. "Christina? Are you all right? Did that bastard hurt you?"

"Me?" She was the last person she was concerned about. "Justin, the wind! It's come, it's finally come!"

"And thank God too. I heard the shouts and I felt the movement and all I can say is thank God! These walls are—"

"But, Justin, we'll reach Australia now and . . . and they'll send you to prison and . . . and I'll never see you again—" She stopped and covered her mouth, her voice choking on her tears.

Justin chuckled, could not help himself. She was by no means the first woman he had reduced to tears but never had he felt taken by such a tender display of emotion and concern.

"What shall we do, Justin? I . . . I just can't bear it—"

"Hold on, hold on, sweetheart," he said softly. "I assure you, I have no intention of spending my life in prison."

"You . . . you don't?"

"No, Christina. Two of my ships are at this very moment probably about fifty miles off and heading

43

this way. My ships have been suffering these same doldrums out there, but now they should be here by tomorrow afternoon, the day following at the latest. I'm a fortunate man." He smiled unseen. "Each of my men would gladly risk his life for me and none of them would ever rest until I was free."

Stunned and then confused, Christina was reduced to silence. He must be imagining things. It was wishful, fanciful thinking or perhaps—she gasped—he had lost his mind.

"How do you know this?" she asked haltingly, "that your ships are out there?"

"It's a rather long story," he shrugged, thinking of his very influential father, Lord Winston Phillips. England would always protect its aristocracy, even at the expense of some principles. While his father could not openly support his bastard rebel son, the old man had certainly operated behind the scenes before, during, and after the trial to make certain his son was both spared a hangman's noose and never saw prison. Not that his father's help had really mattered, for Cajun, Jacob, and the rest of his men would have managed even without help. "Suffice to say, the *Defiant*'s course had been made known and my ships have been paralleling her. They would have been here far earlier, except for the dead weather."

Christina had no idea why this information frightened her far more than it relieved her. "Captain Forester," she thought out loud, "is not going to let you go without a fight."

Justin merely laughed at this. "The *Defiant* stands not a chance against one of my ships, yet alone two. Captain Forester seems a fair and smart man and I'm

44

sure he'll surrender without a fight. But, Christina, I want you to know—"

She suddenly gasped as two strong hands lifted her bodily upright.

"Miss Marks! What in God's name are you doing talking to Mister Phillips!" Captain Forester never gave her a chance to answer. "You should be ashamed, Miss Marks, ashamed—a young lady of your position and background. Well! I've had just about enough out of you! You're to remain in your quarters."

Chapter Two

Justin's dog Beau, a huge Saint Bernard known for his ability to outsmart people and an occasional heroic deed, lifted his body onto the deck rail of the *Athena*. The ship glided effortlessly over eight-foot crests. Sails flapped madly, greedily fed by a strong wind. A gray dawn broke over the open sea and yet a mysterious strip of black settled between the gray sky and the darker sea. For Beau, though, it was the smell; the scent of sea and air were wrong and he barked, growled, and then whimpered, concerned.

Jacob Robbins had just been called on deck, having given the order he was to be awakened as soon as the *Defiant* came into view. Standing alongside Cajun, Jacob looked for the *Defiant* off windward on the far horizon, and once he spotted her, he enthusiastically began a discussion of its easy capture.

The two men, Justin's longtime friends, presented an arresting picture. Nearly as tall as Justin, Jacob had a long and thin, not unhandsome face. A scar slashed across his cheek and many more appeared on his muscled arms and chest, evidence of too many fights. Golden colored skin set off light blue eyes, but he had silver hair and brows. Not gray but rather that pure metallic color of precious metal, a color at direct odds with his youthful face. His father had been a wealthy Italian shipping merchant, his mother of the fiery Irish ancestry, and the only thing he loved more than fighting and ladies was the sea.

Cajun stood in direct contrast to his friend. He possessed a strange, almost mystical air and no one could ever guess his origins from appearance. One might say Oriental from his fine almond-shaped and dark liquid eyes, Indian from the smooth caramel color of his skin, Negro from his unusual height, large white grin, and deep bellowing laughter, and Arab from his famous surprise attacks and the ever-present saber on his side. And always he stood with his legs apart, his arms folded across the huge expanse of his bare chest, seeming as though he was separated from his surroundings, but a passive observer in this world. It was a misleading impression, one that was often a fatal mistake of his enemies.

"Captain!" a man shouted from the lookout, stopping Jacob mid-sentence. "To starboard!"

Jacob and Cajun, along with the rest of the crew, quickly assembled on the starboard. For several moments Jacob simply refused to believe the phenomenon taking shape there, a phenomenon that Cajun prophesied in one of his dreams. Two days ago, Cajun had dreamed of seeing a huge dragon devouring the ships and neither Jacob nor he had known what to make of it.

Like many others, Cajun though had never witnessed the sight and he had no idea what to make of the small stripe of darkness on the gray horizon.

"A storm?" someone finally questioned, breaking the ominous silence.

"If it only was just a storm," Jacob muttered under his breath.

Looking like a gathering from the Tower of Babel, the men remained in an uneasy silence as they watched and waited. Dawn spread slowly against the barren gray desert of ocean. Wings of light reached from one corner to the next, but the darkness, still but a sliver of black on the most distant horizon, remained untouched by sunlight. An impenetrable black void.

"Well, w'at in God's name is it?"

"That mate," Jacob explained, "is the opening to hell."

After weeks of nothing but an empty blue sky and windless sea, a storm was heading their way. All passengers were confined to quarters until further notice, and each passenger had been given ropes to tie themselves to the bunks. While these measures had frightened all the other passengers, Christina's fear grew from a far graver concern.

Despite the captain's warning of danger, there existed a collective calm in her small quarters and the five young women pretended nothing was wrong. Christina sat on Hanna's bunk finding a strange comfort as Hanna took a brush to her loosened hair. Hanna stroked methodically, almost absentmindedly, while she chatted with Elsie, Marianna, and Katie. On the bunk above, Elsie swung stick-thin legs to and

48

fro, rocking with the ship's growing movement, while amusing them with stories of her mistress's ludicrous pretensions, speculating out loud on how Lady Knowles might be faring in the face of danger.

Hanna and Elsie, so brave and unconcerned, Christina thought. They might have all been sitting safely by a warm fire in a cozy parlor back home. How she admired their daring and recklessness.

Like her mother before her, Hanna May Haley had been in service to the Everetts as long as anyone could remember. Elsie had arrived at the house later and the two women, so alike in temperament, had become fast friends.

Christina often marveled at how strikingly similar they were in character while completely opposite in appearance, and once she had tried to render Hanna and Elsie in her sketchbook. Hanna had a tall voluptuous figure, bordering attractively on plumpness. Tight red curls framed her round, pleasing face and her cheeks were always flushed; her bright eyes always danced with laughter. Elsie was her opposite. She was small and thin with an abundance of dark brown hair haloing a pixy-cute face, a face that revealed all the mischief in her heart.

Christina had been dissatisfied with her sketch and had given up. Elsie and Hanna had come out looking somewhat humorous. Somehow her emotions and feelings always prevented her from rendering the stark realism she sought.

No one ever told her this was the gift of an artist.

Marianna and Katie, while laughing softly at Elsie's fun, had a bit more trouble dismissing the increasing motion of the ship. The two women sat

49

closely together, Marianna's arm resting protectively over her friend's shoulder to brace against the rocking. Katie's small white hands wrapped tightly around Marianna's arm. She had tried to be sick but none of them had eaten more than bread rolls and Christina worried as the young lady's pallor blanched whiter still.

Marianna and Katie were both in their late twenties, as close as sisters, and for most of the voyage had kept to themselves. "Katie's all I have in this world," Marianna once said to Christina. The two women had been orphans, raised together in a poor house and eventually had become "house mums" there. While they tried to speak of the poor house with humor, Christina—sensitive to the meaning hidden in the words—knew the humor covered despair and loneliness of two children trapped in an unkind world. Together, they had both opted for marriage by posting in Australia rather than face certain spinsterhood in England. Spinsterhood not the result of their appearance or manner, for indeed both women were fairly attractive and pleasant, and each owned a Christian education. But their lives presented precious few opportunities to meet eligible men.

Katie might even be considered pretty. She was small, with baby-fine chestnut hair and pleasing features, although many scars from a bout with childhood pox marked her skin. Marianna was unnaturally tall for a woman, but her somewhat ungainly features were softened by a warm smile and pretty blue eyes.

Christina could not fathom what Marianna's and Katie's lives would be like. The idea of entering into the sacred union with men one didn't know scared her. The two men were supposedly good Christians and, like Christina's uncle, they each owned small farms not far apart, so at least Marianna and Katie would have the comfort of each other. Christina often wondered, though, what if their husbands were unpleasant or even cruel? What would happen without the protection of family, or indeed even congregation?

Christina would have been shocked to discover that both Marianna and Katie, along with everyone else who could weigh their respective circumstances, saw her own future as far more uncertain and potentially unfortunate.

Hanna lifted Christina's hair to the side and began braiding a small portion, creating a fetching chignon, as she joined Elsie's musing. "Oh aye," she laughed, "I kin just see me mistress and ole 'enpecked 'Enry now—" Hanna called the lord by that affectionate title. "No tellin' w'at ole Lord Henry will do once 'e gets the lady tied to a bunk. No doubt 'tis the poor man's first opportunity in years." With the exception of Christina, they all laughed. "I suspect the ole guy is a avin' the time of is life right about now. Why I kin just 'ear that shrill voice of me lady's: 'Enry, stop it! Stop it I say! I'm warning you . . . Oh! Oh! Oh . . ."

Christina was hardly listening as she turned her cruel fate over and over again in her head. Justin's men would rescue him today and she would never hear of him again. If only she had a chance to view his person. Just once! She would draw him immediately. How she would cherish a picture of him to carry with her always.

She often tried to imagine what he looked like. In

her mind's eye she created a picture of a man not very tall, but medium height like her father. He would possess a slight, perhaps even slender physique, though she could not say why she thought so. Perhaps because his intellectual facilities were so keen and sharp. She dismissed the trouble Justin had caused fighting the crew and Mister Carrington as patently not true. There must be a mistake in the telling. Justin, kind and gentle and so very compassionate, would not be capable of any such violence. Nor would he be handsome, though surely she'd find him attractive with his soft blue eyes, eyes that were at once intelligent and—

A tremendous explosion jolted the ship sharply on its side, throwing Christina, Hanna, and Elsie above hard against the wall. Katie screamed and Marianna hugged her tightly while bracing as though for a blow to the face.

" 'Tis cannon fire!" Elsie cried as she recovered. They all braced themselves and waited, listening to the shouts, orders and running feet heard above, sounds that were small and weak against a fierce howling of wind, rain, and a raging sea.

Captain Forester watched the sleek sailing ship draw boldly alongside the *Defiant*, while the *Hero* drew along starboard. The two ships' cannons were manned, readied, and aimed, seemingly at his very person, as he stood on quarterdeck giving orders. A lifeboat was being lowered into a menacingly churning sea.

"Bring the prisoner to deck," he ordered and then to young Ensign Gibson, "Warn the passengers that we are being boarded by pirates. All cabin doors

52

should be bolted locked."

"Aye, aye!"

The battle had been over before it started. The *Defiant* would lose to one of the ships, two merely assured the end would be quick. There was nothing to be done, save enduring the humiliation of the audacious act.

Young Gibson raced along the dark hall, wet from the rain and nearly shaking with fear. He called into each cabin to explain pirates were boarding the *Defiant*, that the captain ordered all doors bolted and shut.

Christina gasped and stood in mute panic while the other ladies jumped up at once. A heated debate ensued. Hanna and Elsie wanted to catch a glimpse of the pirates and refused to bolt the door. Scared witless, Katie and Marianna not only wanted to bolt the door but also insisted on securing their trunks against it.

Captain Forester felt an impotent fury as he watched Justin Phillips reunited with his men on board the *Defiant*. Like his two ships, the young man had a startlingly bold and commanding presence and seemed unexplainably unaffected by his long days of confinement. Standing in the rain and conferring with his men, Justin Phillips ranked easily among the tallest of men and his muscled frame, clad only in white breeches, a torn canvas vest, and black boots, spoke of unleashed power. The captain watched as Justin swung into action, first leveling orders at his own men, then securing a pistol and a dagger to his belt as he turned and approached.

Justin stopped in front of the captain and addressed

him forthright: "Captain Forester, have you ever sailed into a monsoon?"

"What's it to you?" came a cold answer.

"To me nothing; to you, this weathered ship, your crew, and passengers, quite a bit. A monsoon is like no other storm. One must ride full sail into a monsoon, with just enough loose sail for steerage and with sails ready to go up as each rips. You lose masts rather than steerage. And the way you're rigged now," he pointed to the sails, "you won't survive."

Captain Forester looked up to his lowered sails. "I never heard of such measures. One weathers storms with lowered sails and while you lose steerage—"

"Not a monsoon," Jacob interrupted at Justin's side. "I got me the color of my hair from the last one Justin and I went through," he said, lifting a wet lock of silver hair. "Over two years ago; four of the most terrifying hours of my life—sixty footers, gale winds that would flatten a mountain, men drowning just from the rain. I saw men crushed from the size and force of freak waves that hit them. It's worse than sailing around the horn in the dead of winter. You've got to steer the ship almost full billow and a sail at a time, 'cause your only hope of seein' daylight is if you blow through it and quickly, and even then we all have but the slimmest of chance."

Captain Forester looked out to the darkness, growing ever larger on the horizon. He had spent his life at sea and had never heard of such a storm, winds that would flatten a mountain or men drowning in rain. It was impossible, simply impossible.

"There is another chance," Justin said. "Are you aware your ship has drifted at least a hundred miles north off course?" he asked, and immediately saw that the information came as a surprise to the captain. "There is a small chain of islands," he explained, "fifty miles into the monsoon's course. With any luck the *Defiant* can keep some semblance of bearing and reach them." He then motioned to Jacob. "Jacob?"

From his canvas cape Jacob withdrew a folded paper wrapped protectively. "The bearings to the island," he said as he handed it to the captain.

Captain Forester's surprise, as well as his doubt, were written plainly on his face. It was incredulous; too incredulous to be believed. Why would men known for their ruthlessness and deviousness, for spreading unmitigated terror wherever they traveled, endeavor to save his ship? Why would Justin Phillips give a damn?

"Rumors are for idle old women." Justin read the captain's thoughts. "Do not be misled. Neither I nor any of my men negate the value of human life. Take my advice—"

"It will be a cold day in hell before I take your advice, Mister Phillips!"

Justin, knowing lives would be lost from the captain's inexperience, wasted several more minutes trying to convince the stubborn man. Unfortunately to no avail. Frustrated, Justin finally ordered two of his men to explain the situation to the passengers. Anyone, even the crew, who wanted to board the *Athena* was to be permitted. He then demanded to know where Christina's cabin was located.

"What do you want with Miss Marks?"

"To see her alive."

"You lay a finger on her or any other passenger, it

55

will be over my dead body!"

Justin lost all patience with the man and leveled a cocked pistol at his head. "That could be easily arranged."

Christina heard Justin's voice in the hall and, unable to bare the suspense, she quickly scurried between the bunks and wall. Her position afforded a view but kept her hidden. A man swung open the door and stepped quickly inside.

Christina stopped breathing.

He was the most devastating and frightening-looking man she had ever witnessed, every bit the pirate of her imagination. So tall and half naked like a savage, his masculinely lean frame radiated a shocking strength and violence, a violence pronounced by his weapons. His dark hair and beard accented sharp aristocratic features and as his fine dark blue eyes looked from one face to the next, his lips curved with an amused smile. He could not be Justin, she knew, but even the fact that he must be one of his men shocked her.

Justin refused to believe any of these women was Christina, for there would be no mistaking that hair. "Christina?" he asked.

Christina gasped and pressed herself against the wall, closing her eyes at once. It was his voice! No, it just couldn't be! This man unconsciously imitated Justin's voice, probably in admiration of his captain . . .

Justin's gaze flew to her hiding place and he chuckled, knowing it was Christina even before his eyes fell on her. She would be hiding at such a moment.

56

He stepped quickly in front of her and then for the longest moment, he just stared, every bit as surprised as Christina.

"I had heard others say you were lovely—but this?" He ran his hand casually over her face and down the long length of that hair as his gaze fell over her slender figure in ready appreciation of the ever-so-feminine proportions. No, he hadn't expected such startlingly beauty.

Christina shivered and could not make sense of all she felt, except that shading everything was fear. He stepped closer, and she still could not look at him, feeling his strength tower over her. His hand lifted her face to him and her fear intensified twofold.

He just stared, stared at the delicately boned face, the high cheekbones flushed with a soft blush, and her lips! Lips pouting and sensual, the color of dark red wine and trembling slightly with uncertainty.

"Look at me," he said, wanting to see the eyes hidden beneath the long black lashes. She glanced up quickly but retreated instantly, allowing him but a glimpse of her eyes.

"Perhaps my fondness has clouded my judgment, though I don't think so. All I can say, Christina, is had I any idea, our ah, friendship," he smiled, "would have taken a markedly different turn from the start."

Elsie and Hanna giggled nervously but she barely heard. She had no idea there was a name for how his gaze claimed her but she felt possessed and without will, as though he had locked invisible chains around her wrists to force her bound and helpless. She wanted to cry in protest, run from him this man, a man she could never call Justin.

The ship took a sudden lurch on its side and she gasped as his arms came around her, pulling her against his hard frame. She froze mutely, startled, then scared by the sweeping warmth his body pressed on her. He seemed not to notice.

"Listen carefully, ladies," he addressed the others. "We are headed into a storm; not just any storm but a monsoon. We run a slim chance of surviving. And to make matters worse, your captain seems bent on destruction. I guarantee that if you stay aboard this ship, you'll be joining that great silent majority, so I am offering passage aboard my ship. While I will guarantee none of you safety from my crew," he smiled, "I can assure each of you better odds. The choice is yours."

Elsie and Hanna exchanged frightened, excited glances. "What do we have to lose?" Elsie whispered to Hanna.

"My lady!" Hanna replied.

"Our ladies or our lives!" Elsie retorted.

Christina watched in stunned disbelief as Hanna grabbed Elsie's hand and both women jumped from the bunks to join Justin. He smiled, turned to Marianna and Katie.

Jacob stepped in the doorway. "Last call—" He stopped, took one long look at Christina held intimately in Justin's arms, and two silver brows lifted. "Is that your Christina now? My but the lass is a sight for sea-weary eyes!" He grinned in appreciation, while bowing formally in address. "Miss Marks, 'tis a true pleasure. We're all indebted to you for caring for Justin."

58

Justin chuckled when Christina looked down and flushed. "She's very shy, Jacob. She hardly speaks to others," he said, brushing his hand affectionately through her hair again.

"Shyness be fine in a woman, so long as it lifts beneath the covers." He smiled and in the same breath he turned to the others. "Which of you ladies are going to save your souls and come with us?"

"These two." Justin pointed and then looked to Marianna and Katie. "How about it?"

The two women had the least to lose. Katie bit her lip uncertainly and looked nervously at her friend. Marianna looked to Justin and he only nodded, convincing the women not with words but with his very manner. Marianna nodded to Katie, and suddenly all the women turned to packing.

"Just what's necessary," Jacob warned, "and hurry it up now."

"Where's your trunk, Christina?" Justin asked.

Christina shook her head but dared not glance up. "I'm . . . I'm not going."

"What?" he asked, staring down at her and suddenly aware of what was running through her head. "Jacob." He smiled slowly, amused. "I do believe my looks have frightened her. Just what were you expecting, sweetheart? A slight dandy of a gentleman in tailored clothes bearing polite social pretenses, a bouquet of flowers for his lady?"

"Ah, Christy." Jacob too chuckled. "You're the first lady I've seen who found disfavor with Justin's looks, though personally I quite agree with your sentiments. I don't care what the ladies say, I've never seen anythin' handsome in him."

Christina wished the sea would in fact swallow her up, so great was her embarrassment. A pained embarrassment that could not hide the real pain of a shattered illusion. All she knew was she refused to go with him, that she would rather die than to do so.

Justin ignored her fear and ordered the ladies' possessions placed in Christina's trunk, silencing her protest by placing a hand gently over her lips.

"I'll be damned if I'm going to let that idiot captain list you among the dead," he said, but added honestly, "though truthfully, I'd take you with me without the threat of a storm."

She looked up in panic, unable to believe that. But Jacob led the ladies out and two men came in for the trunk. "No," she said to the two men, "that's mine! All my things—"

Justin merely nodded to his men and the trunk was carried away.

"I don't want to go with you!"

"This refusal might bother me had I given you a choice." She gasped and tried to pull away but he stopped her. "No, sweetheart, you have no choice; you're coming with me." And he lifted her effortlessly into his arms and carried her through the door.

"No . . . No! Please, please, Justin, put me down!"

"Not a chance," he replied and when she cried out and struggled in earnest, he merely chuckled and tossed her over his shoulder. He brought her quickly to the deck. Rain fell in torrents from a darkening sky and within a minute they were soaked. The wind was fierce too and the sea already churned beneath huge fifteen-foot waves. Four of Justin's men held Captain

Forester at gunpoint, forcing the man's officers and crew to watch passively as Justin made his retreat.

With one hand on the ladder rope and one arm keeping Christina securely to him, Justin quickly shimmied down the side of the *Defiant*, and Christina screamed, clinging tightly to his neck. With inexplicable grace and ease, Justin dropped into the lifeboat. Her feet never touched the bottom, even as he set her on a seat.

Each of Justin's four men in turn dropped into the lifeboat and then they were off. The lifeboat, as large as a fair-sized house, made slow progress between the two ships, climbing over ten-foot swells, then sliding down. Waves occasionally crested and collapsed inside the boat.

Jacob moved quickly to secure what he called a floater over her, a stuffed jacket. He hurriedly tied it around her waist and chest and he then pointed behind her. She turned to confront what could not be imagined.

Darkness devoured half the sky, black against gray. It looked like the opening to a dragon's mouth, sheets of lightning like a lashing tongue and thunder its fury. The monsoon.

Ten men rowed. The women were placed protectively between them. Justin stood at the stern shouting orders to his men, his tall frame seeming to defy gravity and rules of balance, making him look once colossal and heroic.

Captain Forester had already forgotten Justin.

His voice was a weak cry in the angry wind as he stood on the quarterdeck immersed in readying the *Defiant* for the fast-approaching storm. The captain would never permit shots to be fired at the boat, considering the female hostages there, but one man no longer considered orders or obedience or chivalry.

Carrington slid his broken leg to the side, seeking a balance nearly impossible between the motion of the ship, the gale winds, rain, and his injury. And only the sheer force of his will could find it.

He just wanted revenge. After all the monsoon spelled death as surely as starvation and thirst. What did it matter? An expert marksman, he raised his pistol and waited.

A shot, but a small whiz against the tremendous roar of wind and rain and sea, grazed Justin's arm. Moving with a flash of speed, he ducked down, bringing Christina beneath him while shouting the order to take cover.

"Someone's a hell of a shot!" Jacob shouted, raising his pistol and searching the distant deck for the culprit.

"But not quite good enough," Justin replied just as he spotted the man, leveled and aimed his pistol.

Another shot hit one of Justin's men and Katie screamed as the man in front of her collapsed, blood washing over his face. Seeing Justin kneeling in front of her about to kill another human being and compelled by something she didn't understand, Christina cried out, "Nooo!" and jerked his arm just as his shot fired.

Justin's shot, a shot that would have proved him every bit as good a marksman as the man firing from the *Defiant*, ricocheted from the side of the ship just as lightning cracked furiously and a huge wave collapsed inside the boat, nearly capsizing it. Nature warned all that the real battle was to be fought with her.

Justin's gaze found his man, Roberts, lying dead against the side of the boat. He turned to Christina and in a single sweep of motion, he lifted her up. He held her hard against his body and forced her terrified gaze to confront the gruesome sight. "Look at him! You might have been responsible for that!"

Shutting her eyes tight, she cried in protest, trying desperately to twist from mercilessly strong arms but Justin held her still, nodded to Jacob, and the dead man was quickly thrown over the side. Then he turned her to face him and said what she could not believe.

"I'm willing to tolerate a lot more from you than I would from any other women, but I will never tolerate interference in my actions. I'll warn you once; the next time you elicit my anger the consequences will not be pleasant. Do you understand?"

And her nightmare began. She managed to nod through a silent scream. Justin set her back in the seat. She started trembling with fear. A fear born not of the storm or its promise of doom but of him. The real Justin Phillips frightened her more than any storm in heaven or on earth could.

Strong arms and thick ropes hoisted the lifeboat up the side of the great ship and Justin instantly became an essential actor in the bustle of activity. Everything not built into the ship had to be secured to something that was. Jacob and two other men led the women beneath deck and into a small cabin. Four bunks, a tiny closet and porthole, that was all.

Each woman in turn submitted to being tied tightly

to a bunk's pole. Christina sat on the floor with the pole to her back and her legs stretched in front of her, while Jacob tied a rope around her waist and chest, leaving her arms free. As he worked to secure each woman in turn, he explained that their small chance of surviving rested in a slim hope that the masts and sails withstood an unimaginable force of gale winds just long enough to see the ship through the center of the storm's eye. "The danger lies in the waves. You'll feel the ship rock on its side real soon now and this here room will turn upside down. Don't be afraid now, for we're only in trouble if she don't right herself, 'cause then the next wave will crush her under and, madonna," he shook his head, "if that happens just say your prayers, ladies, 'cause we all goin' ta hell for bein' such sinners—present company excluded, of course.

"The trick is keepin' the ship on keel and knowin' when she goin' under before she does, then at least the lifeboats might be some hope, if only a slim one. I swear, though, ladies," he surprised them with a sudden grin as he stood up, "if there's any chance of seein' the next day, it's with Justin. Young as he is, he's got the damnedest intuition and the sharpest senses I've ever watched. He'll know when our time's up."

Jacob left and for a long while no one had a word to say. They suffered silently as the monsoon's forces gathered and grew stronger by the minute. The wind howled savagely, unceasingly, and the ship rocked violently. Eyes widened and faces paled as the room slowly darkened; the black outside penetrated their small sanctuary and destroyed any feeling of safety.

Katie seemed to be getting sicker. She shook visibly as though with chills and this despite the warm air of the storm. Her pale face was drawn, a ghastly pallor covered her skin, and Christina was becoming increasingly worried for her.

She had no idea how long they sat in silence, perhaps an hour or more, but suddenly the door swung open and in walked Justin. Water fell unnoticed from his person and he looked taller, even more devastating in the small room. The strain of the battle showed on his face, making his sharp features harsher somehow. There was an unmistakable air of anger about him. This was owed to having just lost his sixth man to the storm, a responsibility he bore himself.

The anger dissipated when his gaze fell on Christina and he smiled. He called out behind himself. The largest dog she had ever chanced to lay eyes upon pranced excitedly into the room. Christina caught a brief flash of mischief in the small brown eyes just as the huge creature shook its long white and brown fur and caused the first screams to sound. She might have laughed at the dog's mischief had not circumstances been so frightfully terrifying, survival so precarious.

Justin pushed back his dark hair and wiped the moisture from his face. "Ladies, may I present my sorry excuse for a dog, Beau. I'm afraid he's going to keep you company for the duration of this . . . ah, ordeal. Over there, Beau," he pointed next to Christina. The dog obediently complied and assumed a sitting position at her side, and Justin quickly tied a rope through Beau's harness and secured it around her pole.

He then knelt in front of her, brushing a stray lock

of wet hair from her face. For a long moment he just stared, wondering how she could still look beautiful soaking wet and in black widow's rags. "Are you all right, sweetheart?"

Christina looked to him with surprise, then uncertainty. He was no longer angry and it was the voice she loved, the voice she had heard seemingly so very long ago through that small hole on the deck of the *Defiant*. She smiled weakly, indeed could not help herself. "Yes, I'm fine," she replied but looked over to Katie. "I don't think Katie's well, though."

Justin went to Katie's side and first untied the ropes binding her chest. Marianna gasped in shock as he tore open the buttons of her worn yellow day dress. "To hell with propriety, ladies, she's got to breathe." Removing a jeweled dagger from his belt, he quickly but carefully slid the knife through her chemise and corset and before a protest could be uttered, he pulled the offending garment off and tossed it to the side.

Katie nearly swooned with the new freedom and, for a moment, it seemed to nearly overwhelm her as she felt the first breath flow through her lifeless body.

"Better?" Justin asked, and received a smile and quick nod. "Put your head between your knees and breathe deeply. Someone should be coming soon with bread and water but I don't advise you to have either for a while."

Returning to Christina, he knelt in front of her again, bracing on the pole against the motion of the ship. He removed a shiny gold chain from his neck and placed it over hers, lifting her long wet hair from beneath. She lifted the tiny gold whistle to her gaze and stared, dazed by its delicate beauty and workmanship. The gold was inlaid with sparkling rubies and tiny diamonds, which formed an exquisite pattern of little flowers and leaves.

"It's . . . beautiful," she whispered.

"It was a present from the queen of Ethiopia," he smiled, "but don't let its beauty fool you. That is the loudest whistle you will ever hear. If something happens in here, I want you to blow on it and keep blowing until I come."

She nodded and set the small treasure against her bosom, but kept her hand around it. She looked up at him and was about to thank him but his dark eyes held her and she felt her heart stop.

"I don't suppose you've ever been kissed," he half stated, half asked in a whisper. Alarm instantly lifted on her face. She could not believe the question much less venture a reply and he chuckled lightly, having no doubt of the answer. "God forbid I waste what might be my only chance to taste those lips."

Too frightened to move or protest, she froze mutely, as his strong hands cupped her face and he leaned toward her. At first his lips did no more than brush lightly over hers, filling her with a heady taste of brandy mixed with a salty taste of the sea. A small shiver leaped through her. Confused, bewildered, she gasped and, without knowing it, her lips parted to accommodate him.

Justin needed no other invitation. His lips covered her and his tongue swept skillfully into a honey sweetness that was her, and for one timeless moment the world ceased to exist. There were no other people in the room, no storm threatening them; there was only him and this, the gentle attack of his lips.

67

It was not enough for him. He wanted more and the kiss, at first so tender, probing, compelling, flared with sudden passion. His lips devoured her with force, and sent a silent cry rising in her throat. Life and will quickly drained from her and she felt like she was drowning, just drowning, abandoning herself to what could not be resisted.

Acutely aware of her surrender, Justin finally broke his kiss but kept the intimate distance between them as his gaze caressed her with a desire he felt grow by the instant. And this despite the circumstances. Unleashed tears sparkled like bright gems in her eyes, making them large and misty, as though painted with watercolors. He brushed a hand over her flushed cheek and whispered, "God, how I want you, Christina."

She crossed her arms protectively over herself and trembled slightly. Not only had she never known a man and his desire, but she had never imagined such a thing, and while she had but a vague idea of what it meant, it was enough. Enough to scare her senseless and she barely managed to say it. "You're scaring me so . . ."

"I know, sweetheart," he said and leaned over her to catch the first tear with a gentle kiss. "I wish I could tell you there was no reason to be afraid of me." He stood up reluctantly and almost smiled, leaving without a glance back.

Numbly, certain that everyone stared at her in horror, she buried her face in her hands to hide her tears, suffering a montage of emotions. She felt frightened, confused, and helpless, terrified by a man she did not know and did not like, a man she had once held in the highest esteem and considered gentle, thoughtful, and compassionate, actually likening him to her very own father!

How could she have been so terribly, terribly mistaken?

Beau tried desperately to keep his balance as the cabin turned at hear eighty-degree angles and he howled back at the wind, then barked, warning that he would fight. Satisfied his message was received, he turned to Christina. He cocked his head to the side, confused by the emotions she felt, emotions his nature allowed him to know.

Steadying himself, Beau placed a heavy paw on her lap, whined, and shifted, leaning his great weight against her. The dog's unexpected concern broke something deep inside her and she wrapped her arms around him and buried her face in the long silky fur, crying softly for another time and place gone forever.

The storm grew in intensity and the monsoon, now like the hands of a wicked child, played with the proud ocean-going vessel like it was but a small toy. Wind and sea and rain raged furiously; rain pounded like hard rocks against the deck, the wind howled with one loud and long scream, and the ship lifted over fifty-foot mountains of water. The cabin spun nearly upside down.

"Please Christy, don't cry," Hanna finally cried out in desperation. "We're all in this together and 'tis bad enough 'avin' to listen ta those two . . . but you, Christy, you 'ave to be strong. You're always the strong one."

Christina looked up in surprise. The room was pitch-black and it came as a mild shock to realize that

69

the others had known she had been crying but assumed that, like Katie and Marianna, her distress owed to the imminence of certain death. And then, only then did she perceive the real danger of the storm.

The ship jerked violently to its side, the cabin spun upside down, and Marianna screamed. Holding tight to Beau, Christina held her breath, waiting for the inevitable lurch back. When it came, Marianna burst into an incoherent fit of hysteria. "Lord have mercy, 'tis the end—the end! We shall die . . . die . . . I'm too young, I—"

"Quiet! Hush now!" Elsie screamed back and even louder, causing Marianna to break into quiet sobs of desperation. "Christy!" Elsie then yelled to be heard over the storm, "kin you see Katie there? Is she well? I keep 'earing her wretching."

"Katie? Katie?" Christina called out. There was no answer but she heard pained rasps coming from her side. One would swear the motion of the ship was just too violent to cause sickness. "Dear Katie, please try to answer!"

When no answer came, Christina panicked. "Should I blow the whistle?"

"No one could 'ear it," Hanna replied and added strangely, "Even if there was a soul alive up there."

The suggestion that they were the only ones left alive sank abruptly into her consciousness just as the cabin spun backward. Beau howled and Marianna screamed again and for awful long seconds, Christina's weight, as well as Beau's, was held from crashing into the hard wall only by ropes. She closed her eyes tight, dug her hands into Beau, and waited,

waited for the room to spin back and Elsie to stop Marianna's screaming.

They would meet their ends, she knew, and soon too. She confronted the fact with but mild surprise and, even more oddly, she wasn't afraid. They would die and that was that. The knowledge somehow filled her with a strange peace and from that she found strength.

She said her last prayer, praying first for Madelyne back home, hoping the old matronly lady was cared for and appreciated in her new position. She then prayed for Marianna and Katie, who seemed to be suffering the worst. The last prayer was a hope that the end would be quick and painless for all of them.

In the midst of the tumult, the furious noise, and the terror, she tried to comfort Katie. Though no sound now came from that dark corner. Elsie and Hanna both worked to quiet Marianna's hysteria, a hysteria that rose and fell with the wind and the waves.

Hours passed. While she never thought she slept—for surely sleep was not possible—consciousness became ever fuzzier, like a dream. How long since they had proper food and water? A day? Two? A week? She couldn't remember. She began slipping into periods of blissful unconsciousness, always waking at a sudden jolt of the ship, Beau's howl, a boom of thunder, or Marianna's sudden fright.

She woke once and Jacob was kneeling over her, trying to brace himself as he held a cask to her lips. "Come on, darlin', take a sip or two. 'Tis been far too long without it." She hadn't realized how thirsty she was until that moment and she tilted her head back

71

and drank and drank.

"Justin?" she asked, but somehow knew the answer.

"Oh, he's still fightin'. Takes more than a monsoon to put him out." A sadness filled his voice and he added, "We've lost a lot of men though. Can't even say how many."

"I'm sorry," she whispered. Jacob squeezed her arm and rose to cautiously make an exit. "Jacob," she stopped him, "please do check Katie there. She's not well."

Jacob glanced at the pole, realizing it was too dark for Christina to see. "Don't worry about the lass, darlin'. She's farin' better than the lot of us."

She heard Jacob's footsteps stumble to the door, barely making out the silver hair disappearing through the door. She looked around. It was so dark. Nothing but black shapes on black. Katie must be unconscious.

"Elsie? Hanna? Are you awake?" she called out. There was no answer. Beau licked her face as though to assure her she was not alone. She smiled weakly and hugged him. "What a fine brave friend you are," she said softly.

She lifted the gold whistle and clutched it tightly in her fist. She hugged her knees and buried her head and prayed yet again.

"Higher!" Justin ordered and the two men on the opposite side of the mast heaved, struggling to lift the heavy weight of the half-mast two precious inches higher. Justin seemed not to struggle with his side, the weight resting evenly on his braced arms, legs, and

72

shoulders.

Jacob, tied to the main mast twelve feet above, waited for the pole to rise those two precious inches. An odd-shaped hammer and ten-inch metal spikes hung from his belt, waiting to be pressed into use to secure the torn pole to the mast, in hopes of raising another sail.

It was a frightening experience twelve feet above the decks. Rain stung like a bombardment of pellets, the ship rocked with a dizzying motion, and waves crashed over the side, making him gasp like a woman, expecting to see the men below washed over. The gale wind was even worse. He had seen one man pushed over the side by a freak gust and the strength in his arms, the ropes binding him to the mast, all seemed but a precarious security against the same fate.

The pole lifted but dropped as the ship rocked back and Justin, managing his side, shouted at the men again. Jacob swore and loudly cursed Cajun who could not be found and who was the only man strong enough to hoist the pole. Before he had even finished his colorful damnation, Cajun appeared and as always seemingly by magic, just suddenly there.

The huge man took hold of the pole opposite Justin and, exercising an ease of strength surpassing even Justin, he single-handedly hoisted it into place. Jacob wasted no time in positioning a spike and swinging the hammer with all the strength he was worth, still cursing Cajun. No doubt the savage was smiling, amused by his fellow human beings' inferiority.

The pole was finally secured and, not for the first time, Justin wondered what benevolent god had sent Cajun into his life. All his men were good, though, the

73

best to be had, and, thinking of this, he felt a sudden surge of hope. After eighteen hours of the fiercest battle of his life, the ship had passed through the eye of the storm and while she had lost two masts and nearly all sails, she had survived.

They had survived!

Justin raised his voice above the wind and ordered the sail secured before he turned to Cajun with gratitude. "We're going to make it!"

Always" came an expected reply.

Justin almost laughed and felt his triumph ride his exhaustion. He was just about to turn the ship over to Jacob and head for the small cabin when suddenly he heard Jacob shout what could not be believed. "Land ho!"

Justin braced himself as that sound filled the air, louder than the storm. The hellish sound of wood crashing on rock. The ship jolted on its side, throwing men hard to the deck and, before anyone could get to their feet, a huge wall of water carried them into the churning black water.

Elsie screamed suddenly and Christina woke with a start. The sound came from the very bowels of hell; not the wind or waves or rain but all of these, with a deafening grating sound of two unyielding forces, smashed together. Then the furious crash of a wave, more grating, and the room turned sideways, not quickly as before, but slowly, frighteningly slow.

Christina froze as Marianna screamed. The room was dimly lit by some unknown source, one she couldn't identify, for the violent black night had seemed to be forever. Hanna and Katie were both unconscious. Elsie's small face was frozen with shock or fright and, while Marianna's hands covered her face, she could not stop screaming.

"What's happened?" Christina cried out.

"A crash . . . the ship crashed on something, but . . . oh my God!"

The door, now where the ceiling had been, burst open and a huge wave of water spilled into the room. Christina watched in horror as the water swiftly filled the room and within short minutes Beau and she, occupying the far end of the room, were waist-deep in a pool of water. The waterfall continued, the danger obvious, and while Christina stared in mute horror, Beau struggled against the ropes, growled and barked viciously at this.

"The whistle, Christy!" Elsie cried. "The whistle!"

Christina brought the whistle to her lips, covered her ears, and blew long and hard. Beau cried in sudden intense pain and fell desperately into the water to escape, head and all. The whistle dropped from her mouth and, not knowing what had happened, she reached forward to pull the dog up. She could only get his front legs and had hardly enough strength to budge him.

Beau lifted his head from the water and shook. Seeing he was all right, Christina lifted the whistle again, but just as the whistle touched her lips, Beau growled and in a single quick movement, snatched it in his mouth and jerked it from the gold chain.

"Nooo!"

It was too late. With whistle in mouth, Beau shook his head furiously and then sent the offending noisemaker into the water. Christina cried and desperately

75

felt in the water to retrieve it. Another wave crashed over the ship, the room tilted more, and water began spilling in with greater force. Marianna's scream halted abruptly, her head dropped forward, and she fainted, blissfully rendered unconscious.

Adrenaline burst through Elsie's small figure, making her terrified brown eyes nearly white, sending her heart and pulse racing. Water reached Christina's neck and while she knew Christina's fate was eventually her own, she felt with an odd certainty it would be easier to drown herself than to watch sweet Christy.

"Christy, your ropes! Get your ropes off!" she yelled unnecessarily, for Christina had started frantically struggling with her bindings. "I'm comin'! Don't panic now," Elsie warned herself out loud. "Just as soon as I get me own bloody ropes . . ."

" 'Tis no use!" Christina cried. "I've loosened the ropes at my waist but I can't reach my chest—"

Water lapped over Christina's chin and Beau barked, growled, barked again, now practically swimming on his short lead. He knew to rescue drowning people—rescue anyone—for this was bred into his blood. Rescue was his purpose in this life and he knew this one could not swim as he could.

Beau ducked his head in the rushing water and grabbed her arm in his mouth, trying to lift her higher. No upward motion was possible with the ropes and, realizing it, he submerged, barked once for air, and ducked under water.

Powerful jaws tore at the rope, and with a strength few men even owned, paused only to lift his head for necessary gulps of air. The rope that bound her loosened bit by bit but she was gasping, choking,

76

desperately struggling to hold life to her.

Unable to reach her chest bindings either, Elsie shut tight her eyes, covered her ears, and screamed at the top of her lungs for help.

Hanna woke abruptly to the sound of Elsie's screaming and the feel of water swarming around her. She suffered but a moment of disorientation. She first gasped seeing Christina's mouth and nose beneath water, but then, unlike her friend, she never paused long enough to panic.

Jacob had noted, with a gleam of admiration, Hanna's voluptuous proportions and, so as not to cause the lady any undo discomfort, he had taken care to tie her chest ropes beneath her arms but over her bosom. After quickly loosening the waist rope, Hanna merely raised her arms, swallowed a deep breath, and slipped beneath the water to freedom.

Justin fought the ocean for what felt like an eternity. He reached the surface for air but before he could see his position, a wave crashed over him, sending him tossing and turning beneath an unimaginable weight of water. Once it subsided somewhat, he swam with all his great strength, but the tumult of water spun him in every direction and abruptly he realized he had been swimming down instead of up. The same frightening sequence was repeated over and over. His lungs burned and his body stiffened, hardening like lead in a refusal to fight without air. Just as water was to be his last breath, he felt himself rising upwards and up and up. With some surprised awe, he realized he had been a good forty feet under. Like a cork, he popped to the surface and never but never had air tasted so sweet.

The ship was sinking and Jacob, along with what men remained on board, worked frantically to lower the lifeboats. Cajun, staring into the black water, waited and waited and, and with quick thanks to his god, he spotted Justin just as his head submerged.

Cajun had never wasted a single effort in his life. The life line hit Justin in the face. Justin grabbed onto it and was pulled so swiftly through the water he knew without a doubt Cajun was on the other end. Cajun secured the rope to a pole and pulled Justin up the side, lifting his friend over.

"Christina!" was all Justin said and the two men raced to what remained of the hull. The lifeboat was lowered and Jacob and two others quickly followed.

Hanna fell on Christina and, thanks to Beau, she had only to tug once on the ropes and then lift Christina to air. Sputtering and gasping, and scared, just scared, Christina held to Hanna, who embraced her tightly in return. Christina trembled with the struggle for life. Every fiber of her being was alerted and mobilized to fight. She had never known she possessed such strength. Water still poured into the cabin and, recovering somewhat, she broke away and flew into action. "There's no time! We must get help!"

Hanna hurried to Elsie, crying now, and then to Marianna, while Christina first rescued Beau and then Katie. Desperately, Christina slapped Katie's face. "Wake up! Wake up!" Katie's head dropped forward and her skin felt unnaturally cold to the touch. With great effort, Christina maneuvered Katie's lifeless form, trying to pull her to the safest point in the room.

Upset by her actions, Beau barked, then whined, and tried to nudge Christina's hands from Katie. "Stop it! No, Beau, no!" The dog persisted and Christina turned to the others. Marianna, too, remained unconscious, despite both Hanna and Elsie's efforts at revival.

" 'Tis no use, they're out of it. We need to get help."

Christina nodded and all three gazes lifted to the ceiling where the door now was located. The waterfall continued to fall into the room, threatening drowning for all of them, ropes or not. "We can't get out and w'at if, w'at if—" Hanna stopped, not daring to finish the sudden frightening idea that no one was left to rescue them.

"We'll boost you up," Christina said to Elsie. The three women scrambled into position, and Hanna and Christina each took one of Elsie's legs and lifted her. Elsie grabbed onto the slippery ledge, salt water pouring over her chest and arms. She closed her eyes, trying desperately to get a grip.

"Jesus!"

And suddenly Elsie's weight was lifted from their arms and Justin was there.

He lowered himself into the room, dropped to the floor, took one look at Christina, and pulled her into his arms. "My God, you're all right! I thought—" He too never finished, there was no reason to, and instead he just held her tighter and for precious long moments he could not let go.

The second those strong arms came around her, his unexplainable warmth securing her to him, she nearly swooned with sudden intense relief. Relief at what she knew not; that he was alive, that they were saved, that all would be well. Though she would have been perfectly content to drown in his arms.

She never wanted him to let her go.

"Come on now," Jacob called down. "I know she's probably the sweetest thing your blackguard hands have touched, but the fact is we're goin' under and none too slowly."

"The ship's wrecked on some rocks or a reef, we can't tell," Justin quickly explained as he glanced around, first spotting Marianna. "We can't see it but land can't be far away. We're going to reach it in the lifeboats." He lifted Marianna into his arms and Christina watched as two dark muscled arms lowered into the room. The powerful hands swept gently under Marianna's stilled form. Jeweled fingers flashed magnificently in the dim light, and Marianna suddenly disappeared through the door in the ceiling as if taken by a whisper of the wind.

Justin lifted Hanna next and the same jeweled hands lifted her with an ease that defied explanation. "Over here, Beau," Justin ordered his dog beneath the opening and, obediently, Beau complied. He tossed up the rope attached to Beau's harness and then lifted the dog's hind legs, while Cajun pulled up his front. As the dog went up, he called out, "Jacob, get Diego before it's too late."

Cajun and Jacob exchanged a glance in which a world of meaning passed. So many had met their death in the storm; why could not Diego be left to meet a merciful death? Jacob had no answer but he would not question Justin's direct order. He shook his head sadly and left to brave the storm long enough to see Diego to the lifeboat.

Christina suddenly remembered and turned abruptly to the other side of the room. "My whistle," she said, distress filling her eyes. "Beau snapped it from my neck and dropped it there." She pointed.

Justin looked confused for a moment but then a smile lifted to his eyes. "Thee will be other trinkets," he said, and gently kissed her forehead.

This startled her. Until that moment she had never nurtured a selfish thought and, despite the situation, the fact that the battle to survive was still being fought, she wanted that whistle. She hardly understood but didn't care.

"I don't want other trinkets," she said simply. "I want the whistle."

"I don't believe this," he chuckled, and wasted no more time. His hands completely circled her small waist and he lifted her into the air. Christina gasped as those same dark hands fitted under her arms and pulled her through the hole to her feet. The hands remained under her arms as though uncertain of her balance, and Christina found herself looking at a most remarkable man.

Cajun looked to her life the manifestation of a genie in the glass vase. He was a giant of a man, oddly wearing only loose jewel-studded red silk pants tied by a gold sash, the sash too laced with shockingly large jewels: diamonds, emeralds, rubies, or sapphires, she hardly knew which. His caramel skin was dripping wet but he seemed strangely separated from the surrounding disaster. Dark liquid eyes held her and she watched his bright white smile lift in stages. "Ah, Justin's treasure; the other," he said.

Justin had never before experienced any difficulty

refusing a woman's whim and looking at the water rapidly filling the small room, he cursed his sudden weakness. And then he dove into the dark pool. It didn't matter that the wasted minutes could cost life and limb. All he knew was that if they survived, he wanted to see the smile in those gray eyes when he returned the whistle.

Jacob, along with two other men, had already taken the others away and Christina remained in the same intimate position with the man who introduced himself as Cajun.

"Are you very afraid, *la niña*?" he asked.

La niña. My little one. The endearment caused her eyes to fill with smiling curiosity. It was as if he knew her or had known of her, and was offering her a special friendship. "No, I'm not afraid now," she realized suddenly. Then, as though she had never known a moment's shyness or temerity, as though they were a million miles away on safe ground, asked him, "Are you very afraid?"

Cajun threw his head back and laughed, a wonderful sound that instantly won her affection. "No *niña*," he replied, pleased, "I am not afraid of what can be seen or heard or felt."

Beau barked as Justin jumped and lifted himself effortlessly through the hole. Cajun and he immediately swung into action, tying a rope from Justin's belt around her waist and then attaching Beau's leash to his belt.

"You'll have to hold yourself to me, Christina. The wind has died somewhat but it's still fierce enough to lift you."

Christina nodded but looked to the door, confused.

82

"Katie, you've forgotten Katie!"

"She died some time ago," he said softly.

Christina's eyes searched his face to ascertain the truth of this, and then her knees buckled under and she collapsed.

"No, Christina," Justin said firmly, holding her upright. "You must be strong for me!"

She nodded weakly, though she suddenly felt overwhelmed, exhausted, and the only strength she felt was his. He lifted her to his arms and she clung tightly to his neck. Beau followed at Justin's side and Cajun moved silently behind them.

She would never forget those long minutes it took to reach the lifeboat. The rain felt like a thousand bullets stinging her skin and she needed a strength she did not have to fight the force of the wind to keep to Justin, for he could only hold her with one arm as he braced against the upturned side of the ship.

Beau's leash was dropped to Jacob, who waited in the lifeboat and the dog was ordered in the water. Beau obediently jumped into the churning blackness and, with some effort, Jacob pulled him back. Holding her firmly, Justin grabbed onto the rope and lowered into the boat. Cajun came next. Christina looked up and gasped just as Justin threw her to the floor and came on top of her, a split second before a twenty-foot wave crashed over the boat. It was the last thing she remembered.

Chapter Three

The soft gray light of pre-dawn shaded everything, sky and sea and land. A gray overcast sky melted into a grayer sea, and, while relatively calmer, the ocean still raged in the aftermath of the storm. Large waves crashed onto a ravished beach. The wind had died to a warm breeze. Nature signaled the end of her vengeance with a sound that woke Justin. He heard the song of birds, a thousand chirping birds.

He woke to the pleasurable tightening of his body's full arousal and he smiled. Sleeping soundly, Christina nestled intimately against his warmth and in a position suggesting she might have slept with him for a good ten years. She wore only the remnants of her chemise and a petticoat, tattered and torn now. Clothing that hid little from his gaze.

The lifeboat, held up on its side by their sticks, served as a makeshift shelter for twenty-two people sleeping beneath it. Accounting for the four women, only eighteen men of a crew of seventy-eight had survived. Some had been lost on the short trip in the lifeboat to the island. The boat had capsized twice and it had been all he and Beau could do to keep Christina alive and breathing until his legs touched the blessed shores of the island.

Christina had remained unconscious, even while he had moved the torn remnants of her dress, undergarments, and boots to check for broken bones. She had no broken bones, but multiple bruises and scratches marred her lovely skin. Somehow by a miracle of God or fortune, they had survived.

Christina nuzzled closer to the warmth, lost on the sweet shores of a dream spun from memories of a time not long ago. She could see it all so clearly. A bright springtime sun shining over Hollinsborne, the quaint village in Kent that had been her home. The huge stone church—her father's church—rose from the center of town, with its steep bell tower touching a pure azure sky. Row upon row of small thatch-roofed, Tudor-style cottages lined the narrow tree-lined cobblestone streets. Then she saw her home, similar to all the rest, except two stories high and in the far corner of town. A small gate surrounded her father's well-tended garden. A garden made with a smooth blanket of neatly cropped lawn and flower beds: geraniums, daisies, delicate monkey flowers and roses, dozens of roses blooming pink, yellow, and white beneath the springtime sun. Madelyne hummed as she went about the day. She heard the familiar sound of the clip-clop of horses as carriages drew to the gate, friendly greetings extended by a parishioner or neighbor come to call on her father.

She sat behind the house with her ever-present sketchbook, drawing the wilderness that encroached

85

there. How often had she sat there like that, staring at the meadow of tall green grass surrounded by dark woods, tall cedars, ash, and gangly oaks? What had she been dreaming of then? Her father had teased that he lost her to the dreams of a young girl becoming a lady . . .

Her father! She loved him so! She sat on a stool while he rested in the huge easy chair by the hearth after supper, listening as she read out load. Madelyne appeared with cider or tea and some sweet treat, an apple tart, cake, a dish of trifles, or eclairs. Like old and comfortable friends, the three of them sat around the fire. She felt so warm and secure . . .

Justin endured the exquisite pressure of the soft form against him for as long as possible. The gentle swell of her breasts brushed against his chest with each of her small breaths and watching, feeling this, became a torment he had never imagined he could, much less would bear. Every fiber of his being wanted and was ready for her, and yet he would force himself to wait.

He had never before had a virgin and the idea that he would take her innocence stirred strange emotions in him, not all of them pleasant. And presently the one bringing the most discomfort was knowing he had to awaken her to love slowly and gradually.

Had he ever waited for a woman's love?

No, he realized, and it would be as new to him as love was to her.

He shifted, hoping to relieve some of the pressure and, to his surprise, Christina nuzzled back against him. This was decidedly too much. He ran his hand over the curve of her small waist, stopping beneath her bosom, teased where the chemise interrupted his pleasure. He let out his breath in a low groan and then brushed his lips against her forehead and whispered, "Wake up sweetheart. You've been asleep too long now."

Christina stirred but before she opened her eyes, she heard the call of exotic birds and she smelled the delicious fragrance of a garden washed by rain. So she had gone to heaven! How odd, she had always doubted there was really such a place. She smiled and opened her eyes.

The smile disappeared instantly and she gasped, bolting up, only to be caught by a strong arm gently easing her back down. "Easy does it," he whispered. "You've been asleep for a day and a night and you'll have to go at it slow."

"A day, a night? . . . What happened?"

"The ship wrecked on an island reef and sunk about a mile off shore." He glanced toward the ocean, his eyes suddenly filled with sadness, perhaps regret. "We reached the lifeboat. You must have hit your head in the boat, for you've been unconscious since. I was getting worried," he smiled, his hand lightly touching her face, "until you did me the favor of opening your eyes."

Consciousness brought back the terrifying events, all of them—the storm, nearly drowning in the small room, Justin, Jacob, and Cajun finally coming for them and Katie, poor Katie dying. She looked past him to see the twenty or so people sleeping alongside them beneath the lifeboat. She saw Hanna, Elsie, Marianna, Jacob, Cajun, and many others she did not know. Beyond them she saw a deserted stretch of

87

beach, lined by lush green foliage and palm trees, all flattened by the wind.

Still dazed and confused, she asked, "Where are we?"

"Your guess is as good as mine. We're on an island in the south seas. Fortunately, it seems to be a large island with an adequate fresh water supply and an abundance of food." He watched as she tried to comprehend all that was said. "How do you feel?" he asked, brushing stray strands of hair from her face. "Dizzy?"

She nodded, still confused and somewhat dazed. "I'm thirsty," she added, touching her lips, suddenly aware of her parched throat. He reached behind her and withdrew an odd hairy shell, shaped like a mug with its top cut off.

"Here, drink this."

She would never forget her first taste of coconut milk. Nothing in the world had ever tasted so good. It was sweet and delicious and she felt the soothing cream slide down her throat all the way to her empty stomach. She finished, and not willing to lose a single drop, she licked her lips and looked at him for more.

Justin chuckled and handed her another shell. He withdrew his knife, cut open the one she had just finished, and sliced off two pieces of the moist white meat. He handed her the piece when she finished. She watched him eat it and there was something about the gleam of amusement in those dark blue eyes that brought a sudden awareness.

"My clothes!" she half gasped as her arms crossed protectively over her near naked figure.

"I was wondering when you would notice."

"You . . . you took off my clothes!"

"I had to, not that I wouldn't have anyway. I first had to cut your skirts and boots when the lifeboat capsized, for they were heavy and pulling you under." His boots, however, rested an arm's length away. "I had to remove the rest later to check for any damage—broken bones and such." He chuckled at her, tossed the coconut aside, and his arms came around her, bringing her back to him. Her arms braced against his broad shoulders and she lifted from him, unaware of the view this afforded him.

"Don't worry, Christina." He smiled as his gaze lowered, caressing the curves she presented to him. "I have seen many beautiful women in my time and I must say I'm very pleased."

He watched shock lift on her features and he chuckled again, shifted so that she was beneath him. Her breath caught and she closed her eyes, terrified by the sweeping montage of sensations his body pressed upon her. He kissed her, firm and warm, and exercising all the restraint he owned, he drank the sweetness of her mouth with a deep but tender hunger.

She froze in sheer panic but his kiss brought a warm rush through her and she felt herself melting again, suddenly limp and passive and helpless. His own desire rose with an urgency that shook him and he shifted to his side, bringing her with him and kissing her still as his hands slowly roamed over her small back, the curves of her waist.

She trembled beneath his touch. He broke his kiss but his lips lazily explored the contours of her face and neck while his hands continued to caress the softness of her form. She felt flushed, scared by the small flame leaping through her, and scared even more when his hand reached to the small of her back, pressing her against the hard length of his desire. She stiffened dramatically, instinctively knowing and yet not knowing. "No . . ." She tried to twist away. "No . . . please, I—"

"Shhh, sweetheart," he whispered, keeping her gently to him as he looked into the terrified gray pools of her eyes. "Yes I want you, perhaps more than I ever wanted a woman but no," he almost smiled, "I'm not going to take you amongst twenty other people. Nor," he added, brushing his lips over her forehead, "will I have you with this fear in your eyes."

She bit her lips, waiting helplessly, afraid he was going to kiss her again, but suddenly Beau raced up from the forest. Excited, the dog stopped in front of Justin and dropped a dead bird at his feet, obviously as an offering. The first sign that life would not be as she had known it. He barked again, pleased with his catch and Justin stood to his feet as everyone else began to wake up.

The first day began.

Christina pulled herself into a tight ball to hide her naked figure. The torn chemise and torn petticoat, all made of thin cotton material, barely covered her thighs. She had nothing on beneath. While her hair was still partially braided, it fell in a mass of disastrous tangles. She noticed various cuts and bruises and she felt hungry and stiff. She first looked around to find something to cover herself in.

The men gathered around Justin, while Hanna and Elsie came immediately to her side, joyously exclaiming over the fact that she was well, that they had all survived.

"Christy, you had us worried so when you wouldn't wake, but Justin kept sayin' you would be fine, but that 'ead injuries sometimes take time and to leave you be, but—"

"But we didn't know," Elsie broke in. "Kept thinkin' that a wrap in the 'ead kin do a soul in—you know, leave 'im without their wits but you're fine now, aren't you?"

Christina smiled at their concern, nodding. "Yes, I'm fine. I don't even think I really did suffer a head injury." A hand reached to her head and, save for a certain heaviness, she felt no pain there. "I think I just fainted."

"Well, little wonder. 'Twas a terror! Never thought we would live to see this day, but 'ere we are!" Hanna spread her arms to embrace a day she never thought to see.

A smile lifted to Christina's eyes and suddenly she laughed too. "Yes, we have been spared!" The same joy at having survived certain death suddenly filled her; she was alive and she was glad! "But how are you? You two look—"

She was about to say awful. Hanna had on only a tattered chemise and petticoat too, though the full skirt of her petticoat was still intact. The young lady's plump figure was noticeably thinner from the ordeal and various cuts and bruises marred her exposed skin too. The thick red curls clustered in a riot of tangles.

"—like we've been through 'ell!" Elsie finished for her, looking every bit as bad as Hanna, though she had both a petticoat and a chemise in one piece. "But we 'ave. There's a stream back there," she pointed.

"We should wash up first thing."

The two women jumped up and Hanna reached a hand to Christina. She shook her head. "I can't," she whispered, glancing down at her bare form, once again acutely conscious of her nakedness. "I can't . . . I would just die . . ."

"Oh, Christy, we're all 'alf naked. Even the men. There's nothin' to be done. Jacob says first thing Justin will do is try to bring up as much of the ship out there as possible and maybe then we'll 'ave some clothes but now—now we're all left with w'at nature gave us."

Christina shook her head. She simply could not walk among all these people without clothes. She would die . . .

"Come on, Christy, 'twon't kill you, I pro—"

"You 'ush," Elsie suddenly said to Hanna. "She's not like us. She's a lady and she's 'as a lady's modesty." Christina started to protest but Elsie stopped her. "I have my chemise, you kin 'ave me petticoat."

"Oh no, I couldn't." She shook her head.

"Yes ye can and ye will."

Christina was too poor to turn down Elsie's generosity. She was a good deal taller than Elsie and so once the petticoat was on, it fitted midway between her knees and ankles but a least she could move about now. She knew she looked a curious sight but then they all looked curious, each person wore signs of having survived a holocaust.

There was much work to be done. Justin ordered two men on a journey around the circumference of the island in opposite directions to ascertain its size. Five men were ordered into the interior of the island, each taking different directions. These scouts were to report back on what they found, with the further instruction to keep an eye out for places that would make a good camp, perhaps caves or an area with natural barriers and protection, and one near a fresh water supply. The rest of the men were ordered to gather foodstuffs, whatever could be found. Which was no problem, for the beach was littered with debris, much of which was edible fish.

The arduous task of retrieving things from the sunken ship would begin as soon as the water calmed, probably on the morrow. The venture's success would depend on the depth of the water in which the ship had sunk. Justin was hopeful, for the ship had crashed on a barrier reef, probably in thirty or forty feet of water, perhaps less. They would soon see.

Single file, the three women walked along the narrow bank of the stream and Christina's eyes widened in stages to take in the surroundings. She had never seen anything like it. Washed by frequent rains, the island gave birth to lush tropical foliage: trees, ferns, and plants so dense as to render much of the island impenetrable. Crowding every space, ivy clung to anything with height, hanging like blankets from branches of trees. Exotic plants and ferns fought for sunlight and grew higher than her head. A haunting dark green shaded everything and the air was thick and moist with the scent of the fecund earth. She had never heard such sounds either, exotic jungle sounds from every direction seemed to rise from the very earth itself.

Following Jacob's instructions, they continued

along the bank of the stream until they came to a small clearing at the foot of a steep cliff. A small waterfall fell into a deep pool of water. Huge granite boulders surrounded one side of the pool while trees almost hidden in vines and ferns grew on all other sides.

" 'Tis paradise, like . . . like 'eaven," Hanna whispered, afraid to break the sanctity around them.

"Yes," Christina whispered too. "Like the original Garden of Eden."

They had passed fallen trees, torn vines, and ferns on their way, and debris floated in the pool, but even the fierceness of the storm could not destroy the prolific garden life on the island.

Elsie, too afraid of water, remained on the bank but Hanna and Christina removed their clothes and stepped cautiously into the shallow pool. "Oh, it feels so good." Christina smiled, lowering, then disappearing beneath the surface to wash away the sticky saltiness on her skin and hair. Hanna followed bravely while Elsie watched on nervously, contenting herself to remain on the safe shore of the bank and merely splashed water on her skin.

The quick bath was invigorating and, once out, Christina quickly struggled back into her chemise. There was nothing to dry off on and thin material clung to her wet frame like an extra layer of skin. She wrung out her wet mat of hair, twisted it tightly as possible into a knot on her head, and secured it with a small twig. It fell loose with her first movement. She gave up.

Many things occurred to her as once. They had no comb or brush—surely she would have to cut her hair—but that was hardly the extent of the things they would live without. There were no pots, pans, baskets, or buckets, no tools of any kind, save for the men's swords and knives—no shelter, clothes, medicine, or even bandages and, as her stomach reminded her, no food either.

They would be like savages. Four women and almost twenty men. The ratio gave her a moment's fear, for instinctively she knew it bode ill. What was it her father used to say . . . "Man is separated from his savage roots only by a thin veil of civilization . . ."

Was it not civilization that protected women?

Yes and now there was no civilization.

Elsie and Hanna were each lost to their own musings and Christina, on her hands and knees, stared intently into the dark pool of water, suddenly seeing an unpleasant future.

Justin wanted her as a man wants his wife. She was helpless to stop him. How could she fight such a man? How could she fight a man who owned the strength to break a man's legs, to fight dozens of equally strong and able-bodied men? A man who tossed her hundred or so pounds over his shoulder as though she were but a feather pillow. A man who led hundreds of hardened men already living by the savage rule of might?

No, she could not fight him. When he held her she very nearly swooned by the strength radiating from his tall frame, the power in his muscled arms, that warmth of his. And even if she had equal physical strength, she would lose the battle with him. The sheer force of his will would overwhelm the most formidable opponent . . .

Oh, she hated her helplessness! She was a pathetic creature indeed, too timid to raise her voice yet alone her fists. Not that any action would prove anything but futile pitted against him. How she would love, though, to tell him what she thought of him. She had fallen in love with him, she knew, but only a small part of a much larger picture. The real Justin was forceful, cruel and—

"Mean!" she said out loud, suddenly slamming her fists into the water.

Elsie and Hanna exchanged confused glances. "Christy?" Hanna asked.

Christina looked at her two friends, both startled by her outburst. The haunting sounds of the jungle seemed to dim, sounding like an eerie echo and nothing but nothing stirred. Apprehension caused fear and her fear looked for a concrete source that wasn't there. Alerted, Christina looked past them and stared into the forest beyond. It was not real, yet real, and she imagined she could see him. Elsie and Hanna turned around too and stared, feeling the exact same thing. A ghost was watching them from the forest.

"Who's there?" Elsie asked after a frightened pause.

Only the breeze echoed in the silence.

"Jacob?" Hanna ventured. "Jacob, is that you teasing us?" Her realization that it was not Jacob came as a chill up her spine. She felt it; they all felt it, a certain wrongness . . . like evil. She turned frightened eyes to her friends. "Me bones are chilled to the core like . . . like I've seen a—"

"Ghosts!" Elsie put to words what she felt as she jumped to her feet and grabbed both Christina's and

Hanna's hands. They never considered it, and, acting as one, they were suddenly running, running as though a demon from hell chased them.

The jungle flew past them, ferns and branches grabbed at them, scratching and cutting their bare feet and still they ran, knowing only a collective fear that caused the instinct of flight. Hanna stumbled and Christina fell into her, recovering quickly to help Hanna up. Elsie stopped just ahead and turned. From the dark shadows behind them came an imagined sound of laughter, mocking, echoing with the sounds of the jungle.

Christina froze as blood pounded in her temples. She looked at her friends to confirm her terrified senses. And Elsie did so with a panicked, "Run!"

Looking like madwomen, they burst on the beach and dropped to their knees, breathless and panting. Christina could not catch her breath, but suddenly she started laughing and laughing. Fear melting into near hysterics, the situation suddenly tickling her funny bone to the core of her being. "I don't believe it! Here we are, marooned on a deserted island, a thousand miles from the nearest civilization, from the nearest person and we—we think we're being watched by—"

"Ghosts!" Hanna added and suddenly laughed too. "I even imagined I heard a wicked laugh but 'twas you, Elsie." She turned an accusing finger. "You thought it was—"

"Me?" Elsie cried in incredulous protest. "Hanna May Haley, in all my days I've not ever seen a soul run as fast as you, like you was chased by the very devil, you were . . ."

The men stared at the women curiously. Justin turned over a piece of fish cooking over a fire and rose, moving quickly to them. Christina had turned onto her back, staring up at the gray sky, simply amazed at how ridiculous she had been. Beau, feeling their excitement and thinking it as a signal of play, half bounced, half ran to her and lowered to his haunches, barking and licking her face affectionately, causing more peals of giggles as she tried to fight him off.

Justin stared at the sight of her like that. It was not just that her dark gold hair spread like fire around her flushed face or her figure lay before him like an offering; the wet cotton material all but transparent. It was her laughter, the most innocently seductive sound he had ever heard.

He bent over and lifted her to her feet. "Christina?" he asked curiously.

"Oh, Justin!" She clutched her bosom dramatically. "You wouldn't believe what happened. We were washing by the pool back there." She looked into the forest, then back at him. "And suddenly—I don't know why—but we thought someone was watching us through the trees—"

"Like the devil or a ghost," Elsie added, "and then we started running, like . . . like it was chasin' us!'"

Justin looked from Christina to the two others. Cajun had come behind him, and with a nod of Justin's head, Cajun turned and disappeared into the forest.

"Did you see anything?" he asked Christina.

His seriousness instantly subdued her. "Well no. How could we if there's no one on the island except us? That's what was so funny—"

"It's not funny," he interrupted. "I've assumed the island was uninhabited—most of these islands are—but I won't be certain until my men report back." He stopped short of sharing the rumors of cannibalistic savages and said instead, "Until I'm certain, none of you are to go anywhere without someone with you. Understood?"

Christina nodded, as did Elsie and Hanna.

"Good. There's plenty of fruit and fish over there," he said. "I'll be back in a while. In the meantime, see what you can do for Marianna. She's still in shock, and if you can't get her to eat, we'll have to start force-feeding her."

Justin followed Cajun into the forest. Christina turned to see Marianna still lying beneath the lifeboat. She had forgotten Marianna.

"Marianna?" she asked as she came to her side and knelt. Marianna lay perfectly still but with wide-open eyes that stared blankly ahead. "Marianna, can you hear me?"

"She's been like that since the storm," Elsie said, coming alongside Christina. "The poor girl. I daresay 'twas from seeing her friend die. Katie was her only friend, like a relation. So sad how many people died . . ."

The two fussed over Marianna for some time, trying to get a response but to no avail. Christina tore off a strip of her petticoat, soaked it in the stream, and gently washed Marianna's lifeless form, talking sweetly to her all the while, whether or not Marianna heard. Marianna's lean figure remained limp, the wide hazel eyes stared straight ahead, seeing nothing or seeing everything. So lost was Christina in her

99

concern, she failed to notice Elsie had left to join the gathering by the fire.

"Oh my, she will get well again, won't she?" Christina asked out loud.

A deep male voice startled her from behind. "As with all of us, she rests in God's hands."

Christina turned to confront Cajun. He stood with his feet apart and his hands on his hips, an unnatural ease in his towering frame and wisdom in his dark liquid eyes. She thought again there was something so majestic, even magical about Cajun, a man who looked part savage, part the genie of her imagination.

"But surely with care and in time . . ." She stopped and, not understanding why she needed his confirmation of her hope, she searched his features. He remained silent, though, incapable of answering what was not known, incapable of condescending to lie to ease a woman's concern.

Finding no answer, she rose to stand next to him. "Is he also not well?" she asked, looking at a man curled up in a tight ball and still sound asleep under the lifeboat.

"No, he is not well."

"Is there something we might do for him?"

"No," Cajun replied as a strange sadness filled his voice. "What must be done can only be done by Justin."

She looked at Cajun curiously, waiting for an explanation.

"For he," Cajun's gaze dropped to the pitiful sight, "is Justin's curse."

Christina's eyes shot to the man too, as though to see evidence of this, and when they returned to ask

100

another question of Cajun, he was gone. She looked back at the sick man and felt a twinge of apprehension. What did he mean by that? Was this ill, helpless man Justin's enemy? Had he wronged Justin in some way?

She shivered and turned to join the gathering, suddenly not wanting an answer to her questions. A huge pit in the sand had been dug and filled with logs and branches and sizzling on the logs were a variety of different kinds of fish. She had had precious few opportunities to taste fish, and had never cared much for it, though now her mouth watered at the sight. She at once became acutely conscious of her hunger.

Jacob, Hanna, Elsie, and two other men, a blond-haired man named Eric and a dark-featured man with an Arabic name she could not pronounce, all speared pieces of the fish with twigs, plopping it sizzling into their mouths. Cajun, at her side, handed her a twig and smiled encouragingly.

"Go on, Christy, it's good," Hanna said.

"What kind is it," she asked, pointing to a flat piece of whitefish.

"I don't know," Jacob replied. "Tastes like bass, but it's not. This here is shrimp," he pointed, "and this is what one finds on a victor's table—it's called crab. These waters must be rich, for this is just what had washed up on the beach. No tellin' what we'll get once we set up some fishin' traps and nets."

It was absolutely delicious. She would have thought so even if she had not been so hungry but, because she was, the food was the finest fare she had ever enjoyed. The men had also gathered these orange melons or fruit—she did not know which—larger than a hand

101

and sweeter and juicier than a peach. There were smaller green fruits, too, not as delicious but just as satisfying. And everything was washed down by the delicious coconut milk, which seemed in abundance.

Justin, followed always by his Beau, returned and before she could move or protest, he swung his long legs around her and sat down, placing her possessively in front of him. She flushed and looked down, hardly noticing how perfectly she fit against him or the comfort of such an intimate position through her embarrassment and a sudden acute modesty. No one else seemed to notice, or if they did, they gave no sign.

"I couldn't find any tracks and Beau never seemed to catch a scent of anything," Justin told Jacob and Cajun both and added, "Though God knows, the dog's worthless when it comes to tracking."

" 'Tis not the first time a woman's imagination led her to hysterics and, I daresay, 'twon't be the last."

Hanna socked Jacob so hard he fell back, chuckling into the sand. Justin laughed too and then speared a shrimp and asked her if she had tried it yet. She shook her head. Watching her with that ever-present amusement dancing in his eyes, he brought it to her mouth, once again leaving her with no choice. She took a small bite and discovered what any fisherman knows—shrimp is one of the tastiest and succulent of the shellfishes.

The men talked of the endless things to be done. Hopefully by tomorrow the sea would be calm enough to begin retrieving things from the sunken ship. They needed ropes, nets, buckets, and tools; in short anything they could get to survive. When his men returned with information about the island parameters and terrain, fires would be started and forever maintained on the four sides of the island to attract any ship that might someday pass by the island. The remainder of the day would be spent making temporary shelters in which to sleep.

Cajun began making an unappetizing mush of mixed fruit and fish and Christina knew at a glance it was to be used to feed Marianna. She finally had her fill, felt ever so pleasantly full, and before she turned back to attend to Marianna, she asked Justin for his knife.

"What for?" he asked.

"We have no comb or brush and my hair," she reached a hand to the tangled knot of hair, "I have to cut it."

Justin just laughed. "Over my dead body."

Christina looked at him with surprise, and then hardly knowing how to respond, she quickly lowered her eyes. Justin studied the long hair tumbling in an attractive chaotic disarray, and the problem was immediately apparent.

"I can carve the ladies a comb," Jacob said.

"Even if she 'ad a comb, she couldn't get it through," Elsie said with years of experience fixing hair. "She needs rose oil, and that doesn't grow on trees."

"I have to cut it," Christina said firmly.

Justin sighed with irritation. He had enough to worry about without worrying about her hair. He only knew he'd be damned before he'd see it cut.

"Well now, I do believe I have a solution." Jacob chuckled mischievously. "Justin, don't you remember those beautiful brown-skinned women with their long black hair on Cook's Island?"

"It's not something I'm likely to forget," Justin assured him, and the men suddenly laughed. Even Cajun smiled at the memory of the voyage.

"No doubt," the Arab added with a huge grin as he addressed Justin. "You had lines of them outside your hut, waiting to take your seed and all in hopes of having children of your skin color! A harem that would make a king in my country green with envy." They all laughed as he added, "I never cursed my dark skin before."

"The hardest thing we ever did was get you off that island. You, Justin—" Jacob laughed, "always impatient with the speed of things, nothing ever moving fast enough, no one ever working hard enough to satisfy you and suddenly you can't understand the rush to get off the island and around the horn before winter hits." The men roared with good-natured laughter while Christina blushed profusely, shocked by such a story and having no idea what it had to do with hair. "Hell," Jacob continued, "Cajun had to knock you out—the only man who could have done it too, and—"

"The point, Jacob?" Justin interrupted impatiently, though he too was grinning at the memory.

"The point is the lasses' hair."

Justin lifted a strand of Christina's hair. "Yes," he chuckled, "their hair, so long and black, and always smelling of coconut."

"They smashed up coconuts to make oil for their hair," Jacob said, tossing a shell into the air, catching it and smiling. "We need oil for cooking and," he looked at Hanna's pearl-white skin, skin like Christina's and Elsie's that had never seen the sun, "probably for sunburns too."

With the matter thus settled, the gathering soon broke up to begin tackling the day's tasks. Christina never paused for a minute. Cajun taught her how to care for Marianna, for that would be her job. The men began constructing small wood shelters, like tents, while Elsie and Hanna gathered more food for the night.

The sky remained cloudy all day, but when dusk settled over the island, it brought a strange quiet. The wind stopped completely, not even a breeze stirred, and the ocean waves grew gradually smaller and less fierce.

Christina sat on the warm sand near the stream, watching the ocean darken by the minute. Jacob had carved her a wooden comb and presented her with the first batch of coconut oil. She had soaked her hair first in water and then worked the coconut oil through it, and now she struggled to comb it. Her thoughts traveled far away.

So many people had perished in the storm, hundreds, maybe. Justin, with unmasked grief in his eyes, said the *Defiant* and probably his other ship the *Hero* had probably met an unkind fate. She could hardly imagine so many tragic deaths.

In the afternoon, an older quiet man named Brahms had led a brief memorial service. Justin had been noticeably absent. While brief, the service had been poignant, even poetic. Brahms had likened the passing of so many people to watching a ship sail into the horizon. "Finally, the great white sails are but a small cloud on the most distant horizon and then it disappears all together. Is it gone now? No, others are watching it arrive on the opposite horizon, waiting to greet the passengers."

It seemed to effect Hanna the most, for she had started crying. Despite her good-natured goading of her lord and lady, she confronted the certain fact that they had perished with sadness and grief. "They really were good to me and my mum, truly . . ."

Christina herself could hardly bear the thought of so many deaths. Captain Forester and Dr. Michaels, the others she had come to know, even the Ladies Knolls and Everett. She thought optimistically, though, that perhaps fate had intervened for them as well; perhaps the ships had been somehow spared, or at least some of the crew and passengers.

Her musing was interrupted by Elsie's laughter, which drew her attention to the campfire. Elsie stirred a fish stew in an old tortoise shell she had found washed up on the beach. Eric was at her side, apparently causing her laughter. Jacob and Hanna had gone off to gather moss for the four small tents of sticks the men had constructed. She did not know where Justin had gone.

Justin! She closed her eyes and imagined another Justin, the man she had known through a small hole on a doomed ship. How she had fallen in love with him—that other Justin! Her heart broke with the duality. She worshiped a part of him and disliked— nay hated—the whole. She reached a hand to her lips and remembered his kiss, sometimes so gentle and other times forceful, both equally devastating.

She panicked at the question of what the night would bring.

Don't think of that now . . .

Night fell with abrupt swiftness. Christina took a place at the campfire. Justin and the others returned, gathering around the fire for the evening meal. The flames of the campfire danced like gypsies in the night and tossed long shadows up and around the small party. Shells served as the plates they had all known in a world now lost. The fish, cooked slower to soak its own juices, tasted even more delicious and Elsie and Hanna had found numerous other fruits to add to the fare.

The men conversed about all nature of things: the tasks at hand on the morrow, retrieving items from the ship, the conditions on the island, what the other men would report finding when they returned, and the subject that would be popular for a long time—the prospects of rescue.

Christina hardly listened. Even when he addressed the others, she felt his gaze upon her. Would he force her to sleep with him? No surely . . . he wouldn't do that. Why then was she so terribly frightened, a fear that seemed to engulf her entire being?

Justin was well aware of her fear written plainly on her features. An inevitable fear, he knew, and he was quite confident of putting it to an end—and tonight, a night of unspoken promises. He had thought he could wait; he knew with sudden certainty he could not. Not for a week, a day, an hour.

He could only wonder how the firelight accented her beauty so. Bathed in the soft light, her long gold hair, drying now, fell in neat waves down her back and, so long, the ends curled in the sand. She sat with her legs folded under her and she stared into the fire with a faraway look in her eyes that was part trepidation, part something else he couldn't identify.

One by one the men left to retire beneath the lifeboat. Then it happened. Christina watched in shock as first Jacob and Hanna rose, retreating to one of the shelters, then Elsie and Eric. She had not expected it, at least not so soon and her eyes shot to Justin in apprehension.

"It's for the best, Christina," he said, not having to guess at her thoughts. "There are two things a man will fight for: fortune and women. Had either Hanna or Elsie not chosen, and soon, my men would have been like a pack of wolves, the women their catch. That would not have been pleasant."

She refused to believe this. "Would you ever do that?"

"Until now, no. I've never cared for a woman enough to fight for her," he said with masculine simplicity. "But now, I think I could kill a man and for the mere thought of touching you."

The words jolted her, scaring her with an ominous portent of something horrible, too horrible to contemplate. Fear grew on fear; her heart started pounding, she felt cold and shaky all at once. She watched him lift a stick that had moss wrapped tightly around the end. He set it to fire. With torch in hand, he stood up and took her hand. She hesitated, seemed to plead for something he was not willing to give.

"I'm not asking" was all he said.

He led her to one of the shelters and stopped in front, leaning over to plant the torch in the sand outside the opening.

She had to stop him. Somehow, some way, she had

to stop him. She thought first of begging but then she looked into the darkness that was the forest.

His gaze returned to her and he chuckled, reading her thoughts. "I am perfectly capable of chasing you down. Spare yourself the humiliation."

She stood frozen, just staring at him, hating him, his height and strength, his threatening masculine presence outlined in the firelight, hating most of all his amusement as he considered her, and wishing she could run. Tears threatened, she could not help it, and when Justin saw this, he went to her and lifted her into his arms, carrying her into the shelter.

He laid her on the thick cushion of sweet-smelling moss, and lay down next to her, careful to keep her partially beneath him. He stared down at her and unmasked tenderness showed in his eyes, confusing her almost as much as the sweeping warmth that sprang so quickly between them.

"Christina," he whispered, gently brushing his hand over her forehead, then through her hair. "This fear of yours, is it just a maiden's fear or is there something more?"

She could not answer him through all she felt and she tried to turn from him, but he stopped the movement. "No, don't turn from me, sweetheart. Close your eyes and pretend we're back on the ship. I want to know."

"But that's just it," she cried in a whisper. "We're not on the ship and you're not the . . . the Justin that I . . . I—" She stopped, for to finish would be a confession she was not willing to make.

"Fell in love with?" he questioned with sudden understanding. He smiled. "Christina, I can make no apologies for who I am but I assure you, the man you fell in love with is the same man lying with you now."

"No." She denied it adamantly. "He would never . . . never force me."

He ran his hand along her side, stopping beneath her breast, pleased with the small shiver his touch brought. "The only thing I will force is your desire."

She shook her head and braced her hands against his shoulders to stop him. "You can't," she vowed with sudden passion. "I can't stop you but you can't make me . . . make me want you like that."

"You are so innocent," he kissed her lips lightly, all too unconcerned, "and it will be my pleasure to prove you wrong."

He took her hands and gently pinned them to the ground, careful to rest his weight on his elbows. For a long moment he stared down at her, loving her even then as she stared back in defiance, almost daring him. But unable meet his stare for long, she retreated behind lowered lashes in obvious pained submission.

"It will not even be hard, Christina," he whispered, "for know it or not, I already have your heart."

His lips found hers, his tongue slipped into her mouth and he kissed her with a tenderness he had never before shown her. He drank the sweetness that was her—a sweetness he could never get enough of and filled her with the taste of him. It was her undoing; she could not fight the effect, not even for an instant. Warmth spread through her. As his lips broke from her to travel slowly along her neck and teased there, she felt a rush of wild tremors. She held perfectly still, frightened and yet—

His hand untied the laces crossing the front of her

chemise. He parted the flimsy garment, marveling at her partially unclad beauty. She stiffened and forgot to breathe. His hand slipped lightly over her breast, caressing her in a way she had never imagined, a way that made her draw a sharp breath, then bite her lip hard. Almost lazily, with but a casual touch, he caressed until he was answered. With a half groan of pleasure, he smiled. "No, it will not even be hard."

Her eyes opened in protest but she met his bold desire, mixed with a hint of amusement. She shut her eyes tight again, fighting the continuous rush of shivers from his touch, frightened by all she felt.

He undressed her slowly, savoring every long moment and for her, forced to endure it passively, it felt like an eternity. He untied the strings of her petticoat and pulled it from her, his hands brushing her skin with fire. Her chemise was lifted over her and all the while he touched her in a manner that made her breath come in small quick gasps. She quickly crossed her arms over her nakedness but he gently forced them back, allowing her no modesty as he lifted from her to give the sight of her unclad beauty shrouded in the soft light of the torch a long thorough appraisal.

She could feel it! She felt his gaze travel slowly over her, her skin grow taut in his path, the effect every bit as devastating as his touch.

He drew a sharp breath, unable to believe how beautiful she was to him. He shrugged out of his breeches and turned her to him, pulling her slender figure against his hard length. She started, then gasped at the feel of his lean muscled body on her skin, the hard swell of his manhood pressed against her nakedness.

"Yes, Christina," he smiled at the virginal response, "I want you to feel me. To know how much I want you."

And then his magic began.

He kissed with a deep longing as his hands came over her in a slow exploration, careful to keep his desire under tight restraint, wanting to awaken every part of her to his lovemaking. She was unaware of his restraint; she only knew he was kissing her again, that his touch, light and curious, was leaving her awash in sensations. She felt hot and cold and shaky and all at once. That melting feeling spread through her as a hot flush. Tremors rushed from a tight ache building deep inside her, making her twist restlessly beneath him.

Feeling this, seeing the sultry darkness fill her eyes, Justin rolled over, effortlessly lifting her with him. He slid her slender body slowly over his length. She arched against him as a shocking hot warmth gushed through her. It made her mindless and breathless, crying, no more able to stop herself than she could him. She was suddenly like a wild supple creature in his arms, and witnessing the birth of her passion overwhelm her innocence, he nearly lost himself. He lifted her higher and took her breast in his mouth and she gasped, clinging to him, crying softly for something she could not yet know.

He could barely restrain himself and while he still had her slowly, there was nothing casual or leisurely about the way he began caressing her. His lips played over every inch of her skin, his hands touched and caressed, forcing her to tremble with rhythms of pleasure at his command. But when his hand gently slipped between her thighs, where nothing had touched before, she panicked and tried to pull away. "No, Justin . . . please, I—"

"Shhh," he whispered, forcing her still, gently biting her lips before kissing her. He slowly caressed her there. Flames leaped from his fingertips and her back arched instinctively, as though she knew this game. She broke from his kiss, clung to him ardently, as that sweet ache of desire grew, swelled, blossomed, then suddenly, mercifully collapsed only to return again and again.

He pursued his pleasure relentlessly, skillfully pushing her passion to a breaking point, savoring the swell of this sweet measure of desire, amazed by the complete surrender of her small body to his demands.

He finally came over her, brushing light kisses on her forehead. She was too lost to be afraid anymore until he entered her with a long, hard thrust. Instantly he stopped, startled by the tightness of her, the almost imperceptible burst, and shocked by the sheer intensity of this, their first joining.

She felt only a hot searing pain, and without a conscious thought, she had bit his shoulder hard to stop her scream. Tears sprang in her eyes and, unable to stop herself, she tried desperately to twist from him but he lifted and thrust himself slowly into her, forcing her open to him.

"I won't hurt you anymore, sweetheart," he whispered like a soft wind. "Give yourself to me. Let me have you."

She closed her eyes and he filled her, forcing the pain through her and away, pulling completely from her before slipping back, filling her with a hot searing warmth. With each slow movement her heart pounded, her breath and pulse raced and, terrified by the intensity of it, she clung to him, desperately trying to keep him to her.

Understanding her fear and alarm, he gently forced her arms back and held her still. "No, sweetheart," he said softly, "don't fight me. Not now. Let it happen." The words coaxed her to almost relax and he then continued his slow, steady thrusts. She felt that ache grow again, swelling to an unimaginable height. Waves of desire washed through her and she felt a surge of want; she wanted his lips, his weight, the full force of his ardor, and she cried for him, her soft cries begging for what he was afraid to give her. But when her slender hips began moving to meet him, his passion unexpectedly pressed toward explosion. He thrust harder, hungrily, answering her impassioned cries and suddenly her ache burst into violent ripples, flooding her mind, body, and soul with ecstasy. Seeing, feeling the intensity of what seized her was all it took for his passion to explode and with a force he had never known before.

She was vaguely aware of him sliding off her, of his hands reaching under her arms, pulling her back to him. He held her tight and she lay perfectly still, surrounded in the warm afterglow of their lovemaking. She gradually became aware of the swift steady beat of his heart, the rhythm of his breathing and the tender and soothing stroking of his hand through her damp hair.

She felt joined to him in a way she had never thought possible, and the warmth of his closeness consumed her; it was both physical and emotional, intense and complete. But with it came a sadness,

114

swelling and swelling from deep inside her. He had forced her to love him and it was over. The beginning was her end, for she knew even then that her love would bring no peace.

Lost to his own emotions, Justin felt her slender figure shake softly with silent tears—a virgin's tears—and his arms tightened around her. He could only wonder at the passion hidden in her innocence, a passion meeting his own. His lips brushed against her forehead and he could not stop touching her, even after she finally lay still in his arms, asleep.

Once would never be enough with her and sometime in the midst of the dark night, a dream intruded on her sleep. He was touching her again, kissing her again, slowly igniting a warm fire in her. She woke on the very real shores of her dream.

"I want you again" was all he said, all he had to say to start the fires of her love. He had claimed her. She was owned and possessed and that—not her love—was, and she thought would always be, against her will.

Chapter Four

It was yet another hot tropical day. A hot sun filtered through patches of billowing cotton clouds and, like a large quilt, the overcast sky trapped the heat over the island. A light breeze felt like bursts of warm breath and Christina, sitting in pleasant shade on the edge of the forest with Cajun, kept interrupting his teaching to wipe the small beads of perspiration from her brow, then cast an anxious look out to sea.

Seeming to know everything, Cajun was teaching her the fine art of basket-weaving. After he had demonstrated the pattern a few times, she watched long nimble fingers expertly weave long strips of near-dried leaves. He might have been an old woman who had spent her life weaving baskets to sell in a village marketplace. She quickly caught on.

They worked in companionable silence for some time and soon Christina found her own fingers flying through the work as though operating of their own volition. She stopped only to swat the bothersome mosquitoes. After two weeks on the island, they had discovered the roughly ten-square-mile sprout of green that was their home was in fact deserted and the only beings that thrived on the island were insects. All kinds of insects lived here and in troublesome numbers, some of which were too horrible to have appeared in her worst nightmare. Some were even as large as small rodents.

Despite this, Christina's first impression of the island remained. It was like the Garden of Eden—an exotic paradise—and the sea and land supplied a never-ending abundance of food. Life had fallen into a strangely comfortable pattern here too. Elsie, Hanna, and Christina spent most of the day gathering and preparing food and tending to those not yet well— Marianna and Diego Santiago. The men left each morning in the lifeboat for a day's work to retrieve supplies from the sunken ship and returned in the afternoon to fish and hunt the two or three species of birds that they had found edible.

It seemed there was a natural rhythm to their life. It was as though the situation unleashed some long-ago-forgotten instincts and way of being. Cajun once commented that human beings were meant to live as they did and she thought this must be true, for she sometimes felt that she had been separated from Hollingsborne, England, and civilization for many years, instead of the mere handful of months.

Which was not to say the small group of survivors lived in perfect harmony; they didn't. The situation also seemed to unleash a certain savagery among the men. Arguments and even fights were not uncommon. Needless to say, Justin's men were not the type of gentlemen a young lady such as herself would likely

117

meet in a drawing room in England. Justin himself was no exception, though Cajun said Justin's strength and harshness in relation to his men was necessary to keep order and "to protect what can not be shared." While she chose not to think of this, she had some idea of what he meant. It was the reason she was never but never left alone. If Cajun or Jacob were not at her side, then Justin was there.

Hanna and Elsie returned carrying the evening's supply of fruits and melons in a blanket and Christina was just about to laugh at the rather ribald song they sang when she caught sight of the lifeboat coming in. She jumped to her feet and chewed her lip nervously as she watched the slow progress.

Frightened, she clasped her hands together, not knowing what else to do. It was so unfair! Jacob would never force Hanna, nor Eric, Elsie. She had tried pleading with Justin but he had just laughed and promised she would learn to enjoy it, that she would eventually find pleasure in it like him! Pleasure!

"Oh, Cajun, what can I do?"

Cajun both knew and understood her fear. "Submit." He smiled. "You cannot fight him."

Submit . . . "No," she vowed in a whisper. "I won't . . . I can't." She looked into the darkness that was the forest and suddenly preferred meeting those awful spiders to Justin. "Tell him I'm hiding in the forest and that I'll not come out until he promises to leave me be!"

Before Cajun could advise against such a measure, Christina turned and disappeared down the narrow jungle path. After their two weeks on the island, the

118

path running alongside the stream was considerably wider and Christina reached the waterfall pool quickly. But this was the last place she wanted to be. She ran through a small clearing to take up an even narrower path on the opposite side. The men used the path for hunting. It paralleled the ocean for a bit, then gradually led through the denser jungle of the interior.

She could not run. She had to walk to clear the vines and growth from her way. The jungle sounds were no louder than the pounding of her heart. Excitement pushed a faster pace. Flushed and breathless, she began looking for a place to hide.

A fat-leafed tree, with an accessibly wide trunk that slanted slightly for an easy climb, stood off to the side. She suddenly smiled at the thought of how many unexpected survival skills she was accumulating: gathering wild fruits, catching seafood, preparing and cooking it over an open fire, making coconut oil and juices, baskets and the like, and now climbing trees. She wondered again what her father would think.

With the easy agility of a monkey, she scrambled up the trunk and climbed past the first branch to the second. It was more hidden from the ground. She assumed a nearly comfortable position on the branch and leaned against the trunk to wait.

Thus comfortably—and safely, she thought— seated and listening to the exotic bird calls of the jungle, she continued her train of thought. It was odd, and certainly unexpected, how quickly she had become accustomed to the island's way of life. Civilization invited unfavorable comparisons to this new life on the island too.

Would any drink ever taste as sweet as coconut milk? Would she ever be able to wear corsets, layers of underclothes, those long, awkward dresses, and boots again? All of which struck her as absurdly unnecessary now. Would she ever be able to even hide from the warmth of the sun beneath a bonnet again? Would any bed—any bed in all of England—feel as wonderful as lying on sweet-smelling moss beneath a star-filled night, wrapped in the warmth of his arms?

She better not think of that now . . .

Once the thought surfaced, however, she could not stop it. She smiled to herself, wondering what she had thought of love before Justin. What all proper young English ladies knew: little to nothing. She had thought she'd be married, that her husband would be gentle and considerate concerning those things she knew nothing about. She had known he would kiss her but she never harbored so much as an idea of what came after a kiss; her ignorance had been that great. And even though she had read all the great romantic poets, she never knew love was so . . . so passionate . . .

Justin and his men saw the shore boat on shore and the prizes from this their last day of retrieving safely up on the beach to dry. They had met with considerable luck. Jacob, Samuel, and himself had finally managed to secure the ropes around Christina's trunk, a stunt that had required dozens of forty-foot free dives to complete. Then, on the last dive, he caught a small glimmer of gold at the bottom of the wreckage . . .

After shouting a last order to his men, Justin made his way to Cajun, followed always by his dog. He passed the two wood tents that housed Marianna and Diego and stopped to look inside. The woman had remained in the same state of shock since the storm; she remained perfectly still, staring blankly into space, unable to respond to anything or anyone. Sometimes she sat up and rocked and it seemed if they let her, she would remain in that position indefinitely.

With remarkable persistence, Christina cared for Marianna day in and day out. She refused to believe Cajun, who thought Marianna's spirit had abandoned her body. She kept her clean and fed, she talked to her, and, twice daily, solicited his help in making her walk. Christina was, he had learned, the eternal optimist.

Justin glanced in on Diego and, as each day, he stared in pained horror at the transformation of his much-loved friend. His mind quickly helped his heart and substituted memory for the reality. Where Diego's emaciated form lay frail and weak from fighting that hellish pain, where his face was pale and bruised from Cajun's merciful blows, Justin saw Diego as he once had been, strong and quick and able, that devilishly handsome face, those dark shining eyes filled with laughter and pleasure whether fighting or wenching, it didn't matter.

Justin refused to believe fate was so capricious as to take Diego like this. Diego and his laughter would return. And he would wait for this. No matter what the cost.

Christina was not the only eternal optimist . . .

Justin found Cajun sitting cross-legged in the cool shade and, after a quick glance around, he saw that Christina was nowhere in sight.

"Where's Christina?"

With an amused grin, Cajun related Christina's message.

Now Justin was torn between irritation and amusement. Irritation that he would have to find her, amusement that she would try to defy him. It wouldn't have happened just two weeks ago. She was changing and it was his single pleasure to witness the shy young girl becoming the woman he loved.

Cajun, watching the emotions on his friend's face, stopped his work to explain. "She is hiding in a tree about half a mile down the hunting path off the pond."

Justin laughed as he and Beau disappeared into the jungle. Halfway there, Beau caught a fresh scent of something and ran off the path in chase. Justin watched him go, knowing that, like everyone, his dog was getting tired of just fish. Sometime soon he'd have to find time to set up a trap for one of the island's wild boars.

Christina shifted, becoming increasingly uncomfortable perched on the branch like a bird. She looked at alternative branches but none looked any better. He would never find her, but, just to be certain, she supposed she should wait until nightfall to climb down. At least this would teach him that she would not be his willing victim.

Her gaze shifted back and forth between a colorful bird loudly chirping away and the branch and leaves above her, searching for spiders. The bird abruptly took flight and, as though sensing the cause, her gaze dropped to the ground and she gasped. Without any warning, moving with that quiet grace and ease, he was just there staring up at her and with that infuriating amusement.

Why she felt like a foolish child with a guilty finger caught in the molasses jar she couldn't say. Then, knowing he saw her as prey, she was suddenly washed in the nervous excitement of a trapped animal. She would try stalling. "How did you find me?"

"You might do well to remember that I will always find you. Now get down."

She couldn't tell if this was a request, order, or threat but it hardly seemed to matter. "Not until you promise to leave me be."

"I will never leave you be. And you're not in a position to bargain with me. Nor will I repeat myself again—get down from there."

Her eyes filled with sudden mischief and she shook her head, sending her long hair tumbling over her shoulder. He chuckled suddenly and she shrieked as he simply jumped up, grabbed on to a branch, and effortlessly pulled himself up. She scrambled back from his reach and started to fall but his arms wrapped tightly around her. She half screamed, half gasped as he swung down and dropped to the ground.

Justin was about to take her by the arm and drag her away, exactly as he imagined cavemen once led unwilling victims away, but to his utter surprise she was fighting him. Fighting like a cat. He held her off the ground by hands that wrapped completely around her small waist and he carefully kept her at arm's length.

"Let me go! Let—" she cried in a voice still soft despite the intensity of her desperation and, with clenched fists, she struggled to pry loose his unyield-

123

ing hands, kicking furiously. "Loose me! Loose me or I'll—"

"Loose you or you'll what?" he queried and rather too sweetly.

"Oh you . . . you—" She could not think of cruel enough words. She renewed her fight and sent fists into his chest, kicking her legs furiously. She was so frantic she never even realized he was holding her off the ground.

Justin just laughed and, seeing she was willing to exhaust herself, he pulled her against him and stopped her struggles. She squirmed helplessly but he tightened his hold. "You shouldn't waste your small strength like this, sweetheart. You're going to need it for what's coming."

She went limp in his arms all at once and flushed, somewhat breathless. She looked up to confront that infuriating amusement in those sharp blue eyes. Small strength indeed! She wasn't about to give up easily. She'd try pleading again and if that didn't work—

"You would force me against my will?" she asked softly.

Quite suddenly he fought a different kind of battle. With her nearly unclad figure against him, that long hair spilling wildly over his arms, and those large pleading eyes . . . How could he—after making love to her all night, every night—how could he want her so badly, so often, and with the intensity of their first joining? He lowered his gaze to the rise and fall of her bosom pressing against the thin material, then to her flushed face, her lips, and suddenly . . .

She bit her mouth to stop from smiling. He was weakening, she knew, and, maliciously, she pressed

124

herself even closer. She reached a shy hand to his shoulder. "Justin, you just don't know." She pretended distraction. "It scares me so and, and I know I'll just die! Oh please don't make me."

"Christina. I—"

"Please?" She pressed as she reached up on her toes to slide her arms around his neck.

Justin suddenly swore, knew he had lost, and didn't care. He lifted her into his arms and carried her around the trunk of the tree to what appeared to be a soft cushion of moss. He lowered her, thinking only of how quickly he could get her clothes off until—

Until, unbelievably, he found himself staring into a look of triumph, a look that spelled out just how she had just manipulated him. "Why, you little—"

It was too late. Christina jumped to her feet and ran for her life, laughter betraying her emotions. Stunned by what she had just done to him, Justin wasted little time in giving chase. Only now he would show no mercy.

Christina screamed as his merciless strong arms put a quick brake on her flight, and before a cry could be called, he tossed her over his shoulder and began carrying her to a certain devastating fate.

"No . . . please!" She pounded impotent fists in to the broad expanse of his back. "I'll drown, I know I'll drown!"

"I'm not going to let you drown, if only to make you pay for playing me the fool."

"I will, though! I will! 'Tis unnatural for a woman!" she tired to explain again. "I've never heard of a woman who could swim. I will drown and then, then you'll be sorry!"

Justin only laughed at this and, within a minute, they were at the side of the pond. He still held her on his shoulder and with his free hand he removed his breeches, seeing no reason why he should get them wet. He wished he could do the same with her clothes but there would be no swimming lesson with her that bare to his gaze.

He stepped quickly into deep water where he knew she couldn't touch bottom and brought her in front of him. He securely held her small frame to him but she clung tightly to his neck, with not just a fear in her eyes now but near panic too, as she anxiously looked over the water that surrounded them. She loved bathing but only if she could touch bottom and she quite honestly believed women—by some mysterious act of nature—could not in fact learn to swim.

"Please don't let me go," she whispered.

"Never." He saw the very real fear now and he brushed his lips over her forehead. She had to trust him, to relax somewhat. "You know I would never let you see harm, much less hurt you."

She nodded reluctant acknowledgment. "But—"

"Shhh." He stopped her protest before it could be uttered. "We are living on an island surrounded by water and there are dozens of ponds. I can't be with you all the time to make certain you don't fall in." He kissed her again. "And I'm not going to lose you. Now trust me, sweetheart. It won't even be hard."

It seemed once again she had no choice. Once when she was but a child of eight, her father, Madelyne, and herself went on a holiday, visiting her father's friend in a distant parish. Madelyne had taken her to a lake for a picnic and there she had witnessed a father teaching his son to swim. She would never forget the boy's scream as his father quite literally tossed him in deep water to sink or swim. The boy nearly drowned too; he splashed and splashed, desperately trying to keep above water. It was actually Madelyne's frantic cries that finally convinced the bewildered father that his boy was going to sink rather than swim.

Her own experience of being submerged beneath water and unable to breathe pressed on her consciousness as well. She had imagined Justin tossing her into deep water like that father had done to his son. But he did no such thing.

Justin first showed her how to float. She was startled by this. She didn't even realize the first time he slipped his hands from her and yet there she was—floating on the surface of the water and effortlessly too! After a few times, she came up laughing and, instantly, his hands were there to hold her up again.

He showed her how the muscles in his body were too heavy and therefore prevented him from floating. Yet he could still swim. She had a definite advantage, which he taught her to use. Within a hour he had her gliding from the shallows to him and back again. She began moving her arms and legs and soon she was swimming.

After the longest distance, Christina stepped up on shore and turned back to him. Oh, Justin." She smiled with a different kind of triumph. "It is fun! I never thought I could do it . . . I thought . . . well, I just never knew it would be so easy."

Justin was hardly listening. After two short weeks, her petticoat had long since been torn irreparably. All she wore was the chemise cut to a short skirt and, wet now, it was transparent. Every ounce of her was revealed.

He stepped back a few paces but then saw her apprehension. "Come on now, you can do it," he encouraged. "This will be the last time."

She bit her lip nervously, but with a courageous dip, she glided out and began kicking and kicking and kicking. Just as she was about to panic, she felt his hands reach under her arms and she was pulled safely to him. She came up laughing, breathless and laughing, as she braced her hands against his broad shoulders. But then his strong arms wrapped around her and he pulled her hard against the smooth muscles of his body, shocking her with the hard swell of him on her body.

Justin chuckled lightly at her response, knowing somehow that no matter how many times he made love to her, he would always see that look of innocent surprise at his desire. Which had nothing to do with what followed, for in all his years never had a woman's desire met his own like Christina's. It was all so unexpected from her. Her innocence mixed with a hidden sensuality and, taken together, it was an alarmingly potent mixture.

It was just a moment but in that small space of time she was aware of everything. The setting sun cast them in an unearthly glow and the cool water seemed to warm in stages. She was aware of him, of the power and strength of the hands gently caressing her back, of his gaze darkening with intensity and bearing into her.

His arms crossed over her back as his hands

brushed through her wet hair. He pulled gently, and her head tilted back with the offering of her lips, parted and inviting.

Then his mouth was on hers and he was kissing her with a raw animallike passion. Their tongues met, played, teased. Her arms tightened around him to draw him closer and, in acknowledgment, he pressed his mouth to hers even harder. Fire swept through him as she yielded to the hunger of his kiss, her entire being at once melting into him.

She had not a thought, only feeling, emotions, sensations. His passion radiated from his huge frame, engulfing her, then sweeping through her. Her blood raced and her heart pounded; she was lost to him.

"God, how I want you," he whispered, his lips brushing against hers, stopping to catch, then gently biting hers. The feeling was definitely reciprocated but she could not for her life speak through the force of all she felt. She wanted his lips again and desperately but they were suddenly elusive, brushing over the contours of her face, moving down along her neck.

She closed her eyes, washed in sweet shivers of heated anticipation. His lips never left her skin, except as he unraveled the laces of her chemise and pulled it over her head. He tossed it to the shore. Through the veil of water he watched a flush of anticipation rise visibly over her. He pulled her makeshift undergarments from her legs, and these too were tossed to the shore.

Desire burst into a crescendo of need. His hands came over her form, keeping her to him while he caressed the inviting curves. Her flesh ignited beneath the hunger of his hands and the insistence of his lips drank the moisture of her skin.

She cried softly for him, arching her slender hips against him where he now held her, lifting her higher. His lips traveled over her skin, sparking small chills, yet she felt her blood would burn through her skin. His mouth found her breast and he played there softly at first but then with a pressing hunger that sent shudders through her.

Warmth gushed through her in waves. The loving assault of his knowing hands and mouth continued until she was crying, crying for all of him. He would not deny her. His arms crossed over her back again, pinning her soft body to him, pressing her breasts against the wide expanse of his chest, then lifting her legs around his waist. She tensed as he parted her, felt a swirl of water rush into her before he lifted her hips for his entry. She wrapped her arms and legs around him tightly and cried softly as she felt the smooth hot pressure of him sliding back and forth over her. That exquisite pleasure pulsated through her, rising, cresting, falling, only to rise again and again.

He finally answered her soft maddening cries and slipped long and hard into her. Instantly he stopped, and for one long unbelievable moment, they clung to each other desperately, startled by the intensity of feeling brought by their joining. Then he shifted, moving with a deliberate slowness, lifting her all the way from him before slowly filling her.

There was a wild untamed carnal element to this love, coming less from the surrounding jungle and more from the sudden unleashing of desire. The force of unleashing intensified and she was crying, clinging, trying to keep him to her, afraid of what was overwhelming her. But he was kissing her and she him, with a kiss that did not stop until breathing was all but impossible. His own desire forced a harder and faster pace and finally, mercifully, ripples of pleasure exploded in her, washing mind, body, and soul and she was swooning, drowning, unaware of his last thrust, the violent shudder of his huge body in her.

The sun had sunk beneath the horizon, leaving them amidst the soft darkening colors of twilight. She could not, would not, let go of him. She knew only that the feel of his body on hers was as essential as air. And there was no other thought.

For a long while Justin held her gently, caressing her back, staring at her intently. Despite the great warmth between them, a warmth that defied both elements and explanation, he knew she'd be chilled soon, and without a word, he led her out of the water.

Justin pulled on his breeches and went to fetch her clothes. She felt his gaze still watching her and feeling suddenly shy, blushing because of it. She looked up with a start when he chuckled.

"Christina, it's not as though seeing any part of you is . . . ah, novel to me."

She couldn't meet his eyes as he fitted the still damp chemise over her, first pulling her wet hair from beneath, then tying the tattered laces of the front. He couldn't tell what she was thinking until she said in a frightened whisper, "You must think I'm terribly . . . forward."

"Forward?" He searched her face incredulously, then chuckled warmly.

She turned from him, embarrassed, wishing she had never said anything, but Justin caught her arm and while he was obviously amused by her train of thought, he apologized. "I'm sorry, Christina, I didn't mean to laugh. It's just that I think of you as anything but forward."

She hardly knew what this meant and she would like to know what he did think of her, of how easily she succumbed to his touch, his kisses. She had learned she could not stop herself and now wondered why she would even want to, for nothing in the whole of her world meant as much to her as the intimacy of his lovemaking.

She wondered if all women felt this way, if she was different . . . or special to him. Sometimes she felt his love wrap around her, enclosing her to him with a near tangible force, and yet he had never declared it.

Justin watched the play of emotions across her face and read the uncertainty of her thoughts. "Come here." He smiled as he sat against a large boulder alongside the waterfall on the mossy bank. She came to him, fitted perfectly between his legs. She leaned against his warmth, waiting for what he would say.

"I too easily forget the limits of your background," he first said. "Nothing in your life could have prepared you for what has happened; it is all so new to you."

She nodded slowly. This was true.

Thinking of this made him smile. He had three older half-sisters and he knew how proper young English girls were raised—in a prison of ignorance. They were given books to read with titles like, *Every Christian Wife's Duty*, books that alluded to the "unpleasant" price a woman must bear for her husband's sanity. Unless the girl caught sight of a chambermaid tumbling with the stablehand, she wasn't going to know just what this unpleasant aspect of her duty was until the very night of her wedding. He supposed this was all very well for those women who— either owing to their nature or their husbands—were never going to experience the pleasure of love.

Obviously this was not Christina's case.

"Yes," he said, more to himself, "you were raised to be courted by some well-intentioned and honest young man, to be married before you gave yourself, all those things I'm not in a position to give you now. The odd things is," he mused thoughtfully, "had I met you under normal circumstances it would never have happened. I would never have known to find you in a shy, very proper young lady. I know it's hard for you." His voice softened as his hand tenderly brushed her face. "I know I forced you to love me—"

She looked away, wanting to deny the truth but unable to.

"Don't worry." He chuckled affectionately at this. "I'm not apologizing for it. I'd have to regret it to apologize and I don't; not for a minute. I do hope to someday make it up to you but, until then, you should know that, yes, I have fallen very much in love with you."

She searched his face to ascertain the truth of this and when she did, love swiftly, forcibly filled her. Her arms fitted around his neck and he held her tightly.

For what seemed an eternity, they remained in each other's arms, content with the completeness of the moment. These moments made her forget the harsh reality of another Justin. A reality that would continue to come back to her like a hard slap in the face.

133

Nightfall began to encroach on the soft colors of twilight. The first stars appeared in the violet sky and sounds of the jungle gradually diminished. The silence was broken only by the barest whisper of a breeze, the steady trickle of the waterfall and, in the far distance, the sounds of everyone gathering on the beach for supper.

"Justin!"

They both sat up to see Jacob standing at the edge of the pond's clearing beneath the light of a torch.

"It's Diego," he said, his face masked with pained concern. "He's worse and Cajun's afraid to knock him out again. I think we should move him for a while."

Christina watched Justin rise and leave with Jacob, without a glance back. Diego Santiago was not a subject anyone mentioned, especially to Justin, though now she knew why. Once she had overheard one of Justin's men say that it was beyond his comprehension how Justin could stand to keep Diego alive, that the man should be killed. But Justin, she knew, could not harbor such cruel sentiments, for obviously Diego's horrible agony was retribution enough for any crime the poor man had committed. Justin rose above his personal animosity to exercise mercy.

Christina pulled herself into a tight ball, watching the darkness descend around her and selfishly not wanting to leave the quiet sanctity of the pond for the beach where she would witness Diego Santiago's suffering. She wanted to escape into the preciousness of those last moments with Justin.

It was too late. The thought of Diego Santiago sent

her thoughts in tumult. How many times had they all been awakened in the middle of the night to hear his agonized cries? And how many times had she desperately sought a means, any means, of easing that poor man's agony? But as Cajun said, nothing could be done. There were no medicines or pain killers and, indeed, no one even knew the cause of his suffering. He grew weaker each day and as he grew weaker, his pain seemed to grow stronger. It was the dark side of the island and at times unbearable for her. The worst thing she ever felt was the helplessness of watching someone suffer and not being able to do anything about it.

Though, oddly, no one was tormented by Diego as Justin was. He often spent long hours alone with him and he cared for Diego himself, all this despite the mysterious crime Diego had committed against him. They had once been friends too, she knew, for Justin often alluded to Diego when he told her stories from his past. He had met Diego at a boarding school for the sons of European wealthy aristocratic families and, when he was but fourteen, he and Diego ran away to seek the romantic adventures they had read about of a life at sea. They had remained together ever since until—

Until what? What had Diego done that Justin and his men refused to talk about? It must have been horrible if they could not even name it. She had once asked Justin what crime Diego committed. She would never forget Justin's face then; he took on a strange haunted look. "As long as I live," he had finally answered, "I will be asking that question. Why Diego—" He never finished and, instead, had suddenly got up and left their tent.

A dark shape suddenly appeared in front of her and she started, then cried, "Beau! You scared me!" Beau whimpered and thumped his tail as though in apology. She accepted and reached out to pet him. The second she touched his fur, she withdrew. He was covered with a sticky substance.

"Oh, Beau! What did you catch?" she asked, half scolding, as she stood up. "Go on, get in the water." She pointed. Beau barked but complied and pranced over to the pond, plunging ungracefully into the water. He then assumed a sitting position in the shallows, waiting her next instruction.

Christina stepped to his side and gently pushed his head under the water, rinsing his coat of the blood. She could not imagine how a dog of his size could catch anything. One would think creatures knew he was coming for miles around.

She rinsed her hand off and looked apprehensively toward the beach. "Come on," she said. "We should be going back."

At night everyone congregated in a large circle around the blazing campfire for supper. A half dozen tall torches stuck in the sand and threw bright light over the area to give a festive air to the congregational site. Christina found dinner well on its way; all of Justin's men gathered round the pit, talking, eating, drinking.

Justin and Cajun were noticeably absent. Upon seeing her, both Hanna and Elsie jumped up to greet her with the exciting news.

"We were just on our way ta find ye," Elsie first said.

"Did Justin tell you?" Hanna asked. Christina shook her head and Hanna grabbed her hand to lead her away from the fire to the treasure. "They got you trunk up today! All our things: brushes and clothes, two blankets, and even a glass!"

"My books!"

Upon inspection though, it seemed most of the books were ruined by the salt water. The clothes, too, would need a good rinsing or two before they could ascertain the extent of their damage. Jacob cautioned them against unpacking that night, for on the morrow they were all moving to the caves.

Since they were finished salvaging from the sunken ship, they were going to move about three miles south. Christina had not yet seen the caves, but Jacob had taken Hanna one day and the way Hanna described the lagoon and caves and waterfalls made their new home sound like the royal palace. Whether grand or not, it would certainly be an improvement over the makeshift tents.

The three women joined the circle around the campfire and Christina had just finished serving up a healthy portion of the fish stew when Justin and Cajun returned. She felt his tension and one look at the sharp features of his face outlined in the firelight spoke of trouble. She quickly fetched two more large shells, served up the fish stew, and handed the food to Justin and Cajun both.

The men sensed the tension as well and the din of conversation seemed to quiet somewhat for a while. Christina finished eating and leaned forward, kneeling on her hands and knees to snatch a coconut from the pile. Justin suddenly cursed and her gaze lifted to find herself the recipient of his angry stare. Instinctively, not knowing what she had done to deserve it, she started back, but he dropped his food and caught her retreat, pulling her in front of him.

"For a young lady who was all blushes and confusion over her immodest state just two weeks ago, you have come far, too far," he said in a low voice so as not to be overheard by anyone, save Cajun at his side. "The only reason I spent two days to bring up your trunk was to see you in something that doesn't solicit lascivious stares from my men. And I want to see you in that something else no later than the morrow."

Feeling blood rush to her face and her lip start to tremble, Christina barely managed a nod. Justin saw this and made no move to comfort her. He wanted to frighten her. Lascivious hardly described the stares of the three men across the fire upon seeing her provocative, all too innocent pose in that flimsy costume. It was a simple matter—either get her clothed or start knocking off his men.

The hot sting of tears filled her eyes and she desperately tried to recover enough to retreat. She could not believe it was him, that he would speak to her like that, and she wished fervently she owned the strength to voice the hundred defensive rebukes in her mind. She had gotten used to immodesty, everyone had, and neither Hanna nor Elsie were any less indecent than she. She didn't think anyone stared at her like that. He made it sound as though she was a . . . a—

She crossed her arms over herself, suddenly ashamed, just ashamed, desperately waiting for her heart and pulse to steady enough to enable her to run and hide. Seeing this, Cajun silently slipped his arm around her. The comfort of his embrace spoke more than a thousand words.

"Ah, Captain." A man named John beckoned to Justin from across the fire. He was a huge, thickset man of about thirty. Hardened and tough, he was known for a reckless flirting with danger, all kinds, operating with what is mistakenly called courage. Like most of Justin's men, John was loyal to the end. He was the kind of man one wanted as crew to sail the seas but one of the last people anyone would choose to be stranded with on a deserted island.

Justin met that bare hint of challenge in the man's tone and leveled a direct gaze.

"I know ye said today was the last day of salvaging but well, me and some of the men here were thinkin' of goin' out again on the morrow."

"In search of what?" Justin asked, though knowing the answer.

The men laughed nervously.

"Why ye know the ship 'ad near five tankards of ale when she went down. Couldn't drink none on Jacob's order during the doldrums. Can't see wastin' it now, can ye?"

The question did in fact hold a challenge, for during the two weeks of salvaging it had become obvious that Justin had refused to bring up any of the tankards. The last thing he wanted to see was this group drunk. But he obviously could not stop the inevitable any longer.

"We'll need the lifeboat by noon to move. You can have it till then," Justin replied.

"Ah, now, that's right generous of you, my man."

John smiled. "Mayhap we'll find one or two bottles as well, anything to help ease our bloody misfortunes—"

"Not a chance," Justin interrupted. "Any rum, brandy or the like will be turned over to Diego. Kafir"—he turned to the Arab, a man he knew he could trust—"will go with you to ensure the matter."

"Diego?" John questioned and then before he thought better of it, he muttered under his breath, "We all know what Diego needs and it's not the relief of a bottle."

The silence filled with a thick tension. Eric immediately grabbed both Hanna and Elsie's arms and rose, bringing them quickly to their feet and motioning them away from the fire. Cajun might have done the same to Christina but Justin abruptly tossed his food to the side and slowly stood to his feet. "Have you got something to say to me?" he asked with a deadly calm.

Cajun immediately restrained Beau, who stood alert and ready on all fours.

John rose slowly, too, but for a long moment said nothing. Then he glanced at the others and found courage in numbers. "Yes," he began gravely. "Since Cajun and Jacob can't say it, I will. If you haven't got the guts to kill him—"

It was as far as he got. Violence erupted from Justin and he moved with such frightening speed no one could accurately say what happened. He kicked his foot in John's face, followed this with a blow to his stomach, and suddenly John was flat on his back, cruelly pinned by Justin's knee, the sharp point of a dagger at his throat.

"Don't you ever mention Diego's name to me again

or I'll show you just how much 'guts' I have for killing."

Christina forgot to breathe.

Justin stood slowly to his feet, releasing his victim. The men were deathly silent and, with the exception of Jacob and Cajun, no one could meet his gaze. "The same goes for each one of you," he warned before turning and storming off into the darkness of the jungle. Cajun released Beau, who quickly followed his master and then he came to Christina's side.

Above the pounding of her heart, she could not reconcile the fact that this was Justin, the same man who could fill her with life and laughter, whose caress could be as gentle as the breeze.

No, it could not be Justin . . .

Cajun lifted her to her feet and wordlessly led her away from the men and the fire to the tent. The last thing she heard was John's startled cry as he tried to sit up. "Geez, he broke me rib . . ."

Chapter Five

Christina woke to the darkness of the cave. She looked up through a wide circular hole in the cavern's roof, much like a skylight. She watched the silent twinkling of bright stars listening to a haunting silence broken only by waterfalls. It was the third night of Justin's absence. He had been gone since the night of the fight.

He had missed their move to what Jacob nicknamed "mud flats." Hanna had not been exaggerating when she described the caverns. A fairly large fresh water river fell over the side of a small mountain, falling into numerous waterfalls that all dropped into a deep pond at the base. There were a half dozen various-sized caves and caverns carved into the side of the mountain. So it seemed the island provided a perfect habitat for them as well.

Their own cave was difficult to consider from the vantage point of a person who knew only civilization and its habitats. Resting on a plateau overlooking the pond, the cave was the size of a large room, with a twenty-foot-high ceiling past the narrow entrance. Their moss bed lay beneath a natural skylight, one that would need a canvas cover with any rain.

Nothing was the same without Justin. Jacob had

forced Hanna, Elsie, and herself to retire at twilight to escape the drunken outrageousness of the men. She had lain awake half the night, listening to their boisterous merrymaking, audible even above the loud sound of running water in the caves. And now here she was awake well before dawn, something she intuitively knew owed to Justin's absence. The absence of his warmth and closeness stole her sleep.

Shivering in the early hour air, Christina rose and quietly slipped outside. The air was slightly warmer outside but still dark and she had to rest a hand on the cavern edge to prevent falling into the pond. She carefully made her way around the wide ledge, stepping beneath a waterfall and then climbing down a ladder to the moist soil surrounding the pond.

It must have been earlier—or later, depending on one's perspective—than she thought, for there was not yet any sign of the softening colors of twilight. She knew exactly where to go to await dawn's light. In the last two days she often found herself escaping to the water's edge, at a spot where the river met the crystal blue water of the lagoon. As she made her way along the river's edge, her gaze scanned the shadows of the beach in search of dark clumps that would be the men sleeping in drunken stupors. The beach was vacant, though, and she wondered if the men actually made it up the ladders to their own caves. She almost smiled at the difficulties that trick surely presented.

The murky ribbon of river connected the caverns with the lagoon. Coral reefs about a mile off shore had created the crystal-clear body of water. The water was so clear one could look into it like a magnifying glass and the day before Eric had taken Elsie, Hanna, and herself out in the boat to view the magnificent sea life in the water's depths, especially abundant around the reefs. But the place she sought now, where the river ran into the lagoon, the water turned a murky blue diminishing with distance from the mouth of the river. Something about the sound of rushing water at that spot made it a favorite place to escape troubling thoughts.

Comfortably seated on the cushion of sand, Christina rested her gaze on the dark horizon, determined to catch the first sliver of dawn's light. She tried not to think of anything—not of the future or of Justin, for those subjects brought confusion of uncertainty. Thinking brought little comfort.

"I'm wondering," a voice suddenly came from behind to interrupt her peace, "just what caused you to wake and wander about in the middle of the night?"

Christina started at the sound of Justin's voice and she rose with a gasp but his strong hands grasped her arms to steady her movement.

"Justin, you're back!"

"I haven't been far really," he said in a whisper as he studied her surprise with a smile. Something in the tone of his voice told her that this was the other Justin, the one she loved. Wherever he had been and whatever he had done, he managed to excise the demons in his heart. She saw this in an instant and suddenly, unexpectedly, a wild rush of emotion filled her, making her at once aware she had missed him, shocking her with just how much. She could almost cry.

He saw the emotion written so plainly on her face

144

and he chuckled warmly. "Could it be you've missed me as much? Does my absence send you wandering aimlessly about in the middle of the night?"

She nodded assent, and as though rewarding such honesty, his lips were on hers and he was kissing her. The kiss was shattering. She was lifted on her tiptoes as the kiss deepened. She felt his thumbs, just his thumbs, slowly caress the sides of her breasts through the thin material of her shift, and as the kiss deepened more, his hands slid down to cup her buttocks and then lift her over his want of her. Desire burst through her in force and then nothing mattered, neither doubts nor uncertainties.

He broke the kiss and let her slide slowly to her feet again. "God," he whispered, thinking he would lay with her, and now on the cool cushion of sand before the sea. "It scares me how much I want—"

He stopped mid-sentence as a scream sounded from the caves. They both froze like animals, alerted. Justin turned, listening. It had been a woman's scream and if his senses were right, the cry stopped as suddenly as it sounded.

"Elsie or Hanna!" Christina abruptly cried.

"Wait here," and Justin was off and running.

With a pounding heart, breath coming in quick jumps, Christina watched Justin's shadow disappear in the night. Hanna or Elsie was being hurt! Attacked! My God, where was Jacob or Eric? Where was Cajun?

Christina could not bear waiting through the suspense and suddenly she, too, started running toward the cave.

With torch in hand, Cajun ran into Jacob's cave but

145

found nothing amiss. Jacob and Hanna were sound asleep. He rushed into Eric's cave. Obviously awakened by the scream, Eric was struggling into his breeches while Elsie sat up, looking around dazedly.

Justin met Cajun as he was rushing out from Eric's cave. Seeing the danger was not from Eric and Elsie, "Jacob!" Jacob said in alarm.

"No—not Jacob," Cajun informed him, already turning toward the only other possibility.

It took Justin a startled minute to comprehend what this meant and then, cursing viciously, he took after Cajun to what they called the sick cave, where Marianna and Diego were housed.

Flames and shadows came alive in the sick room as Cajun's torch added to another. First Cajun and Justin saw Diego, rendered blissfully unconscious from the recently found spirits. Marianna lay in the shadows and for a moment all seemed still, but then the shadows moved and a muffled grunt sounded.

Justin was immediately there, lifting the large man off Marianna and with such force that the man fell against the cave wall, nearly knocked senseless. "What the hell are you doing?" he demanded at once.

The man, known only as Bryce, shook his head as though to clear it, then pushed back his long brown hair. His hand slowly reached up to wipe the whiskers covering a wide-set mouth, and from the lethargy of his movements, his hooded blue eyes, Justin saw at once that the man was quite drunk.

"Weren't doin' nothin'," he finally replied in a slurred cockney accent marked with belligerent tones. "Just 'avin a swipe at the lass." He grinned stupidly, then tried to focus his gaze on Justin. "Not that 'tis

146

any of your bloody business."

"A swipe? My God! She's unconscious!"

The man's next grin brought Justin disastrously close to losing control. "All the better," he replied. "Do not mind a'tall 'er bein' out like that. Only way I ever knows with a wench."

Cajun had knelt over Marianna's form. She had awakened with a scream and for the first time since the shipwreck. But red bruises already surrounded her mouth where the man had stifled her screams. The worn bodice was torn. Red marks and scratches spoke of the man's cruelty.

He quickly checked her pulse. His eyes narrowed. He placed a wet finger over her mouth. He stared for a moment in disbelief, then finally looked at Justin. "She's dead."

Christina ran into the sick room just ahead of Jacob to see Justin at that very moment turn from Cajun to Bryce. "You son of a bitch—" and Justin kicked his booted foot with shocking force into the man's face. The man fell violently against the wall and Christina screamed as the sickening sound of his skull cracked loudly on the cavern wall. Bryce never knew what hit him. He toppled into a lifeless clump on the dirt floor. A small pool of blood trickled from his mouth.

Cajun confirmed the second death of the night.

Christina looked with shock at Justin, not able to comprehend the situation—except that Justin had just killed a man.

"Geez . . . What happened in here?" a stunned Jacob finally managed. Justin turned to him and Jacob knew he was in trouble. He had witnessed Justin's rages before and this looked like it was going

147

to be a fine one.

"What happened in here?" Justin repeated furiously. "I'll tell you what happened. This drunken idiot thought Marianna easy prey for his sick attentions. And now she's dead, Jacob! Dead!"

Christina ran to Marianna's side. Jacob looked from Marianna to Cajun, who nodded confirmation. "I'm sorry." His face became a mixed expression of pain and guilt. "I'm really sorry—"

"Sorry?" Justin shook his head with something akin to disgust. "What I want to know is just what the hell were you thinking signing on a man like that?"

It was well known, especially by Jacob, that Justin cared more about the quality of men sailing his ships than he did even about his ships. While John and the others might not be parlor room dandies, they were a far cry from the stupid, base creature Bryce so obviously had been. Justin would never have let the man scrape barnacles from his ship's bottom, let alone hire him as crew.

"I can explain," he began. "We were in a snatch. I 'ad 'alf a day after your trial to set sail after ye and I was at least ten 'ands short. He, and some others like him, were all I could get."

Justin was not to be pacified by excuses. "A damned wharf rat could have served better—" he began angrily, though in truth his anger rose less from Jacob's indiscriminate hiring than the sheer misfortune of the night's events.

Christina was not listening to his angry tirade, one that stretched into long minutes; her gaze fixed on Marianna's face, strangely peaceful in death. Poor Marianna, never chance or fortune . . .

148

Tears filled her eyes. She was so sick of death, death and violence, the utter viciousness of this life. Would it never end?

"And you, Christina." He turned suddenly to her as Jacob and Cajun were finally dismissed to lift Bryce's body out for burial. "I thought I told you to wait on the beach?"

She stood up slowly, but lowered her eyes. "I thought it was Elsie or Hanna and—"

"No, sweetheart," he interrupted harshly, impatiently, "I don't care what you thought. I don't tell you things capriciously; I mean them. I'll not have you question my orders like that again."

She bit her lip to stop from crying, boldly meeting his gaze. "I can't believe you're angry with me when . . . when Marianna is dead and you," her voice trailed to a whisper, "you just killed a man."

"Believe it." He took two steps to stand over her, then lifted her face. "The last thing I want to see in a dangerous situation is you. You're the easiest way to get to me and it would take but a fool to know it."

There was a long silent pause before she turned to leave. "Was it necessary—" She stopped at the opening. "I mean—killing him?" She seemed to almost choke on the word.

Justin was presently far too preoccupied to consider Christina's feelings, thoughts or values on the taking of life. Her father had indoctrinated her in numerous pacifist beliefs, teaching her that the taking of life was man's greatest sin, that violence begat violence and no good came from it, beliefs she had incorporated into her heart with a naïve passion. He never argued with these views, realizing her experience stood as an ocean of separation from any harsh reality.

"He's not the first I've killed, and I daresay, he'll not be the last." With that seemingly callous statement he dismissed her too. Christina stood with a frightened pause as she assimilated the cruel words she did not want to believe. Once done, she turned and, chased by the demons of her heart, she started running.

The western lookout was a small indentation carved naturally into a ninety-or-so-foot cliff that dropped at a straight right angle into the sea. One reached it by climbing down a long makeshift ladder, secured precariously by ropes tied around a huge boulder at the top. The only reason any man trusted this ladder with his life was because Cajun had made it.

Brahms reached the top of the cliff and called down to Robert, presently on watch. "Relief has come, my man," Brahms chuckled as Robert, a small, lean man climbed the ladder as swift as a spider monkey. They spent several moments shooting the breeze before Brahms took a deep breath, and keeping his gaze securely fixed on the top, he began the frightening journey down, more than a little glad that after the first month of sailing with Justin—two long years ago—hard labor had stolen all excessive poundage.

He jumped the last three feet, thanked God for safe passage, and, after placing fresh wood on the signal fire, he settled comfortably on the small plateau. He removed his favorite pipe from his knapsack. As he leveled his gaze on the shimmery blue vista, he drew on his pipe, pretending as always that it was filled with sweet Virginian tobacco. And had his pipe actually been filled with that tobacco, he might have believed he had journeyed to heaven, so complete was his contentedness on the island.

Like most of life's paths, it had been chance, pure and simple, that he had met Justin and Jacob in Boston two long years ago. Crying in his cups, drunk and destitute and wishing he were dead, he had been tossed physically out of an ale house. He had lain in the gutter for hours, kicked, spit at, and scorned by passersby, and some pitiful part of his soul actually welcomed the harsh treatment. That was until he looked up to see Justin staring down at him, and not all too kindly.

Something about that one look of Justin's suddenly filled him with the decent emotion of shame. He had tried to struggle up, wanting to get away, not wanting to feel anything, especially anything decent. And that was the last thing he remembered. He woke up on Justin's ship, cared for by one of Justin's many pretty maids.

When he was finally given a chance to see the man who had rescued him from the gutter again, Justin had somehow known all about him. Justin knew he had been a reverend, knew of the tragedy—his wife's death—that had stolen his will to live. Justin then made him a straightforward offer: "You can sign up as crew. The work is long and hard, the money is better than good, and since you seem bent on destruction, you might be glad to know it also involves considerable danger. If one could discount my luck, the odds of you surviving the next two years are slim to nil. But you should also know that I won't tolerate drinking by any man who needs it. You'd have to give

151

it up."

Brahms had never been at sea, never thought of going to sea, but he had agreed immediately. And he would never forget that Justin had added as he was leaving: "Someday I hope you come to see that fortune has blessed you. Any man who has known a love bringing him such happiness—if even for a short time—that its loss steals his very will to live, is a man to be envied."

With these words, his new life had started.

Brahms sighed and leaned back, reflecting on the last two full years. Not a day had passed in which he had regret, though no, he would never know that happiness again. It came only once in any man's lifetime. But he had his memories of Beth and eventually he came to learn the truth of Justin's words.

Thinking of Christina, Brahms smiled. It seemed Justin was—or would soon be—a man to be envied. He only hoped, and with all his heart, that instead of such a short time, Justin's love lasted his lifetime. For if any man deserved such a gift, it was Justin.

Brahms drifted lazily into a light sleep and woke several hours later to a darkening sky promising a warm tropical rain. He threw another log onto the fire and stood up and stretched as his gaze scanned the horizon. Instantly, his eye riveted to a spot on the distant horizon.

What was that? Not porpoises . . .

He scrambled quickly for the glass and, standing at the very edge of the cliff, he lifted it into place. And once he saw what was drifting toward the island, he gasped, "Oh my God!"

Jacob found Justin and Christina wrapped in each other's arms, sound asleep beneath a magnolia-type tree and oblivious to the warm rain and impending darkness. Like Adam and Eve before the Fall. He could not fathom—though he did try—the scene that must have transpired to create such abandonment. Now Hanna be a fine lass, he thought, her good nature and humor, her pleasing shape, and even those red curls of hers had all struck his heart in a powerful way he hadn't expected and still he could not imagine getting so lost in a tumble that he forgot to notice it was raining on his back.

Jacob would never think of intruding if the event didn't demand it but it was hard—nay, impossible, even with Cajun's help—to keep the men from falling to chaos without Justin. His youth aside, something about Justin, his sharp wits, strength, and commanding presence like a judge's gavel, could bring order where none previously existed.

"Justin," Jacob loudly called out.

Justin woke with a start. Perhaps it was the primitive response of a man sleeping with his woman out in the open and vulnerable to attack, but he bolted to his feet and held his saber in his hand before Christina had even opened her eyes. His entire body was mobilized for a fight, while Beau, too, had jumped to all fours and searched the area for the cause of alarm.

Jacob laughed at this. "Be thar demons trespassin' through the night?"

Justin relaxed all at once and, spotting his friend through the overhanging branches of the tree, he placed himself between Jacob's view and Christina.

"What is it?"

"You're not going to believe. Brahms spotted a lifeboat from the *Defiant*. Cajun and some others took off in our boat to pull 'em in."

"Oh my goodness," Christina whispered.

"Survivors?" Justin questioned.

"Don't know. Can't imagine any, though. Three weeks exposure, probably without food or water."

Justin quickly pulled on his breeches and secured his belt. He gathered Christina's shift and handed it to her while calling to Jacob for his canvas cape. She slipped the cape over her head and, once dressed, he took her hand to lead her through the jungle.

"Is there hope?" she asked.

"There's always hope."

Cajun quickly separated the dead from the living. Eight people had managed to hang on to a bare thread of life. Except for one man mumbling incoherently, they were all blissfully unconscious, sprawled randomly between twelve dead corpses. He and Kafir lifted the dead out, lowering each unceremoniously into burial at sea. Brahms and another man wasted no time and rowed silently, quickly, to shore.

Brahms thought about objecting to a sea burial, partially because of religious reasons and partially because he was able to imagine a washed-up corpse on the beach. He refrained, though—any objection would waste time and these people needed immediate help if they had any hope in heaven, as Cajun undoubtedly had already realized. He supposed there were enough sharks in these waters anyway . . .

"Allah have mercy," Kafir muttered as he looked

154

down at one man. All the survivors showed the gruesome signs of slow starvation as well as dehydration. They were emaciated skeletons, with all areas of exposed skin covered in ugly red blisters and sores. But this one man's leg looked like nothing but a swollen mass of dead flesh. "What is the nature of it?" he asked Cajun.

Cajun had no idea. The man wore tattered remnants of a soldier's uniform, so perhaps he had been in the exchange of fire at Justin's rescue. He peered closer, lifting a bloodied bandage and saw that it wasn't a bullet wound. "It has been broken."

"He will lose it?"

Cajun nodded. He was more gifted in the healing arts than most surgeons coming out of Cambridge but it took no such knowledge to be amazed that the man had survived with such a diseased limb. He should be dead, Cajun knew, and, sadly, he would wish for death if they could not perform the amputation while he was still unconscious.

Justin, Christina, and the others waited impatiently on shore for the two lifeboats. Christina clasped her hands together as though in prayer and, like the others, she took no notice of the heavy rain falling from the dark sky. She started forward with Justin but he motioned her back. "No—wait here until I call you."

Christina took Elsie's and Hanna's hand in hers as they watched the men secure the lifeboat on shore. Justin shouted orders to the men. Cajun lifted the first survivor, Kafir lifted another.

"Lady Knolls!" Hanna gasped in shock, and before anyone could stop her, she dashed toward the boat to see if Lady Everett, too, was among the living.

Christina barely recognized Colonel Carrington in Cajun's arms or Lady Knolls in Kafir's. Three weeks of exposure and starvation left what seemed the bare skeletal remains of their frames while their face, arms, and the colonel's bare chest were raw with blisters and sores. And the colonel's leg—

"Step strong, *la niña*," Cajun called sharply. "They will need you." Christina swallowed her revulsion and nodded as Cajun called out orders. "Prepare a large mixture of part fish oil, fruit juice, and milk. Warm it over a fire. Also prepare a batch of oil for their skin, gather what clothes are available, and boil a large pot of salt water."

One by one the survivors were brought to the large cave at the foot of the mud flats, where Diego and Marianna were once housed. Hanna and Elsie gathered moss for beds, while the others hurried to carry out Cajun's orders.

Many of the eight survivors roused during their first drink of water. Cajun's warmed food mixture followed the water. One man's throat was too swollen to allow even water through. Justin held the man up and kept his head tilted while Cajun poured minute drops of watered milk into his mouth. It took over an hour to get barely half a cup down his throat but finally his passage seemed to open enough to consume what Cajun hoped was an adequate portion to sustain him.

After the first feeding, the survivors were hand-washed and cleaned, and their exposed skin oiled. The worst sores were bandaged. Lady Knolls awakened as Christina and Elsie gently oiled her face, scalp, neck, and arms. She seemed to be dreaming, though, speaking unintelligibly. "I had to," she said in a nearby inaudible voice. "Don't you see? Those filthy old hands . . . I had to . . ."

"Who is she?" Justin asked as he came to Christina's side to stare down at the only surviving woman.

"Lady Knolls—Caroline Knolls," Christina replied.

Justin tried to recall where he had heard that name.

"She's my lady," Elsie added, "and I daresay, she's the living proof that God didn't favor the good on this trip—"

"Elsie!" Christina scolded.

" 'Tis true." Elsie wrung the washcloth in the bucket, eyeing the woman with open animosity. "Not a kind woman at all. Nothin' was ever good enough for the likes of her, oh no. Uppity and insufferable. She 'ad airs enough for a queen, she did."

Justin chuckled at Elsie's description. "Rest assured, lassie, our island's life-style will have no room for queens, even less for self-appointed ones."

"And I'm thankful for small mercies," Elsie promptly replied.

"Christina," Justin said, lifting her up by the arm. She looked up at him expectantly but he paused, studying her. Her hair was lifted into a loose knot on the top of her head and she wore what he knew was the last item of clothing in the trunk. A pale pink long-sleeved nightdress hung loosely on her frame, tied with a hair ribbon at her waist. He was not altogether comfortable with the angelic look the garment created. It was just that much worse than the tattered chemise and skirt that solicited his men's blatant admiration. And he'd be even less comfortable when he cut the skirt and sleeves. But nothing, he realized, could hide her beauty anyway.

"What are you doing?" she asked as he knelt and removed his knife.

"I'm afraid we need the extra cloth. It's the last left."

"But . . . but what for?"

"Cajun has to amputate that man's leg," he said on the heels of a solemn pause.

She looked over where Colonel Carrington lay. "Oh no . . . Is he certain?"

Justin nodded. "He'll die if it's not done."

"I'm sorry . . ."

Justin looked up to find an expression of guilt on her face. He quickly cut off the skirt as high as he dared, and then rose. "That is not your fault," he said simply.

"But if I hadn't been out on deck—"

"No, I don't want to hear it." He stopped her. "I'll be forever amazed at how women blame themselves, carrying the burden of guilt when it is the man who violates them." He thought of the Arab countries that kill women for being violated, this no matter what the circumstances, and then wondered sardonically if death might not be preferable to the persecution most women received in western countries. "No, Christina, it's not your fault," he continued as he cut each sleeve at the seam. "That bastard should be glad he'll lose only a limb and not his life, for had I not been—"

"No, please," she interrupted in turn, not wanting to hear the rest. Justin thoughtfully looked down at her and then leaned over to kiss her before leaving for Cajun's side.

The torchlight danced over Colonel Carrington's naked body, where he lay on a bed of fresh moss. A pile of various torn clothes, a bucket of hot water, and Cajun's saber waited to be put into use at his side. Cajun's ebony darkness, his half-naked frame, the solemnity in his dark gaze as he knelt in silent prayer at the man's side, all created the impression that some ancient sacrificial rite was about to be performed. Elsie, Hanna, Brahms, and the few others who had been helping had all left, not able to bear witness to the operation.

Christina hastened to join them.

She stepped out from the dwelling to the dark rainy night. No one was in sight but then darkness shielded any sight. The darkness was complete, and while she would like to sleep with Hanna and Elsie tonight, she had little hope of reaching their caves in the rain without light. The ladder up to their own cave was somewhere around the side, but one thought of walking along the slippery edge at the pond in the dark stopped her from any attempt to seek it.

Having no choice, she sat inside the mouth of the cave, careful to keep her back to the inside. She smiled hearing Beau's friendly whimper and feeling his wet fur against her legs. She could barely make out his huge shape. "At least I have some company now," she whispered and petted him affectionately.

She felt the full effects of exhaustion. The air was heavy with moisture but still warm and this, taken with the ever-present luring sound of rain falling into the pond, put her into a light sleep, despite the uncomfortable position. A light sleep that was instantly shattered with a long terrified scream.

All Colonel Carrington saw was a huge, half-naked savage kneeling over him with a raised saber. A vision from hell. He tried to form his scream into a n*ooo* or help or please, but his terror permitted only one expression. He could not stop it. Then hands were upon him—

Christina heard Justin trying to calm the man. She first thought the scream was the result of pain, that the amputation was over, but as Justin tried to quiet him, explaining what had happened and where he was, she realized that the operation had not occurred yet. For several minutes the scream turned into incoherent mutterings and questions until the situation finally became clear.

"No! God no! I forbid . . . I—nooo!"

"You will likely die unless it is removed," Cajun said softly.

"I'd rather be dead! God knows I am familiar with death now. Too, too familiar with death. I have learned to accept it. If I am to die, then so be it. But I will not live as half a man!"

Christina would have been surprised, even shocked, by Justin's strange expression of understanding—an expression of admiration. She heard him say only, "It is his decision, Cajun. Do what you can."

Holding a torch upside down to combat the rain, Justin found Christina waiting outside. He helped her up and brushed back a stray lock of wet hair, answering her anxious look with a smile.

"Will he die?"

"No, I don't think so," he replied with an assurance he didn't understand. The answer relieved her and together they made their way around to the

160

ladder.

"Beau can't follow," she said.

"I'll have to build some stairs for him," Justin replied, petting his dog. "To Cajun, Beau." He pointed. But Beau waited to watch them climb the ladder before turning back with a half whimper, half bark.

The ledge was slippery but wide enough for safe passage under the waterfall and through the opening of the cave. Torches were lit inside and it was dry and warm. A bed of fresh moss covered the middle of the floor, her trunk rested against the side of the cavern and, on it, Hanna had at some point during the long day placed a turtle shell bowl filled with fresh fruit. Directly over the bed and in the center of the cave was the skylight, covered now with the canvas sail to catch the rain. This was their home.

The shadows lengthened and the light died as Justin put out all but one of the torches. He removed his belt and wet breeches, smiling when he caught Christina suddenly lower her eyes. As he came to her and untied the ribbon at her waist, then lifted the wet shift over her head, he wondered about this innocence of hers.

Christina thought he was going to kiss her. But after setting the wet shift on the trunk to dry, he stretched out on the bed. "Come here," was all he said.

She paused in a sudden understanding of something, something important. The passion between them, the startling force of it, came not from her love but from her uncertainty of this love and her fear of him. Without words, Justin understood this too and

161

as though to tip the scales in his favor, he forced her to relinquish everything—self and love, her very will—in each act of love.

She felt his eyes upon her as she came to him. She lay down alongside him, front to front, entwining herself in his warmth with a naturalness that still surprised her. She felt his lips tenderly caressing her forehead. Passion lay dormant, waiting for another time and she closed her eyes and almost instantly fell asleep.

Sleep did not come as easily for Justin. It was not just his ever-present desire for her, especially difficult to suppress with her small figure pressed so intimately against him but his thoughts rested uneasily on his mind. He, too, was thinking of their love and her innocence. She would always be this way, nothing and no one could destroy it. Certainly not time. A part of himself saw, too, that in a strange way he was just as innocent. By the time of his tenth and eighth year and countless couplings, he learned to separate infatuation and lust for women from love. He never made the mistake again.

He knew now that he was in love. And his love for her was both powerful and profound. His vulnerability sometimes shocked him and made him think of Brahms; made him wonder if she knew just how easily she could destroy such a large and vital part of himself.

Theirs was not a perfect match, he knew. The startling gentleness of her person would always find a part of his world frighteningly harsh. But he could not change. He lived in a world he would always have to change, usually from necessity and sometimes for the better, destruction for creation.

Hopefully, she would come to understand this, to accept all of him . . .

Cajun gently pinched one of the colonel's toes and the man grimaced with pain, nodding. "Yes, I can feel it."

"It is a good sign," Cajun replied.

The colonel watched as Cajun first washed his battered leg, then began applying the thick salve, a salve made from God-knew-what concoctions this man had found on the island. It smelled vaguely like rotting earth, though oddly not altogether unpleasant. Perhaps he was just getting used to the putrid scent of it. In any case, whenever the mixture was applied he felt a cool soothing relief soak through his skin, much like the sweet sensation one finds in an after-dinner mint.

After a mere five days, he was getting stronger and, as the savage said, his leg showed signs of mending. Watching the man skillfully wrap his leg in a moist cloth, tightly but not too, he was beginning to see he owed the astonishing fact that he still belonged to the living to this strange man, Cajun. He felt an odd sense of gratitude and this was an entirely new experience for him.

The colonel thanked Cajun, attempting to sound sincere, sounding awkward instead. It was as if the savage knew he had trouble with such sentiments, for with the nod of acknowledgment came a glint of amusement. He had learned, too, that Cajun spoke little, at least to him. As a matter of fact the only time Cajun said anything not related to his health had been the first time he could focus his gaze and he saw Christina Marks.

She looked like a starving man's delusion. Christina Marks had been pretty before but now, with her skin slightly colored, the long hair left unbound, and her figure barely concealed in the short shift, he had thought he was dreaming. Her picture looked drawn from the most exotic imagination, perhaps a fairy queen or some such fanciful creature. His thoughts must have been plain to read, for Cajun had simply said, "She belongs to another. Conceal your thoughts."

He did not have to be warned twice.

Two of the patients had recovered enough to leave what they had taken to call the sick room and only six remained. Each day their recovery seemed to leap in larger increments. Caring for them became easier and more routine. Christina and Elsie had just finished the noon feeding when Christina noticed a cut on Lady Knolls's arm that did not seem to be healing.

"Cajun," she said, coming to his side. "The Lady has a cut that needs your medicine."

Sitting up to finish the potion of daily gruel, Carolyn Knolls watched the huge savage come to her pallet and kneel to examine her bare arm. He held a coconut shell of wretched-smelling ointment. He was obviously intent on using it. "Just what do you think you're doing?"

Spoon-feeding another with Elsie's help, Christina called over, "That cut on your arm needs some medicine."

"I'll not have him touch me."

Christina and Elsie both stopped what they were

164

doing and looked over.

"You heard me," she addressed Cajun. "Just because the others may not care if they are defiled so doesn't mean I would stoop so low. I may be stuck on this god-forsaken island, almost dead—certainly wishing I were—but that doesn't mean I'll let a nigger's hands touch my skin."

"Christina," Cajun called softly.

Christina quickly handed Marianna's food to Elsie, hastening to Cajun's side. She searched his face for a sign of hurt or insult and seeing this made Cajun almost smile. "No, *la niña*, I cannot be hurt by the workings of a small mind." He handed her the shell of salve and finished evenly. "Apply it as thickly as possible, then bandage the arm loosely." And he left.

"It is wrong of you to speak so." Christina finally found her voice as she began applying the salve to the Lady's arm. "Cajun, more than anyone I know, deserves our respect, nay, even admiration. He is good and kind and noble—why there just aren't enough superlatives to describe him, and if not for his knowledge, I daresay you wouldn't be nearly as well so quickly."

"Aye, she's right, my lady," Elsie added. "Cajun be a fine—"

"Quiet yourself!" Carolyn interrupted harshly. "It's difficult enough listening to her impertinence—" she looked at Christina, then at Elsie—"but I'll not tolerate yours."

Christina stopped, shocked by her ill temper, the cruel biting of her tongue. She must be quite ill still; it was the only possible excuse.

"Oh, yes," she said, turning a sly smile on Christina, "that's the Miss Marks I remember—shocked by rudeness, so easily intimidated into speechlessness. The timid little Miss Marks, all insufferable English properness. Of course," her gaze traveled over Christina's scanty dress, the ridiculous orchid in her hair, "we're not very 'proper' anymore, are we? Tell me," she asked in a pretense of nonchalance, "has he at least promised marriage, a life of 'happily ever afters'?"

"I . . . I—" she stuttered and suddenly she was tongue-tied once again, feeling her cheeks flush crimson.

"Oh, I see he has not. Well, I for one admire the men who drop all pretenses. There are certain benefits after all. It's much better to know you're just a whore than to suffer the naïve delusions of a young girl's broken heart. Was he at least kind enough to add the word love to help soften the blow?" The fact that Justin had, registered on Christina's expression. "But then again," the woman smiled, "God knows how many bastards a man like that could leave one with—"

Christina quickly rose and left before another cruel word could be said. Elsie stood up too, and trying to control her temper, she said, " 'Twill be very interestin' to see w'at becomes of the likes of you 'ere on the island. Yes, it will. Very interesting."

Christina could not be found. Elsie searched for nearly an hour and finally gave up. She found Justin working with Jacob to create stairs up to his dwelling that would allow Beau access. The humidity was so great as to be nearly tactile and sweat poured from both men's backs as they chopped away at the side of

166

the mountain.

She interrupted what seemed to be a rather heated argument between the two men. She first related what was said to Cajun but to her surprise neither man was concerned. They even laughed at it.

"Known Cajun for years and I've yet to see him bested by anyone or anything," Jacob said. "He's a rock that I'd wager the devil himself couldn't move."

Justin agreed with the sentiments. Anyone who knew Cajun realized he had a strange peacefulness of soul and this internal elevation would not, could not, be affected by anything external, certainly not the ramblings of a "small mind."

"But that's not all," Elsie continued, then turned her tongue on Christy and it got worse, much worse. She said . . .

At the end of it, Justin interrupted Jacob's cursing to ask, "What did Christina say?"

"Well, that's just it, she got all tongue-tied just like before and she couldn't say anything, let alone deliver the lashing that she-dog deserved. She left and I've been looking all over but 'aven't been able to find 'er."

Justin dove into the water to cool off and then left to find her. He knew just where she'd be. The other day they had taken a picnic up to the top of the mud flats. About half-way up they discovered a wide plateau overlooking the beach, lagoon, and the boundless blue ocean beyond. One of the island's many waterfalls fell from a steep cliff into a shallow pond and all this was surrounded by lush tropical foliage, a chaotic array of wildflowers. It was a picture of tropical beauty and they had spent all afternoon swimming, eating, talking of nothing and everything, making love.

Sure enough, Justin reached the plateau to find her sitting on the edge of the cliff staring out at the ocean. Her back was to him and, not wanting to startle her, he called softly, "Christina?"

Lost in her thoughts, struggling not to believe the ugly truth, she jerked slightly at the sound of her name. She quickly wiped her cheeks before turning around. "Oh . . . Justin, I—" She stopped, wanting to sound normal but unable to hide the tears inflected in her voice. She stood up and turned away to gather her wits.

Justin watched this struggle and moved quickly to her side. He turned her around and gently lifted her face to him, then wiped her cheek. "You've been crying."

His tenderness drew her to him, making her want to collapse in his arms and beg him to tell her that his love was not pretense and that he would marry her someday. But she had not the courage and, besides, such things cannot be asked for, only volunteered. She would never ask him to promise something he didn't mean or want.

Justin sat down and drew her sideways into his arms so he could study her. His hand brushed lovingly through her hair. "Could that woman have given you such doubts? Could your love and trust of me be so fragile?"

She looked up, surprised he knew and wanting to deny it, but unable to.

"How could that be? How could you doubt the depth of my love for you? What are you thinking, sweetheart? That once we're rescued, I would see you to some port, say a pleasant good-bye as I taste your lips for the last time?" He chuckled softly. "I think it would be easier to shoot myself."

Wide, misty eyes met his bluer ones, reflecting the ocean stretched beyond. She felt his love as a tangible force and then the tenderness in his kiss spoke the same message. She wanted it never to stop.

Justin gently lowered her to the ground. She averted her eyes as she felt his gaze caress her in a way that caused her breath to catch with anticipation, waiting for his touch. A touch that effortlessly awakened her to desire.

But for a long while Justin was content to just study the contours of her form, seeing her beauty as yet unchanged but knowing with sudden certainty that she would soon be with his child. He didn't know how he knew, only that he did, and he was less surprised by the thought than he was by the surge of emotions it brought.

He had known few women long enough to know or care whether they came with his child. Most women took precautions, the penny royal tea that forced a bleeding and rid the woman's womb of the unwanted seed. Then too there were always a surgeon's services. Christina was, to say the least, different. As long as he was alive he would see that her innocence kept her ignorant of such measures, for he wanted every child that came from their bed.

He brushed his hand over her flattened stomach, and thought of his own childhood, so thankful that he could give his child a better life.

He had been born in Jamaica to an English lady, Elizabeth Dowell. His mother had died during childbirth and probably to the intense relief of her sister's family whose care she had been under, for there was no marriage and the father had not been named. All Justin knew of his mother was that she had been tall and pretty, given over to books, the writing of poetry, and music. The only thing her sister's family had missed upon her death was her music, of which she had been accomplished, in both piano and voice.

Being a bastard and an embarrassment to the family, Justin had been turned over to a nursemaid and quite literally forgotten for almost five years, left to be raised in the servants' quarter of the huge plantation and not particularly welcomed there either. The greatest shock of Justin's life—one he still remembered—was when his mammy told him, "Youse gettin' too big to pretend youse colored. Somethin'—lord willin'—has to be done."

Nothing was done, though, not until his father, Lord Winston Phillips, returned to his older brother's plantation and chanced to encounter a young five-year-old boy whose heritage was written plainly on his features. Justin often wondered what would have become of him had he not been the exact image of Lord Winston Phillips. The man had picked him up, swung him around and laughed, just before launching into a heated curse of his brother for never telling him that Elizabeth had got with what was so obviously his child. All he had been told was that Elizabeth was dead.

The next week Justin had been on a huge sailing ship—the kind in which he had spent endless hours watching and dreaming of—off to the land of his forefathers, England. Which was not to say he was accepted with open arms into the Phillips's household. Quite the contrary. While he had been introduced as his lord's young nephew, this fooled no one, especially Lady Cynthia, who he once heard comment, "I had always assumed seven children were enough for any man, even Lord Phillips." Nor had his seven older half-brothers and sisters ever let Justin forget—not for a day—his status as a bastard child.

Oddly, it was only his father who seemed glad for his presence in the world and, in a strange way, Justin was his favorite son. His father could not bring himself to place the same standards on the young, half-wild and already quite extraordinary boy, and he never but never managed to discipline the lad—not the first nor the tenth time Justin was sent home from the boarding schools for incorrigibility, various monstrosities to the family name. This was usually fighting to defend the bastard title that preceded his every entrance, or for his undying curiosity, what was often described as disturbing, and peculiar questions, rather too loudly voiced opinions, all of which were, to say the least, iconoclastic in the extreme. Why, his father could hardly contain his amusement those many times Justin ran away, found sometime later wandering the docks like a lost pup, dreaming about the great ships he loved. And amusement could describe the scene of any of the many times he got caught in a tumble with one of the upstairs maids, the first at the shockingly innocent age of thirteen. No, Lord Phillips could only shake his head and laugh.

Thinking of this troubled childhood, Justin suddenly vowed to himself never to leave his child and it caused him to say out loud, "I wish I could marry you, Christina."

Christina suffered a moment's bewilderment. She could not deny their love, neither hers nor his, but as Carolyn Knolls had cruelly made clear, he had not yet mentioned marriage. Did this mean he couldn't marry her or wouldn't marry her?

Justin chuckled at the look of apprehension crossing her features. He rolled over and lifted her lengthwise on him, wanting to feel her body against his. Thoughts of procreation manifest in desire for the act; he wanted nothing more than to spend the rest of the afternoon filling her with his seed.

"No, sweetheart, rest assured I will marry you," he said, brushing his hands through her hair. "What I meant was that I wish I could marry you before you come with child."

Christina searched the features of his face, not understanding. "Then again, God knows how many bastards a man like that could leave one with." She had always thought that a woman's womb would not accept a child unless blessed by the sanctity of marriage. The rare case of the unwed mother was owing to unfortunate mistakes, to . . . to—

She looked at him in shock. It had simply never occurred to her before but it did so now—everything, especially her naïveté and ignorance, and she lifted from him. "That won't happen to me!"

"A woman doesn't always have a choice," he replied softly, seeing her fear and surprised it had not occurred to her before.

"No." She shook her head, though with less resolve. "It can't . . . I—"

Justin pulled her back into his arms, not understanding this at all. "It can happen and it probably will. I am not a man who could restrain himself, not with you, not seeing you like this." His gaze fell over her almost bare form, the long hair spilling over his arms, and then he looked back at her face. "Not being stranded with you on this island." He chuckled. "I could never wait for you," and he kissed her in a way she could not resist. "Is that so bad?"

She couldn't answer. Not only were his lips upon hers again, his hand awakening her to the pleasure of his love, but she had no answer. For part of her did not want to have his child, not now, not while stranded on this island, perhaps not ever.

During the dark quiet hours of that night, Christina lay again in Justin's arms. She stared up at the skylight, seeing a hundred bright twinkling stars, listening to the easy sound of his sleep, the ceaseless lure of the waterfalls and the sea beyond and thinking . . .

She belonged to him, claimed by the act of love, and it was not her place to question him much less refuse. Not that refusal was a viable choice anyway. Oh yes, she loved him; she was drawn to him, drawn to him in a timeless way that she didn't understand and was helpless to stop. As though he was the earth and she was the moon destined for the eternity to be at his side.

And sometimes her love filled her heart, seizing her with a frightening intensity. How he affected her! His smile, his lips and caress, the ecstasy of his lovemaking . . . Was there anything in the world more special than those times at night when they lay in each other's arms laughing and whispering over nothing and everything? Then her love filled every fiber of her

173

being.

She shifted restlessly as the familiar disturbing images surfaced unwillingly in her mind. She saw Justin breaking the colonel's leg with brute strength; Justin carrying her forcibly from the *Defiant*; Justin firing a pistol through sheets of rain to kill a man; Justin turning on her with a violent eruption of anger; Justin over John with a dagger; Justin kicking a drunken man once and that man's lifeless body beneath Justin's dark shadow . . .

The words echoed through her thoughts, "He's not the first and I daresay he's not the last."

How many other lifeless bodies have fallen beneath his shadow?

A dream spun from a young girl's heart slipped into her consciousness and she saw herself as she always imagined she would be. She was married, perhaps to a surgeon or reverend or even a scholar. Life contentedly followed a predictable pattern; days to nights, weeks to years, the peacefulness of this life happily interrupted by picnics and outings and church, celebrations of the birth of children, Michaelmas, May Day, and the like. A happy home filled with warmth and love and peace. Peace . . .

Christina was only vaguely aware of the tears slipping down her cheeks as sleep finally stole this— the last sliver of her consciousness.

Chapter Six

"I can't find my brush anywhere," Christina said as she sat alongside Hanna in the warm sand the next afternoon. She began the struggle to get the comb through a long mess of tangles.

"I 'ope it's not buried in this sand—you'll never lay eyes on it again."

"I was certain I placed it back in the trunk. I asked Elsie but she hasn't seen it either. Honestly, if I lost it, I'll have to spend half the day in company with the comb—oh, look at them," she finished in the same breath.

Justin, Jacob, and a handful of others were playing a ball game—with a coconut shell—in the lagoon. The game was lively and aggressive, the shouts, mostly curses, could be heard for miles. Beau ran up and down along the shore barking encouragement. It was as much fun to watch as it was to play and Hanna and Christina soon found themselves laughing and cheering.

Hanna laughed as Jacob dunked Eric, only to get

bested by Justin and Brahms as his back turned. She rolled onto her stomach, stretched lazily beneath the warm sun, and with dreamy eyes, stared into the dark forest a few feet away.

"Oh Christy," she whispered, "sometimes I don't think any soul 'as a right to such 'appiness. If only me mum could see me—wouldn't she be proud?" She laughed. "Fancy 'er only daughter planning' to wed a sea captain! Who'd ever believe it?"

Christina smiled and turned from the game, stretching out on her stomach too. The two women took to whispering between themselves; intimacies coming effortlessly with Hanna as though they had always been sisters or relations to each other.

The conversation quieted and Hanna seemed to drift into a light sleep. Christina sighed contentedly, closed her eyes, and listened to the distant shouts of the men's game—now in the form of water races. She felt that ever-so-pleasant exhaustion from basking beneath the sun and she drifted into a light sleep herself until . . . until—

Something brushed agains her leg.

Cool and moist . . . She stirred, started to turn and suddenly, with no other warning, the sting of razor-sharp teeth sank into her leg and she screamed. Hanna bolted up in the instant and saw only the lizardlike creature upon Christina, a creature found only in nightmares. Smaller by feet than an alligator, but with jaws as vicious as any shark, the creature was but a frenzy of snapping jaws and she was screaming and screaming, they were both screaming, as Hanna helplessly, desperately grabbed Christina's arm in a futile effort to escape.

176

Justin was moving before he knew what it was, before he knew it was her, before he saw the horror of it. He fell onto the beach running and, then seeing it, her name burst through him like an explosion of lightning. Already running feet ahead of Justin, Beau could not see it but he smelled blood and heard screams; he would defend—defend to the death.

Christina didn't know anything but the merciless snapping of jaws to her flesh. Her arms, legs, her whole body thrashed, convulsed, becoming one scream to get it off, to stop it. Then red, red on green and her blood was everywhere.

Reaching the spot first and with vicious speed, Beau pounced on the creature. The dog snatched a long tail into his mouth and bit down with all his strength, trying to tear it away from her. The creature briefly turned its jaws to snap at this but in a flash of an instant it returned to its first victim, now nothing but an indiscriminate snapping of jaws.

Followed by half a dozen men, Justin raced upon the scene just as Beau bit into the creature's back. The creature turned to snap at the dog and Justin, having no weapon, without a thought landed on the creature to seize the chance. He grabbed the jaws in his hands and using an unnatural strength fueled by adrenaline, he held on for his life. It was John who moved in a sudden rush and joined his strength with Justin's to force the jaws back. For a moment time stopped. The creature hung between them, every muscle in the men's bodies flexed. Teeth punctured fingers clean through. Slowly, inch by inch, the mouth was forced apart. Suddenly, mercifully, the jaws snapped back; blood spurted briefly from a deep recess of its mouth. It was dead.

In the next instant Justin had lifted Christina up and into his arms.

Hot stinging pain shot through her, seeming to come from everywhere except her one leg. She pressed herself against him, burying her face to stop her cries. One leg shook uncontrollably but otherwise she held rigidly still, afraid to move or look, afraid she had lost her leg.

"It's all right, it's all right . . . it's over," Justin whispered as much to himself as to her. But it wasn't all right, it was far from all right, and he shouted to everyone gathered around staring in helpless shock, "For God's sakes someone get Cajun!"

He looked at her wounds for the briefest of moments and saw only blood. He shut his eyes to it but felt the warmth of her life covering the moisture of his skin. He shouted again for Cajun. His eyes were closed though and he didn't know that Cajun was already there, assessing the situation at a glance, acting without words.

Cajun carefully wiped off her leg. He held a cloth to the worst wound and knew at once that like glass cuts, the wounds looked far worse than they actually were. She would live if he stopped the bleeding in time.

Cajun's orders came with a quick assurance that brought everyone relief. Everyone moved at once, scattering to do Cajun's bidding. Justin snapped to and carried Christina swiftly to their cave. The men all set off for water, both salt and fresh. This one reed plant was needed to strip into threads for stitches. Hanna was too shaken to move. Elsie, who had come running at the first screams, set off for Cajun's medicines and to fetch some other rubber plant leaves. Jacob was told to follow Justin.

Once in the cave, the skylight was lifted and bright afternoon sun flooded in from above. Justin became aware of everything at once. He had been whispering meaningless words of comfort to her the whole time. She had dug her nails into his arm, her teeth in his shoulder, all, he suddenly realized, to stop herself from crying out in pain. And it had to be a lot of pain, for her better leg was shaking uncontrollably.

Operating with his intuitive gifts and keen understanding of all things medical, Cajun, too, was acutely conscious of her pain.

She would have to be knocked out.

Justin watched Cajun's fist clench in a silent signal that he was to hit her. He looked back at Christina. Her pain . . . her pain . . . Yet he could not do it. Not even to save her.

"I can't."

"You must."

Justin hesitated, then tried to shift her. Her nails dug in harder and she cried in a gasp of pained whispers, "No, don't let me go . . . please—"

"Christina, I have to . . . Just for a moment—"

She cried out again, weakly struggling to press harder against him. Not altogether coherent, all she knew was the sharp memory of not being able to get it off her. She was safe in his arms. Justin saw this and he looked at Cajun and Jacob for help.

Neither man had ever seen him helpless, as he was now.

Jacob and Cajun exchanged glances and Jacob stepped forward. With both alarm and urgency, he shouted once. "Christy!"

Christina jerked her head around with a gasp, expecting to see it or her leg or she knew not what, and in that instant, Cajun's fist hit her head.

Justin stared in shock, for it seemed Cajun had barely touched her and yet she went out. That was all it took. Relief swept through him. Relief that she was unconscious. Relief that he hadn't hit her, for he would not have known how little it took.

She first felt it brush against her, cool and moist, and before she could move, she felt the vicious biting. She bolted up with a scream, arms and legs thrashing to get it off . . . get it off—

And almost in the same instant, his arms came tight around her. "I've got you . . . I've got you. It's only a dream, a dream . . ."

She collapsed all at once against him, trembling and scared, just scared. It took several long minutes but with the security of his arms and the gentle coaxing of his voice, she began to calm down at least enough to feel her leg and arm wrapped tight in bandages and the dull sting of multiple cuts.

"My leg . . ." she whispered. She couldn't feel it. "Is my leg—" she couldn't finish.

"It's fine, you're fine. Cajun stitched you up good." He smiled at her, looking with tenderness and concern. "Here, drink this. It will help the pain," and like the first time she woke in his arms, he reached behind her and handed her a coconut shell. "My men volunteered the last of their rum. Drink it quick, without tasting."

She did as he bid and, with her eyes closed, she

180

swallowed and swallowed, not feeling the hot liquid until it burst like fire in her stomach. She coughed but managed to keep it down and almost immediately she felt its warmth spreading through her.

"Better?"

She nodded, tried to smile.

"Does it hurt much?"

She shook her head.

"Liar." His hand brushed tenderly through the long hair. It had taken a good hour of washing to get all the blood out. "Do you remember what happened?"

She closed her eyes. "Only not being able to get it . . . off, to stop it. I remember you grabbed it, and then John—what was it?"

"We don't really know. Much like an alligator, only smaller and about a hundred times more vicious. Samuel claims he once overheard some men talking of alligator hunting, when another man mentioned a rare creature that lives on the South Sea islands, like an alligator or a giant lizard, as yet even unnamed."

Justin stopped short of the rest of the story: that a ship sailed to the islands to get fresh food supplies, stopping for just overnight. Two men, land starved, chose to sleep on the beach. Their screams alerted the crew but by the time the crew reached the beach, all that was found was this lizardlike creature devouring the remains of two bodies.

"I had my men pound through the bush looking for others like it but nothing was found."

"Beau? Is Beau all right?"

At the sound of his name, Beau rose from the foot of the bed and came to Christina's side, thumping his tail in greeting. "He's fine, just a few cuts," Justin replied. Both he and John had puncture wounds through their fingers to attest to the creature's frightening strength. Beau's thick fur had protected him far better than their mere skin.

Christina shifted to pet him and Justin felt a shiver go through her. Cajun had said having lost so much blood, she'd likely be chilled upon waking, and that it was important to keep her warm.

Elsie had gone in search of the only blanket on the island and eventually found it in Carolyn Knolls's possessions. Despite the circumstances, the woman refused to turn the item over. Elsie had to call him to forcibly take it from her. Justin was beginning to wonder if there was no limit to that woman's malevolence.

"Are you very cold?" he asked, tucking the blanket around her.

She nodded, staring to shiver uncontrollably.

"Here, drink another cup of this." He pressed a coconut shell to her lips, which she drank from thirstily, finding the rum mixed with milk this time. Then she tried to press herself even closer to his warmth. Justin brought his leg protectively over her and embraced her tightly.

"Don't ever let me go," she whispered on the edge of sleep.

"Never."

Christina, comfortably nestled in Justin's arms, tried to follow the conversation between Justin and Jacob. It sounded important. The small effort proved taking; she felt exhausted and, staring into the amber coals of the campfire, she found herself drifting into that pleasant consciousness—not quite sleep but not wakefulness either.

After two long weeks of recovering, she was doing much better—at least she knew she'd live and if Cajun was right, she'd be walking in another week. After the multitude of cuts healed the only permanent damage seemed to be scars. Two large scars on her leg, a long one on her stomach, side, and arm, and a very small one on her chin. One Justin swore could not detract from her beauty.

But then, there was that nightmare . . .

"I'm tellin' ya," Jacob's voice rose suddenly to jolt her awake, "your Mister Robinson is the shrewdest and most greedy bastard I've ever known. And I wager he's spent your fortune twice already."

"Not a chance," Justin replied after a sip of ale that his men had drawn up from the shipwreck that day. "True, he's a shrewd bastard but that's why I employ him. However, I do trust him. He agreed to wait seven years before he declared me dead and I believe he will."

"Who's Mr. Robinson?" Christina asked.

"The man I hired to manage my fortune."

"Aye, manage it—spend it." Jacob laughed. "Take my word, you'll return to Boston to find not only did Mr. Robinson declare you dead and buried, but the bastard will have forgotten your name."

"I'm not worried," Justin replied with an easy shrug. "Should that happen, I'll just have to round up the men and start over again."

Jacob laughed in earnest and tossed another log into the pit. "Justin, you're the only man I know who could lose that much with a shrug. Over five years of our hard work, and you would just start over again."

"I would and I could, Jacob, for I have plans for that money."

Christina knew of some of those plans. Justin had said his money was being invested in various holdings in the New World: mines, mills, and some munitions factories. More ships too. She tried to stifle her natural response to someone who would make money for money's sake, for such efforts were considered sinful by most, merely distasteful by others. Justin had laughed at such sentiments, said they were archaic English notions and would soon die, for "what could be more noble than building things and seeing men to work?" His men had readily agreed and she would like to believe this true but still . . .

Their small party was soon joined by others. Eric and Elsie returned from a walk, then Brahms and Kafir returned from hunting. Having caught three plump birds for supper, they immediately set about cleaning. Christina liked both Brahms and Kafir tremendously; Brahms's stoic peacefulness and his kindness, and Kafir's good humor, nothing and no one excluded from his quick tongue. Knowing them, it made sense that these two men should prefer the company of Justin, Jacob, and Cajun, rather than the other group that was presently engaged in a boisterous, surely drunken party somewhere down the beach.

Eventually Cajun joined them, silently slipping into the light of the fire. He mentioned something to Justin, who nodded in turn. It was something about the men down the beach but she couldn't catch what, for suddenly everyone seemed to be talking at once.

Elsie was lamenting about a fresh rip in her now hopelessly battered chemise; how in no time they were all going to be left stark naked. The men, for some reason, began a discussion of the European political situation, Napoleon's war with England, and America's response and this oddly, inexplicably, somehow turned into a heated debate over what foods were missed most. Cajun rolled his eyes with a smile at this inane twist in the conversation and Christina laughed when Jacob described his mother's strawberry tarts and Justin said it sounded as though he was talking about a woman.

"Well, since Hanna's not here I can say I might be willin' to trade one or two nights with the lass for just one of them sweet strawberry tarts."

Justin chuckled and pointed to who stood behind Jacob, obviously having just overheard his remark. "Trade me in for a lousy tart, will you?" Hanna asked and then Christina gasped as Hanna dumped the contents of a coconut jar directly over Jacob's head. Jacob cursed, jumped to his feet, and to everyone's amusement, a chase was on.

All this detracted from who Hanna had brought from the sickroom to join the campfire. Still weak and thin but sufficiently recovered, Carolyn Knolls sat down on a log. Wrapped in the blanket, only her frail face showed to the others. She looked decidedly uncomfortable and indeed was. The only reason she let Hanna talk her into coming out was to escape persistent frights from spiders in the cave. On the other hand, too, this was the only society on the island and she might as well start to get used to it.

Conversation continued but there was no denying

the tension her presence brought to the group. Carolyn Knolls never ventured a word, nor did anyone attempt to engage her. Everyone knew of her rude, ungracious, and often cruel comments and unpleasant disposition, except when she wanted something. Wanted something like her own private house some of Justin's men were building for her. Jacob had said the house was going to cause a riot of trouble. Christina had not understood the comment; it was one of the things she had planned to ask Justin about that night.

"You know," Justin suddenly commented with but mild interest, "I thought the Knolls name sounded familiar. I knew your husband's father. A Lord Knolls often visited my father at Ash Manor," he explained, "and I met him once or twice while home on holidays. He was a kindly old man and a fair chess player, and I remember once how he helped me out of a pretty bad spot . . ."

Justin drifted momentarily with the thought, remembering the day and the man. He had been in a particularly bad brawl with three older boys, including his older half-brother, Clinton. Their taunting over his bastard status had been particularly cruel, and not only did he get the worst of it in the brawl, but Lady Cynthia was willing to have him bear the brunt of the punishment alone—three days locked in a room. But Lord Knolls, having overheard the entire incident and acting for his father who had been gone that day, interceded on his behalf. More than that, the old man seemed to sense it was one of the few times, perhaps the only time, Justin had reached the end of his rope. He wanted to return to Jamaica, hating Lady Cynthia, his half-brothers, England, and all that meant, hating life and himself, wishing he could be someone else, anyone else.

"Ah, they got to you this time, didn't they lad?" the old man had first said, kneeling to press a damp cloth to his bruised eye and bloodied lip. Justin still remembered the violent heaving of his chest as he tried to fight the tears that he never allowed anyone to see. "Son, it's a hard lot you have in this life and I daresay, you're going to be called a lot worse before you're through. You've got to remember that it hardly matters what others call you. What counts is yourself, what you make of yourself." He smiled. "I have a sneaking suspicion the lord is making you suffer now, so that you can become someone special. Does that make sense?"

He had nodded and desperately hoped it was true; that he was someone special. The old man had chuckled then. "Damn, but I wish I had been blessed with a son, and I'll tell you, I'd want him to be just like you—not some dandyish fop who had everything handed to him on a silver platter . . ."

Justin looked up from his thoughts with a smile. "I didn't know Lord Knolls had a son?"

"He didn't," Carolyn replied simply.

It took Justin a moment to assimilate this and when he did, he chuckled. "Ah, the lovely things money and title will buy a man." Carolyn remained silent as did everyone else. Justin asked with renewed interest, "Tell me, will the good lord be waiting for your return?"

"I shouldn't think so. He's quite dead now."

"I'm sorry," Justin said sincerely.

"I'm not," she added, not wanting Justin Phillips—

indeed anyone—to think she ever cared for such an old fool.

"No, I see you wouldn't be." Justin felt Christina tense at the cruel remark, saw her look away in embarrassment. He knew such sentiments shocked her, but he wanted to see how far this woman would go. "I knew the lord wanted a son. It's too bad your ah, marriage couldn't accommodate him that far."

She wasted no time in replying. "No one but no one has that much wealth," and she shook her head with a shiver of disgust. "Believe me, nothing on earth could ever persuade me to let those old hands—" She stopped but not in time.

Justin had one last question. "And just how did the good lord die?"

She met Justin's gaze directly. For some reason she wanted him to know. She, like all of England, knew of Justin Phillip's reputation; his bold courage, the ruthlessness, his traitorous activities, his clever ability to make all things English look foolish. Having neither the mind nor the inclination to examine the values behind Justin's activities, she foolishly thought she'd gain such a man's respect by confessing.

"Wouldn't you know," she began and in a rather seductive voice, "the good lord died suddenly and I must say 'quite unexpectedly' in his sleep." She paused for effect. "Some short time after he finished his will."

A thick silence descended over the campfire and everyone, even Cajun who always seemed unaffected, was taken aback by the woman's admission of cold-blooded murder. Everyone but Christina, who completely missed the point, missed it because such an idea was quite literally unconscionable.

Justin rose suddenly. "The air grows cold and foul suddenly. Christina?" he said and swept her up to his arms.

Carolyn Knolls was forced to see that she'd made a horrible mistake and, to her surprise, she felt an honest blush of shame rise in her cheeks.

Everyone else rose as well. Moving with the others, the men were heard muttering things like, "Thank God women like that are few and far between."

" 'Tisn't natural, I say . . ."

Once in the privacy of their cave, Christina ventured, "I don't believe she really meant that."

Justin looked down at her. He had thought she hadn't grasped the meaning of the woman's last statement. "Meant what?"

"That she's not sorry her husband died. Oh perhaps at first she truly did marry him for his wealth and title. As awful as that is, many families still arrange marriages for that reason," she informed him. "But, well, I'm sure after a time, she cared for him a little. Especially if he was, as you said, such a kind and good person."

Justin could not imagine any artist drawing a more startling contrast between two women than that which existed between Christina and Carolyn Knolls. He gently lifted back her head and stared at her intently to whisper with a strange intensity, "I love you, Christina."

Christina woke to the dark space of the cave. She knew immediately what had awakened her. Justin, both his arms and his warmth, was gone again. The

189

stars shone bright through the skylight and except for the ever-present sound of the waterfalls, all was still. It was surely the middle of the night.

With hands bracing on the cavern wall, she lifted herself slowly, always cautious of tearing the stitches but especially now that they were almost healed. The floor of the cave felt cool and moist on her bare feet. She limped awkwardly to the mouth of the cave and stared out into the dark night. It was so quiet. The moon shone a bright ribbon of light over the sea in the distance. Not a breeze stirred.

She listened intently for a sound, that sound, the muted cries of Diego. The sound that would take Justin from her. Almost every night now those cries would bring Justin, and often Jacob and Cajun as well, to Diego's hut. Moving him into a small hut down the beach hardly helped, though it did bring some peace to all others.

The silence suggested once again that Cajun knocked the man out with a blow. A blow was sometimes the only merciful thing to do. She had heard though that a blow to the head can cause one to lose their wits and make them simple. Repeated blows surely caused more damage.

How long could Diego last?

If it was up to Justin's men, Diego would be murdered immediately. She still heard rumblings from the men to that effect, at least every time Diego's gross pain was heard in his cries, and this despite his obvious suffering, the equally obvious fact that he was a dying man without help of a murderous hand. How could they think Justin's mercy as weakness?

Wondering and concerned, she limped back to bed

and carefully lay down. But sleep was elusive. It was not only the tumult of thoughts about Diego, wondering still what crime he had committed, but more to the present, it required the sheer force of her will not to scratch the stitches.

"Jacob! I'm warning you—" Justin's whispered voice came from outside.

"John was right—I'm your friend, Justin, and 'tis my place to speak. Lord, you've got to do it, you've got to. 'Tisn't just that Diego—of all men—deserves it, but it's startin' to wear on your men—"

"Damn you! I can't, I just can't! Not yet—"

Christina couldn't hear Jacob's reply but Justin's voice sounded loud and clear with its warning.

"Don't push our friendship further than I'll let it go!"

Silence. The voices stopped as quickly as they started. Christina was shocked; even Jacob wanted Diego killed! How hard it must be for Justin to hold to his principles . . .

"She's leadin' 'em on, prancin' about like a she-cat in heat, practically promising each poor sod a piece once her house is built."

Neither Jacob's crude words nor the disgust in his voice were lost on Justin as he rowed out to the barrier reef that marked the far side of the lagoon. He had been gone two days and two nights to hunt boar again and upon his return, one of his men presented him with the news that a large reef shark fed in the lagoon. One thought of another attack of Christina's legs had determined the day's task, and they hoped to add shark to the boar feast that night.

"I know," Justin replied, not interrupting the athletic grace of his endeavor.

"You know?" Jacob repeated as though unconvinced. "Well that thar house will be finished inside of a week and it don't take a devil's imagination to know what's going to happen when John and the others find 'the lady' has her door barred." The sun was already blistering hot. He took off his straw hat, wiped his forehead, and replaced it. "Well," he prodded, "what are you going to do?"

"I, my friend, am going to do nothing." Justin did not miss a beat with either oar or the conversation. "It's her game and she's played it before. It will be my pleasure to show her what happens when she plays the game with real men instead of an innocent old gent."

Jacob glanced over the smooth blanket of blue water, studying it intently as he imagined a scene played out there. "She's not likely to survive that."

"No, probably not."

Feigning a weak voice, Carolyn called out, "Who is it?" Not that she didn't know.

John chuckled good-naturedly at this, passed the coconut jar of rum to one of the four others, and replied, " 'Tis ye lovers of last resort, my lady."

"I'm not feeling well," Carolyn said, finding it increasingly difficult to conceal her growing irritation at the men's near-constant interruptions. The idiots build her a lousy one-room shack, hardly suitable for a servant and they expect—what do they expect? Surely not that—even these imbeciles couldn't harbor such a notion.

"Oh aye, my lady, we've heard that before, haven't

we, mates?" John received quick agreement from the others. "But that's w'at we've come about," he continued, actually enjoying this game while it lasted. "We've come bearing gifts . . . ah, get-well-quick gifts, ye might say."

Samuel almost lost a mouthful of rum at this. He was not an unattractive man: he was tall and well built, with sandy blond hair and an incongruent smattering of freckles across a strong nose, well-chiseled cheeks. After managing to swallow and wipe his mouth, he corrected John through his laughter. "Not gifts—bribes! We've come to force ye to choose. Which one of us bastards are ya going to make happy?"

"Very happy," another added.

Carolyn's face reddened with anger. So, the oafs did own the bloody gumption to think that she—Lady Carolyn Knolls—would choose from a pack of barbaric sailors, hardly fit to groom her horse yet alone engage in such grandiose speculation. She couldn't believe it, the idea almost made her laugh.

Though she had led them on a bit . . .

"Well, gentlemen," she resumed, dismissing those thoughts, "I am not entertaining visitors today. You may leave," and to make certain they understood their position—"Dismissed."

This was met with wild hoots of laughter. "Dismissed, is it?" John questioned, a bright sparkle in his eyes. "You might not have noticed but we're on a godforsaken island, my lady," always placing exaggerated emphasis on her title. "Aye, and there ain't nowheres to dismiss us—which means—"

"—ye ain't gonna shake us," another man finished

for him.

"Aye, you're stuck," Samuel explained. "You choose one or ye get us all!"

Carolyn refused to condescend an answer. She'd have to speak to their great lord and master about it. The idea of talking to Justin brought a smile and she vigorously renewed brushing her hair, a brush taken from Christina's trunk. If only she had something decent to wear . . .

Laughter followed the brazen murmurings from the men until finally John called out, "We'll leave 'er 'ighness to stew on that for a bit. Just remember, my lady," and he bowed, "we ain't ole men who are likely to die in their ah, sleep!"

She could hardly bear the laughter that followed the remark. God, she should have kept her mouth shut about that! She had just wanted Justin Phillips to know the old lord never found his way to her bed . . .

After helping Christina with her line and tossing his into the lagoon, Justin settled back against the cliffs, shifting to take Christina into his arms. "Come here," he said.

Christina looked anxiously about, misinterpreting his intentions. Oh yes, she'd like nothing better than to spend the morning making love but just last night . . . and then too they weren't exactly alone on the beach. Hanna and Jacob were nearby searching the shallows for shellfish, along with some others. The shadows of the cliffs offered only partial protection.

"Justin," she whispered apprehensively, "I don't think . . . I mean, we shouldn't—"

"Shouldn't what?" Justin smiled, knowing exactly

what she was imagining.

She blushed. "Well, you know . . ."

"Know what?"

He was making her come out and say the words. "I don't think we should make love again."

"You don't?" He grinned. "Ah, but you are thinking about it a lot, I see."

"Oh no, I wasn't . . . well, I was but . . . I—" She grew flustered and he chuckled. "Are you, I mean, were you planning on—"

"Ravishing you?" he interrupted. "I wasn't, but if we keep talking about it much longer, my plans will definitely change. As a matter of fact, it's already getting rather hot and the forest back there looks shaded and cool—"

"No! No!" she said quickly. "I won't mention it again! My lips are sealed."

They laughed and Christina took a seat in his arms. The morning dawned bright and beautiful again. Conversation came easily, easy-shifting and flowing, though each subject became a backdrop for wild flirtations and laughter. Sometimes they could be like two children together and she loved it then—loved him then. Perhaps an hour or so passed and, two fine fish later, Justin was about to make good his earlier threat when they were suddenly interrupted.

"May I speak with you?"

Carolyn Knolls stood several feet away, obviously having overheard much of the intimacies between the two. Christina blushed, partially because of this and partially because of the lady's state of dress—or rather lack thereof. She wore only a cloth binding her breasts and a shockingly short skirt, like . . . like a harem girl, Christina thought, knowing a harem girl's costume from one of Kafir's songs. And thick blond hair was pulled to one side to fall in lovely mass over a shoulder. Her color and weight gain spoke well of a remarkable recovery.

Carolyn was thinking the same thing about Christina. She was obviously well, nothing but a few fading scars remained. One on her leg looked particularly nasty but, unfortunately, the others hardly detracted from her beauty.

"Alone," she added after a brief glance at Christina.

Christina didn't understand the strange look that crossed Justin's gaze. It was an unconscious look reserved for those times a woman—whether lady or ale whore—sought his attentions without his desire she do so. "Anything you have to say to me might be said in front of Christina."

"I'm afraid not."

"That's all right," Christina said, standing to leave. "I should be off to see Cajun anyway."

Carolyn watched her go, then returned her gaze to Justin, finding herself a recipient of his gaze—was that amusement in his eyes? However he was looking at her, it caused her some brief uncertainty. She paused a bit too long, lowered her gaze, and to her horror, she felt herself blushing.

"Yes?" Justin prodded lazily.

He was standing now, leaning against the cliffs, striking a pose so casually disarming that for the first time in her life, she felt she wasn't in control. "It's about your men," she said, determined to recover.

"My men," he repeated rather than questioned.

"Yes, they're at my doorstep like a pack of hounds.

They've even begun threatening me."

Justin was about to say something about the stench of a she-dog in heat, but decided against such tactics. "Well, I understand that," he said instead. "You're an attractive female on an island regrettable short of that very commodity."

"Commodity?" she repeated in a whisper part incredulous, part alarm.

"Yes, commodity." He barely smiled. "Surely I don't have to explain that to a woman such as yourself?"

She was very nearly speechless.

"Just how did my men threaten you?"

"I don't see how it matters," she said.

"I'm interested."

She paused long before explaining. "They said I must choose one of them or . . . or—"

"Take all of them," Justin finished for her. "I wouldn't call that a threat; I'd call it sound advice."

She looked shocked, then angry. "If you think I'd ever—ever—choose one of those imbeciles . . . I . . . I don't believe this!"

"Believe it, my lady. Reality—especially an unpleasant one—has a way of pressing into consciousness, with or without one's belief." And with that, he left.

Having left Justin with Carolyn Knolls, Christina set off down the beach in search of Cajun. The day dawned like a rare summer gift—too easily taken for granted on the island.

The island teemed with life. Noisy birds hopped from branch to branch, tree to tree. Gulls flew against an azure sky. Strange flying fish lifted unexpectedly

197

from the sea to skim a few feet before disappearing as one again. Small sand crabs scurried back with each receding wave.

The sun felt warm on her face, the sand warm on her bare feet. She felt happy and lighthearted, for lately there seemed to be only one Justin present—the one she loved. And this thought brought a smile to her lips.

Until she passed Diego's small cabin.

He was up! Through the large opening of the hut—like a window that looked onto the beach, she caught sight of his dark shape standing up. She had never seen him up and about before and while no one was supposed to care for him besides Justin and Cajun, something, perhaps just curiosity, compelled her to approach to see if there was something she might do for him.

She stood for a long minute in the doorframe unseen. Diego sat on the bed of moss, holding his face in his hands as though in some agony of indecision. His long dark hair and beard had not been cut for several months. His skin looked unnaturally pale and what once must have been a strong physique was now ravished by the mysterious disease. He looked like he had been starved.

"Good day," she ventured softly and added quickly, "I was just passing by and saw that you were up. I wondered if I might bring you something?"

Diego looked up slowly and with no surprise, not speaking for long moments as he considered her. His eyes were dark and clear, but troubled. Troubled oddly by this brief lapse of his pain. Like a convicted criminal waits the noose—he waited for its inevitable return. And the pain was always worse after a lapse, as though its retreat was only to redouble its effort.

But he abruptly smiled at her and she found what many other women had found; Diego's smile affected her like few others.

"I knew you were lovely," he said to himself, dropping all pretenses and propriety. "But so young?" He had never thought Justin capable of losing his heart but should he ever have imagined such a thing, he would have thought the woman would be much older and sophisticated, perhaps a widow, someone confident of herself and what would surely be a limited position with Justin.

Christina was a complete surprise.

"Come here," he beckoned. "Set with me for a spell. Tell me the story of how you came to win Justin's heart."

Diego knew the story, of course, knew quite a bit about Christina, but he wanted the chance to discover her for himself. He knew, too, all about her shyness and he witnessed the firsthand evidence of this presently. Christina shifted nervously, lowering her gaze, feeling suddenly timid with his unexpected request for her company. But few men understood women better than Diego, and this understanding gave life to irresistible charm, a charm Diego knew how to use and use well—one had only to count the number of broken hearts left in his trail.

While it took considerable prodding and encouragement on his part, Christina soon found herself opening up to him. They first swapped stories of their background; Diego's relating of his colorful past filled the room with Christina's laughter. She soon felt relaxed and at ease, telling of the auspicious first encounter with Justin, their friendship, the turn of events that eventually marooned all of them on the island.

Having searched most of the island looking for Christina, Justin was passing by Diego's hut when he heard the familiar and much missed sound of Diego's laughter, then Christina's. Well aware of Diego's charm with women and not wanting to break up one of Diego's rare moments of laughter and comfort, he stopped quietly outside the door and for a while contented himself just to listen.

"I cannot describe my surprise, nay—shock upon seeing Justin that first time on the ship. He looked so . . . so." She laughed. "Well, before he spoke, I couldn't even reconcile the fact that he was one of Justin's men, yet alone him. And I don't know why I imagined him so differently, for I knew of his background, his fighting and all, and I was there when he grabbed the colonel's leg. Somehow, though, I had thought he'd be slight of build—" Diego laughed at this and Justin smiled unseen, "and . . . and, well, just gentle and—"

"Dandyish," Diego finished for her.

She nodded with a smile.

"Justin does look the savage these days, but believe me, he owns many faces. I have seen him look quite the gentleman, both refined and noble. You'll see once you're rescued from here."

Christina looked down, unconsciously scratching the cut on her arm while her other hand held the whistle at her neck. Not for the first time she wondered what that would be like.

"I imagine, though," Diego said softly, seriously, "that some of my friends' ah, faces can still frighten you?"

She looked at him directly, startled by his understanding. She nodded. "Yes," she whispered, turning away. "Sometimes . . ."

"Christina." He took her hand, seeing an expression that revealed all the trouble of a young girl's heart. "Justin has many faces because he has to. You know he would never hurt you—"

"No, of course not," she replied still softly, solemnly. "It's just that sometimes I feel there's two Justins; one that, yes, scares me so, and one . . . one that I fell in love with—" She waved her hand, suddenly embarrassed by the intimacy of her conversation. "Oh, you must think me quite ridiculous."

Diego shook his head, smiling at her self-effacing withdrawal. Nothing could be further from the truth and he was just about to tell her so when a strange look crossed her face, part curiosity, part concern.

"I was wondering," she began, not able to imagine a crime, any crime, that he could possibly have committed—

"Yes?"

"What has occurred that causes . . . friction between you and Justin?"

"That's between Diego and myself, Christina." Justin startled her as he stepped through the door. Then to Diego, "You're better."

While startled, Christina caught the unmistakable intensity of Justin's simple benign statement, and Diego's sudden tension. It was as though "you're better" was a demand. Just as suddenly, Diego re-

201

laxed and smiled at Christina as he replied, "What man would not feel better with such company? I've enjoyed our visit immensely, Christina."

"I should like to come again. May I?"

"You'll have to ask Justin that." He looked up at Justin and the tension immediately returned. "For in truth I'm not always this, ah, well."

Christina looked up at Justin, too, as though for an explanation. He only smiled and took her by the arm to show her off. "Come, Diego needs his rest."

She bid him good-bye, leaving Justin with him, wondering still. She never wondered how long Justin had stood by the door listening, though she might have known. For that night Justin kept his passion down to make love to her with a startling gentleness that lasted long into the night.

Chapter Seven

Stealing the knife had been easy enough. Most of the men—what Carolyn called the wolf pack, a pack that now included all the men who had been on the *Defiant*'s lifeboat—had gone off on a hunting trip. The men craved red meat as much as the sight of the merry streets of London. Only two men had remained and they remained solely because they had one precious bottle of rum left and they had not wanted to share this treasure. After a drunkenly boisterous night, the two men had finally fallen asleep and she had simply slipped quietly by their sides to steal one of their daggers. A knife she would use to demonstrate that she was perfectly capable of defending herself.

After all, she had killed for far less reason and while she'd prefer the gentler, easier means of poison, the situation called for far more drastic means. So, when the pack returned and they forced her to pick one of them, she'd charmingly, sweetly oblige. She knew which one too; it would be their leader; she'd pick the man named John to die.

She supposed they could kill her in turn and probably would but she would infinitely prefer death than to ever, ever condescend to choosing one of them.

Thinking, plotting, thinking, Carolyn Knolls stepped out into the warm morning sun, vigorously fanning flies and mosquitoes from her person. She turned at the sound of laughter and caught sight of Justin chasing Christina into the water. Laughing, Christina ran to the water's edge, dove in, and began swimming out. Justin caught her within a few feet. Christina's arms came around his neck and the embrace was completed with a kiss. Long and passionate, as though they had not a care in the world. And watching them sent her thoughts turning in a different direction . . .

Why did he dislike her so? And what in heaven's name could a man like Justin Phillips see in such an insipid, silly girl like Christina Marks? She was pretty enough, she supposed generously, but so timid, so utterly ridiculously feminine! What was it Lady Everett used to call her?

Oh yes, a "scared little mouse."

Too bad those scars didn't leave a bigger mark . . .

And him? What was it about Justin Phillips that attracted her so? She had certainly known far more handsome men—at least more handsome in a refined way. Which was not to say Justin Phillips lacked anything, anything at all. But it seemed more his manner than anything else, his unusual masculine strength. He was the only man she had ever met who was stronger than her, and at least as sharp. The only man too, who didn't succumb easily—or at all for that matter—to her charms. He was a challenge. A worthwhile challenge if he was only half as good in real life as he was in those dreams she had been having.

Perhaps after she settled this other problem, she'd see what she could do to get little Miss Marks out of the way . . .

Christina didn't quite understand. After eating fish for so long and an occasional piece of fowl, she didn't have any appetite for the wild boar Justin's men had killed and brought back to the camp. A much larger pit was created for the catch and it had been hanging over the flames, cooking slowly since morning. Even the rich scent seemed distasteful.

It was a warm and pleasant moonlit night, filled with a festive air. With one exception, everyone on the island gathered around the campfire waiting for Samuel, who had been ship's cook, to begin the carving. The English soldiers now mixed amicably with Justin's men and one could not tell the two groups apart. Even the colonel seemed a changed man. He was quiet and reflective now and though Justin watched him closely, he never gave Christina more than a passing glance. And to Justin's amusement, the colonel made many attempts to lure Cajun into conversation, some successful too.

The men broke into a loud cheer as Samuel stuck the pig and announced it was done. They quickly formed a loose line and, with a long dagger, Samuel began the carving.

Watching this, Hanna whispered to Christina and Elsie, "Don't look so good to me."

"Me neither," Christina replied with a wrinkle of her nose. "Even the smell is somehow distasteful."

"I don't know what it is," Elsie agreed, sharing their sentiments. "I used to love a nice piece of pork or bacon, but now, after so much fish, it's like . . . like—"

"Eating dead flesh," Hanna finished for her.

"Oh Hanna!" Christina half grimaced, half laughed. "I wish you hadn't said that. I fear I'm going to be ill."

"What are you ladies going on about?" Jacob asked incredulously, overhearing. "My mouth's been watering all day just thinking of our first decent meal in months! Can 'ardly wait to sink me teeth into—"

"Wait's over," Justin interrupted, presenting him a large piece on a shell. "As for me, I haven't tasted anything so good since," he looked at Christina," our last kiss."

"Oh dear, my kisses are being compared to—"

"A bloody boar's!" Hanna laughed as she declined a piece. No amount of persuading could tempt any of the ladies to even taste it and they instead picked on the various fruits accompanying the feast. Justin gave Beau a large leg bone and the poor dog seemed almost overwhelmed by the present. Beau fit the treasure securely in his mouth and looked to both sides to determine who might be willing to fight him for it. Seeing no immediate threat but not willing to take any chances anyway, he pranced down the beach to devour it in the safety of privacy.

By the time all the men were served, half of them were up for seconds and for a long while it seemed no one could get their fill. The festive air continued as all manner of compliments and exclamations over the fine fare continued.

"Reminds me of my sweet Susan's cooking," one man, Henry, said in a tone of sadness, reminiscing out loud. "Every time the ship sailed into port, I'd just wander over to 'er rooms above the tailor shop and don't know 'ow she always knew, but she always 'ad a feast fit for a king just waitin' for me. Lord," he added after a pain-filled pause, "she must think me good as dead."

Another man added, "I remember your Susan," he said, wanting to lighten the mood, "and that ain't all she 'ad waitin' for you!"

The men laughed at this and immediately they broke into a ribald sailor's song about the love-starved lass waiting patiently for her sailor. The song put everyone in a sentimental mood and no sooner had they finished than another man spoke up on this, their most popular subject.

"Never thought I'd miss home like this. Was 'ardly feeling me land legs a day afore gettin' the urge to sail the seas and now, now—"

"It's all you can think of," Brahms finished, asking rhetorically, "Shall we ever see those merry shores again?"

Pleasantly full, Eric leaned back into Elsie's arms and, like everyone else, he thought longingly of a place called home, then the prospects of rescue. Abruptly his gaze turned to Cajun, Cajun and his prophetic dreams. "Cajun, have your strange dreams spoken to you?"

A quick silence settled over the men as they each turned to Cajun in anxious wait for the answer to a question no one previously thought to ask. Each was familiar with Cajun's auspicious talent and while some like Justin chalked it up to coincidence or clever after-the-fact interpretation, no one would discount any hope he might give. And it was hope they waited for, waited for so intensely that Christina felt the entire group hold their breath as one.

Cajun stared intently into the fire and Christina had the unmistakable impression he was deciding something, weighing the choice: to tell or not to tell. "Yes," he finally answered. "I had a dream not long ago, one of a ship coming to the island." He added before anyone could respond to this good news, "But it offered few of us any hope. In my dream I saw a British military ship."

"A man 'o war! Geez—"

"Wouldn't that be beggar's luck," John said, kicking sand in disappointment.

"Hell, I'd be 'alf willin' to take my chances with the noose than to stay on this godforsaken island," someone else added.

"I don't advise it," Justin said with an ironic smile. "I daresay they'd bring back the keel haul for the lot of you."

The men laughed in agreement at this, no one wanting to even think of the horror of being stripped and dragged around the keel of a ship, your skin scraped by a million barnacles only to feel the sting of the salt water; a horror few men had ever lived past their first screams to tell about. It was an outlawed means of maintaining discipline among the hardened, the lowlifes, the criminals—men most common of the sea—and presently an effective deterrent among Justin's men for ever risking stepping on to a British military ship.

"I have the solution." Carrington's voice rose above the general murmurings of the group. "Should Cajun's dream come to life, I and the others from the *Defiant* can still enjoy safe passage to England. You," he directed his gaze at Justin, "must tell us whom we should speak to about your deliverance from the island."

"Aye!" two of the men from the *Defiant* declared simultaneously.

A different kind of silence then fell over the crowd as each man waited to see Justin's response to the unexpected offer from the unexpected source. The events leading to the animosity between the two men were commonly known and then, too, it was a British military officer offering this hope. The opportunity for deception and treachery were plain, and no one knew how to take such an offer. They all looked to Justin for their cue.

By this point Christina was thoroughly confused. She had no idea what a keel haul was; she was certain she didn't want to know. She vaguely understood that Justin and his men could not leave by British military ship—because obviously they were considered criminals—but the idea had never before occurred to her. But Carrington's suggestion made sense to her, for he could surely send word of the island's location to one of Justin's other captains. So why the tension and hesitation?

"I shall take your offer at face value," Justin first replied. "Should that scenario unfold, you should see a Captain Eli Steward in England or a Mister Richardson in Boston." Justin paused with a wry smile and his men remained silent, each knowing there would be more; each knowing their captain. Justin would not leave himself or his men open to deception.

For Justin had yet to be bested by anyone or anything; the victories and successes of his ventures spoke for themselves. Except for that one time his ship was undermanned and stuck on a sand bar and then met with no less than three British men-of-war—the situation that had resulted in his capture—Justin had never let his men down.

Nor did he let his men down now.

"You made the offer, Carrington, and I shall hold you to it—should a British military ship actually venture to this island. And so I should warn you; if you alert the military to our presence here, you will cause a bloodbath such has not transpired on earth or in hell. And I will personally see that you are one of the first to go down. Make no mistake, as small as my group is here, our reputation speaks for itself. We are perfectly capable of defending ourselves."

A chorus of unanimous "Ayes" rose from his men but Justin silenced them. "However," he continued, "it occurs to me that your offer gives chance for different kind of deception. You might simply decide not to tell anyone about our presence, leaving us marooned here. So, if we are not rescued within six months of your departure, when I get off this island—and believe me, I will get off this island—I will track you down and if you are not already dead, you will certainly wish you had been."

The men responded with low murmurs of approval but Christina looked away in horror, frightened again by this—the other Justin. She had no doubt he could, would, cause a bloodbath or track a man down only to leave him wishing for a quicker mercy that never came. Crimes he had probably already committed. This was the man with whom she had fallen in love.

How was it possible?

"I understand your threats," Carrington coolly replied after a considerable pause. "I assure you that I have no intention of deceiving you or your men, for—" he turned now to Cajun, "I owe you my life, perhaps even a good deal more." He more than anyone was aware of how much he had changed. This was all he said, and then with surprising dignity, he rose and left the campfire.

Hanna and Elsie began gathering the shells, placing them in a large fishing net to take to the pond for washing, quietly talking over the evening's events between themselves. Christina made no move to join them and instead watched as Justin, Jacob, and some others strolled down the beach for a private discussion, one surely involving plans. She then turned to Cajun.

She found Cajun staring at her, perhaps through her, and for a moment she thought his look of concern was owing to the fact that he had read her distress.

It was not. Cajun was still remembering his dream, the unspoken part. He saw Justin standing on the island's highest peak to look down to the water where Christina stood on the deck of a British military ship. Cajun's remarkable capacity to empathize allowed him even in his dreams to feel all the pain and anguish and anger written on Justin's face as he watched her go.

"Cajun, why are you looking at me so?"

Cajun at first made no reply but she had a horrible feeling he was looking at her unkindly. She started to question him but before a word was uttered, the man John drew attention to the campfire.

"Lads, the night calls for a celebration," he loudly suggested. "One with toasts. First to our 'imminent' rescue and secondly," he smiled, "to this night, the night of our lady's choice." He stopped the men's response by holding up his hand. "Sammy here and I wouldn't want you to have to toast such a fine night with babe's milk so we brought out the very last— honest to God—tankard of ale."

It was becoming the common joke. It seemed almost every night someone would manifest what they swore was the very last—honest to God—tankard of ale. No one actually knew now many of the twenty or so tankards had been stashed away, but it was beginning to seem like the island had a never-ending supply.

While the men laughed heartily, raising their cups in toast to what the night might bring, Christina, knowing it was no longer a place for a woman, left to be alone.

Carolyn Knolls had listened to much of the night's discussion. She made her own plans based on her own need for retribution. Should that nigger's prediction come true—unlikely but just in case—she would leave and once she saw the shores of England, she'd not hesitate to make it known and to the highest military official just who was stranded on the island. This, even if she did manage to suddenly find favor with Justin Phillips. After all, should she have him, Justin would merely be an interesting diversion, hardly more than a pastime and certainly nothing more. And to turn him in would even the score for all her trouble and humiliation.

Trouble she saw coming to the door.

She carefully placed the dagger underneath the makeshift moss mattress and close to the edge for easy retrieval. These things could be tricky, she knew. She shook her hair loose from the knot and brushed the attractive locks smooth with Christina Marks's stolen brush, a brush the poor chit had imagined lost in the sand. She had enjoyed watching the girl vainly comb the sands for over an hour, indicative, she thought with self-disgust, of how little it took to amuse herself these days. Hoping her skimpy dress and unbound hair were enough to deceive the wretched monsters of her intentions, she went to answer the door.

Cold blue eyes greeted the men and she stood perfectly poised in front of them, a catlike smile on her lips.

"A very good evening to my lady," John said magnanimously, blatantly pausing to enjoy the fine looks so seductively revealed. His smile spoke of his pleasure. "Well now, we've come to hear your choice as you know. To make it easier on yourself, what is surely 'a lady's sensibilities,' " he sarcastically emphasized her title, "we've narrowed the selection to the five of us who built your house for you. Seems only fair after all. Gentlemen," he said in mockery, motioning behind him.

The five men she had ever so coyly convinced would gain her favor if they built her a house stepped forward. She suddenly found herself enjoying this evening's game, thinking of each of their faces when they found a dead man in the morn.

Carolyn eyed each one in turn and silently wondered if she might have made a mistake by selecting John. Big and muscular, not an ounce of fat and obviously capable of handling any number of wenches, John might prove difficult. Of course each man looked uncommonly strong and capable; Justin Phillips made no random choice of his men.

Four of the men—John included—were not unhandsome. Indeed, she saw that a low kind of woman might find them tolerably attractive. Though one man had something wrong with his eyes; they did not seem to work together and this bothered her. She eliminated him, and then another man for what seemed to be a clubbed foot. It was a wonder anyone had survived birth with all their wretched defects. She hardly bothered a glance at the man she considered too unattractive.

Carl witnessed her silent rebuke and stepped back without a word, feeling quite the fool. She had said so many things to him about "hard-working men" and "if she could just have her own place built" and then that warm smile of hers, promises that she'd favor his visits . . .

He knew many names for such a woman.

This left Carolyn only Samuel and John. Though she liked Samuel's fair looks and could imagine many a maid finding his freckled face handsome in a boyish kind of way, he was even larger than John. Thus her original choice was confirmed.

"What's a lady to do with so many fine prospects," she finally said as though she was a young girl with her first dance card in hand. "But if I must choose—

214

and I see that you do insist—I'll waste no more time and I'll get on with this ah, adventure with you." She pointed at her victim.

John both hoped for and suspected such a decision, and with a quick good-bye and a smile, he stepped through her door.

She smiled sweetly in turn, reminding herself to use all her strength, for flesh yields uneasily to cold metal. The door was shut.

The men were disappointed as they joined the others at the campfire, some laughing, others scowling but all muttering unkind testaments to what was wholeheartedly agreed upon as a poor choice. A colorful discussion of women sprang to life as the men finished their cups, one that soon focused on that kind of women. It was Carl who came closest to understanding the viciousness of the lady's heart, and he was the first to suggest that it wasn't fair the only unspoken for female on the island, one who possessed such a blatantly malevolent nature, should get away with, 'spreadin' 'her thighs for just one of us'

"The likes of 'her should 'ave the lot of us and not one less. Might teach the uppity wench a lesson."

"It's amazing how we're planning as though Cajun's fantasy was already brought to life." Justin laughed as he and his men returned back to the caves. "No questions asked. Even I'm acting on the premise that his dream has become reality."

"I've lived through too many of the savage's dreams to doubt anymore," Jacob replied. He thought of the dragon and monsoon, one and the same in his mind and he looked out into the clear star-filled night and was thankful again for drawing breath. "But it makes sense on a rational level too."

"I know. Cajun's dreams spring from a sharp mind, that's all. Of course a British military ship will find us. They'll be scouting these seas for the missing *Defiant*, searching each island for survivors of what could only be either a pirate's capture or a shipwreck. Cajun's far more logic than magic."

"Aye and in any event, time will tell."

"It always does."

They reached the campfire. A warm wind blew across the beach, and the red flames of the campfire leaped and lashed out a greeting. The primitive light on the men's faces, their half-naked and muscled frames, taken with the laughter and heated cursing as each fought for the attention of the whole, all created a scene that seemed taken from man's past. An ancient and savage past.

Assuming Christina waited in their cave, Justin was about to turn in when caught the drift of their conversation. He stepped into the light of the fire with Cajun and Jacob stepping behind him. "I see our, ah, 'lady' has chosen," he addressed the group at large. He noted John's absence with surprise, surprise that she actually picked anyone. "Let me make this clear. So long as she has picked, she's not to see any harm— much as she deserves otherwise. Understood?"

For a moment silence reigned and just as reluctant ayes were called a man's astonished howl broke into the air. All heads turned toward the small shack down the way, though Justin and Jacob first thought it must be Diego and they looked in the opposite direction. Suddenly there was cursing, loud cursing that could only be John, and then a furious shuffle, a lady's cry, and pounding against the wall.

"Geezus! John must be beatin' the lass!'" a man exclaimed.

"I ain't never known John to harm a woman—any woman—"

"Hell no! He puts them on a pedestal, treats 'em like they were queens—"

The inane discussion of John's amorous practices came to an abrupt halt as John burst from the shack, dragging Carolyn in front of him. He held a dagger to her throat. Naked except for a thin cotton loincloth, she struggled vainly against John's hold. He quickly brought her screaming to the crowd of men. Carolyn closed her eyes in stark humiliation and fell silent, though she still thrashed in a frantic effort to free herself.

"She tried to kill me," he announced, cruelly tightening his hold to stifle her squirms. "Thrust a dagger in my backside!"

Indeed the knife held to Carolyn's throat held bloodstains and John turned, bringing her with him as he did so. Samuel lowered a torch to his friend's back and the crowd gazed at the nasty, though far from fatal wound.

A low angry murmur rose from the men . . .

Christina's thoughts were nothing but a tumult of chaotic confusion and anxiously she searched for some balance, an equilibrium if even temporary. She just needed something to calm her fears and put her heart at ease long enough to know what to do, what not to do. She found no such peace at the water's edge and she started back to the caves in search of Cajun. Cajun would help her understand and then, then maybe she could face Justin.

Christina stopped dead in her tracks, and with wide eyes, she took in the horrifying scene. All she saw was John holding a naked Carolyn Knolls before a crowd of men.

"I did try to kill him!" Carolyn suddenly burst in near hysterics as John swung her back around to face the crowd. "I did! I will kill any of you for coming near me! You're not fit to wipe my boots! Do you hear me? Not fit to look at me!"

This outburst caused no small amusement among most of the men. "We may not be fit, but we sure are capable!" one man shouted.

Christina's wits returned all at once and she rushed to Justin. She tripped facedown in the sand, picked herself up, and ran, practically falling on Justin. "Stop them! What are they doing? Justin—"

Justin hardly glanced at her but he motioned to Cajun. "Get her the hell out of here." And before she could react, Cajun was lifting her into his arms to bring her quickly away from the scene.

Carl stepped forward and in a low, nearly inaudible tone, he vented an anger he had held in his heart for long years. An anger that rose from the fact she did not consider any of them fit to wipe her boots; an anger rising from the cruelties of an ancient class system.

"Not fit to wipe your boots, ye say? I remember me own father was hung by your kind . . . hung 'cause 'e broke 'is bloody back tryin' to feed eight mouths and pay your kind's taxes, hung so that your dogs could eat better than people, hung 'cause one day 'e gets so tired of watchin' 'is own flesh and blood die of starvation that 'he goes out and shoots a partridge on some 'igh and mighty lord's land! Hung! The poor bastard was hung 'cause of you and yours!''

Silence. Then suddenly Carolyn, with a reddened face and a futile twist in John's arms, simply spit in Carl's face. "That's what I care about your father!''

Carl's gaze bore into hers as he calmly wiped his cheek. He straightened, raised his arm, and swung hard into her face. Carolyn cried fury, struggled fiercely to free herself from John's arms. John glanced at Justin for permission and an almost imperceptible nod passed between them. And then it started.

John laughed at her struggle and tossed his baggage to another man, who in turn tossed her to another and so on. A loud ribald chorus rose from the men, drowning her predictably desperate cries as she felt one set of greedy arms, then another and another.

Justin and Jacob turned away and, seeing the end, she cried hysterically, "No! Don't leave me with them! Nooo! I'll . . . do anything . . . any—''

Jacob shook his head in disgust. "Lord, if any woman deserves what she's going to get, 'tis 'er.''

"She has indeed dug her own grave.''

Beau was oblivious to all this, still devouring the femur bone in blissful privacy far down the beach, and after a few futile calls, Justin climbed the ladder. He made his way around the ledge, under the waterfall, and into the torch light of the cave. Obviously distressed, Christina jumped up and ran to him. "What was happening? Did you stop it?''

Justin first stared at her dispassionately, then somewhat incredulously. "Stop it?" He strolled to the trunk and sat down to remove his boots. "No, Christina, I didn't stop it."

"No?" she questioned with incomprehension. "Why not? Is it over? Is she all right then?"

Justin made no reply, though he looked at her with some hint of amusement. Her innocence still startled him and he was beginning to see he might have a problem here.

With confusion written on her features and not understanding why he wouldn't answer, Christina moved to the opening of the cave to listen for sounds rising from the beach. She could barely make out the chorus from the men above the waterfall. "I—"

Suddenly a scream broke over the island.

"Oh my God!" she gasped, turning back to him. "They're hurting her! You must do something." She ran to him, dropping to her knees in desperation. "Why aren't you doing—"

"Shhh." He gently laid a hand to her mouth. "I'm not doing anything. I'm going to bed."

"But I don't understand? I—"

"No, you don't understand," he cut her off. "It's fairly obvious that your innocence keeps you ignorant. And I'm not about to change that."

Her eyes widened in bewilderment but she backed away shaking her head. The next scream snapped her head around. She paused for a moment to listen and then enlightenment came with a sudden gasp.

"Nooo," she whispered. "You couldn't . . . you wouldn't . . . I don't believe it—" She was backing away from him in horror, then suddenly she turned and ran, thinking only that she would stop it. Justin swore and rose to give chase, catching her just at the waterfall.

"Let me go! Let me go—" she half pleaded, half cried, prying desperately at his arms. "If you don't stop them, I will! I'll do it—"

"You'd likely become part of the meal. You're not going anywhere near there."

He brought her back to the cave and sat her feet to the ground. She seemed to collapse all at once and he loosened his hold as he watched tears filling her eyes.

"How could you?" she cried in a whisper. "How could you—"

"She deserves it, Christina."

"Nooo! No woman deserves such a thing—no one!" She shook her head. "Just because she has a condescending manner—"

"That's hardly the extent of her crimes. Among others are asking my men to build that house in return for her favors, then denying them, doing her best to humiliate them and finally trying to murder John. And had she murdered John, it would have been her second murder. Christina," his tone emphasized the fact, "she killed the poor old man who was foolish enough to marry her!"

She looked up with disbelief and a pause. "How . . . how do you know that?"

"What I haven't witnessed, she's told me herself."

"I don't believe you. And, and it doesn't matter. No matter what she's done—" She stopped at another sound of a scream—this one a half cry, and she felt all the horror any woman would feel. "Oh please, Justin!" Her clenched fists pounded haltingly against his chest. "Please, I can't bear it—"

"You can bear it and you will. That's enough—"

"No." She panicked. "If you don't, I'll—" Another scream caused her a choked cry. "I'll never forgive you," she cried in a sudden passion. "Never!" She tried frantically to twist away, hurt and angry and afraid, afraid it was true. "You're mean and cruel and—"

"Is that the best you can do? Mean? Cruel?" He questioned lightly. "It's an embarrassingly poor performance sweetheart," he said as though she were but a small child. "You must remind me to teach you . . . ah, more convincing adjectives—"

Nothing could have shocked or hurt her more than his sudden amusement and she half cried, half gasped and twisted one arm free. With surprising strength, she slapped him in the face. Now Justin was surprised. It was completely out of character for Christina. He lifted her off her feet, and with two strides, he lowered her to the low bed of moss and pinned her beneath him.

"Stop fighting me."

Tears streamed down her face but she could not stop fighting him. Fighting not just him but all of it, the ugly cruelty of the men on the beach, the cruelty of Carolyn Knolls that solicited such treatment. The cruelty of a harsh reality she simply could not face.

Justin was far more grounded in the here and now. The small body twisting beneath him created a more immediate conflict, one that he would end.

"You stop fighting or—" he warned, "I'll find some way to occupy you."

The threat brought a quick awareness of his desire. She stopped abruptly and looked at him through the

222

blurred vision of her tears, fearful that he actually meant such a threat. The last thing she wanted was to be forced to make love to him, for her mind was filled with ugly visions of what must now have happened on the beach and the comparison was neither farfetched nor pleasant.

"Yes, Christina, I want you," he said in an altogether different voice, suddenly not caring, not caring about anything but her. And how could he not want her so? Her hair captured the flame's red light and spread as a wide golden halo around her head, her face was flushed, and her eyes wide, misty, still wild with her fight; wild in a way that just begged to be tamed.

She shook her head almost frantically but he laid his hands on the blanket spread of her hair to still the motion. And then he kissed her, lowering his weight to stifle her brief struggle. The kiss was long and thorough and she squirmed in rebellion, trying to cry out against the tender assault of his lips. Until it became clear that any movement only added fuel to his passion and, once realized, she went limp, completely limp.

Feeling this, Justin lifted partially from her. Amused eyes met enlivened, angry ones. "It won't work, Christina," he whispered against her ear. His lips caressed the long line of her neck and she closed her eyes as shivers passed through her. "Other women might be able to participate passively, but not you." He gently bit her lip. "Never you . . ."

Holding her arms in one hand, he rolled partially from her and began slowly unbuttoning the tiny buttons of the flimsy shift. She closed her eyes again and said nothing as he untied the waist belt and parted the garment. And still she said nothing, even as he released her to lift the shift from her, stopping only long enough to drink the salty moisture of her tears.

It was sometime close to the dark hours before dawn when he finally released his claim on her and he pulled her unresisting body against him. She cried softly and she trembled slightly, this despite the warmth radiating from him. She felt her heartbeat spiral slowly downward, seeking a peace that could only come with sleep.

Chapter Eight

Jacob called Justin to Diego's hut early in the morning and Justin, thinking Christina asleep, left without a word spoken. Which was fine with Christina, for she had not a word to say to him. She rose and knew what she must do. While the task caused no small amount of trepidation, it dictated urgency and she dressed quickly, stopping only to take a quick cleansing bath and not bothering to take the time necessary to get a comb through her hair.

She made her way into the bright sunshine and found Hanna and Elsie finishing a morning meal of fruit at the pond's edge. They both looked tired and solemn, suffering the effects of a long sleepless night. Neither spoke nor offered Christina a greeting as she approached.

"Will you come with me?" Christina asked softly.

Elsie diverted her gaze.

Hanna looked at her feet and, distractedly, she buried them in the soft mud. "Don't want anything to do with 'er," she explained in the same solemn whisper. "Don't want to see her or to think about it. I just want to pretend it never happened." And with that, she got up and left.

Christina watched her go, then turned to Elsie. "Elsie?"

A haunting minute of contemplative silence followed Christina's beckoning.

"I suppose you're afraid to go alone?" she asked quietly.

Christina nodded.

"I am too. I know 'twill be a 'orror, it will." But she stood up. "I'll go. Though I don't know why we're wastin' our sympathy on 'er. Lord knows, if anyone deserves—"

"No," Christina said in quiet fortitude. "Don't say it, please don't say it. I don't care what she's done. No one deserves that. Not the most wicked person in the world."

Elsie's soft dark eyes considered this. "You're too good, Christy, too good. You're like a misplaced angel, you are, and sometimes I don't think you belong here on earth with us. Come on." She stopped to pick from the basket of fruit. "I don't suppose she'll be hungry, but just in case."

They made their way to Carolyn's small hut and knocked softly on the door. There at first was no answer, though they heard a shuffling from inside. They knocked again, louder. "It's us—Christina and Elsie. Can we come in?"

There was no answer and bracing for the worst, Christina slowly opened the door. It was dark inside. The reed shades were drawn tight against the morning sun. At first they saw nothing. The room looked vacant. Only a bed of moss, a chair from Justin's ship, and a small makeshift table as furnishing. A bouquet of dying flowers wilted in a coconut shell on the tabletop. As their eyes adjusted to the dim light, they spotted her in the same moment and Christina could not stifle a gasp.

Completely naked, she crouched in a tight ball in the far corner of the room, shaking still. She was watching them wearily through red and swollen eyes while hiding herself like a tormented and frightened mouse hides from a cat. Upon approaching, they saw the various bruises marring her pale white skin. Her hair—the thick blond tresses that any woman would consider her best asset—had been cut, cut by a cruel and careless knife.

"Go ahead! Stare at me! See what they've done to me!" she cried through trembling lips. She covered her face in her hands. "I don't care . . . I don't care . . ."

"Elsie," Christina whispered, "run to Diego's cabin and fetch his blanket, and then get a bucket of warm water."

"Aye," Elsie replied, staring still as she turned to leave.

Christina knelt by her side, staring with wide, worried eyes. She cautiously reached a hand to the cut tresses. Carolyn looked up, and in a moment of desperation, she fell against Christina in a torrent of tears, reduced to a frightened and hurt child. Christina's arms came around her and she held her tight, then gently rocked her, as she whispered words of comfort.

Carolyn could hardly speak through her tears. "I'll

227

kill them for this . . . I'll kill them, I swear it! No
. . . matter what . . . I'll see them hanged . . ."

"There, there."

Darkness claimed the light. Cloud cover hid the
night sky and promised rain, but the air was warm
and unnaturally still. Justin made his way up the
beach toward the campfire with a torch light, followed
by his dog. It had been a long hard day, one of
Diego's worst and he had only just seen Diego finally
to sleep.

Merciful sleep.

Thinking of Diego and in a foul mood to say the
least, Justin cursed out loud to himself, to God, to
whomever was listening. Damn, if even Cajun wasn't
beginning to look at him to do what was unconscionable.

It was a small, noticeably quiet group gathered
round the campfire finishing dinner. Christina was
not there and Justin asked Elsie forthright. "Where's
Christina?"

Elsie did not look up. "She's still sittin' with 'er."

"Has she eaten yet?"

"Not that I know of," and with an accusing tone,
"awful 'ard to eat when ye've been sittin' with a
ruined woman all day."

"Lord," Jacob groaned. "I'm tired of the tither you
lasses have been in all day," he said more to Hanna
than to anyone. "That woman survived and that's a
hell of a lot more than she deserved."

Elsie and Hanna both cast Jacob hard stares as
they simultaneously rose and left wordlessly. Jacob
leaned back in the sand and he announced with a wry

smile, "I can see it's gonna be a long lonely night for me."

Carolyn had finally fallen asleep. Christina sat in the chair just outside the door planning to stay the night in the event Carolyn woke. A torch blazed overhead and she worked furiously on weaving a basket. Not that they needed another basket, they didn't. She just needed something to do. She looked up briefly as Justin approached but returned at once to her work.

He stared at her for a few minutes, watching her fingers attack the task. Her anger was obvious and though Justin rarely entertained banal thoughts, he did so now. She was beautiful even angry.

"Come on, Christina, we'll get you some food."

"I'm not hungry," she said softly, not bothering to stop her work or look up. "And I'm quite able to look after myself."

"I'm hardly convinced," he replied dryly.

She pretended not to hear.

"Christina," he tried again, "I'm tired and want to retire."

"I'm going to stay here the night."

"No, you're not."

She stopped her work but still didn't glance up. "I don't want to sleep with you anymore."

Justin paused to consider her, the statement, and all it meant. "That may be," he finally replied, "but I'll be damned if you're sleeping anywhere else, with anyone else. Now you can walk or be carried."

Christina's gaze shot up to him. Those very same words he had used that first night together. And he looked exactly the same, so tall and threatening and, yes, slightly amused. "You would force me to sleep with you?"

"Yes. Now move."

Christina froze for a brief moment in an effort to control herself. Then, without a word, she dropped her work, stood up, and began walking toward the cave. Justin followed behind with the torch, not seeing how she bit her lip to stop it from trembling with either tears or fear or anger, she did not know which.

He watched the long hair falling neatly over the small proud back, the gentle sway of her hips, the ever-so-feminine gait of the shapely bare legs, and he suddenly sighed, wondering just how long his enforced celibacy could last.

Hopefully not past the morning sun.

Christina slipped inside the cave while Justin left to pull the canvas over the skylight in case it rained. She lay down on the bed, turned away, and curled up into a tight ball. Nervously, unconsciously, she gnawed on a finger of her clutched fist as the humiliation of the past night burned on her cheeks.

She could not bear it! He would force her again! Make her want him like that, forcing her to love him when . . .

When she no longer wanted to. This she knew for a certainty. She could not escape the nightmarish vision of his callous indifference to Carolyn Knolls's screams, his amusement at her pain. She didn't want him to touch her and yet the moment he kissed her—

What could she do?

Justin returned and eyed her position with some patient amusement. He calmly removed his boots and clothes and lay down beside her. It was time for a talk, a very long one, he supposed. He moved about to take her into his arms and position her backside against himself in the way that they often talked, for not seeing him while hearing his voice somehow permitted her startling intimacy. But suddenly he saw that she was crying.

"Christina," he said as he gently forced her around and held her face to him. She kept her eyes closed, biting her lip and obviously afraid. Afraid of him. "What's this?"

"Please . . . don't force me again. You don't know what it's like—"

"To be raped?" He was furious at her obvious train of thought. "No, I don't know what that's like, but neither do you. I'm forcing you to sleep with me, that's all, and the only reason is to prevent that very thing."

"I thought—"

"I know what you thought. Rest assured, I shall endeavor—somehow—" he added sarcastically, "to keep my hands from you." He paused to watch her embarrassment and confusion yield to fresh tears. "Look at me," he said in a different voice. She looked up slowly to confront both his anger but, yes, concern too. "I'm willing to wait for you—I have no choice. But, Christina, I'm at my wit's end with this fear of yours. You must learn to trust me."

She searched his face for a long moment. The torchlight danced across his features, accenting and highlighting his dark hair and beard, the dark brows arching over finely shaped and intense blue eyes. He was indeed every bit the pirate of her imagination. She turned away to hide her thoughts, then frantically searched her mind for the comforting image of another Justin, the one she had loved.

No such image surfaced and she hugged herself tightly, finally facing the fact that the other Justin existed only in her imagination.

She wondered if she did love him anymore, or if she did could such love be a mistake? She wanted to tell him this, that should he wait for her, he would have a very long wait. Words were not easy though and the matter seemed far better demonstrated than spoken.

Justin's increasing frustration manifested in his dreams. Common everyday glimpses of Christina formed vivid pictures in his sleep: Christina brushing out her hair till it flowed like gold silk, Christina stepping out from the pond, her thin cotton shift molded to her form to accent every delicious curve; Christina lying naked beneath the sun—that warm, shy smile of hers just before he lowered his lips to hers—the sound of her laughter as they played in the waves. And these innocent pictures inevitably led to not so innocent ones.

Each morning, he woke from just a dream to find Christina sleeping soundly in his arms. He cursed softly, and dared not to move to relieve the pressure. She'd only come back against him and any movement disastrously heightened his frustrations. He lay perfectly still, watching her sleep and wondering—not for the first time—how much longer he could last. He had never been very good with celibacy for any length of time but after just a week of it with Christina, he was very near his breaking point.

Perhaps if he showed her just what he went through

each blessed day, night, morning . . .

Again, despite her vows, her nightly promises to herself, she woke up in his arms. Sometime in the middle of the night she inevitably came against him, seeking his great warmth, some primal comfort she was certain she didn't understand. And now, like every morning for the past week, she found herself nestled intimately against the long length of him, enduring the amusement in his dark blue eyes as he in turn considered her and her dilemma.

She looked at him accusingly.

"You can hardly blame me, Christina," he chuckled lightly, lifting the long braid of her hair, drinking the sweet scent of coconut. "Can I help it if your desire manifests as you sleep?"

Somehow his amusement, the long week of enduring his constant teasing and baiting, only increased her determination to make him accept the sad fact that her affection had irrevocably changed. But it had become clear this was impossible; he steadfastly refused to take her or the matter of her heart seriously. And this both hurt and infuriated.

"Please . . ." she said, shifting to pull from his arms. The movement brought sudden awareness of his aroused manhood pressing against her abdomen, only the thin cover of her shift between them. She looked at him, part startled, part frightened.

He made no move to disengage her. "Tell me, Christina, which frightens you more, my desire or yours?" And as he asked this, he ran his hand lightly over the beckoning tips of her breasts, smiling at the easy response this brought. Alarmed, she tried to pull back, bracing her hands against his shoulders but she was suddenly held still.

His hand traveled over the curve of her waist and hip and she drew a sharp breath, managing only a weak "Nooo . . ."

"No what, sweetheart?" he asked innocently as his hand slipped beneath her short shift.

"No . . . you promised—" She started up but stopped, gasping as his hand slipped gently between her legs. She clasped her legs together but her movement only clamped his hand against her. Justin chuckled and held her immobile with ease as he skillfully began caressing her there.

"Promised what?"

"No . . . I—" She stopped as a shocking tremor of warmth shot through her, then another, and instinctively her back arched to permit him greater access.

"You seem to be having trouble speaking, sweetheart," he noticed with lazy indifference as his fingers slowly flamed the fire of her desire. She caught her breath, weakly trying to twist away from his most insistent touch, only finding that any movement heightened, ignited the fires he caused. Her mind tumbled in confusion, though her body was quite certain of its part in this and she moistened in an ever so painful answer to him.

Far more than an adept lover to begin with, and after hundreds of hours of pleasure with her, Justin knew every inch of her body and just how it worked. And he used this knowledge to expertly bring her to an edge, then carefully keep her there until her arms swept unwillingly around his neck and quite obviously mindless, she softly cried for him, for all of him.

And abruptly he stopped.

"Speak up, sweetheart. What's on your mind?"

His voice pulled her from the sweet depth of passion he had just so effortlessly brought her to. She opened her eyes and suffered a long moment of confusion.

"Hmmm? What is it?" he queried, then questioned hopefully. "Is there something you want from me?"

Sudden embarrassment spread on already flushed cheeks. Oh, she could die! Just die! How could he do that to her? Forcing her desire, and against her will, then, then making her ask for his touch!

"No! No!" she blurted, but embarrassingly soft, her voice never able to convey harsh emotions no matter how she tried. "There's nothing—nothing! that I want from you!" And torn between tears and fury, she forced herself away from him, stopping just short of slapping his amused face again and only by sheer force of will.

Justin merely laughed and rose to don his breeches. "I could have sworn there was something you wanted. If you happen to think of something—anything—by all means let me know." And with that, and still chuckling, he left to start the day.

Christina still fumed over Justin's morning shenanigans as she bent over beside Cajun to pick roots. They were lost in the jungle's forest in search of herbs, roots, and plants that Cajun might use for medicine. She was thankful for the task, more thankful for Cajun's silent companionship. She thought she would cry should she have to talk.

Patches of huge billowing clouds pushed against an expansive blue sky, a bright afternoon sun. Like shades drawn against light, the moving clouds caused intermittent darkness and bursts of sunlight to fall over the island. It was still warm, even hot, and the ever-present humidity was a challenge to endure uncomplainingly.

Cajun, who often had to use his saber to hack a way through the profusion of lush growth, exercised his keen sixth sense to discover things she would never have found by herself. He constantly amazed her. He stopped but rarely, knowing exactly what was worth picking to place in his fishnet and what was not.

The outing was proving to be an ordeal. She eyed the thick foliage distrustfully, startled by every slight sound and watchful of the changing areas around her feet. Ever since her attack, the jungle had become dangerous and frightening as well as beautiful and exotic. Though she knew she would always be safe with Cajun nearby, every small lizard—and the island was covered with them—sent her heart pounding in fright.

She had to force herself to keep moving. She never would have come on such a venture had she been able to bear seeing Justin after the morning's humiliation. She had met his laughing eyes only once and she knew she had to escape, if only for the day.

Cajun spotted something and leaned over to lift a blanket of moss from a moist bed of earth. His deep chuckle drew her attention and she hastened to his side to peer over his shoulder. Tiny, queer-looking mushrooms grew in the moist bed. Cajun pulled one from the dark soil, turned it around for a close examination, and then chuckled again while shaking his head.

"What are they?"

"Mushrooms." He stated the obvious. Mushrooms for which men will pay a fortune to own. A small sack could bring as much as a thousand licras in some places. He had never known where the valuable toys—for he thought of them as such—grew. It was a well-guarded secret.

"Well, what are they good for?"

"Many things." Cajun smiled strangely. "Primarily for increasing one's . . . ah, appetite."

"Oh, like a spice? Are they tasty?" she asked as she reached to pick one of the tiny globes.

Cajun's hand came over hers to stop her. "I wouldn't know. But you, *la niña*—" and this made him laugh, "do not need such things. We will leave them for now."

Cajun turned and moved away to a promising group of rubber trees, but Christina was hardly deterred. Her appetite was indeed fine and she might not need them, nor Elsie nor any of the men. But, on the other hand, Hanna had lost all her pleasing plumpness. Hanna simply could not eat enough on the island and more than once Jacob complained, threatening to turn Hanna in if she lost another ounce—just as soon as trades were possible.

The mushrooms might be just what Hanna needed.

Christina knelt and picked one. She plopped it into her mouth, wondering if the taste dictated it be mixed in Hanna's food or given to her directly. She chewed and chewed, then swallowed. They seemed curiously bland. She put another one in her mouth and chewed and suddenly—

"Uuugh!" she gasped as suddenly a horribly bitter

aftertaste hit her palate. They were awful, just awful! She wouldn't give one to Hanna if it were covered in chocolate! After a quick glance around, she spotted Cajun nearby. While his back was turned to her, it would hardly do to spit in front of him—in front of anyone.

She swallowed and got it over with. She needed something to wash it down with. Already she felt her stomach turning in revolt.

Definitely not a spice.

Sometime later Christina sat on the beach with Hanna and Elsie, sipping coconut milk and finally feeling her stomach settle down. Her friends were engaged in a heated discussion about Carolyn Knolls's latest predicament. It seemed John had decided she was to be his personal servant. He made her see to his every need—washing his clothes, fixing his food, even carrying his fishing pole, giving him back rubs and the like, fetching this and fetching that.

Yesterday the men had a good laugh upon catching sight of Carolyn walking a respectful distance behind John, carrying his fishing pole and net.

"It seems we have a real live taming of the shrew," Justin had laughed.

Christina remembered her absolute fury at the remark, the situation—as if the poor woman hadn't suffered enough, and she demanded that Justin stop it.

"Stop it?" he had chuckled. "Why, Christina, I'm thinking of adopting his method."

Hanna and Elsie were still upset over it and Chris-

238

tina thought she should be but why something so upsetting to her yesterday seemed humorous today, she didn't know. But it did and she giggled suddenly, the idea of the grand Lady Knolls carrying a fishing pole for a man like John striking her as somehow wonderfully absurd.

"What's tickled ye?" Elsie asked, unable to see anything funny in the situation.

"She is a shrew!" Christina cried. The idea made her fall back over with laughter. "Why, I bet she ends up in love, just like Katherine."

Hanna and Elsie exchanged shocked glances.

"That's not very funny."

"No, it 'tisn't," Hanna agreed, confused. "After that 'orrible night, I don't see anything funny a'tall."

"No, no, you're right," Christina quickly agreed, trying somewhat unsuccessfully to humble her laughter. Oddly, she could not seem to focus on the horror of that night at all. It seemed a distant vision, elusive and yet . . .

"What's wrong with ye?" Hanna suddenly asked, looking at Christina's wide, vacant eyes, her flushed face.

"I don't know . . . I feel so . . . so warm," she decided. Her blood seemed to be warming in stages and she had the strangest sensation of actually feeling her blood flow through her veins. She felt excited and agitated and ever so happy all at once.

Hanna reached a hand to Christina's forehead. "Well, you're cool to the touch. Don't know w'at it could be."

"Island fever," Elsie explained in a heavy sigh. "We're all gettin' stir crazy here, trapped on this rock.

If we don't get rescued soon . . ."

And the conversation shifted easily to this popular subject.

But Christina's thoughts had already traveled miles away. She was acutely conscious of all things: the warmth of the sun on her face and the warmth of the sand on her feet, the sweet taste of coconut milk in her mouth, the delicious fragrances of flowers and earth and sea, the soothing rush of the river water. And she was thinking that life suddenly seemed pleasant, so pleasant indeed.

She shifted uncomfortably, abruptly remembering the morning. How effortlessly he had conjured her passion and how effortlessly she had succumbed! She remembered his warmth, his caress, his lips . . .

Her heart started beating faster, her blood flowing furiously, and a blush spread across her cheeks.

She best not think of that now . . .

She couldn't seem to stop though. For a long while and despite her best effort, she found herself lost to memories of his lovemaking. She was so lost to memories, such vivid memories that she suddenly sat up and crossed her arms over her bosom, glancing at her friends. They were oblivious to her oh-so-obvious train of thought. She glanced out over the lagoon to where Jacob and Justin sat fishing in the lifeboat. Justin . . .

She didn't care anymore.

She stood up in a rush and skipped to the shoreline, waving and calling out to him. She suddenly just wanted to see him. She had an irresistible craving just to look at him.

The thought of seeing him made her so excited that

she never wondered at the sense of it.

Justin finally looked up and caught sight of Christina waving on the shoreline. He stared for a moment, surprised by her summons considering the week-long animosity and then the trick he played on her this morning. Something must be amiss.

Justin dove in and quickly swam the mile or so. He reached the shore and came quickly to Christina's side.

"What is it? Is something wrong?" he asked, breathing deeply and glancing behind her and around for something amiss.

"Nooo," she said too slowly, staring not at his face but at his body. His skin was so smooth and bronzed, small beads of moisture sliding off his muscles. His muscles! She felt suddenly fascinated by his muscles, muscles everywhere. He was so strong . . .

"What is it?" he asked again.

"Your muscles . . ."

"My what?"

"Your muscles . . ." She raised her arm to run a single finger from his shoulder down his arm.

Justin watch the finger in confusion. "My muscles?" he repeated, following her gaze over his body. He looked behind her again, thinking, "You want me to lift something for you?"

"Nooo," she said, again too slowly. She looked up to his lips. She reached a hand to her own lips, vividly recalling the taste of his kiss and suddenly all she wanted was for him to, "Kiss me!"

"Kiss you?" He stared for a long moment in disbelief. "Oh no, Christina." He shook his head, laughing. "If you think for one minute I would let you get away with the trick I played on you this morning—"

"Oh no! No trick . . ." She stopped, finding it difficult to talk because it was impossible to think. She giggled at herself. "I only want you to kiss me." She reached a hand to his chest, and ran a single finger teasingly there. "If you kiss me, then I'll—" and she reached up on to her tiptoes to whisper something he simply could not believe came from her mouth.

He stared at her in stark disbelief, confusion, and no small amount of amusement. There was something wrong here. She would never say that. Until now he would have bet his life she didn't even know the word for it. He was all for the suggestion and to say the least after this long week, he would more than happily comply but there was something wrong with her. Even if she wanted to make up, even if she suddenly found herself desiring him as much as he did her, she would not have said that.

He continued to stare down at her, waiting for some explanation.

Christina giggled at his obvious stupefaction. "What's wrong?" She reached her arms around his neck and lifted back on her tiptoes so that her hips pressed against him and the tips of her breasts touched his chest. She felt his quick response and giggled again. "You do want to kiss me, don't you?"

This was too much. Too unbelievably much. Something was definitely wrong. "Yes," he said, "but after I find out what's wrong with you." And he lifted her into his arms, calling for Cajun even as he moved to their cave.

Justin had just set her to her feet inside the cool darkness of their cave when Cajun appeared at the opening. He bent his huge weight and stepped inside, straightening to stand in wait.

Justin was staring down at her, trying to hold her at some small distance long enough to get to the bottom of it. But he could not seem to turn from the seductive mischievousness in those eyes. "There is something wrong with her," he explained. "Christina, say something to Cajun."

"I don't want to talk to Cajun." She could think only of his kiss, how much she wanted to feel his hands on her again. Though abruptly it occurred to her how rude that was! "Oh, Cajun," she giggled, not understanding the sudden feeling of dizzying excitement, how she couldn't get her mind off . . . "I don't mean to hurt your feelings and, and I always love talking with you but, but—" She looked back to Justin with a smile, "right now I just want—"

"I know what you want," Justin quickly interrupted. He stared at the sultry desire in those wide gray eyes, a smile that all too easily revealed her thoughts and he suddenly laughed, trying to keep control just long enough to know what happened. "What I want to know is how come?"

It required but a few moments for Cajun to know what must have happened. "Christina," he said with a smile already lifting to his dark eyes, "did you taste any of those mushrooms I pointed out to you?"

Christina was finding it increasingly difficult to concentrate on anything but Justin. She stared intently, confused and frustrated by this long wait for his arms, all these questions, Justin's own curious mixture of confusion and amusement. Every inch of her skin seemed waiting to feel his touch, his kiss—

"Christina, sweetheart, can you answer Cajun's question?"

"What question?"

Justin chuckled and shook his head. "Mushrooms, sweetheart, did you have any?"

She nodded absentmindedly as she reached for him. And Cajun suddenly started laughing. Justin quickly stopped her hands and momentarily contented her by holding her against him, but keeping her anxious hands firmly behind her back. "What were they, Cajun?"

"The answer should be becoming obvious. The only true aphrodisiac I know of."

Justin shot a shocked glance at him, then looked back at Christina with a widening smile of disbelief. He too suddenly laughed. "I don't believe it. My God, I was born under a lucky star."

"Ask her how many she ate."

"How many mushrooms did you swallow, sweetheart?"

Christina decided she was going to die if he didn't stop talking and start kissing her. "Justin, please, I don't understand why we have to talk of food and stars and things when I just want—"

Justin buried her head in his chest and through his laughter managed to ask his last question. "Just tell me how long it will last."

"Longer than you, my friend," Cajun bellowed with laughter as he left, "longer than you . . ."

Thinking that would be a most interesting challenge, Justin listened to his friend's laughter all the way down the ladder. Then he finally turned his complete attention to her. "Now tell me just exactly what you want."

And Christina's laughter, her freed hands, made this perfectly clear.

The first thing she felt upon waking was hunger. A ferocious hunger such as she never before experienced. Then as she moved, her body registered exhaustion, utter, complete physical exhaustion. She stretched and turned in discomfort only to discover a soreness as if, as if she had spent the entire night making love . . .

The memory crashed into consciousness at the exact moment she heard his chuckle.

"Ah, my sleeping beauty has finally awakened. I was beginning to get worried but then," he chuckled again, "you did earn your sleep."

Christina sat up. Her hair fell in a mass of wild tangles to hide her nakedness but then nakedness was not on her mind. Justin leaned casually forward with a mug in his hand, standing with one leg bent and resting on the trunk. His unconcealed amusement confirmed her worst fears.

"So, how do you feel?"

"I . . . I—" Her eyes shot up to him as a hand reached to her bruised lips. She stared in marked disbelief as memories of unabashed, uninhibited, wild lovemaking floated one by one into consciousness. She didn't do that . . . no, she couldn't have done that and he—

She suddenly blushed profusely.

"Speechless I see," and he laughed at her. "Well,

what can one say about such a performance as yours, except that it was extraordinary, just extraordinary," he repeated with feeling.

A blush burned on her cheeks and she covered her face in shame.

"Don't look so distressed, sweetheart." He was enjoying this immensely. "I quite enjoyed myself. My only question is when can I expect an encore?"

"Ohhh," she said as if in pain, his amusement intolerable. "Never . . . never . . ." she vowed, burying herself in the moss.

He only laughed. "Never say never. I don't like to threaten you, sweetheart, but those mushrooms do solve any problem I might have with celibacy."

She turned slowly around. "You wouldn't?"

Justin moved to her and leaned over, lifting her face to his. "Let's just not tempt me, hum?" There was unexpected seriousness in his tone but this was quickly replaced with amusement and, still chuckling, he left her alone with what felt like undying humiliation.

She collapsed back to the moss. Emotions, emotions, emotions swelled, then raged through her. She felt dangerously close to tears and so tired of it. Tired of battling him, tired of always losing, tired of being torn between her love and yes . . . hate.

She was being ripped apart.

She didn't know how she could face him now. In truth he was starting to threaten her. And perhaps that frightened her more than anything, for that could destroy her love like nothing else, leaving her with only . . . hate. And she didn't want that, no matter what, she didn't want that.

Somehow she faced him, though throughout the morning she could not meet his amused gaze. It wasn't until she talked to Cajun—his stoic disinterested manner easing her embarrassment—that she learned she had slept for a day and a night after the day and night of lovemaking, missing a whole twenty-four hours, which explained her hunger. Ravenous, she spent a good portion of the morning satisfying her hunger.

By late afternoon Justin and Jacob disappeared to attend Diego. Diego's condition, or at least his pain, had worsened, Cajun quietly explained, as he watched Christina's gaze follow Justin down the beach. Concerned eyes turned to him and she stood up, thinking she might help too. "No." Cajun stopped her. "It is difficult for a man to bear pain in a woman's company. And Justin needs to be alone with him now."

She wondered if Cajun's words meant Diego's time had come but she knew not to ask, for like everyone else, Cajun shrouded Diego's illness in mystery. He always eluded her inquiries. The thought of Diego's interminable suffering finally ending in death caused a wave of sadness in her heart, humbling her own troubles in its wake.

She was not helpless and somehow she would survive this. For the while she could do nothing about this conflict of her heart, just as Diego could do nil about his pain. But the world was not stagnant but rather forever changing. Sooner or later it would end. The situation would alter itself, an opportunity would present itself, and then, then she would know what to do.

Jacob returned after nightfall and without Justin.

247

He went directly to the campfire and reported to Cajun. "Diego's finally asleep now but still his frame is wracked with convulsions." He pushed long fingers through white hair and sighed, looking inexpressibly sad. "Justin will stay with him through the night."

Relief swept through Christina.

"That is," Jacob added in a strange tone of solemnity, "if the night lasts to the day."

Cajun's gaze shot to Jacob with a fixed stare.

"You're right, Cajun, you're always right. Justin is at his rope's end; he knows he must act. Aye," he said to himself, falling into the sand exhaustedly, feeling as though he had borne the pain he had only witnessed and knowing it was so much worse for Justin. "Diego is Justin's curse—the only man to show him that he can't always have what he wants."

Christina diverted his gaze to hide her alarm. So Jacob thought Justin would soon act against Diego! Is that why Cajun thought Justin needed to be alone with "his curse"? And does reaching his "rope's end" actually mean Justin would end such a helpless, doomed life as his men thought he should?

No, she almost said out loud. Justin would not kill a weak or defenseless man. A man who, no matter what crime he had committed against Justin, had once been his friend. He was not capable of cold-blooded murder, if even for revenge.

She told herself this vehemently over and over again.

But doubts crept into her thoughts.

She excused herself early, pleading exhaustion, and sought the privacy of their cave. Once in the hallowed darkness of the cavern, she lay on the bed of moss to stare up into the star-filled night, just thinking. Time crept slowly past. She knew not how long she lay there tossing and turning, lost to an unending stream of unpleasant thoughts, but it was long enough to hear everyone retire.

Sleep continued to prove elusive. Anxious musings kept her tossing and turning. The soothing lure of rushing water could quiet neither mind nor body, no matter how hard she concentrated. Hours flew past midnight and finally, when she realized she had watched the progression of a bright crescent moon rise to the equinox, she got up.

A long walk on the beach would serve as a sleeping potion.

She stepped quietly outside and down the steps to the pond, then alongside the riverbed heading to the ocean. The campfire had died to hot red embers but the bright crescent moon cast long shadows. The sand felt cool on her bare feet but the air was so quiet and still; that perfect temperature, neither warm nor cool. Small waves gently lapped onto shore. She breathed deeply at the water's edge and felt her thoughts slow. All tension was absorbed by a near mystical calmness of the quiet night.

And quite suddenly it shattered as she heard it, that cry, Diego's cry sounding from the far distance. She stared in helpless horror at the natural jetty separating their beach from the beach that housed Diego's small hut. Another cry sounded like a desperate plea. She heard Justin reply and though the words were inaudible, his tone was not.

He was angry.

Alarmed and knowing she should not, she found

herself moving trancelike to the jetty. The voices grew ever louder. Diego was begging for mercy! Hearing this, having no idea what she would do, only knowing to stop it, she scurried out in the water to escape the jetty rocks. She made her way around the rocks and then stopped dead in her tracks.

Outlined in the light of the crescent moon, Justin's tall frame towered over Diego, who had collapsed to his hands and knees in the darkness of Justin's shadow. The poor man's arms could barely support his position and he was crying, not with pain, but for mercy.

"My God, don't do this to me! I beg you, Justin . . . I beg—" He collapsed to the sand, his frail body racked with either pain or tears, she didn't know. Justin remained unmoved, his gaze focused on the dark stretch of beach ahead as though unable to bear witness to this—the sorry reduction of his friend, and Christina watched transfixed, wanting desperately to run from it but held immobile by the need to know what he would do.

It seemed the battle between the two polarities in Justin; between the man she loved and the man who frightened her to the depth of her soul. Diego was begging for mercy; begging for his life. Justin played as a god; capable of vengeance and a quick death or mercy and forgiveness. She would know what he would do.

Diego struggled and each pained gasp for life pierced her heart. He finally lifted himself enough to grab on to Justin's legs. "You were my brother," he deplored. "I loved you, I—"

Justin seized him by the arms, lifting him to his feet

to embrace him with all the fierceness of his being. Tears swam quickly to her eyes, and she clutched herself tightly.

How could she have doubted him? How . . .

Shame washed over her for having ever questioned him, and just as she was about to turn away, Justin's arm lifted back and, with Diego still held in an embrace, he thrust his dagger forward.

Christina's scream never left her throat. Cajun stepped behind her at the exact moment and clamped his hand hard over her mouth. She hardly noticed, her terrified eyes held to Justin as Diego's body fell lifelessly at his feet.

With the bloody dagger in hand, Justin turned to see who Cajun held in his arms. His gaze bore into her. She had an unmistakable impression he dared her to pass judgment. But abruptly the moment passed as Justin turned, merging into the darkness that was the forest. It might not have happened; she suddenly could not say for certain that he had even seen her.

Cajun looked down at her. It was the first time she had ever seen anger in those dark eyes. "You should not have been here."

She searched his face, not hearing and not caring because, "He killed him!" she cried in a sudden rush. "Diego was begging for his mercy—"

"Yes." Cajun stopped her. "And finally it was given. You do not understand, *la niña*," he added softly in answer to her confusion. "You are but a woman and a young one. Until the gods paint the world black and white, until you have perfect understanding, you have no right to pass judgment against any man, especially the man who has chosen you."

Confused and frightened, she tore from Cajun's arms and cried, "How can you speak to me so, when it was Justin who so cruelly passed judgment on life?"

He just stared at her. She was too young and innocent for a man like Justin. He would do no more explaining; it was not his place. Justin would do so and in his own time.

Cajun merely shook his head in answer and turned away. Leaving her alone and frightened, frightened by a man and his harsh world, a world that offered no escape.

Christina was lost in a debilitating numbness that could not overcome an increasing anxiety. Justin had been gone for three days now and no one had seen him. For this she was glad and had it been in her power to snap her fingers and disappear, never to see him again, she would not hesitate. But she would see him again, and soon.

What would she do? What would she say? She didn't know; didn't know how she could know. She could not escape the nightmarish vision of that night: Justin standing over a man who had fallen to his knees, helpless with pain and begging for mercy. Then, Justin cruelly lifting him to deceive with an embrace before . . .

Christina started, realizing she had been staring numbly into the gray depths of the lagoon for nearly an hour, lost to the vision that haunted even her sleep. Fresh water rushed into salt. The morning's gray sky painted the lagoon and the ocean beyond gray, a bleak and dismal gray that seemed to offer no hope.

Christina had been sitting by herself on the beach

for a long time, too long, Hanna thought. As she made her way down the beach toward her friend, she had known something troubled Christina for some time. Christy had been all to herself since Justin went hunting and the ill man had been buried. While Christy had taken a fancy to Diego, she seemed far more troubled than grieved. Something was wrong, she just knew it. She had tried many times to earn her friend's confidence but to no avail; Christina would only say it was of no real concern.

Hanna beckoned softly from behind. "Christy?"

Christina turned and saw Hanna. In that moment and for no apparent reason, the world suddenly came into sharp focus and she knew what she would do.

She would leave him. Until that was possible, she would avoid him. There would be times when avoidance was impossible; mayhap he would force his company upon her, physically or otherwise. There was little she could do to stop him. But she could disappear perhaps for days on end if she hid in the wilds and at least then, when the opportunity came to leave him, it would come as no surprise.

As for her love, a love she suddenly knew as real and passionate and undying, she would just have to accept it for what it was—a mistake. This was not a paradox, for she quite literally loved him against her will, but she would not submit to that love—no matter how powerful—with a lifetime of anguish.

"Christy?" Hanna beckoned again, disturbed by the determined stare, "why are ye lookin' like that?"

Everything came with the fresh vision of a babe in arms. Hanna, sweet Hanna. The island had transformed her as well. Whereas Lady Knolls had tumbled down the formidable class structure, Hanna had been elevated. Once merely a plump, jolly maid, now elevated to the lofty position of a sea captain's wife. A great equalizer this island was; shifting and shaping lives irrevocably.

"Have you noticed how much we've all changed on the island," she asked quietly.

Hanna could not fathom where this question arose from but determined to engage her friend in any conversation, she brightened and quickly agreed. "Oh aye." She first laughed, running a hand through her red curls. "I've lost my plumpness and gained a sea c'tain for me 'usband. As soon as we're back, I'm gonna purchase the fanciest rags imaginable, rags fit fer a queen. Then I'm gonna walk into the finest shop in all of London and I'm gonna say, 'I want this and that and this and oh heavens no! Silver 'twill never do, never. Must be gold, real gold, fer nothin's too good for the likes of me,'" and she curtsied, "a sea captain's wife."

Christina smiled at the song and dance, the first smile in what felt like a long time. Hanna was lovely now, no doubt about it and she was certain to do fine as Jacob's wife—provided she had voice lessons. Nothing separated class as much as elocution. Hanna lost weight and gained the status of a sea captain's wife; she lost her innocence and gained an unwanted love.

"Do come see your cave, Christy." Hanna tried again to cheer her friend with the news that Jacob just finished making a table and chairs for them. "All the fixin's are in and whilst the table and chair would 'ardly impress a lady, they be real nice and Elsie and I

254

fixed a fresh bed for the two of you—"

That was the wrong thing to say. "I don't want to," Christina interrupted unkindly and abruptly turned back around.

Determined, Hanna tried again. "Then, what say ye, we go check the traps and pick some fruits?" There came no reply. So she added hopefully, "Jacob says 'twill be the last chance before the storm comes."

Christina translated this into the last chance she might have to escape. Justin would surely return with the storm and if she could lose Hanna in the forest . . .

"Very well," she said shortly.

Losing Hanna proved easy business. Once in the forest Hanna busied herself with the task, chatting amicably as though nothing was wrong and apparently not requiring response from her. With Hanna's back turned, Christina quietly slipped through the trees and was off, planning to return to the first wood tents three miles up the beach. The tents would provide shelter and no one would think to look for her there, at least not for a while.

A warm breeze blew strongly through the trees as she picked her way slowly through the forest, always watchful of the lizard beasts. The first sight of a small lizard scurrying over the ground almost sent her running back. Should she suffer one of the those nightmares alone . . .

She stopped, unconsciously rubbing the scar on her leg. No, she could endure it alone; she had to.

Suddenly, a muted cry—distinguishable from all outer exotic calls of jungle—broke the quiet. It came from the interior of the island. She listened, waiting at first, hearing only her heartbeat and even breathing against the backdrop of birds, trees rustled by the wind and a small stream burbling somewhere behind her. Then it came again.

Someone was in agony or pain . . .

Without thinking what it might be, she started toward the cry, at first moving slowly but then faster and faster as the sound grew louder. She began running as much as this was possible through the thickness of the jungle. Arms fought to clear a path through the overhanging vines, ferns, and towering rubber tree plants seconds before her bare feet touched moist earth.

A wide trunk, strangled by vines and thereby hidden, lay menacingly across her path and she tripped and flew crashing to the ground. She fell hard; her shift caught under her knees and ripped at the seams. For several seconds she remained on her hands and knees with her face reddening, staring at the large tear in the only "decent" garment left.

The next agonized cry bid her quick recovery and she scrambled to her feet and was off. She stopped after some distance and, realizing she had passed it, she waited for the next cry to orient directions. It was very close now. An animal in pain, she realized, turning toward it and now exercising caution.

She finally reached a small clearing along the banks of a trickle of a stream and she stopped, stared, needing several long seconds to grasp what it was. The cries seemed to come from the very earth itself. Nearby, hanging grotesquely from a tree, was a dead bird. Its belly had been slit, blood and entrails spilled to the ground. Suddenly she saw there was a huge pit dug in the earth, camouflaged with leaves and twigs. Attracted by the bird, the creature had fallen into the pit and was now crying for escape. She slowly inched forward, afraid of what it might be.

Picking up a stick, she poked the earth in front of her, not wanting to make the same mistake as the creature of slipping on insecure ground. She came to the edge and peered inside, gasping instinctively.

It was a large piglike creature, wider and almost as large as Beau, another one of the island's boars. His cries had died to helpless whimpers and her heart broke as she watched his hoofed foot paw futilely at the loose soil of the earth. Sensing her presence, he turned his head and locked small dark eyes with hers. There was no fear or anger or threat from this her natural predator. Just a weak cry. A cry she knew as one for help.

She didn't know what to do. She should run to fetch Cajun, who could probably dig him back out, but she wondered if there was enough time. The poor creature could be injured from the fall but surely he would die of fright before then . . .

She looked around for a means to bring him water, hoping this would hold him over until help came. Finding nothing, she glanced at her skirt and never hesitated. She tore the skirt completely from the seams, doubled it over, and turned to the stream. Using the material like a cast, she filled it with water and hurriedly brought it to the edge of the pit, then lowered it by the ends until the knapsack of water reached the creature's head.

The distressed creature cried out at this new torment but then, realizing what it was, he thirstily

257

lapped it up and Christina smiled.

"Get the hell away from there, Christina!"

Christina's startled eyes shot up to see Justin moving swiftly toward her. She dropped the wet skirt on the boar's head and stumbled back to a stunned sitting position. Tall and now so dark from the long months in the sun, clad only in breeches and with a bow swung around his chest, he looked like a savage. A dagger and a saber hung from a thick black belt at his waist.

Frightened and not knowing exactly why, she tried to scramble to her feet but not in time. Like an angry hawk, Justin swooped down upon her and lifted her to safe ground beneath a huge willowlike tree away from the pit.

"Have you no sense, girl?" He stared down at her furiously. "What the hell do you think you're doing?"

Fear mingled with alarm. He might indeed have been a savage, cursing in an alien tongue, the way she stared up at him in terrified incomprehension. She felt the unleashed violence radiating from him, barely controlled, and like the first time she saw those sharp features on his bronzed face, his devastating gaze, or felt his strength, she wanted to run.

"Well?" he demanded harshly.

"I . . . I heard him crying and I thought to bring him water—"

"Water?"

Another woman would have slapped the cruel grin that spread across his face as he considered this. She held herself perfectly still though and dared not breathe, for his gaze lowered to her bare form and made her at once acutely conscious of the absurdity of

258

her half-naked figure. She had on only the torn bodice of an old nightgown and a loincloth, that was all.

Justin almost laughed as her arms crossed protectively over herself. She was the last person he needed to see here, dressed like that and performing the ridiculous stunt of bringing water to a doomed boar. He couldn't trust himself with her; she was the reason he stayed away. Until he found some peace, extirpated the seething emotions of his heart, he knew he could hurt her and badly.

After having lost a fine chase, Beau raced into the clearing. He sniffed out the boar and barked excitedly, prancing back and forth. Justin glanced at his dog and the pit, then turned back.

"Go back to the others, Christina," he said in dismissal as he released her and turned to the pit. "I'm in no mood to play the dashing gent out to win his maiden's affection."

His tone should have warned her but something held her to the spot. She realized in an instant that Justin had built the trap, that Justin was going to kill the poor animal just like—"Don't kill him!"

He swung back around to confront her, standing feet away and in a pleading pose.

"Please . . ." Her voice trailed off and her eyes lowered, both embarrassed and confused by the desperation in her request.

But Justin understood only too well. "Spare the boar and find redemption?" he questioned incredulously, then shook his head and chuckled contemptuously. "You are so innocent, Christina. It will take a damn bit more than a boar to give me redemption. Now get out of here."

He called Beau down. The dog sat back obediently as Justin straddled the pit. He removed his saber and using both hands, he raised the sword over his head. Wide-eyed, terrified, Christina clasped a hand over her mouth to stop the scream in her throat, refusing still to believe he would.

The doomed creature cried as Justin swung the sharp blade into his neck with all his strength, killing the creature instantly, mercifully. A fountain of blood spurted into the air, dying quickly, and the creature collapsed. With some effort, he pulled the sword from the flesh, wiped the blade on moss, and then knelt by the stream to clean the sword thoroughly.

Christina never understood what came over her but it was as close to a crazed madness as she would ever trespass. She forced herself forward until she stood at the edge of the pit looking down as though she had to see to believe. The sight sent her heart pounding frantically, her face reddened, and her fist clenched as she stumbled back beneath the willow tree in repulsion.

"You killed him!"

Justin was surprised she was still there. "Yes, Christina," he said calmly now, "I killed him."

"You killed him," she repeated in a demand for his remorse, guilt, anything but the calm acceptance of the unforgivable. "He was so helpless . . . begging you for mercy . . . and, and you killed him!"

"You don't know what you're talking about, Christina—"

"I do! I was there and saw it . . . I saw Diego on his knees, begging you . . . I heard him—"

"Stop it!" he yelled sharply. "I'm not going to

listen to this from you."

"No." She shook her head. "No, you won't listen to me, like you wouldn't listen to him! Not when he called you his brother, when he said he loved you—"

The words triggered an explosive response that brought Justin to his feet, moving to her in two swift strides. All his pain and anger rushed to the surface, and he stared at her furiously, daring her to say a single other word.

She did not back away and instead cried, "You're cruel and vicious and I hate you for it . . . I hate—"

Justin grabbed her arm and clamped his hand over her mouth, stopping himself from shaking her senseless.

Christina tried futilely to pull free and then in desperation bit her teeth hard into his hand until she drew blood. His hand jerked back from her mouth but it wasn't enough. She was suddenly crazed, wild, sending her clenched fists pounding against his chest as she cried, "I hate you . . . I hate you! I'll never forgive you for—"

Justin grabbed her fists, forcing her assaulting arms behind her back and her entire body into a tight hold against his. Outwardly he seemed dispassionate, but inwardly he teemed with emotions as he watched her struggle for all she was worth. She would not cease, her own emotions fueling a strength she did not normally own.

He could not stop his response. He wanted to subdue her; an act to extirpate his own pain and guilt, if only for the moment. He held her arms with one hand, while his other grabbed a handful of her loosened hair, forcing her head back. She cried out once, the shock of it hitting her as his mouth crushed against hers. She clenched her teeth together but his tongue plunged savagely into her, prying the warm recesses of her mouth open to him.

She tried to fight him—oh how she tried to stop him—but his strength was inviolate and the kiss, given with as much pleasure as pain, seemed interminable. The force of it drained her as his strength consumed her and she felt herself growing limp, weak-kneed, and helpless.

His mouth left hers suddenly and she drew a gasping breath as he lifted her hair back to press moist lips along her neck. Chills dashed along her spine and she cried out softly, whether in protest or not she hardly knew, for she could not separate the fire from the fear and outrage pounding in her heart. Then he was kissing her again while his free hand tore open the buttons of her ripped bodice. A simple tug freed her from the loincloth. And his lips never left her, even as he pulled off his belt and shrugged from his breeches, even as he brought her to the mossy blanket beneath the canopy of a willow tree.

She didn't know when exactly the violence of his passion changed, transformed by the very act itself, but at some point after his joining, his tension and anger collapsed, dissipated, expelled. He began calling her, whispering impassioned words of love and never had she been so vulnerable to him. She could not resist, not mind, body, or soul. He sent her nearly swooning into blackness with waves of ecstasy only to return to feel his final release pierce her to the very depth of her soul.

When she finally lay still in his arms, shielded in

the warmth of his body, listening to the steady beat of his heart, she heard the soft sound of a light rain falling against the earth. Like an umbrella, the swooping branches of the tree protected them and created a peaceful illusion of isolation from any profanity of the outside world, as if they were truly alone. Even Beau would not disturb this peace; he lay quietly at their side.

She loved him, and while her resolve was the same, the stirring of the depth of her love made it that much harder. The thought of just how much she loved him made her suddenly start to cry. Justin's arms tightened around her, his hand combed through her hair. "I'm sorry, Christina. I'm sorry."

"Why, Justin?" she managed to whisper through her tears. "Just tell me why?"

Justin remained silent for a long while. She deserved to understand, he knew. In a perfect world she would have known without being told; or at least her love would have bid her to trust. Trust him; trust him enough to know he would not take life ruthlessly. The odd thing was he knew—even before he told her—that her understanding would still bring condemnation. She would never speak it to him but her heart would condemn killing in any form, even as an act of mercy.

He found no words to begin his tale. Where to start? At the beginning of his friendship with Diego? How the friendship was first filled with times of laughter and fun, adventure and, more often than not, trouble for two young lads becoming men, how over the years Diego became like a part of himself, much as Cajun and Jacob seemed essential parts of his life now. He would do anything for Diego and, when the disease first struck, rapidly and unexpectedly, he brought Diego to every blessed surgeon, medicine man, shaman, so-called healer, in every land they traveled to. Hundreds of cures brought no relief. Relief came only with morphine, opium, cocaine, and the like, medicines which this island could not provide.

If only there had been some way he could have borne his pain for him, he would not have hesitated. He would have done anything for Diego; anything but the one thing he wanted from him, or so he had thought. Diego had been Catholic and, like most Catholics, lapsed until the final call. He could not kill himself. What she saw was Diego asking him to give up hope, an unceasing hope that they would ever laugh as brothers again.

Words were an inadequate vessel to express the emotions of his heart but he knew he must try. "It is difficult to speak of," he finally began, "and I suppose what I fear most—" He turned to her, wiping a tear from her cheek, finishing softly, "is that you'll still condemn me after you understand."

This startled her. Not just that he was afraid—afraid of anything—but that he should fear her condemnation.

"Diego was indeed as a brother to me; I could not have loved him more. We grew to manhood together and—"

"Justin!" The call interrupting him mid-sentence. Justin, like times before, bolted to his feet, alarmed by the excitement in Jacob's call. Christina sat up dazed and tried to cover her nakedness. Jacob raced into view all at once and there was no doubt something had happened.

"A ship off windward, just like the savage said, a man-of-war, and the lifeboats already landing. They spotted our fires."

"Are the men alerted?"

"Nay, 'twas Kafir and meself on the lookout. I came to find you, Kafir went to alert the men."

"Good," Justin responded instantly, already into his breeches and handing Christina her rags, as he snapped off orders. "You fetch Blake, Carrington, and the other men from the *Defiant* and get them down to the beach before a search can begin. They have their story straight, they are the only survivors. I'll round up the men and head for the high ground."

"Carrington?" he questioned. "Are you sure we should let him go? I don't think I trust the bastard—"

"He's my ace, Jacob; I trust him. However, that lady is to be detained—permanently. Find her. Take Christina with you and meet us at the high point."

And Justin was gone.

"Come on, lass, time's a wastin'!"

He could hardly comprehend Christina's distant, even dazed stare at a time like this. For he didn't know that Christina had just realized it was the last time she would ever see Justin again.

"Jacob, I need your cape to hide my nakedness," she said in a disturbingly calm voice.

"Oh aye, but hurry, hurry." He struggled quickly from the canvas cape, grumbling. "Don't want a lady's modesty to cause a bloody war."

She swung the cape over her head. "You go on ahead, Jacob," she said, thinking that this was the last time too she'd ever see his laughing blue eyes as well as his silvery hair, that special grin of his as he teased Hanna unmercifully. She wanted to tell him to take good care of Hanna, to cherish her always. She wanted to wish them both the happiness she herself could not have. But she said only, "Go on! I won't tarry; I promise I'll catch up in a minute. I just have to . . . to relieve myself."

Jacob offered a lively curse to women and their untimely ministrations as he turned to rush on ahead. Christina watched him go with tears in her eyes. Then she turned into the wind, heading for a British ship that would finally take her home. Home to England.

Chapter Nine

Richard Morrison, the ship's surgeon, knocked on what had once been the door to his small cabin.

"Who is it?" Christina asked softly.

"It's me, Richard, I've come bearing gifts for my lady."

Christina turned over on the bunk and wiped her cheeks. "Just a moment, please."

"I'd wait forever," he answered brightly.

She quickly washed her face in the dressing water atop a small set of drawers, not wanting Richard to discern her tears, and pulled the man's coat she wore tight about her person. She opened the door.

Richard burst into the small cabin like a breath of fresh wind, his energy and exuberance following him everywhere. He was a small man, not much taller than Christina, but mayhap one of the most handsome men she had ever seen. Fair, with a crown of golden curls and dancing amber eyes, he reminded her of Fielding's Tom Jones in both appearance and character. He had a quick smile and an easy laugh and yet a sensitivity that astonished her. After just a week of being on board the English man-of-war, the *Kyte*, Christina wondered how she might have fared if not for Richard's kindness and attention.

Taking care to keep his present hidden behind his back, Richard took one long look at her and he knew. "You've been crying."

"Oh no." She thought quickly. "Just a little seasickness. I'm afraid I still haven't got my sea legs back," which was also true.

"Hmmm." He eyed her speculatively and with a doctor's concern. "Well, nothing a little wine and bread won't cure. Which brings me straight to my purpose. The captain has asked you again to share his table tonight. Before you decline," he held his hand up to stop her protest, "I must warn you, I'll not take no for an answer this time. 'Twill just be Captain Shaw and myself, none of the other survivors this time. Make me a happy man and say yes."

"Richard, I can't, not like this." She glanced at the baggy breeches and oversized man's shirt and coat, the only clothes they could find for the only woman on board. But she was glad for the excuse.

"If you had proper clothes would you accept the captain's humble invitation?"

"Well, I suppose, but—"

"Good! Then here it is," and he handed her a large brown package tied with a string.

Christina stared in surprise.

"Open it" came Richard's command.

She slowly unraveled her treasure and lifted a pastel pink evening gown. The exquisite dress had fashionable short puffy sleeves, a low neckline decorated with tiny silk pink and white flowers, an unusually high waist, and flowing skirt. There were matching slippers and ribbons, silk undergarments galore, though no cumbersome hoops.

She was speechless.

"It was Edith's favorite gown."

"Edith?" she questioned.

"Yes, Edith, the general's daughter. I had to seduce the homely thing, then sneak into her trunks to steal it. Yes." He chuckled at Christina's shock. "These," he held up the dress, "are stolen goods. I shall spare you a retelling of the difficulties involved, especially in finding the undergarments."

"Richard!" She almost laughed. "But . . . how?"

"Yesterday in port."

"But I thought no one was to leave ship, except for supplies and—"

"These are supplies. India, that heathen sewer, may not have any dress shops to speak of, but fortunately it has plenty of generals with spoiled, homely daughters who wear only the latest fashions."

She laughed, indeed she could not help herself. She only prayed it wasn't true. "I don't believe it," she said hopefully, after calming down.

"Believe it," he said. "I'm just glad we're safely out at sea, for on the morrow I'm supposed to meet poor Edith for a quick elopement."

Even the fact that he could make up such a tale made Christina's eyes widen dramatically. Richard only laughed, kissed her cheek, and told her he would be back in an hour to escort her to the captain's table before leaving.

A while later, Christina squirmed in her seat,

pricked by the dozen or so pins holding her—or rather Edith's—gown together. Edith must have been a very large girl, and she had not time to make the necessary alterations. She stared at her plate of fish, boiled potatoes, bread, and various odd fruits taken from India's port and felt torn between persistent seasickness and hunger. Hunger won and she dug in.

"It's a horrible ordeal you've been through, Miss Marks, just horrible." Captain Shaw was saying this with a shake of his graying dark head. He sipped from a goblet and left a fine red line of wine on his whiskers, then wiped it promptly with his tablecloth. "At least," he thought out loud as he was oft known to do, "the other six survivors were honorable men. Yes, thank God for that."

Richard eyed his captain kindly, having long since grasped the limits of the man's intelligence. Captain Shaw was an astonishly straightforward man, a good captain but with a temperament unwilling to examine situations or people beyond the obvious, certainly lacking the insight necessary to comprehend the delicacies of a woman's mind. For Richard had no doubt that had Christina been violated repeatedly, she would have reported the same.

Christina blushed shyly and said softly, "I feel very fortunate to have survived when so very many have perished."

"A shame," the captain agreed, "a damn— Ah, well." He stopped to rephrase, hardly accustomed to the propriety necessary to accompany a woman on board. "A true tragedy. Well now," he said, turning to the matter at hand, "Mr. Morrison tells me you have naught plans to go back to Australia to be with your

270

uncle's family."

"No, I think not," she replied, pausing, still startled by how much she had changed from the time of her father's death to leaving Justin—and his love. She could no longer bear the thought of burdening her uncle's family. Somewhere along the way she discovered courage enough to pursue her own life. "I've written them already, though goodness knows how long a post will take from India to Australia. In any event, I told them I was alive and well—which should be good news to them—and of my plans to return to England." England. The very word sounded like sweet music.

"You have other relatives then?" the captain assumed.

"No, but I hope to stay with my father's old housekeeper, Madelyne, until I'm able to secure a position."

"A position?" the captain inquired, already disturbed by the idea. Why he felt responsible for the lovely lady he couldn't say, but he did, uncomfortably responsible.

"Yes. I should like to be a governess or schoolteacher."

"A schoolteacher? You?" Richard asked incredulously and then laughed at the idea. He had never inquired into her prospects, simply because he sensed she had none and while this sad fact had concerned him, he had not a clue as to what to do about it. But a schoolteacher?

" 'Twill never do, Christina!" Richard declared. "You're far too lovely to waste away in some dreary boarding school for monstrous brats and that nobody

271

else wants defiling their home. Wouldn't you agree, Captain?"

"Well . . . I—"

Richard could not wait for Captain Shaw's slow wits to catch up and he turned at once back to Christina. "You're not really a would-be schoolmarm. I know. This is just a clever disguise to distract us from your dark secret." He paused for suspense.

Captain Shaw stumbled confusedly over the twist in the conversation, grasping little of it. He did not like secrets, anyone's secrets, and he was certain he didn't want to hear Miss Marks's.

"My . . . secret?" Christina in turn felt nervous.

"Yes—" Richard smiled, "The truth is you're a displaced fairy princess from a faraway land, destined to usurp the evil witch who stole your throne and deliver your people from oppression. Admit it—" he demanded.

Christina blushed at this attention and to her surprise she bantered back. "You've guessed my dark secret! Now whatever shall I do?"

"Make me your knight, swear me to secrecy and let me fight at your side!" He used his eating utensils to demonstrate his swordsmanship.

"Yes! But of course!" Christina laughed, a sound she had not heard for some time. It was Richard's doing, she knew, and she only wished he could accompany her through the dark hours of night when she had nothing but tears. Not that she was attracted to him in that way; she wasn't. She could never but never love another man after Justin and, besides, for all of Richard's attentions, there was absolutely no hint of attraction on his part. More like they were good friends or even brother and sister. And for this she was more than thankful.

The captain's brows were drawn together throughout the young people's lively banter, a banter that continued for some time. His ship surgeon's flamboyance had always confused him; it had taken him nine months of sailing with Dr. Morrison to finally realize that the young man was only serious at his work. And a fine doctor he was—too good if the truth were known. Richard had studied at the best schools and with the finest surgeons known, and he had had what was reputed to be a flourishing practice in London itself. The King's navy never attracted doctors in his class. Nay—the young man was running from something, something he was glad to know nothing about.

"Well." The captain cleared his throat in an attempt to bring their attention back to the here and now. "I know an agent in London who might help you secure a position, Miss Marks."

"You do?" This was an ever-so-helpful surprise.

"Aye. I'll post a letter as soon as we reach port."

"Oh, Captain Shaw, I hardly know how to thank you," she whispered, overwhelmed.

"After what you've been through, it's the least I can do." The captain truly believed this.

Christina's emotions were as violent as the wind, rain, and sea as the graceful ship sailed around the horn of the dark continent. She was lost to the heavy burden of her memories, the uncertainty of her future. Somehow she had thought that by leaving Justin she'd leave the conflict of her heart too, but it seemed to shadow her days and nights, her every thought.

Memories, a montage of memories, seemed to sustain her very existence. She could not stop. She remembered everything: their laughter and play, those long hours in each other's arms talking of everything and nothing, his sharp, quick intelligence that always understood, always was able to help her understand and then she'd remember his warmth, the way he looked at her when he wanted her, his lovemaking.

And abruptly she'd panic.

She left him! She'd never feel his lips again, know his touch, or hear those three precious words of love. No words could describe that panic, an irrevocable horror that she had made a mistake she'd regret with every breath for as long as she lived.

Then she would try to remember the pain. She forced herself to think of each act of violence. Oddly these memories were not as clear, not nearly as vivid as the memories of his love and those times she thought of them, she found herself excusing each with the exception of Diego. The memory of Justin killing Diego spun clear in her mind and she thought of it over and over again, clinging desperately to the only justification for the pain in her heart.

Still the tears would not stop.

Richard knew something was terribly amiss with Christina and knowing women from a different perspective from most men, he guessed the trouble had to do with something she tried to bury on the island. He was a doctor and by no means modest, and therefore he considered himself her best medicine. He insisted on escorting her for daily walks around the deck—weather permitting—as well as joining her for dinner as often as possible. There were times he succeeded in

274

lightening her spirits and these times he was able to glimpse a young woman with whom he felt certain he would have fallen in love—had it ever been possible for him to love any woman.

The winds blew lethargically across the deck, hardly able to fuel the ship's great sails, and the ship sailed at a snail's pace north, along the west coast of the dark continent. Another three weeks to England at this pace, Richard claimed one day as he and Christina slowly strolled the deck. Richard was chatting amicably, admiring the soft sunshine of the day and Christina's loveliness. He particularly admired the way she wore her hair. Parted and braided, then wrapped around her head like a halo. A common sailor had given her a pretty pink parasol, one saved for his girl but lent to Christina for necessity's sake, and as it shaded her face, it cast her in an enchanting light. He fancied they made a fetching picture together.

Christina stopped suddenly to stare straight ahead. Richard's gaze followed hers to Colonel Carrington. He leaned against the rail, enjoying a smoke, while staring thoughtfully out to a barren sea.

"Is something wrong?"

She turned to him. "Richard, I must address Mr. Carrington, but I—" She paused to hide her fear. "But, well, 'twill seem a silly request—but would you stand by me as I do?"

Richard not only saw her fear, he felt it as well and this confirmed his suspicion that someone, perhaps Mr. Carrington, had hurt her on the island. "But of course," he said, momentarily startled by the intensity of his protectiveness for her. He forced a smile. "Am I not your knight in shining armor?"

A smile lifted to her eyes. What would she do without Richard? How quickly he had befriended her! And how she would miss him once the voyage was over.

She turned toward Carrington and felt Richard's hand slip through hers offering confidence.

"Mr. Carrington?" she beckoned.

Colonel Carrington was at that very moment contemplating the storm, his confrontation with death, life on the island, all the twists of fate that had changed him: both in mind and heart. He wondered how it was possible that a selfish and simple man motivated only by the petty concerns that ultimately mattered not, a man who saw the world in colors of black and white, could change into a thoughtful and contemplative man, one who could see only shades of gray. His experience pronounced this truth and to contemplate it left him shocked.

At the sound of his name, he turned from the sea to encounter Christina in Richard's arms. For a moment he considered the other man, then he turned to her and waited for her address.

"I must ask if you intend to keep your promise?"

He chuckled bitterly and turned back to sea. "I assure you I do, if for no other reason than having no doubt he would carry out his threats. For suddenly I find that I value both life and limb."

Christina considered this and was about to turn away when he turned back around.

"I must say, I was quite surprised to see you here." He looked at Richard and decided he was of no import; surely their intimacy guaranteed his confidence. "Did he know of your plans?"

Christina shook her head.

"I see. It's none of my concern, Miss Marks, but tell me, are you happy with your decision?"

Richard felt Christina's hand tighten in his and he pressed it reassuringly as she answered, "It is as you say, Mr. Carrington, none of your concern." And she started to turn away.

"You might look to your own safety as well, Miss Marks."

Christina could not stop the tumble of her words. "He won't want me after this. He'll never want to see me again—"

"I doubt that, Miss Marks." He eyed her speculatively, "I seriously doubt that. Of course he'll be hurt and angry—any man would, and while those two emotions are by far more dangerous in a man like him, that's hardly the worst of it. Do you know what the worst is, Miss Marks?"

She shook her head slowly.

"He'll be sick to death with worry over your safety, his helplessness to do anything about it. Even if you do not, he knows what could befall any woman on board a ship of men, one left in a London port with naught relations, or protection or even coin, yet alone a young lady such as yourself. Every time he thinks of you, he'll be imagining the worst." He watched the look of desperation as she tried to deny it. "Yes, he will seek you out. If only to end his nightmares."

"It's all nonsense." Richard thought to come to her aide, understanding a surprising amount from the brief conversation. "Any gentleman would see to her safety."

277

"Yes." The colonel smiled. "But then we are not all gentlemen, are we, Miss Marks? Good day."

Christina stared as he walked off, then turned to Richard, who was studying her with concern. "Take me back," she whispered desperately. "Please, I want to go back."

And Richard thought she meant her cabin.

Dark circles appeared under her eyes, her face blanched white, and she held her breath but there was nothing left in her stomach except bile. "I've never been seasick before, not even during the monsoon."

Richard stared into her large gray eyes and carefully measured his words. "I daresay, it's not seasickness that ails you anyway, Christina. The seas are calm, the sailing slow, and one can hardly perceive the ships rollicking."

"I must have caught a flu," she decided then, though oddly she felt fine except for the nagging nausea.

"I think not."

She looked at him with a question.

"Have you missed a bleeding?"

Christina merely stared. Her shock, the lightning speed of her thoughts, had nothing to do with the impropriety of his question. He was, after all, a doctor and after life on the island, she had learned propriety served no real purpose, save to spare old spinsters from falling faint.

She answered him when her arms crossed over her bosom and her eyes lowered to search her as-yet-unchanged figure. "No," she whispered. "No, I just can't be . . ."

Having experienced this many times before in his profession, Richard waited for it to sink in. Women had one of two reactions: overwhelming joy expressed in silly sweet near permanent smiles, or denial. And considering Christina's situation, he was hardly surprised by the latter reaction.

Tears glistened in her eyes and she covered her lips as they trembled. The child was not a reality to her yet, though the situation was a dark one. What could she do? No one could take a governess in her condition, or an unwed woman with a child. Madelyne would not even help her.

A distant memory floated into mind; she remembered a young girl in her father's parish being hit by the vicious tongues of two other women: "Ye wicked slut! Flaunting yer fertile belly with a barren finger, will ye? No man will claim ye and neither will we. Off with ye, before ye corrupt me own girls with yer wickedness. Off I say!" Voicing similar sentiments, her father had gone off to talk to the girl's parents. Madelyne had thrown a tither over the money he lent them to send the girl away, muttering for near high a week about the sins of the mother being spent on the innocent, this being the shame of an unwed mother.

Richard sat down beside her and pulled her into his arms as suddenly tears flowed uncontrolled. "Oh God, darling, don't cry. Please don't cry."

"Whatever can I do?"

"We'll think of something." He felt certain. He first thought of offering to abort the child but she probably couldn't do that, probably didn't even know it could be done. Then, too, he doubted his own ability, for the thought of a little girl, one with her mother's smile and golden red hair made him quickly dismiss even mentioning the god-awful procedure.

Then another idea occurred to him.

It first seemed too good to be true. He tried to think of all the reasons why not but after several long minutes he could not find even one. It would solve her problems, as well as his own. He could live in London's society as he wished, the vicious rumors would be put to rest, and his practice would flourish again! No more wretched sailing! And Darrell would love it; love her. It was perfect!

"Marry me," he said suddenly, and he dramatically dropped to his knees before her. "Oh, you must say yes, darling. You must! It's perfect. I'll provide you with a good home and I'll be the most adoring father!"

Christina stared in bewilderment.

"Oh, I know you don't love me, not like that, but you are fond of me, aren't you?"

Christina nodded, wiped her eyes.

"And God knows, I'm fond of you! I always wanted to marry someone just like you—so sweet and charming and ever so lovely. Oh, do say you will!"

Christina bit her lip with perplexity, but shook her head. "I couldn't, I just couldn't, not after knowin' . . ." Her voice trailed off.

"Knowing him?" he questioned, causing her eyes to lock with his. "Oh, I know who you left on the island, and who must be the father of your child. It's well known who was on the HMS *Defiant* when it went down and, after hearing your conversation with that man, it all became pretty clear. There's only one reason why someone would choose to remain hidden on the island, forsaking rescue, and that's if his name was Justin Phillips."

Shocked, she searched his face to ascertain his sentiments, then grabbed his arm. "Have you gone to Captain Shaw?"

"Heavens no!" Richard shook his head. "I'm not a man who sees to another's demise and as much as I love England, I hate war. My loyalty goes only as far as my wages and, besides, I've always admired Justin Phillips, especially after meeting him."

"You've . . . you've met Justin?"

"About two years ago." Richard nodded. "I was studying under one of the most famous surgeons in London, nay all of England. Mr. Phillips, along with a couple of his men, brought a man in to see Dr. Waughton. It was an awful case, one of the worst I've seen. The man was in horrible pain and, reportedly, it was near continuous."

"Diego," she whispered.

"Yes," he said, surprised, "that was his name. Did you know him?"

"He was on the island. He recently . . . died."

"Well, I can't honestly say that I'm not glad," he said with contradictory sadness. "Mr. Phillips paid a small fortune, not just for Dr. Waughton's services, but for secrecy as well, for they were already wanted by the Crown at that point. It was a shame; nothing could be done for him and the poor chap was so bad off, he asked me to end it."

She paused haltingly. "End it?"

"Suicide, you know," he explained. "Seems he was Catholic and couldn't do the business himself. I might have obliged him, too, had not one of Mr.

Phillips's men stopped me. Seems Mr. Phillips would not have it. Apparently he could not fathom the hopelessness of his friend's condition; he cared for him too much. And I always admired him for that."

Cajun might have been in the room; his warning sounded so loudly in her mind: "Until the gods paint the world black and white, until you have perfect understanding, you have no right to pass judgment against any man. Especially the man who has chosen you!"

Oh God, how could she . . .

"I know you still love him," Richard said softly. "Why did you leave?"

"I don't know, really," she said on the heels of a long pause. "It's all so confusing now. I couldn't bear it, not him but his life. I never meant to fall in love with him but . . . but somehow—oh, Richard." Her tears formed anew. "I'm afraid I've made such a mistake . . ."

"Could he forgive you? Would you want him to?"

She turned away and thought long and hard. "No," she said finally, "he won't forgive me. Nor will he seek me again, despite what Mr. Carrington said. It was not good toward the end. For either of us, I think. I know Justin, he'll never want to see me again."

"My second question?"

She met his eyes directly. "No." She shook her head. "I do love him, I always will, sometimes so fiercely and passionately that—" She stopped and added in a whisper, "But in my heart I know I'd naught find peace at his side."

"Which leads us back to my first question. Marry me. I'll never make any demands of you, except that

282

you be as happy as possible."

She stared into his hopeful amber-colored eyes. Had she misread him all this time? "Do you love me?"

He was suddenly serious. "I care for you, Christina, and probably a good deal more than I've ever cared for a woman. But I've never loved a woman. I know I never will. Our marriage would be one of friendship and comfortable companionship." He smiled. "But that's why it's so perfect. It's all you want and it's all I can offer."

Confusion spread across her features. "Why? Why would you want to marry me if you don't love me? And how can you know you'll never fall in love with another woman?"

"Your innocence is beguiling." He smiled, kissing her affectionately. "But I've known the sad fact that I could never fall in love with a woman ever since I was a young lad. Suffice to say, I'm just not capable of, ah, the intimacies between a man and a woman—any woman."

She again searched his face for meaning, sensing something hidden in his choice of words. He didn't like women but he liked her, he just didn't feel, "Ohhh," she said, still somewhat confused. Was he celibate? Not caring for the intimacies between men and women?

"You see," he waved his hand and turned away. "I had to leave London to escape the rumors—rumors that were affecting my practice and my friend's social standing."

She knew of his friend Darrell, for he talked of him often. "What kind of rumors?" she asked cautiously.

"Please, darling, spare me an interrogation. You

283

wouldn't want the gruesome details in any case."

"Don't you think, I mean if I do agree—don't you think I should know what rumors follow you and if they be true?"

"It makes no difference if they're true or no, so long as people believe them. Oh, darling," he again dropped to his knees dramatically, "don't you see? This was meant to happen! I need you and you need me. We'll make a fine pair! You enjoy my companionship and I enjoy yours—why, we're already such great friends. You need me to provide for your babe, to be a father and, darling," he brushed her cheek affectionately, "you truly have no other choice."

She considered it, all of it. It was true. She had no other choice. 'Twas truly a fantastic offer to be his wife; a doctor's wife in London. And God knows, she did care for him and if she should be with child . . .

Her child! She looked down at her figure and felt the first swift rush of emotion. She turned back to him and said only, "I've never been to London.'

Richard laughed and accepted this as her answer. "Oh, 'twill be grand!" he rushed on in his flamboyant manner. "We'll be the talk of the town! I'll show you off to everything and everyone—men will be just green with envy! And Darrell will love you, I know it, and when the baby's born—" He stopped with this idea, then pleaded dramatically. "Oh, Christina, do promise me you'll have a girl—boys are such trouble. And she must look just like you, with red-gold curls, large gray eyes, and a shy, sweet smile—"

Richard continued but he lost Christina to thoughts of her child. Not able to imagine a feminine version of Justin, she knew he must be a he. He would not be an easy baby either, but she would love him all the more for his trouble. To always have this part of Justin to hold and cherish and love!

And as she imagined her son, a smaller image of Justin, her heart filled with a wild rush of love and joy, begging to be shared. The panic returned twofold and almost caused her to cry out loud: Justin—what have I done to us?

It was too late to wonder, though; she was married that day.

The ship sailed slowly into port. Standing on deck along-side Richard, Christina watched the dazzling sights draw ever closer into view. She nervously smoothed the soft folds of her pink gown for the tenth time, then tipped her hat to shade her eyes from the bright morning sun in order to see better. A bright sun was rare in London, Richard had said, adding, surely, an auspicious welcome.

The docks bustled with activity. Crates and boxes piled everywhere. Carriages and horses added to the confusion. Sailors and soldiers alike swarmed to and fro and people from all walks of life cluttered the crowded space. Haggard-looking men and women sold wares, pushing carts and shouting above the loud drone of noise. Merchants waited for shipments and women waited for men. Beggars lurked in every corner, it seemed, competing with the others for the crowd's attention.

The multitude of sights and sounds overwhelmed but it was the stench that was unbearable. Sewers drained from the streets into the river. Carts of decaying fish, the noxious fumes of liquor, the more pleasant scents of cooking from the taverns, all blended to create a dizzying aroma. For a moment Christina felt on the verge of sickness again but Richard thoughtfully handed her a perfumed lace handkerchief, which was quickly placed over her nose and mouth.

Christina's wide-eyed attention bounced between a nicely dressed man loudly accusing a shockingly dressed woman of stealing his purse and the pathetic sight of a legless man maneuvering about in an odd, though extraordinarily ingenious, four-wheeled cart. Her eyes widened even more as three sailors began exchanging ribald greetings with two disrobed ladies in a window. She turned quickly away as one of the ladies straddled the windowsill seductively, much as a man straddles a horse.

Richard just chuckled.

The ship was nearly in its slip when Richard cried out his excitement: "There he is! Over there—next to that fine carriage there!"

Christina looked in the direction. An elegantly dressed young gent sat atop a fine gray mare. He was bent over chatting with the personage in the grand carriage. The black carriage was indeed one of the finest she had ever seen, obviously belonging to a wealthy personage, someone too who was waiting for their ship.

"Is that your Darrell?" she asked.

"Yes." They were still too far away to call out but Richard's eyes never left his friend. "I wonder who he's talking to? I can't quite make out the insignia." It was red and gold with a capital *P* over two lions. "Oh my." He suddenly realized who it was. "Do you

286

know who that is?"

Christina shook her head.

"It's Lord Winston Phillips, your Justin's own uncle—or father as some might have it. He must have been waiting for days to see our ship—to hear word of his nephew."

Christina swallowed hard, as suddenly her heart started pounding like a savage drum. Justin's own father!

"The captain will say he's dead."

Christina nodded slowly.

"You must speak to him, my darling. Spare the old man his grief."

"I can't."

"You must."

Christina bit her lip, then shook her head. "I'll send a note."

"Too dangerous, it might be intercepted. Besides, it's not really enough; he could hardly believe some anonymous note."

"Oh, Richard—"

"No." He stopped her. "You can't let him think his son's dead when he's not. I insist." Richard could not stand to see anyone suffer, especially unnecessarily. "Darrell obviously knows the family. I'll arrange an introduction. Don't worry," he cautioned her, "I'll stand by you."

He was right to insist, she knew. She owed Justin that much, at least that much. Anxiously her mind traveled to the imminent confrontation and she tried to form the words she would say, tried to remember the words she couldn't say, but all she could think of was that she would be meeting Justin's father. The paternal grandfather to the child she carried.

Distracted, she could hardly manage the formal good-bye to the good Captain Shaw as he escorted her down the plank. The captain had been so pleased with their marriage, one might have thought he was marrying off his own daughter. Her farewell called for a special note of thanks but she could hardly manage it. She was relieved to see the captain quickly lost to the demands of his ship.

Then everything happened at once. With an arrogant crack of his whip, Darrell pressed his mount through the crowd, forcing people to jump backward or be trampled. He swung his leg forward and jumped off his horse, and with a loud yelp of greeting, he fell into Richard's warm embrace.

Darrell was a small man like Richard. He had long auburn curls and amber eyes too, and with the same devilish glint in them. But the similarity stopped there. He was not handsome, his features rather too sharply aristocratic—as arrogant as the crack of his whip. And his dress! Never had she seen such elegant attire on a man. None of the dreary black and brown material that was in fashion but gold: everything a shade of that precious metal. Pale gold velvet breeches, waistcoat, and vest, all of which were embroidered in what must be the real thing, and then ruffles and ruffles of lace on a tailored silk shirt.

She finally watched the amber eyes turned to her with a warm, if not curious smile. "And who might this lovely creature be?"

"Darrell," Richard smiled, taking Christina's hand for a formal introduction. "I'd like you to meet Christina, recently made my wife."

Darrell's expression immediately became a curious mixture of incredulous disbelief and, oddly, humor. "Your *what*?" he demanded in a loud, refined English voice.

"My wife." Richard laughed. "Yes, I'm a married man now. You, my friend, have the good fortune of looking on my lovely wife. Christina, this stunned gentleman is my good friend, Darrell Bradley Cole."

"Pleased to meet you, sir. Richard has said much about you."

"No doubt." His gaze seemed unable to leave her person. "Richard," he beckoned slowly, "I think I need an explanation—"

"You'll get it, but not here. First, I need an introduction to Lord Phillips there and then, then let's enjoy a mid-morning meal at the Five Crowns together. I don't know what I've missed more, you or your culinary dining experiences. Come!" He slapped Darrell's back. "What say you?"

Darrell's eyes still could not leave her, and he said in a strangely hurt voice, "Richard, I'm—I'm shocked; I don't know what . . . to think—"

Richard saw the explanation could not wait. He excused them both and took his friend aside and, for what seemed near a half hour, they talked. Christina heard little of it and cared less, for her attention was riveted on the carriage of Lord Winston Phillips.

Captain Shaw approached the carriage. A footman quickly disembarked and swung open the carriage door. Lord Winston Phillips stepped out and she gasped. Justin was the very image of his father; no one could mistake their relationship. Tall, nearly as tall as Justin and with the same commanding carriage, Lord Phillips seemed but an older version of his son. He had the same impressive features, the same dark hair and brows. While she could not see his eyes clearly from the distance, nor was he as broad of shoulder or as muscular as Justin, she felt she looked upon a love that she had thought lost forever.

She could not hear what Captain Shaw said but he must have gone straight to the point. Seven survivors only, no sign of the English prisoner, Justin Phillips. At first Lord Phillips showed no sign of emotion but he turned quickly, wordlessly away to hide what feeling he had. Like Richard then, she could not bear it, and swallowing her nervousness, willing her heart to slow its pace, she hastened to Richard's side. But Richard must have noticed as well, for he had already urged Darrell forward.

The incessant noise and bustling of activity seemed suddenly to grow louder, more frantic, as she waited. Darrell spoke briefly to the lord and returned quickly. "He sends his regrets but feels not inclined to receive introductions at this time." And at the very moment Darrell spoke those words the carriage took off.

"Oh catch him! Tell him it concerns his son and is most urgent!"

Darrell looked briefly at her and then the disappearing carriage, suffering a moment's indecision. He nodded, took his mount's reins, and mounted to take flight. Another wait. Christina tried to peer over the heads of the crowd to see if Darrell had stopped the carriage. But all she saw was the confusion of the docks.

Darrell returned in short minutes. "Lord Phillips awaits this news. May I?" he said, offering his hand to lift Christina up.

"Shall I go with you?" Richard asked.

She shook her head and Richard lifted her atop Darrell's mount securely in front of his friend. The horse moved slowly through the crowd until it reached the awaiting carriage. Lord Phillips stood outside and even before she spotted him, she felt—she could actually feel it—the intense scrutiny of painfully familiar blue eyes.

Strong hands fitted completely around her small waist to lift her to the ground even as Darrell quickly made introductions. Lord Phillips's hands seemed unwilling to leave her, and she could not for her life meet those eyes.

"You have news of my son?"

Her eyes shot up at the sound of his voice, that voice, a voice so similar to the one she had loved. She nodded, then glanced quickly to her sides.

He understood immediately. "Please step into my carriage. It's the only privacy I can offer at the moment."

The footman helped her ascend and she took a seat opposite Lord Phillips on a plush maroon couch. She kept her eyes hidden beneath long lashes and she, too, got right to the point. "Justin, sir," she said softly, "is indeed alive and, I think, well."

"I know that."

She looked up, startled.

"I know my son," he explained. "If there were any survivors, he is among them. And no matter what Justin insists upon putting himself through, he is always well."

Christina suddenly saw from whom Justin inherited

291

his arrogance. "I see," she countered evenly, though softly. "My intention was to relieve your doubts, even grief, but since you have none . . ." She rose, but felt a firm hand stop her movement, gently guiding her back to her seat.

"Christina—may I call you by your Christian name?" he asked but did not wait an answer. "Do not fault me for confidence in my son's abilities. Besides, you have yet to tell me what happened. You, too, were a survivor, were you not?"

She hesitated.

"Have no fear," he answered her hesitancy, "I have not only a father's pride but a father's love as well. In all truth, I would easier shoot myself than go to the authorities."

What were you thinking,. sweetheart? That once we were rescued, I would see you to some port, say a pleasant good-bye, as I ask for your lips for the last time . . . I think it would be easier to shoot myself . . .

Christina returned to the present and nodded, though this was far from the source of her hesitancy. "Justin is stranded on an island—the island from which we were rescued. Obviously he could not board a British vessel in safety."

"Hence he remains on some faraway island?"

"Yes. However, one of the survivors has promised to alert a certain captain in London to launch his rescue."

"I see," he said. "And is that survivor you?"

She shook her head.

"Is this person trustworthy?"

She paused. "In light of Justin's threats, I think

292

yes."

She was startled again when he chuckled at this. "Tell me, did Justin's two ships go down in the storm too?"

"Sadly, yes. And only a handful of his men survived."

"So, he had already been rescued at that point," he seemed to say to himself. "Are Jacob and Diego among the survivors? His man Cajun?"

She was surprised by how well he did in fact know his son. "Yes, all of them, but Diego—" She paused again, then added quickly, "Diego died recently."

"I am sorry to hear that," he said solemnly, "but then I'm not. His illness was very trying for all who knew him."

There came an uncomfortable moment of silence. Christina thought to leave but suddenly she felt his scrutiny again.

And indeed, shrewdly observant, Lord Phillips was quickly forming his impression of her. The young lady's beauty was startling, her intelligence and breeding obvious. But something was amiss; he sensed her fear. Justin, he knew, had never fallen in love before but he'd have to have been a fool not to when presented with this. And his son was not a fool. He knew in just these few minutes, or at least felt, Christina was as rare a treasure as his own Elizabeth, Justin's mother.

"Tell me, did Justin let you leave the island?"

Startled gray eyes shot up to him. "I . . . I act on my own volition." She hastened to add softly, though with clear trepidation, "Your question seems at once impertinent and irrelevant."

293

"Impertinent yes, irrelevant, I think not." He smiled. "And then your answer is telling. Were you also acting on your own volition when you boarded Justin's ship from the *Defiant*?" he continued his questions. His answer appeared immediately in her large expressive eyes. "I see," he said gently, knowing his son was perfectly capable of such a thing. "But you did fall in love with him and he you?"

Christina could not fathom the intelligence behind such quick reasoning and was at a loss as to how to answer. "Please—" She rose, just wanting to leave.

"Why did you leave him, Christina?"

He watched the startling eyes fill with tears and then saw her hand move protectively across her abdomen, an unconscious gesture with women and one in which he—being the father of eight—was intimately familiar. "Christina—" He reached a hand to her but she shook her head.

"No, please. It's too late." She bit her lip, not thinking of the words that came unbidden from her as she left. "I'm married now. I'm sorry. Tell him I'm . . ." She couldn't finish through her tears as she stumbled out of the carriage.

Lord Winston Phillips watched her go, knowing he could not stop her. The situation definitely required discreet inquiries. Anything to prevent his past from being Justin's future. He only hoped and this with all his heart, that in fact it wasn't too late for his son.

Chapter Ten

After lighting a warm fire in the nursery, Betty Mae Jones peered into the crib for the tenth time to make certain her young charge still slept. She smiled at the lad's sweet angelic face—a face markedly different from the little devil he was during waking hours. Only five months old and he was already into everything. She then set about finishing her chores. The supper dishes had yet to be cleaned and she had still to tidy the gaming room after yesterday's party.

Downstairs a huge bin of water in the pantry waited for the dishes, but the matronly lady first opened the front door and stepped out into the chilly night air.

"Beauty! Beauty!" She called her mistress's dog, his name tripping uneasily on her tongue. How can any mutt that size be a beauty? Still less than a ten-month-old puppy, the Saint Bernard filled the fashionable but regrettably small townhouse on London's west side and, la, she thought not for the first time, the miserable creature made her cleaning that much harder, what with his fleas and fur and all. "Beauty!

Ye get in 'ere afore I feed ye supper to the cats! Beauty!"

That threat seemed to do it, for she first heard its bark, then saw the white and brown puppy lumbering clumsily toward the house. The dog climbed up the steps, wagging her tail in anticipation. " 'Ow is it our mistress loves ye so, I don't know," she complained out loud as the dog followed her happily into the pantry. "But love ye she does—second only to 'er babe upstairs."

Beauty barked at this, never bothered, though often confused by the old woman's tone of irritation. The old woman sounded mean but acted nice; she always saved a bone, always brushed her coat, and always kept the back door open. The old woman was part of the pack, as affectionate as their mistress. So why all the fuss?

"Don't look at me with those big droopy eyes!" Betty snapped as she worked the dishes. "I can na 'elp it. Ye 'ave more fleas than a blind beggar and ye fur's 'tis always fallin' on me clean carpets, it is. I canna ever get the house straight with ye and I like a clean house. I do—nearly as much as I like my one or two glasses of sherry a night."

One or two? The dog looked confused again. More like three or four.

"No sherry fer the likes of me tonight—la!" She shook her head. " 'Twould never do to fall asleep with deaf ears to the little master's cry. Not since this is the first night our sweet lady trusted us alone with the lad. No, sir . . ."

Betty continued to keep the dog company while she went about tidying up the gaming room, determined all the while to resist indulging her master's abundance of spirits. She had just finished dusting and setting everything in its place when she heard the first sounds from upstairs. "Hear that?" she asked Beauty. "Them be the first grunts afore he works up 'is wail. And my how that bairn can wail," she laughed, moving quickly into the pantry. She dipped the suckling cloth into milk, this laced with a goodly amount of sugar, and rushed up the stairs with surprising speed for a woman her age. She flew into the nursery and lifted her charge from the crib mere seconds before he sounded the infamous wail.

He smiled at her familiar face, second favorite face after his mother, and greedily grabbed the suckling cloth into his hands. Betty took her bundle to the rocking chair by the fire and while the little boy contented himself, she sang and rocked and talked. The little lad soon grew bored with the cloth and dropped it unceremoniously to the floor. With a huge grin he turned to amusing himself with his own voice, his favorite trick of making Betty's face laugh back at him.

An insistent knock sounded at the door.

"Oh heavens! Not another call for the master," she muttered to herself, having just watched the thick black lashes close over dark blue eyes. It could only be yet another emergency at this hour, she knew. Must be a full moon out tonight, she thought, rising from the chair to make her way downstairs.

With her charge hanging limply over her arm, she opened the door and she started. For a long minute the man she was looking at stole her breath. Handsome didn't quite do it, but devastating, frighteningly devastating. She might have been a country virgin meeting the devil himself.

Uncommonly tall, the man's imposing figure was clad in a wealthy gent's traveling cloak, the fold of one side thrown over a shoulder to reveal black breeches, boots, and a richly tailored white silk shirt. None of the fashionable frills. He had short dark hair and brows, dark eyes hidden in the light, and his sharply defined features spoke at once of arrogance and aristocracy. She took in everything at once, including the strange way he stared at her charge. She suddenly wished she had not put Beauty outside again.

"Good evening, madam. I've come to see Mr. or Mrs.—" He paused at the title, "Morrison."

His gaze seemed unwilling to leave her charge, even as he spoke. She looked past him to the mounted men on the street. " 'Tisn't an emergency, is it?"

"No, but it is urgent."

"The doctor's not at home presently, sir, and I don't expect him till near dawn."

"And Mrs. Morrison?"

"Oh, well, she's at the governor's charity ball—she was on the committee, ye know, fer all the poorhouses and all. This is the first night she left me with the young master—" She smiled at the babe, now sound asleep. "Ye can leave a card—"

"No, I'll wait," he informed her and turned at once to his men with quick commands. "It should be awhile. Cover the streets and one of you find out what's delaying that carriage. I want it here within the hour."

Having little choice, Betty stepped aside as the stranger stepped inside the hall. The house seemed suddenly to shrink. The man first removed his gloves and handed them to her. Her arms were full and just as she suffered the indignant thought that all in his class assumed servants had ten hands, he surprised her.

"May I help?" he said, motioning to the sleeping child.

"Oh aye, fer sure," she said, carefully placing the babe in his arms. She made a fanfare about placing his gloves in the decorative glove box, hoping he'd notice the fine quality, disappointed when he did not. His gaze was still fixed on the child.

Justin expected to feel something the first time he looked at his son's face. He had imagined he'd feel father love and joy and pride, and indeed he did; but what he had not expected was the intensity of these feelings and it shocked him.

This was his son!

He could not account for all he felt. Perhaps most surprising was how familiar his son looked to him. Just familiar. Familiarity that seemed beyond the fact that he was looking at his own face in miniature: the same dark hair and brows, the same shaped face, nose, and mouth. No, it was felt as though he knew him already and inexplicably. He thought of the Hindu's strange belief in reincarnation.

"Here, I'll take him off ye hands."

"That's not necessary. I don't mind."

Betty was quite suddenly charmed. " 'Tis a rare man that likes babes." She smiled. "Don't usually notice 'em till they start talkin'. Please, come sit in the parlor," she motioned.

Justin followed Betty into the parlor, and still

holding his son, the questions began. "How old is he now?"

"Just after his fifth month."

"Is he small for his age?"

"Small?" Betty laughed. "I can tell ye haven't been around many babes. Why, little Justin might be eight or nine months for his size."

He had, of course, known the child's name from his father, though actually hearing it gave him a long moment's pause.

Betty saw that this seemed to please the man. "May I get ye a drink?" she asked, adding hopefully, "Myhap some nice sherry."

"Only if you join me," he said, though still his gaze kept to the child.

This was most unexpected coming from his kind and she smiled generously. "Oh, thank ye, don't mind if I do." She returned shortly with two glasses of sherry.

"He looks healthy! Is he?"

She laughed again. "One has only to hear his wail to know how healthy he be. The little master keeps his mum on her toes, he does. Why, he's already crawlin'—if ye can believe that! Everywhere! And I've never seen a babe that demands so much attention from his mum. And I've raised three of my own."

"Really!" Justin exclaimed, pleased.

"Oh aye. 'E looks an angel now that he's asleep, but believe me, there's a devil in those eyes—"

"What color are his eyes?"

"Blue, dark blue, just like—" She stopped, midsentence to look at Justin with sudden visible shock. She suddenly recognized the man in her mistress's sketches, minus the beard and the long hair.

Oh lord . . .

Like all servants, she knew the secrets of her house. She had known her mistress's child was not her husband's. Not just because little Justin neither resembled the good doctor in either appearance or temperament, or even because of the separate bedrooms, but the good doctor, for all his fondness, showed none of a father's keen interest in his child.

Keen interest such as this man was showing.

"I better take the lad upstairs to his crib."

"Must you?" Justin asked, unaware of the change in the old woman's tone.

She nodded.

Justin reluctantly handed his son over to her and she excused herself. He rose to check on his men but on the way out, he spotted a sketchbook sitting on the window seat.

He could not stop himself. He knew it belonged to Christina; he remembered she was always sketching as she talked to him on the *Defiant*. He recalled, too, numerous attempts on his part to coax her into sharing her work but to no avail. In her usual self-debasing manner, she claimed to pursue drawing for her own amusement and "my works I fear are immature, drawn by an unskilled hand, and truly they could be of no interest to anyone but myself."

Justin picked up the sketchbook and flipped slowly through the pages. He had his father's appreciation of fine art; he owned the ability to recognize talent. Christina was definitely talented; he was startled by just how. The landscape sketches of Hyde Park were impressive, good enough to place her in the finest art academies if she were not a woman. In between these sketches were ones of his child, small letters indicating his age—three days, two weeks, one month, and so on. He smiled at these; the progression was plain.

There were other sketches too. One particularly impressive picture of an old beggar woman selling apples on a busy street. An odd subject. Christina somehow captured the old woman's despair as well as the passersby's indifference. Very talented indeed.

The last part of the book was sealed, bound by thin strings. He knew what he would find as he untied the gold lacings. Sketch after sketch of a man he recognized only too well. Each was drawn from memories, each offered a different impression; some pleasant, most not. A vision haunting her dreams.

Yes, Christina, you have frequented my dreams as well . . .

The door opened and Justin set the book down. Richard was heard cursing and calling for Betty as he hung up winter bindings. "Betty! Betty, where are you? God, but that's the last time I render service to paupers."

Upstairs and in a panic, Betty would not descend for her life.

"I deliver them a beautiful healthy baby girl and it sends them all into tears, even the blessed mother, crying because she was not a he. Betty!" He threw off his coat and turned into the parlor, still angry over the ordeal. "A simple cobbler thinking himself King Henry . . . imagine, needing an heir to a cobbler throne—"

Richard took one look at who stood at his mantel and he stopped. It required a long minute to ascertain the certainty of his vision and then he fell limply into a chair. "Oh, God," he whispered to himself after the long pause in which his mind raced over the implications and consequences.

"You know," he finally looked up to Justin. "I half expected you to show up at some point."

"I imagine you did," Justin replied in a voice both calm and impassive.

"I suppose you've come for her."

Justin nodded.

"We're married, you know."

"Yes, I know."

The ship that had finally rescued them carried a message from of all unexpected people, Mr. Carrington. The brief note told of Christina's marriage as well as alluding to the gossip and rumors that followed her new husband. It hadn't taken great leaps in speculation to imagine the benefits of such a marriage for both parties. And these suspicions were confirmed when he saw his father, who, much to his surprise, had kept updated information on Christina and his grandchild, starting from the day he had met her and guessed all.

"I also know," Justin added, "that annulments are possible within the Church of England."

With arms resting on widespread knees, Richard continued to stare at his hands. He did not venture a glance up. "Need I ask on what grounds?"

"I don't think you have to."

Richard expected this and nodded. "It will mean a public confession. It will ruin me, you know."

"I'm sorry. I see no other alternative."

Richard's gaze shot up at the sound of the sincerity

303

of Justin's remark.

"I'm not a blind fool, Mr. Morrison," Justin answered his surprise. "Believe me I know only too well how much I owe you." And suddenly he could not hide his pain. "God knows what would have happened to her had not you come into the picture. I would offer financial compensation—"

"Oh please, Mr. Phillips." Richard shook his head. "That's hardly the problem. It's my reputation. What's the old saying? A man's reputation is better than gold." He sighed emotionally. "It so true. Despite my personal proclivities, I love my work. And I'm damn good at it too."

These sentiments won Justin's respect. He was not a man interested in another's personal proclivities; he judged a man mainly by his actions and Richard's actions had probably saved Christina's life, if not her well-being and the well-being of his son. This was all he cared about. "If this is true," Justin resumed, "if you want only to practice your trade, I would suggest a move to the New World."

"The New World?" Richard questioned with proper English indignation. "You mean America? Good God, I'd rather die than find myself among those barbarians! Criminals, religious fanatics, the like. Oh no, I can't see that at all—"

"Come now, Mr. Morrison." Justin almost smiled. "For an educated man, who himself has been the victim of rumors produced by simple minds, I'm surprised." Then his voice changed. "Truly, it's a wondrous country. Land stretching endlessly west, as boundless as the opportunities and possibilities. A government that's practically nonexistent." He looked at Richard directly. "Thousands of people, all there for the same reason—to start fresh. And God knows, we need doctors there. The only doctors to be found are self-appointed ones, ones ignorant of anything written in a book." He paused for a long while to let Richard weigh his words. "I could also make the proper introductions for you and with my connections in Boston, there's the possibility of a university position."

Richard could hardly believe this. "I'm taken aback by your generosity, Mr. Phillips," he said at once, "and I must say I hardly expected such a reaction. The New World . . ." To be sure they would need doctors there; disease surely ran rampant among such lowlifes. The idea of a university position! He had always wanted to teach medicine! "Then too, it seems I have no real choice," he said out loud. "And speaking of choices," he ventured hesitantly, "I'd like you to know that while our marriage was arranged for the benefit for both of us, I care for Christina. I care a good deal. Will Christina have a choice in this matter?"

The fire had died to bright embers, and standing at the mantel, Justin was now hidden in shadows. Richard could not see the emotion in his face when he replied, "No, she will not."

"I see." And indeed he did. He wished he could protect her somehow, and he felt like he had failed her. He suddenly needed a drink, and knowing Betty probably lurked just behind the door listening to all, he called for her prompt service.

Christina raced ahead of Darrell and flew through the door, still laughing at Darrell's teasing. Not

305

thinking anyone was home but Betty, and having suffered only one thought the whole evening, she rushed straight up the stairs and burst in the nursery.

Justin saw only a brief flash of the maroon velvet of her gown.

Darrell stepped into the parlor. "Ah, Richard, you're back," he said, falling with an exhausted laugh into the chair—ignorant of Richard's company. "Well, that's the last time I do you the favor of escorting your wife anywhere! She had them beggars lined up all evening and I—imagine it!—nearly got called out twice! Seems no one cares that a lady's married anymore. My word but she was such a success! And imagine if you had let me dress her properly—" He noted Richard's sad expression. "What's wrong, Richard? Oh dear, did your patient die again?"

Richard shook his head but glanced toward the shadows where Justin stood. "I have company, Darrell . . ."

Justin climbed the stairs quietly and slipped unnoticed into the nursery. Christina leaned over the crib singing a soft lullaby to his son as she gently rocked him in the crib. The vision of her at that moment would be a memory that lived with him for the rest of his life.

Firelight lit her face. The long hair was braided and simply wrapped around her head like a thick crown haloing the delicate features of her face. Her skin was pale and her cheeks were flushed. She smiled as she sang and a mother's love for her child shone in her eyes.

He no doubt had men lined up for her attentions. It mattered not that her husband could ill afford rich silks or tailored gowns, or that she wore her hair so simply. The dark maroon color of an obviously homemade gown accented the paleness of her skin and its simple lines accented the startling femininity of the shape beneath. And God, how nature had rewarded her for service! Motherhood pronounced her beauty and changed a girl into a woman and, unbelievably, the woman was so much more desirable.

Christina finished her song but remained staring at her sleeping child's face. How many hours had she spent looking at him? Would she ever tire of it? Each hour filled with a strange mix of both pain and joy at his arresting likeness to his father . . .

The silence suddenly warned her that she was not alone.

She slowly looked up and then confronted the man who haunted her dreams. Time stopped and forever existed in seconds; she could neither move nor speak. She could only stare at a dream brought suddenly to life before her.

The emotions rushing through her were suppressed by her shock. Shock that he was standing there. Shock at how very changed he was. She had only known Justin bearded, with long hair and dressed like a savage. The finely dressed gentleman staring back at her was a stranger and yet as familiar as her own image.

"Don't look so surprised, Christina," he said softly. "You must have known I'd come—if not for you, then for my son."

Thoughts and emotions, thoughts and emotions, all clamored for her attention until, until the shock finally gave way to her greatest fear. One she had lived with throughout. She slowly shook her head as the full magnitude of it crashed into consciousness.

"Nooo," she cried in a pained gasp and in sheer desperation, she rushed to him and dropped to her knees. "Don't take him from me! Please, Justin, I beg you! I—c—c—" She choked on the words.

Justin stared with shocked incomprehension as her eyes filled with tears.

"I couldn't live . . . I would die—"

And abruptly he understood what he didn't want to believe. "God, girl, is that what you think?" He seized her arms to lift her to her feet. "That I would take him from you? Unlike you," his words lashed out like a whip, "I'm not capable of the cruelty necessary to separate you from our son."

"But . . . but . . ." The fear still pounding in her breast made it impossible to trust his words. "Then you will leave him?"

"No."

It was flat and inexplicable and her eyes were wide and enormous as she searched his face for the understanding that eluded her. He would not separate them, yet he would not leave him with her. He didn't know. "I married," she whispered on a frightened pause. "I married Richard—"

"So you have." He released her and turned away to hide what he fought desperately to control. "Thankfully your husband has already agreed to an annulment."

"An annulment?" She drew back, this new shock causing her to practically stutter, "But how? How is that possible? On what grounds could annulment be possible?"

"The marriage has yet to be consummated."

"How . . . how do you know that?"

"Can you deny it?"

She looked down, and to his utter disbelief, the answer was written in shame. Shamed that her husband had not wanted her, as though this was a personal failure on her part. He could almost laugh at the bitter irony of it. He had lived through hell imagining her in another man's bed. As long as he lived he'd remember the intensity of his relief when he learned that—of all the men in the world—she found the one man who would leave her untouched.

She nervously twisted her hands, still unable to look up. "Richard has agreed to this?"

"Yes."

"And then you would . . . marry me?" she finished in a whisper.

"Yes. But make no mistake, Christina—I will marry you only for our son. I'll not let him carry the burden of his parents' sins nor the title of bastard. Only for those reasons will I take you as my wife."

The words were delivered so casually as though the cruel reality could be of no consequence to either anymore. She felt her lip tremble slightly. She turned away suddenly.

Justin went to the window overlooking the quiet street. Fog rolled beneath the street lanterns. The carriage and his mount waited in front of the house. From a small red glow of the driver's pipe, he knew it was Brahms in the driver's seat, one of the best drivers he had. Jacob and his men would be hiding somewhere down the street. There was nothing amiss. Still it could not be long.

309

He turned back to her and was about to tell her to pack in haste when he saw her lips trembling with what he knew would be an apology.

And he lost control of it.

"Oh no, Christina. Don't you dare say you're sorry. Sorry will not cover the hell you put me through. And it was a hell, Christina," he said with sudden feeling, coming to stand before her, holding on to her as though afraid she would run again. For a brief moment the depth of his pain, anger, and anguish showed in the intensity of his eyes and she almost swooned with the knowledge. Abruptly, he shoved her aside and turned, concealing all signs of emotion in a sudden near-stoic manner. "Love is a strange thing; I don't think I knew what it was before. Do you know what it is, Christina?"

Another person might have been misled by this—the dispassionate tone he suddenly adopted—but not her. She felt the violence in it, the readied violence of a wounded creature waiting to attack again.

"Love," he answered for her, "is when a man gives himself—the most vital part of himself—to a woman to care for. The act requires trust, for it leaves one vulnerable. Never," he emphasized, "is a man so vulnerable as when he is in love. Thanks to you, Christina, I will never trust another woman again; I will never be that vulnerable to a woman's deceit again. But stealing my love like that aside, I will survive."

"That was not the worst of it. Oh no." He shook his head remembering the irrepressible agony of those endless days and nights. "The worst of it was imagining what was happening to you alone and unpro-

310

tected. You, who I loved with my very life. Do you have any idea of what that was like for me? Do you?"

She shook her head, crying now and scared, just scared, more scared when he was suddenly there, his hand reaching under her chin to force her face to his.

"The simplest questions drove me mad! Mad!" His voice hardened with fury. "What would she do to eat? What would a man make her do to eat? The visions that followed—you lying naked and hurt and bloodied, raped not by one man but by ten—"

"No! Stop it . . . stop it!" She struggled to pull away but he held her still. "It didn't happen . . . it didn't—"

"But it did, Christina! It happened in my mind over and over again! I lived with that and damn you for it! Damn myself if I ever forgive you for it!"

He held her small weight up, and she was shaking as tears fell to the floor from her closed lids. His hell was not over and he knew it would never be over, for now he had to live with her. And that would be anything but easy, for— "And God, even after all that, I still want you—"

Her eyes opened in shock, confusion, a question, and he answered in a haunting whisper. "And I hate myself for it."

Nothing hurt more than that single statement and if his purpose was retribution, he was successful; she might have chosen death easier. A silence followed, broken only by her tears. A silence that made him wish for another time and place when he could have pulled her into his arms and comforted her with a love he now disowned.

A rush of horses suddenly sounded from down the

street. Justin reluctantly tore his gaze from her, then stepped quickly to the window. He pushed open the glass and called down to an alarmed Brahms. "How many?"

Brahms swung around. "Too many!"

"Stay where you are. Alert the others and tell them to hold fire. I'll handle it from inside. Fetch a cloak," he said to her as he withdrew a long pistol from a holster hidden in his cape, still watching the street. Christina was frozen on the spot, for still dazed by the turbulence of emotions shaking her, she could not comprehend what was happening. "Move it. We won't have much time."

Brahms could make no sense of this but he knew better than to ever question Justin's orders. If Justin thought he could handle a dozen or so redcoats alone, no doubt he would. He quickly signaled with the carriage lantern to hold fire. Too late. A shot ricocheted from down the street, then another and another. A man cried out, the sound buried in the clamoring of horses' hooves.

Instantly Justin's voice thundered from above. "I ordered no fire!"

"Aye, but—" He stopped as soldiers rushed up from down the street. No less than twenty men on mounts, with others behind them. They quickly surrounded the carriage and Brahms found himself looking at five pistols aimed at his head. Men scrambled off their mounts and within seconds the house, too, was surrounded. Soldiers raced up the front steps.

Christina heard the shots from the other room. She suffered the only thought a mother could have and she rushed back into the nursery, thinking only of grab-

312

bing her child to hide under the bed. She flew through the door and immediately Justin placed his son in her arms. Little Justin partially woke from his sleep and felt the comfort of his mother. He half smiled and unbelievably fell back to sleep.

Richard burst in the room. "Soldiers! Everywhere! What should I do?"

"Do, Dr. Morrison?" Justin questioned all too calmly. "Why, do what any man would do seeing his wife and child abducted, but do make the charade good, my life will depend on it."

Richard watched in frightened stupefaction as Justin stepped behind Christina and holding her tightly to himself, he raised his pistol to her head.

Christina blanched white and pressed her child to her bosom. "And oh—" Justin suddenly remembered, "get those annulment papers to Boston as soon as possible."

A half dozen soldiers burst through the front door with a frantic clamoring as they immediately started to search for Justin Phillips. Darrell was heard screaming murder, identifying himself and his connections—everyone who was anyone in court—all of whom were going to be notified of this outrage against Dr. Morrison's house.

"Scream, Christina."

She turned frightened and confused eyes to him.

"Do as I say, sweetheart," he whispered.

She screamed.

"Dr. Morrison, please—add to the clamor."

Richard suddenly made sense of it. He turned and raced down the hall to the stairs. "My wife! Help me! He's got my wife!"

Justin pushed Christina through the door and down the hall to the top of the stairs just as two soldiers started up at Richard's call. Everyone stopped at once at the sight of Justin Phillips holding a pistol to a young lady and her child. The room was abruptly still. Betty simply fainted, quietly falling in a heap at the doorway.

"Gentlemen," Justin addressed the crowd at large, "have you ever seen what a pistol does to a head? Not a pretty sight," he assured them, looking from face to face for the one man—and there was always one—who would play the hero to attempt a rescue. "Unless you've a curiosity for it, I suggest you grant me passage."

She could not believe this was happening to her.

The soldiers seemed to be waiting for someone else to give orders. "Oh, God!" Richard cried strategically, positioned between the soldiers and Justin on the stairs and holding his chest as though about to suffer a seizure. "Let him go! Dear God, don't let him hurt her—let him go!"

Justin was impressed by Richard's performance. "Don't doubt it, gentlemen," and then in that commanding voice, "Now move it!" The soldiers slowly fell back. "In there." Justin indicated the parlor and to a young man wearing a lieutenant's uniform, "Tell them outside. And oh—do drop that pistol."

The young lieutenant stared angrily for a moment, unable to accept his impotence, and Justin saw suddenly the hero. The young man dropped his pistol, turned in a sudden rush to the door. "He's got a woman and a child," he called out. "Stand back and allow passage."

314

"My driver too," Justin ordered.

The order was related and Brahms, held by the pistols of four men, found himself suddenly released. He climbed back to the driver's seat and quickly took the reins, knowing this would be a hasty departure if ever there was one. The soldier's attention was fastened to the house; no one noticed the driver fussing with the carriage lantern but the neighbors who watched from the safety of their windows. It would be a story they told for years to come.

Justin made his way slowly down the stairs, Christina and child held firmly in tow. Richard kept in front, looking every bit the terrified husband. "Back up, lieutenant," Justin snapped as he neared the door. The young man slowly backed toward the parlor, waiting his chance, while Justin, careful to keep his back to the wall, progressed to the door. He kicked the lieutenant's pistol out of the way, then purposely turned his back at the door frame to allow the young lieutenant this one opportunity to play the hero.

The opportunity was instantly seized. With hands firmly on an already drawn sword, the young man charged at Justin, and at the exact moment, Justin swung around and slammed the butt of his pistol into the lieutenant's face. And before anyone else could move, Justin had the pistol back to Christina's head again.

Little Justin woke with a start. Sensing his mother's fear and the cold night air, he started crying. Christina clutched him even tighter to herself. Any minute the soldiers would decide she wasn't worth the price of losing Justin Phillips. They would fire indiscriminately, and oh God—

Brahms calmly withdrew two pistols from the driver's seat and ordered the soldiers to drop their weapons. Reluctantly, one by one, each man tossed his pistol to the ground.

After a quick assessment of another dozen or so soldiers disarmed outside, Justin pushed Christina down the steps toward the carriage. "Should anyone follow," he stopped to warn them, "I shall shoot them both and escape with less of a burden. Do not doubt my ruthlessness; history should speak for itself."

Beauty could not believe the nerve of the cat sitting snuggled in the tree. Just feet away! She barked furiously at it, wanting to make the cat see she would tear it to pieces, but the cat just sat there, watching the foolish effort with but lazy indifference.

Beauty barked, jumped, barked.

What? What was that?

She stopped barking to listen to the unfamiliar sounds. She sniffed; too many humans for this hour. Sounds of humans coming from the direction of down the street . . .

The hair slowly lifted from her coat and she started running.

With Christina still held at gun point, Justin slowly made his way down to the carriage. A dog barking sounded from the near distance. Closer. Christina's head snapped around to see. Beauty ran toward her to attack him. No warning or stalling, just a great rush. She saw it even before it happened.

"Beauty! Nooo!"

Justin had no choice. One shot fired and Christina screamed at the same moment Beauty cried out and fell with an ugly jerk to the ground. Christina started forward with her scream, but the wind was knocked from her as Justin thrust her forward to protect her with his life.

"Don't anyone move!"

Brahms enforced Justin's order by aiming his pistols at any number of the helpless soldiers. No one moved. Justin quickly pushed Christina and his son inside the carriage with himself and instantly the carriage jerked forward. So taken by the rush of events, not one of the soldiers wondered why—if Mr. Phillips had truly intended to shoot the lady—he had placed himself in the line of fire those tense moments after the dog went down.

Justin quickly slipped out the opposite door to join Brahms in the event someone followed. The carriage was joined by his men. It would be a long ride to Portsmouth, where his ship sat waiting to take them to Boston.

He shouted to Jacob, who nodded and drew back to make certain no one followed. He turned back and settled in the seat beside Brahms, watching with some disbelief as the man attempted to rekindle his tobacco beneath the wind and moist fog, the terrifying speed of the carriage.

"Anything for a smoke," Justin commented dryly.

"After that, I deserve it," Brahms in turn called against the wind. "I suppose you already know who informed the authorities of your whereabouts?"

Justin nodded.

"Not one of ours?" Brahms queried.

"What do you think?" Justin asked rhetorically.

"No, but I can't figure who then."

"Someone from my father's house. I was suspecting

317

it. God knows there's enough rivalry and jealousy to warrant it."

Justin would not be surprised if his father's entire house—from the stable hands to Lady Phillips herself—knew every intimate detail concerning Christina and her child. His father had never been very careful to guard the secrecy of either his personal or business matters, a subject he would definitely bring up in the next letter. If Jefferson's Embargo Act got through congress—and he thought it would—he and his father would be partners in one of the grandest smuggling adventures yet. He would need his father's complete trust.

"It makes sense," Brahms said finally as a cloud of sweet-smelling tobacco disappeared into the moving fog. "If it had been one of our men, they would have taken us at the ship."

"Exactly."

Brahms expertly guided the horses around sharp bends and twists in the road and Justin still found himself bracing the driver's rail for each. Danger was suddenly a force with which to contend with Christina and his son inside.

"Well, that was a close one for sure." Brahms laughed, managing reins and pipe simultaneously.

Justin didn't know he meant the last turn or the run-in with Britain's finest.

"Had it been anyone else but you, I'd have wagered my life they'd have got you. Christina? She's all right?"

"I think so." Justin stared straight ahead.

"That must have been her dog." Brahms thought out loud. "It looked just like Beau. She must have got it because she missed the old fellow."

This thought had also occurred to Justin.

"And that was your son in her arms." Brahms steered the conversation as well.

Justin nodded.

"I couldn't take my eyes off the redcoats long enough to look. But you've seen him?" Justin nodded again and Brahms laughed at his expression. "Now that's a father's pride written all over you. Let me guess—he's big and healthy and he looks just like you."

The carriage raced along and as Justin waited for Jacob's return, he related to Brahms all he had been told of his son, including that strange sense of familiarity he felt upon seeing him, as though he had already known him.

Brahms was interested in this. "Well now, either Cajun's heathen beliefs in the reincarnate soul are right or—" he grinned—"the feeling comes because he is already so much like you. In which case, I bet he's a handful for his mother."

Justin smiled. "That's what her maid said."

Brahms added purposefully. "The two of you will be fine parents—that boy is bound to be spoiled rotten."

"Yes. At least if I have anything to do with it."

Brahms laughed just as Jacob returned to signal all was clear. The carriage slowed to an even pace and Justin rose to return inside the carriage.

"Is Christina nursing the babe herself?" Brahms asked.

Justin had no idea.

"If she is, she'll be thirsty. Take her this cask."

"How the hell do you know that?"

"My wife." Sadness marked his features. "She was a midwife before she died. Babies are one thing I know all about."

Brahms reached a hand to stop him and Justin stared at it, illuminated by the carriage lantern directly above. Long and thin, his hand looked like a musician's or scribner's, too delicate for a man whose life was at sea. A wedding band tied the hand to a past which its owner would not forget. The calluses looked oddly misplaced and it reminded Justin that Brahms had never been meant to do the hard labor he demanded of his men.

"I know something else too." He looked directly at Justin. "I know she put you through hell—everyone does—but don't lose her. God, Justin, don't lose her. I had no choice," he added, "but you do."

"It's a different story, Brahms."

"Is it?"

Justin made no reply.

Christina was remembering the day she had gotten Beauty. She had yet to be showing then and Richard and Darrell had taken her out for an open air carriage ride in Hyde Park. She spotted the little boy on a corner standing alongside a dog much larger than himself, a dog exactly like Beau. And in his arms was the last puppy.

"Stop! Please stop!" she had called to the driver. The carriage stopped and before either Richard or Darrell could guess her intentions, she flew out the door and straight to the dog.

"Oh, just look at him," she said to no one but

herself as she knelt to rub the huge head with both hands. "He's just like Beau!"

The boy saw that he was finally going to rid himself of the last pup. "E's a she mum and this," he said, knowing well his business and placing the bundle of living fur in her arms, "is 'er pup. Genuine Saint Bernard. Bred pure."

"Oh, Richard," she said as the two men approached, "just look at her!"

Richard was looking; looking at the size of what he feared was the mother. "Oh God, I think I'm in trouble."

The puppy seemed to sense that this was a momentous occasion and enthusiastically licked Christina's face. The mother barked happily. From the looks of their dress, the boy began an assessment to guess yearly income. And Christina turned to Richard with wide hopeful eyes.

"Oh God, I know I'm in trouble."

"I do have that sense," Darrell agreed.

"No doubt it's owing to all those mothering chemicals in her body."

"No doubt," Darrell agreed, then asked, "Did you know the Greek word for womb is hysterica?"

"It makes perfect sense suddenly," Richard replied.

Christina was used to their teasing but this was important. "Oh, Richard, please, I promise I'll never let—"

"Think of its fleas!"

"I'll bathe her regularly, I promise!"

"Where?" Richard wondered.

"Oh, Richard, she just reminds me of another dog I knew and, and I want her so badly—"

Darrell laughed. "If you can resist those eyes, I can not. How much?" he asked the boy.

Christina laughed and jumped up holding her treasure and kissed Darrell's cheek.

"A quid even," the boy said.

"A quid?" Richard screamed, "Why you cunning little thief—"

"That's the pick of the litter, sir!" the boy argued.

"The pick? You mean the runt! I'll give you—"

And on and on the bargaining went until finally a price was found. Once they were settled back in the carriage and Richard saw how happy Christina was, he knew in truth that had she wanted a hundred of those mongrels, he would have bought them. Such was his fondness for her.

"What will you name her?" Darrell had asked.

"Gargantua?" Richard suggested.

Christina knew already. "Beauty. Her name will be Beauty."

"Beauty?" Richard questioned with distaste. "How insipid!"

"Innocuous at best," Darrell agreed.

Christina looked from one face to the other. "Oh you two! Really," she sighed, "I don't know how I ever get along."

But she had gotten along and wonderfully. She thought of all she had lost: Richard and Darrell, Betty and Beauty. She loved them all and with all her heart. She could not believe it was over.

It was over though; it had been over the minute he walked back into her life. Peace shattered like a hammer to porcelain. He walked into her life and brought with him his violence . . .

They would be married, bound together forever by the single act of vows. They would live together; they would see each other every day in the intimate circumstances of man and wife. Yet he hated her. The very sight of her solicited his loathing.

Did he know this would be the cruelest punishment?

She could live without him, nourished by a thousand precious memories and the joy and pleasure of raising his son. This was how she had foreseen her life. Peaceful and quiet, filled with the small pleasures of daily life. She could have survived with this.

She could not survive with him and his hatred of her. It would be a slow death, as insidious as Diego's and just as painful. Love and hatred, two forces clashing in destruction—her destruction. Yes, it would be her end; he might more easily shoot her, certainly more merciful.

And she did love him! She had always and would always love him. Love had been the only constant throughout the tangle of feelings, thoughts, and motives, the unfortunate twists in fate that made her turn toward the wind to a British ship that carried her away from him and his love. Thoughts and feelings and circumstances that seemed but a jumble in her mind now, fuzzy and elusive like a dream upon the waking. And now the only clear thing in her mind was her love and his hatred, a future that was as cold and barren as a snow-filled desert.

The carriage door opened with an icy burst of wind and Justin slipped into the seat opposite her. She did not wipe her tears fast enough, though he would have known she was crying anyway. It seemed his fate to bring tears to those soft gray eyes.

"I'm sorry for putting you through that," he said sincerely, though in a permanent tone of animosity.

She nodded, not venturing to speak.

"Brahms said you'd be thirsty." He handed her the cask. "Here, let me," he said, lifting the bundle from her arms. She drank thirstily as he stared at his son's sleeping face. When she looked up again, she found him staring at her.

"That was your dog, I suppose."

She nodded.

"I'm sorry about that too. I had no choice."

"No," she whispered softly, "you never do."

That was not lost on Justin.

The carriage bounced over a hole with a loud thud. Little Justin woke and first stretched in his father's arms, arching all the way back. Justin watched with interest. He yawned, then lazily opened his eyes to see who held him. He stared in acute interest at the new face and then, as though reaching some happy conclusion, he grinned ear to ear and reached up to touch.

Justin chuckled and introduced himself, and for the next twenty or so minutes, Christina watched their relationship develop. She could not help but be surprised by both parties' quick affection; she hadn't expected it, at least not so soon. She had not expected the bittersweet joy of watching this.

Amazing Justin with his small strength, his son squirmed, and realizing how hungry he was, he abruptly started screaming. Justin was not intimidated. He leaned back and looked at Christina.

"He's hungry," she explained softly, her gaze anxiously fixed on her son's signs of discomfort. Then to

324

make it perfectly clear to Justin, "I have to nurse him." Nursing was done in private. Richard and Darrell, even Betty, would excuse themselves from her company.

Save for the intensity of his gaze, Justin made no move, making something else perfectly clear. He would do what he wanted with her; she had no say. The subjugation of her will was not by choice or certainly desire, but rather came by design the day she bore him a son. The only choice she had was to leave him again, but now that meant leaving her son.

She stared in silence, understanding his message all too well. Her eyes dropped to the child in his arms, squirming in frustration. Then her gaze lowered altogether.

Justin watched as both her arms reached behind to unbutton the buttons of her gown. The gown finally slipped from her slender shoulders to hang loosely at her waist. She wore no chemise, only a corset, one laced in front. Her hands slowly untied the strings and, still without looking up, she parted it and leaned forward with extended arms to receive her child.

A jeweled whistle adorned a sight from which he could not take his eyes.

She waited; the seconds seemed interminable. Justin finally rose, placed his son carefully in her arms, and left wordlessly, wondering only who was the victim.

Chapter Eleven

The long journey to Boston was slow and trying for Christina. The seas were wild, the ship met with frequent storms, and more days than not the cold winter winds and rain prevented even short walks on deck. She and little Justin were for the most part confined to their cabin for the duration.

She met animosity at every turn. Justin hardly spoke to her unless it concerned their son. She expected this. Only it was so much worse than she imagined. From watching Justin play with his son, she saw how very important a father's love was. Justin thought to do things and play with him in ways she had not the inclination or idea to do. The pain came only when little Justin—with a smile or scramble to her—tried to include her in their fun, then how quickly and easily his father would distract him until the capricious little fellow forgot his mother altogether.

What she hadn't expected was the cool indifference, sometimes even rudeness, from the other men whom she knew intimately from the long days on the island. This hurt most from Jacob. He seemed unable to meet her eyes and the only time he ever addressed her was when Justin first showed him his son. "He's a beautiful boy, Christy. Ye did well." That was all. When she inquired about Hanna and Elsie and Eric, he said only his new wife was waiting in Boston while Elsie and Eric were now married and apparently living with Eric's parents in Holland, part of the Prussian empire.

"And are they well?" she asked hopefully.

"I don't see how it matters much to you. After all," he replied softly, " 'twas ye who left us, not the other way around."

"But I didn't leave you." She tried desperately for his understanding.

"When you left him, you left us," he cut her off. " 'Tis that simple." And he excused himself before she could say anything more.

Only Brahms seemed willing to forgive her and she cherished the few times he kept her company. He told her everything of Boston, describing at length the climate and the terrain and especially the people, the similarities and differences with England. He also filled her in on the details of everyone's life; details no one else was willing to share.

He described Hanna and Jacob's wedding, making her wish she had been there. He told of Eric's hard decision to give up life at sea—surely owing to the terrifying hours of the monsoon, the subsequent stay on the island. Eric opted to take his father's trade—of all things, horse trainer for the Prussian army.

The fate of Carolyn Knolls surprised her most and

she made him tell her twice before she believed it. John had forced Carolyn to stay on the island with him. He planned to "fill 'er with a string of brats before he'd let her go," and he asked Justin to send a ship by in a few years. Justin promised to do just this. Christina could only imagine Carolyn Knolls's fury at such a long imprisonment, one with such unpleasant consequences for her.

"Cajun?" was who she inquired about first.

"Well, apparently he's somewhere in India right now. After we were rescued, and Justin received the letter from his father and Carrington telling him you were safe, Justin decided to sail to Boston before coming to England. And Cajun and Justin decided to part paths at that point."

"But why?"

"Any number of reasons, I suppose. First, Justin is not going to be sailing anymore. Oh, he'll have his ships out, but he won't be on them. And Cajun knows he doesn't belong in the so-called civilized world."

"What do you mean?"

"Why, just imagine Cajun walking down the streets of London or Boston! He looks a savage and partially is. I've even seen him don proper clothes a few times, but he still doesn't fit. Cajun has never felt comfortable where his color matters. The English-speaking world can't accept his dignity; they would try to strip him of it, beat it out of him, and when they couldn't they'd kill him. No," he shook his head sadly, "a man like Cajun belongs in Arabia or India where his color doesn't matter."

She never thought of this but intuitively knew it as a sad truth. "Will Cajun never see Justin again?"

"Oh no. Cajun and Justin are as close as two men can without being—" He stopped, remembering her husband, then finished, "Cajun will show up again, no doubt."

Christina hoped this was true and wondered if, when he did show up, if he would have found it in his heart to forgive her. She cared most about Cajun and in an odd way, his opinion mattered most. Redemption or prosecution.

She was lonely and the ship kept her from any means she might have of coping with her loneliness. She had no sketchbook or even knitting or embroidery to do. Justin kept few books on board. If not for the joy of caring, nursing, and playing with her son, the joy of watching him unfold a little more each day, she could not have borne it.

Christina was up in early morning before dawn, suffering from yet another night's sleep interrupted by—how many times had little Justin roused her? Five? Six? Her nursing could no longer sustain him and he needed solid food, food that was not available on board the ship.

Already washed and dressed, sitting in a chair with little Justin in her arms, she was lured into a light sleep by the ceaseless motion of the ship on the water. The call of land sounded loudly from deck and Christina woke, hearing the excited cheers of the men. She jumped up from the chair. "Finally!" She laughed out loud. "Land, Justin! Did you hear it? We're going to see our new home!"

Little Justin tried desperately to figure out what he just did to cause his mother's excitement. Perhaps it was a gurgle. He gurgled again and grinned, then waited for her reaction.

Christina stopped herself from going up on deck, knowing she had to wait for an escort. Surely he would send someone soon. She sat back down in the hard wood chair and waited, trying to contain her excitement. Excitement coupled with a bit of apprehension. Excitement that she would be seeing the New World for the first time; apprehension because she knew not what it would bring.

Time passed miserably slow until it became clear Justin had sent no one to escort her up. She swallowed her disappointment. She told herself it didn't matter; in time she would have to see it.

Finally the door opened and Justin himself walked in.

Gone were the faded breeches and vest, the windblown hair, and the unshaven face, the familiar costume he had again adapted the day the ship set sail. The gentleman to replace the sea captain, and the contrast was startling. His thick dark hair was brushed neatly back and his face was clean-shaven. He wore a crisp cotton shirt, finely tailored brown breeches, the kind loose only at the knees where they were tucked into shiny black boots. A gentlemen, but not. His shirt had none of the fashionable frills, no lace or ruffles or neck collar. Then as though such stark masculinity needed accenting, a pistol hung from a worn leather shoulder holster, a jeweled dagger hung from a black belt.

Justin greeted his son and took him from her, and then addressed her forthrightly. "Since we'll be disembarking by late morning, I should explain a few things to you. Boston, Massachusetts—like any major port city—holds a diverse conglomeration of people. However," he continued to the point, "the Puritan historical influence is still strong and you'll find the social stratification every bit as rigid as England's. For these reasons, and until I receive the annulment papers, you will be introduced as my wife."

This information was what Brahms had told her. Brahms had added the amusing fact that, unlike the rigid hereditary lines of English elite, all of Boston's upper echelon's wealth came from "privateering" English ships during the revolution. Some brave captains found themselves not with one ship but ten, and suddenly wealthy. Then they remembered all their uncles, aunts, and cousins who were dukes, duchesses, lords and ladies of the English court.

Christina watched little Justin fondle the ivory handle of the pistol. She held her breath. His father didn't seem to notice or care.

"As you know," Justin looked at her to say seriously, "the only bond between us is our son. I don't know how that will affect him—I suppose one day he'll ask us about it and we'll tell him."

Christina looked away uncomfortably. She had already thought of this. The day would come when Justin would ask why his father didn't like her. She knew this; what she didn't know was how she could possibly explain it.

"I want this to work. With the exception of certain social obligations arising from my work and politics, as my wife I'll ask nothing from you."

She knew this too. After the night in the carriage, he had made this perfectly clear. She tried to tell herself she was glad. Physical love with hostility could

331

only be ugly, if not even terrifying.

"In other words," he finished, "I hope to live as amicably as possible."

Christina nodded in acquiescence. The speech held nothing unexpected, and was delivered with no outward hostility but rather calm indifference. As though he had accepted the sad fact that he disliked his wife—nay, hated, she was certain of this—and he would make the best of his misfortune.

Little Justin abruptly decided he was bored with his father's long stream of words, words he sensed had little to do with him, and he began squirming with all his strength. Only to discover what he already knew—while his strength caused his mother some concern, it had absolutely no effect on his father. He laughed and playfully socked his father's face.

Justin laughed too, tossed his son in the air, and swung him around, receiving a peal of laughter as reward. "Would you like to see the new land?" he asked as he turned toward the door.

Christina did not wait for an invitation to join them.

"And, oh, one other thing," Justin remembered. "A carriage should be waiting to take you and Justin to the house."

Christina lifted her eyes to him.

"My house is in Middlesex," he explained, "about fifteen miles from Boston. I also keep a household in town for convenience. I'll be staying there for a few days."

"I—" She couldn't believe he would do this. "You would send us to your house alone?" she asked on the heels of a frightening pause.

332

"You've demonstrated your ability to travel far greater distances without me. I don't see why it's a problem." And with that he left her alone.

But he did know. She knew he understood. To be forced to a new household alone—why, she didn't know a soul, not a single soul. She didn't even know if he had servants, and if he did, what would they think of her arriving alone without her husband on such a momentous occasion? It was unheard of. No introductions or even a trunk and her dress—

She looked down at the miserable state of her dress. It had once been the prettiest dress she had ever owned, but the fabric had not been made for travel. Her only garment showed every day of its excessive wear and was as stained as any beggar's rag. And her hair—

She felt her hair. She had not wanted to bother him and therefore she had never asked for some fresh water to bathe. He had never offered the luxury, only dressing water and salt water in which to wash little Justin's clothes. It had been over a month since she had washed it and it showed, despite the tight braids wrapped around her head.

She looked a pathetic creature indeed. She would not blame anyone for finding her a source of ridicule, even laughter—if not to her face, then behind her back. He thought she deserved it. He hated her that much.

Tears swam unwelcome to her eyes and she covered her face in her hands.

An hour or so passed before Justin returned his son for feeding and, no doubt, changing. He left without a word. It was Brahms who finally came to escort her up.

A cold biting wind greeted her and little Justin as she stepped onto deck. The sky was a crisp blue that comes only in winter. Clouds hung in the far horizon, drawing her gaze to take in her first sight of the new land.

She had never seen a port as large as Boston. Over thirty wharves and numerous docks. Ships docked everywhere. Quaint, whitewashed buildings mixed with brick ones and these stood in the foreground of thick green forests. Marshland spread to the right as far as the eye could see. She clutched her cloak tight around herself and her child, marveling at the sparkle of the rooftops, how very clean and uncluttered the lovely town looked compared to London. It was breathtaking.

The ship slipped slowly into dock. The men crowded around the rail, already calling to the sizable crowd waiting for their arrival. The clamor of metal sounded as the great anchor was lowered, this requiring the strength of five men at the turn wheel.

Justin finished calling the last of his orders and came by her, lifting Justin from her arms. He looked at her almost quizzically. She quickly turned her head, not wanting him to discern her tears. Too many tears had been shed. This was her fate and she, too, must learn to accept it.

As Justin led her down the gangplank, she found herself looking at a dozen or so faces, all of which seemed waiting for him. Everything happened at once. At the same time the crew rushed down, the crowd rushed up, two surges clashing. Greetings and noise and confusion. Everyone rushed forward with greetings and Justin was suddenly surrounded. She was forgotten.

It became painfully obvious Justin did not intend to introduce her to anyone in the large gathering that surrounded him. He must be embarrassed, she realized, clutching the folds of her cloak tight about her. She stared hard at the tips of her worn slippers, wishing the earth would open to swallow her up, so great was her embarrassment. She prayed no one noticed her and if they did, that they wouldn't connect her pathetic lot with him or his son.

She finally heard Justin explain in a loud voice that he could not receive guests till the evening. The crowd disbanded one by one until she finally looked up and saw only Jacob; and in his arms was a lady.

She was beautiful and lovely and looked ever so different. She wore a fashionable day dress of pale green, gloves, and a matching darker green cloak. Her hair was styled into pretty ringlets around her face. Christina might not have recognized her but it was her—it was Hanna!

A surge of emotion rose through Christina and it was all she could do not to run into her arms. She had missed her so much! And if only Hanna didn't disown her friendship, if Hanna could forgive her . . .

She could not swallow this hope as she approached the small gathering. Hanna lifted little Justin from his father's arms and, for several long minutes, she happily engaged in the traditional conversation and exclamations one makes to an infant. Justin suddenly left, seeing another friend, and just as Hanna's eyes finally fell on Christina. Christina held her breath, seeing her concern and worry and—

"How do you do, Christina?"

"Fine . . . I'm fine. I, oh Hanna—" She reached out to her.

"He's a lovely boy," she replied too quickly as she handed Justin to her and turned at once to Jacob. "We've got to rush on."

Christina's heart broke swiftly in two.

Not wanting to make matters worse, Jacob nodded and quickly steered Hanna away. In mute pain, Christina stood suddenly alone with her child in her arms.

Her gaze swept the crowd for Justin. She found him several yards away talking to someone in a fine carriage. He leaned forward. A lady leaned her head out. Beautiful did not come close to an apt description of this woman's loveliness. She reached a gloved hand to his face and, laughing, she kissed him.

Christina barely remembered anything else.

Justin returned to her and quickly led her to another carriage. He exchanged a lively greeting with the driver, introducing the handsome colored man as Chesapeake. She barely managed. He saw her into the carriage and, after kissing his son good-bye, he motioned Chessy forward. The carriage bolted forward and, as it fled past, she caught sight of Justin just as he climbed into the lady's carriage.

Why did it shock her so? She should have known he had a mistress; that she would be rich and beautiful, probably witty, intelligent, and charming too; that he would flaunt his affairs publicly—he cared so little for his wife.

Then why, oh God, did it hurt so badly?

Chesapeake shook his head sadly and, determined

to reach the house by dusk, he cracked the whip across the mare's back, pushing the horses to a faster pace. He just couldn't fathom it, no sir. How in tarnation could a man be so good that he captures slavers and frees people of color and yet so mean to a young lady who was his very own wife?

Makes no sense, really.

'Course, he thought to himself, he hardly knew his employer, Mr. Justin Phillips. He knew the rumors, everybody did; he knew of his employer's reputation, a reputation that would do any man proud if you could believe it. Mr. Phillips made his wealth in the time-honored Boston tradition of privateering. Then, too, some said Mr. Phillips came from a wealthy family—some or 'nother lord or something. Near everyone who was anybody this side of the 'Lantic had one of them in their family—them lords and ladies must breed like mice in a wheat bin.

He knew somethin' else about Mr. Phillips too. Over two years passed since Mr. Phillips's house was built and staffed. Two years of absentee landlord and employer; two years of gettin' paid for no work. First they was told Mr. Phillips got caught by the British and hung. Fine but they still got paid. Then they was told Mr. Phillips didn't get the noose but died in a storm on his way to prison. And still they got paid, as though a dead man's goin' ta need a driver, house servants, cooks, and gardeners!

Someone, it seems, had the good sense to know a dead man wasn't all that dead.

So, sure 'nough, three months pass, the dead man shows up, but only to say he's leavin' again to fetch the new mistress and his son, and, lickety-split, the

337

man's gone again.

Now he's back.

Chesapeake shook his head, feeling his dander rise like a rooster in a cockfight.

He didn't care how great they all said Mr. Phillips was—he didn't take kindly to no man who treats his wife mean. No sir. Lordin' it over her like that. First flaunted that lady right in front of her, then the worst, sendin' her into her new house all alone, no one to introduce her proper but the damn driver! Why, it's just not done! Everyone's gonna know right off, the master don't care for the mistress and if the master don't care, then no one else does either. That pretty little lady's gonna be lucky if she don't have to wipe her own floors.

She was sure pretty, too, and young! Whooo, did she look young. What in tarnation could possess a man? Was he blind? Didn't he see how sad and hurt and pained she looked?

Lord, it was a shame. Ain't no excuse, no sir . . .

Thinking on it, Chesapeake worked up a frightful anger, and wanting to help his mistress, to do anything he could, he stopped the carriage and tied the reins. He jumped down and went around the side to open the door.

"Howdy." He grinned generously.

Christina looked surprised. "Is something wrong?"

"No, ma'am," he assured her. "Nothin's wrong. But it's a long trip out and I just thought, well, I thought you'se might be hungry or thirsty or somethin'. Hope—she's your cook," he explained, "packed us a fine fare. Fried chicken and biscuits with honey and two huge slices of her apple pie. Maybe you'se

338

hungry?"

Christina studied the long Negro face, his kind brown eyes. She could not guess his age but his concern was all too apparent. She immediately saw in him a friend and God knows, she needed a friend, anyone who might help her face the others.

"Yes, I am," she replied with a shy smile in turn. While she had not had much of an appetite for some time, she could ill afford to lose any more weight. And then too, they had forgot the morning meal as soon as land was sighted. As a matter of fact, once her attention was drawn to it, she was astonished by how hungry she actually felt.

"If there's enough?"

"Always enough with Hope around." He smiled and then, peering inside, he asked, "Is your young'un asleep in there?"

Justin was sound asleep in the seat drawer and she nodded.

"Well, how about riding up front with me?"

Christina brightened but— "But, is it done?"

"No, it ain't, to tell truth." He smiled. "But I won't tell if you won't."

Christina gladly accepted his offer, desperately trying to lift from her despondency. Once in the driver's seat, Chesapeake set a large basket on her lap and he got the horses moving again.

The fresh air was inviting and the road had been deserted for some time, except for two young boys with fishing poles. Thick forests of elm and oaks grew on both sides of the road. They had passed a foot traveler and a farmhand with donkey in tow, an occasional meadow and glen. The houses were buried down the shaded lanes. So different from the pastoral splendor of the English countryside.

"I'm sorry," she first ventured. "I don't think I caught your name?"

"Chesapeake Freeman—Freeman coming from two generations of freed folks," he explained proudly as she passed him a chicken leg. "But call me Chessy, everyone does." And Christina was then given the exciting history of the Freeman family, starting with his own pappy's wild trip north on the underground railroad. Chessy, in turn, was given a glimpse into his new mistress's person to discover she was every bit as sweet as she looked.

"Oh! Oh! Here she comes! The carriage is pullin' into the driveway now!" Aggie told all the others. Finally! After waiting all day.

"Take your places," Rosarn called excitedly to the others. "Someone call Mary from upstairs! And get old Hope out from the kitchen! Hurry now," she called above the sudden chatter of the sixteen other servants who scrambled into line according to rank. Rosarn ran her chubby hands over the gray muslin work dress and took a deep breath, sucking in the ample evidence shown in her waistline of Hope's fine cooking. Her long gray hair was fitted neatly into a bun and she pinched her pale fleshy cheeks for color. The first impression was lasting, she knew. And if only she hadn't lost her front tooth last week, she thought wishfully as she felt the large hole gape in her mouth.

They had drawn straws to determine who would peer through the window. It would be unseemly for all sixteen heads to be seen there. And Aggie had won.

"Can ya see 'er yet?" Rosarn asked Aggie.

"No, not yet. Just the carriage, but—lord!"

"What, what?" Rosarn asked.

"Well, there's not a trunk to be seen. Must have taken the master a whole 'nother carriage to get the lady's things out," she quickly reasoned. "Oh! Oh! Chessy's goin' round now!"

Everyone fell silent. Rosarn nervously eyed the appearance of the others, looking for any small fault their new mistress might find.

"Well? Do you see her?"

"Yes! My word, but she's young!"

"Is she pretty?"

"Can't see from the distance but I—yes! She looks as pretty as they come, but—"

"But what?" Rosarn could hardly bear it.

"Well, she wearin' a common cloak. Can't see her dress but it must be her. She's holdin' the babe."

"Is she comin'?"

"Why no. She's just standin' there like she's in a stupor, staring at the house. And oh my, but I do believe she's alone! He's not with her!" She turned to the others with shock.

Eyebrows raised and nearly everyone looked at their neighbor in line for an explanation for this, an explanation that no one had.

Christina was staring and in shock. All the small confidence she gained by Chessy's quick friendship drained the moment the carriage turned down the lane. Nothing could have intimidated her more than the sight of what Chessy assured her was Justin's house.

What could she say? Two stories high and plastered and whitewashed in the shape of an open rectangle. It was one of the grandest houses she had ever seen. The beautiful manor could easily stand among any of the grand English manors. Manicured lawns spread on each side of the oak-shaded lane. Stairs led to a wide portico, proud Greek pillars in front. Beautiful and magnificent, and she wanted to run and hide.

The sun had just set as the carriage passed down the lane and through the darkening dusk—she had glimpsed it all. Stables and barn, two stories high and whitewashed too, surrounded by bales of sweet-smelling hay. Five horses in the corral and how many more in the stables? There were cows out at pasture. A vegetable garden of perhaps two acres, fruit trees, and a whole apple orchard in the distance. There was a large building she guessed was the servants' quarters and another building that must be a huge kitchen. There were small houses behind that for servants with families, each with its own nicely tended gardens. The lane finally rounded a circular drive in front of the house she could not believe would be her home.

Christina looked to Chessy for help and she felt Chessy's hand on her arm. "You'll do fine," he said softly. "Just remember who's the mistress and who ain't."

Christina nodded and she boldly marched forward. She had not taken two steps, though, when she heard a dog barking. The house stood on a hill, overlooking a clear fresh water lake, and she turned to see him running up from the water with all the enthusiasm his huge heart could afford.

She instantly handed little Justin to a surprised

Chessy. "Beau!" she cried, kneeling down, as she opened her arms to receive him.

Beau had been down at the lake trying to catch an elusive bass when he heard the carriage and caught her scent. Changed, but the same. He remembered her, remembered that he loved her, and he had started running.

Barking with excitement, Beau raced to Christina and knocked her to the ground, and just like so many times before, he lavished kisses on her. He received the happy sound of her laughter, shrieks, and, this special time, even tears.

Christina didn't know why—perhaps because of Beauty, perhaps because of days lost or maybe simply because he was the only one to forgive her, but even after he let her up, she could not stop touching him. "Beau, my fine friend." She buried her face in his thick fur, hugging him tight. "Oh, but I missed you so—"

She stopped, as over a dozen people rushed on the scene.

"Oh my God, she likes him!" someone cried.

"We 'alf thought he was killin' you!"

"Oh no," she thought to explain, "Beau and I are friends from way back." She stood up and suddenly saw their shock. She looked to Chessy.

"This is Mrs. Phillips, our new mistress." He quickly diverted their attention. "Seeing hows Mr. Phillips is . . . ah, detained, I'll make introductions."

Aggie was staring hard at the young lady's dress. Why, she had a nicer dress than that! And what a sight she was! Why she wasn't even wearing gloves or a hat, like Asherella, she was.

Rosarn, entertaining similar thoughts, elbowed Aggie hard and drew her attention to the matters at hand. The assembly, all of them, withdrew to line up once again inside.

Christina followed Chessy and little Justin inside. She stepped through the wide mahogany doors, and with unabashed curiosity, she took in the first set of rooms. The servants were lined up in the wide hallway, large enough to be a parlor. She tried to take it all in at a glance. Elegant candelabra. Turkish carpets over polished wood floors, a gilt-framed looking glass reflecting a startlingly bold seascape opposite it. The wide douther side opened to show a study and parlor respectively, or at least she thought it was a parlor—a very large parlor. Wide stairs led up, dividing halfway to the east and west wings.

Through the open doors she caught glimpses of the rich mahogany furnishings, velvet hues of blues and greens—the colors of the sea. She would have liked to examine the paintings and woven carpets. Now was not the time.

Chessy introduced her to each new face. She felt the intense scrutiny of each set of eyes. She offered a noticeably shy greeting to each, thankful to have caught Chessy's disapproval the first time she curtsied. Mistresses did not curtsy to servants.

"This is Hope, our cook," Chessy said.

Christina stared at the old, frail-looking colored woman with open astonishment. She just looked too old. Her face seemed absolutely timeless and her slight frame seemed all bones, robbed of flesh by time.

"You'se surprised, I kin tell." She showed a wide,

toothless grin. "I may look old and I am, but just everyone likes my cookin'. I spin meals like the Bible spins yarns!"

Christina laughed at this and complimented her chicken right off. Hope, too old to care a whit about propriety and the like, had already reached a conclusion about her new mistress. She was as sweet as a honeydew melon in spring, that was all and that was enough. The other dullwits were not as clear-sighted as she, she knew, and she sought to win them over for her new mistress. Hope pointed to the babe. "Why, ma'am, just look at your young' un thar." Everyone turned attention. "He ain't never seen dark skin afore, I'll wager, and it looks like he's taken a likin to it."

Indeed, throughout this whole time little Justin had been staring at Chessy's face with a mixture of plain awe and bewilderment. He reached hands to it and discovered it felt the same. Then he laughed and stared and laughed some more.

The minute Christina laughed at this, everyone else did too and the tension broke immediately. Christina showed her son each dark face and introduced each person. He was clearly impressed, deciding he liked dark skin better or at least as well. Anything for variety.

Rosarn stepped forward to inquire about her trunks.

"Oh . . . I'm afraid I don't have any." She lowered her gaze and blushed. "We left England in such a rush," she whispered. "I have only what I'm wearing."

This confession instantly won the sympathy of every

woman in the room. Sympathy that was reinforced throughout the following days. Christina turned out to be the least demanding mistress any of them ever had and certainly the most agreeable; compliments were generous and criticism unheard of. They, especially the household help and Hope, began fighting to find things to do for her.

Of course, they all knew something was terribly amiss. That had been clear the day she arrived alone, wearing common clothes and with no one but Chessy to introduce her. No one was insensitive to her air of sadness either, a sadness that seemed only to lift when she played with her son. She spent far too much time alone as well, buried in a book in the library or out on long walks with only a dog to keep her company. Then, as the days passed, it became increasingly clear someone made a horrible mistake on top of everything else. Not a single calling card came for her, as though her arrival was being kept secret.

Everyone tried to fathom the reasons for this and it was a main subject of conversation. It was reasoned and generally agreed upon, that Master Phillips had married her because of the child. It was a common enough tale. But why would anyone treat such a sweet lady so terribly? Even if it was a loveless match, what could she have possibly done to deserve it?

Christina walked up to the house from the lakeside, returning after an unusually long walk. The cold winter air was invigorating, though she was told it was an unusually mild winter for Boston. There was hardly any snow, at least none that remained on the ground. She was coming to love the thick surrounding woods, the peacefulness she found at the lakeside. The long walks provided a few hours' escape, and she always felt better afterward.

Beau dropped the stick at her feet and she picked it up and tossed it again, thinking of her letters to Richard, wondering how they were received and what had happened to him after the escape, how he and Darrell and poor Betty had fared and all. As she turned onto the lane to the house, she saw the horse and carriage and the single mount sitting out front.

She stopped for a long moment. Justin was back. She wanted to turn away, hide in the woods and forever. How would he treat her? Would he even say a good day? Or would he simply ignore her very presence and pretend she wasn't there?

The only reason she forced her feet forward was because she had no choice.

After finally seeing his son to sleep, Justin had returned to his study and stood looking out the huge picture window, thinking of all his work ahead. Just as he had expected, Jefferson had managed to get his embargo act through congress.

The next four months were objectively among the most important, and perhaps ominous, of his life. The day after the morrow he would meet secretively with his six best captains to discuss, decide, and assign the next shipping runs. There was much to be done before then and yet like a curse he could think of naught but her. He had not completed even the first set of calculations, calculations that were so simple for him, Jacob often joked he could do them in his sleep.

The danger and risks in smuggling was directly proportional to the rewards: the greater the risks, the greater the rewards. No more so than now after Jefferson, desperate to stay out of the war between England and France, had gotten the Embargo Act through congress. An act Justin saw as disastrous for the country, yet simultaneously a fantastic opportunity for anyone with the brass guts to run the blockade.

England and France both desperately depended on American trade and shipping. Throughout the past five or so years both countries had enacted laws forbidding American trade with the other. American ships were seized at every opportunity, the cargo confiscated and the crew impressed. Well over four hundred ships had been lost to date, but none of them, with the single exception of the time he had been captured, had been his ships. And because he picked his captains and his runs so well, because he had both the talent and boldness to outrun and outmaneuver the French and English alike—opportunely chose one as bedfellow, one as enemy, then switching on the next run—he had made his fortune.

Jefferson's Embargo Act changed all this. Desperate and determined to see that both England and France grant American ships freedom of the seas, to stay out of their war, Jefferson and his well-meaning but foolish bank of lawyers got their law through congress. No American shipping in any form, to any port, at any time. They hoped it would force England and France to renege all laws restricting American shipping but he knew all it would do was bring gross depression to the country as a whole, especially Boston, but with unemployment and suffering to Americans everywhere. Except for smugglers. For men like himself, more than willing to take the risk, it meant money and a lot of it.

Justin's plans were secret. Only Jacob and his secretary, Mr. Richardson, knew the details. And if he could keep the plan concealed, he'd have amassed just enough to launch the rest of his plans.

He caught sight of Christina in the distance as she turned onto the lane and he watched her hesitancy once she saw that he had returned. Her picture looked drawn from some sad fairy tale: she looked slight and forlorn and, God, ever so beautiful, standing there all alone, staring off at the house with apprehension and, no doubt, fear as well.

He cursed softly under his breath.

Justin heard the door open and shut quietly. He could not hear her footsteps, she walked so quietly. But then there came a strange flip-flop sound, a shuffling. He did not know she was tiptoeing in trepidation of disturbing him, hoping to disappear in her room unnoticed—and the strong sound was the worn sole of her only pair of shoes.

Christina reached the top of the stairs when Rosarn called up to her. "The master! He's home." Christina nodded at her and turned back up the stairs. "He said to send you into the study as soon as you got back."

Christina froze, then took a deep breath and descended the stairs. Rosarn watched from below, noticing her hesitancy, the telling sole on her shoe that had ripped apart. Lord, the poor lady had not even a decent pair of shoes. A real life Asherella, just as Aggie said. Thankfully she had already taken the liberty of talking to the master about it.

Christina thanked Rosarn quietly and slipped

349

through the study doors. Justin was waiting for her. Her gaze swept up from the shiny black boots, the tailored black breeches, and white silk shirt, a face that was still familiar and strange both. She immediately perceived his disapproval. She wondered what she had done now.

"Good day," she ventured in a whisper, then awkwardly, stupidly, "I hope all is well?"

"Yes, all is well." He paused, moved in front of his large mahogany desk, and leaned casually against it, folding his arms. "I see you made it here in one piece," he first said, pointedly ignoring the social niceties.

She nodded.

"I also see you have managed to win the collective concern of the household. Rosarn found it necessary to ask me if she might send for the dressmaker. She should be here tomorrow."

She looked up, startled.

"In the future," he continued, "I'd ask you to manage your own affairs. I don't want to be bothered with them."

Christina's eyes quickly responded to his cruelty. Her gaze lowered to the floor. "A dressmaker is not necessary," she whispered. "If I could just have a roll of fabric, I could make my own dresses." She had done so her whole life.

"I think I can afford to clothe my own wife," he replied sarcastically. He suddenly thought of Darrell's comment on her clothes—"imagine if you let me dress her properly . . . she had them lined up all evening."

"Besides," he added, looking at her dress and suddenly angry, "if that is the sorry result of your industriousness, it will be money well spent."

Christina jerked slightly as though slapped, and his punishment came as he watched her desperate struggle not to cry.

She wanted only to win her struggle but this the evidence of how much he hated her could suppress tears for but a moment. Her lip trembled and she caught it. Then she nodded quickly, stupidly, as though this ended the conversation, and turned to leave.

"I'm not through yet, Christina."

She stopped but did not turn around.

He was silently cursing himself, knowing that if their sham of a marriage was to have any chance of working, he would have to control his baiting anger. Another woman might snap back, rebuke him, throw a tantrum or something but not her. Not the shyest, most gentle and feminine creature it was ever his mistake to lose his heart to.

"As soon as you have a proper wardrobe, I'll see to having you introduced to society. It will mean a ball, I suppose, and God knows how many dining invitations. Are you up to it?"

Still with her back to him, she nodded.

"And, Christina," he said in a different tone, "it will hardly do if you fall into tears every time I talk to you. You must try to control that, as I must try to temper my words."

She nodded again and he said softly, "That's all." She quickly departed, leaving him lastly with the sight of her torn shoe, flopping sorrowfully with each quick step away.

Justin fell into a chair. It was not going to work.

Her very presence, every time he looked at her, brought such an avalanche of unwanted emotion: pain and hurt and anger, the anguish from her betrayal, and some, like his anger, he could barely control. He, who never had trouble controlling anything, least of all himself.

How could they possibly last?

He would gladly give his entire fortune to erase the past, all of it, with the exception of his son. For his son, he would bear it. Perhaps time would erode his feelings, leaving him with blessed indifference to her.

He could not imagine indifference to her, though, even coupled with time. Anything and everything but indifference. For desire was the monster that raged with all other feelings; for even when she stood before him in a tattered dress and cloak, her hair tightly wrapped around her head like a matron's cap, dark circles under those large gray eyes, he wanted her. Her beauty might have first attracted him but love had carried him far past that point. She might be an old woman wearing every blessed sign of sixty or more years and he'd still want her. Other women he kept in his life hardly helped. If anything, they exacerbated the problem by offering blatantly bare comparisons. And even if time stole all other feeling for her, how could he feel indifference with such intense desire?

The only possibility was to separate as soon as Justin was old enough, arrange visits between two households. Yes . . .

The idea provided long-term hope and brought him some small relief but left the immediate problem unanswerable. As he turned back to his work, he had to wonder just how he could get through a single night, yet alone the long months.

Weeks later, Christina lay on her stomach atop the huge overstuffed feather bed, staring into the fire in the hearth. She tried to refrain from looking at the open carved wood doors of her clothes closet where over twenty beautiful dresses hung neatly in rows. The dresses had just arrived from the dressmaker that day. Not only dresses but petticoats galore, chemises, corsets, undergarments, and a smattering of frilly nightclothes. There were hats, gloves, cloaks, and slippers, too. They were things, all of them things, and she wanted nothing to do with them.

What she wanted and desperately was a sketchbook. A simple sketchbook. Sketching was the only way she knew to cope with loneliness. It had worked throughout the long hours of childhood and she knew it would work now.

Little Justin filled many hours, it was true, and her growing son brought the only joy and happiness she felt. But a small child was hardly enough. Not only did she loathe the idea of depending on her son for her happiness and well-being, but there were long naps and other caretakers as well, Rosarn and Aggie and Justin himself—those times he was home.

She supposed the arrival of her clothes meant the onset of socializing. There would be parties and balls and dinners and plenty of chances to meet friends. How she would love a friend! Someone to talk to and confide in, someone with whom to share things! Someone like Richard and Darrell, or like Hanna and Elsie had been.

There was little hope of making friends at any

353

social function Justin arranged. Like their household—with the noted exceptions of Chessy and Hope, Rosarn and Aggie—the people would be polite but distant, turned away as soon as they observed Justin's animosity toward her. And they would notice it, she knew, for Justin could not even look at her without feeling disgust. She wondered how he could bear presenting her as his wife.

Reluctantly, she eyed the small fortune represented in the closet. Had it been hers to trade, she would gladly trade the entire wardrobe for the few coins a single sketchbook would cost. But they were not hers to trade, they were his and bought for his purpose. She had not a penny of her own. She owned nothing but a jeweled whistle and the ring left from an annulled marriage.

Her ring . . .

She looked at the small gold band on her finger. She slowly slipped it off, and holding it up to the firelight, she smiled. Oh surely she could get a few coins for it! Richard would not mind! He always knew how much her sketching meant to her!

Justin was not home and since he was not home, she saw no possible way she could ask his permission. Now was the time! She bolted out of bed and threw on a robe and slippers, then quietly slipped down the stairs. The house was dark, quiet, and no one was still up, but she knew from Chessy that there would be a card game going on in the servants' quarters. She would ask Chessy if she might join him on his next trip to town.

The servants' quarters were divided into two parts: colored and not, then upstairs for women and downstairs for men. All those who had families lived in separate houses on or near the property. She quickly made her way through the chilly night air.

Everyone pretended not to notice the oddity of their house mistress, dressed in nightclothes and holding a lantern, knocking on the door to the colored servants' quarters at the late hour. Everyone but Chessy. He swung open the door and was just about to ask worriedly what was amiss when he noticed something. She was happy; happiness was etched into her face and he wondered if he had ever seen anything quite as pretty.

"Oh, Chessy, good evening! I'm so glad you're still up."

"Mrs. Phillips?" he inquired.

She glanced behind him to the card table and whispered, "I was hoping I might go with you on your next trip to town?"

"Oh . . . well, sure thing . . . why?" he asked all at once.

"I've not seen Boston except for once and there's something I want to purchase. When are you leaving again?"

"On the morrow."

She could hardly believe her luck. "Oh good! Before dawn, I suppose?" Chessy nodded and Christina, after promising to meet him on time, turned and raced back to the house. She set the lantern carefully back on the latch. The huge front door slammed shut. Happiness and excitement brought a smile she could not suppress, made her skip like a young child to the stairs.

She stopped abruptly.

Justin stood at his study doors. His gaze fell over her slender figure shrouded in pale rose silk, the long unbound hair cascading in ripples over that. He quickly grasped the designs of the uncommon material used for her nightclothes. It teased with the hint of transparency but just a hint, leaving a man with only one thought—that of taking it off.

Hope shattered the instant upon seeing him, while his brass scrutiny caused nervous hands to clasp the thin folds of her robe tightly at her neck.

"What are you doing outside at this hour and dressed like that?"

The question came as a demand. She stumbled awkwardly. "I . . . I went to talk with Chessy."

"About what?"

"I wondered if I might go into town with him on the morrow?"

"Hmmm." He hardly heard.

She was certain his pause was in search of reasons why she couldn't go on an outing, and she held her breath, bracing for some cruel rule that would prevent her from going anywhere.

While Justin was finding it a considerable struggle to think past the rose silk, he finally triumphed and returned to the question. He wondered if Chessy was enough escort for her; he supposed he was. Boston's streets swarmed with a growing number of unemployed sailors and he knew better than most that unemployed men and trouble went hand in hand. Though probably two or three in every ten men working, worked for him. At least one of his men would be at every corner.

"If you don't think I should—" She turned.

356

"No, no I'm sure you'll enjoy an outing."

She looked at him in shock.

"I was only hoping though that I might persuade you to leave Justin home. I haven't seen him in a long while and I'm probably going to be rather busy in a few days."

She paused in plain stupefaction.

"Christina." He smiled, misunderstanding her expression, "I'm sure he'll survive a day without you."

She nodded slowly and then before he could change his mind, she started quickly up the stairs.

"And, Christina—"

She stopped but did not look around, nervously crossing both arms and fingers in a fervent prayer that he would not now renege.

"Don't let me see you wearing things like that outside your bedchambers."

Christina smiled with relief, almost laughed, and managed to nod before racing up the stairs. Justin found himself fighting not to follow her. He combated this battle by forcing unpleasant memories back to mind.

For a long moment he stood at the bottom of the stairs looking up, just as he had once stood on a mountain looking down with a question wanting to be yelled: "Why, Christina? Why did you do this to us?"

"You ain't goin' in thar!"

Christina looked from Chessy to the window of a small shop pushed between one of Boston's poorer printing shops and what seemed to be an ale house. In England such shops were called "swap shops." Here it was a bootery and trading post combined. In small print beneath the signpost read: Gold and Jewelry, Bought and Sold. This was what made her stop Chessy.

"Why not?" she asked innocently.

"Why not?" he repeated. "It just ain't done, that's why. That shop if fer desperate po' folks and fools, lowlifes, the lot. Folks like you just don't have to be swindled by the greedy vermin that run those shops."

"I just want to see."

"See? What's thar to see but folks' treasures bought fer a nickel of what thar worth, being sold fer a dollar more. I'm tellin' ya, it just ain't done."

"Well, I'm desperate enough to do it."

"What you have to be desperate about?"

She paused in exasperation. "It's too hard to explain. I have to; we just won't tell anyone."

Chessy watched her gather the soft folds of her pale beige day dress, matching brown velvet jacket, and reticule. The brown hat she sported reminded him of a painted picture he once saw of a bandit named Robin Hood, with its feather and, hell—it alone was worth half as much as the whole damn shop.

Chessy glanced nervously over the busy street, already imagining the bustling passersby's interest in the carriage and its occupant. The group of old bats across the way had already fallen into whispers. He smiled generously, tipped his hat.

Lord, he would hear about this one.

An hour or so later Christina sat on a bench outside another store waiting for Chessy to return from his errands. A sketchbook sat open on her lap and she, for the longest while, contented herself with just staring at a pure blank page. Then, furiously, she

358

began drawing.

Two sketches later, she was still consumed with the vision in her mind. She did not notice the man watching her intently. Finally and with a frustrated sigh, she slammed the book shut.

Why would her vision never transform to paper?

Wondering what was taking Chessy so long, she looked up and her eyes fell on the arresting face staring back at her. He wore a life's passion on his well-lined face, in the intensity of sharp dark eyes, these accented by severe dark brows. Dark hair, liberally streaked with gray, was brushed straight back from an unusually long forehead and gave a fleeting impression of madness, but only fleeting for the intelligence written on his face was plain as well.

"Let me see," was all he said as he reached a hand to her book. His fingernails were stained with paint. While he studied her two sketches, she looked at him. He wore no jacket against the chilly winter day. Well-worn clothes were covered by a smock that showed a smattering of multicolored paint. Paint was encrusted on his boots, too, as well as beneath his fingernails.

Beneath one arm he held a carefully wrapped box, one he had just picked up from the store. She was certain it was paint, ordered all the way from London or Paris.

He looked at her, then back at the sketch and back at her with a quizzical expression. "You trapped the man's greed well." It was a sketch of a trade shopkeeper, a man he often had to deal with.

The compliment filled her, somehow she knew he offered them but rarely.

"And I saw you were dissatisfied with it. Why?"

359

"It never comes out like the picture in my mind," she said with feeling as she looked at the sketchbook.

"You hold the pencil too lightly, as though you are afraid of telling what you see." Christina's eyes shifted and told him that this was true. "Do you paint?"

"No, I've not ever had the chance."

The answer was telling. He would not normally even ask the question, for no woman painted. Women of her class merely passed their leisure wasting good paper with bad drawings, desperately trying to convince themselves they were not useless. He had already known she was different, as unusual as her talent. Now he knew she had the desire as well.

"You need instruction," he said and glancing at her clothes, "and I need your wealthy father's or husband's money."

She blushed with shock and embarrassment.

"Spare me the display of such shallow emotion." He did not smile. "I have neither the time nor the inclination to attend to propriety. Your clothes tell me you were either born into or married someone's fortune, probably both. A simple fact. Another two facts—you need instruction and I need your money. Make no mistake, though," he cautioned. "I'd not offer my instruction for money alone. No, you have a rare talent, made rarer by the sad fact of your sex. Had nature not made such a blatant error in assigning you the female sex, you could join my weekly class where I—in vain—attempt to instruct a sorry group of idiots who have—for some unfortunate reason—the shared delusion that they are artists. Society, however, would hardly stand by such an arrangement. Women are not expected to have minds to think with, yet alone talent. Beautiful women even less so. So, we will have to make private arrangements. You may call on me at any time."

Stunned speechless and in a daze, she passively accepted her sketchbook back and watched him turn to leave. "Wait," she suddenly called out stop him. "You must be very expensive?"

"Yes." He watched her expression drop with plain disappointment. "Young lady," he began with condescension just as plain, "if you haven't learned to use your feminine wiles on a man yet, I was mistaken about your wits. What husband could refuse you?"

Hers . . .

"Who is your husband?"

"Ah . . . Mr. Phillips, but—" She was about to say that wasn't the problem, only it was exactly the problem.

"I should have guessed."

"You know of him?"

"Yes. He's had the good taste to buy three or four of my paintings. You should be glad. Not only would he encourage the pursuit of talent—even in his wife— but he's also one of the few people in this godforsaken country with the wits to appreciate it. And if anyone can afford what I'd ask, it's him."

He left Christina without a word of good-bye, which was good, for Christina could not now speak, intimidated into speechlessness when it occurred to her just who he was. Charles Paton. Two of his paintings hung in the house, one in Justin's study, and one in the hall. Both were seascapes: pictures of a ship battling a raging sea; disquieting and violent, man's smallness pitted against an omnipotent nature.

She had studied the paintings for hours, with both admiration and envy.

She thought on the conversation the entire trip back and returned to it many times in the next few days. With her usual self-effacing manner, she first tried to tell herself that he saw talent in her sketches only because he—like most artists—was in need, seeking to solicit a gullible pupil with flattery. Artists were always poor; sadly few paintings were valued in any given artist's lifetime. He had simply wanted Justin's money.

She dismissed the subject from her mind time and again. What did it matter anyway? She had naught to pay him. She had bargained for nearly a half hour with the man in the shop, finally leaving with just barely enough to purchase a sketchbook and a proper pencil. There was not a ha'penny left. She could never but never bring herself to ask Justin for such a frivolous indulgence as painting instruction.

As many times as she dismissed it as wishful thinking, the subject persisted to intrude on her thoughts. To actually paint on a canvas! Put colors to her sketches! She had always dreamed of painting but never as a reality. Her father had thought she wasted too much time in her sketchbooks as it was and then too he could never afford painting instruction, even if there had been someone in Hollingsborne who could provide them. Richard loved to indulge her every whim, but throughout her time with him, she had been consumed with a new mother's fascination of her first child. The idea had never occurred to her then, but even if it had, she suspected Richard would think it ridiculous for a woman to want to paint.

Thinking again on the subject one morning while watching little Justin play in his nursery, she wondered what Justin would think if they were on terms? Would he—like Richard and her father—think it was a waste of time? An unnecessary indulgence? "You should be glad, not only would he encourage the pursuit of talent—even in his wife, but he was the wits to appreciate it." This could not be true. Men never thought women capable of art. Some part of herself wanted not to believe this. Some part of herself longed for a chance to show them wrong.

Little Justin was immersed in his blocks, fascinated by the possibilities. Christina returned to her sketchbook, reminding herself to hold the pencil tighter, always seeking a boldness that evaded her.

She heard Justin's two guests taking leave downstairs. Their mounts were called up from the stables. The nursery was directly over the front porch and through the open window, she heard Justin as he saw the two men off.

"You'll know tomorrow?"

"For a certainty," one of the men replied.

"Good. Bring it to me as soon as possible. And tell your Mr. Lowell I am not mad."

She wondered if she imagined the hint of anger in Justin's tone, or if it was real. Perhaps ill tidings were brought. He never confided in her about his work, or anything for that matter, and though she always wondered, she certainly knew better than to ask. Looking at her caused him discomfort, speaking more so.

Though lately . . .

She dismissed the thought outright.

He would never forgive her.

A short time later Aggie appeared at the door, looking nervous. "The master wants to speak to you, madam. Right off too. I'll look after the boy."

Christina bit her lip and looked at Aggie with a question.

" 'Fraid so," she replied softly. "He's in a fit about something."

Christina looked with apprehension toward the door and rose. Aggie placed a reassuring hand on her arm as she passed and for a moment their eyes locked. Comfort and understanding were transmitted and Christina decided in that instant that no matter what she had done or didn't do to solicit his anger, she would bear it. No tears. No matter what she would not cry.

She quietly entered the study. Justin sat at his desk, leaning back in his oversized easy chair and with his long legs crossed on the cluttered desktop. He was reading some papers. He did not notice her.

"Yes?" she beckoned softly.

He looked up. "Sit down," he motioned as he swung his legs over the desk to stand up. He closed the study doors and came in front of his desk, studying her with a mixture of anger and, yes, she read perplexity in his expression as well.

"Some business associates of mine just left. Several minutes of my time was wasted as they found some amusement in relating to me the latest rumors concerning you. Needless to say I'm not normally concerned with what some man's foolish wife prattles on about at the supper table."

"Rumors?" she whispered, alarmed. "What rumors?"

Justin did not bother relating the most current consensus among the gossipmongers. Word had it that Christina was the lovely and pious daughter of a poor reverend, that he had fallen in love at first sight, had her kidnapped and kept on a deserted island until she got with child and was then forced to marry him. He had almost laughed out loud when he had first heard it, for it presented such a curious and arresting mixture of truth and fiction.

"There are many," was all he said presently. "Apparently interest in you is at a peak and I'm sure you'll be a smash at your presenting ball next week. However—and to the point—the rumor that concerns me is the one currently circulating through town, one that I'll have you deny. The rumor has it that my wife was seen entering a common peddler's shop, where she bargained to trade a gold band for mere pennies."

He stopped to wait her reaction. She stared at hands that were suddenly twisting a lace handkerchief. She couldn't speak but her expression spoke for her.

"I see. Now, did you do this with the malicious intent to embarrass me or is there some other motive that I cannot for my life fathom?"

"No," she said in a barely audible whisper. "I didn't mean to . . . to embarrass you."

"No? Surely it must have occurred to you how it would look to people seeing my wife selling a piece of jewelry for mere pennies?"

"I didn't think—"

"That is obvious!" he said, causing her to jerk visibly at his tone. "What's not obvious is, what then

365

was your motive in entering a shop like that?"

Christina struggled hard for long moments to keep composed, focusing hard on Charles Paton's painting hanging over the mantelpiece. It hardly helped. Metaphorically she saw Justin as the sea—violent, raging, and ever so forceful and she, like the pitifully small ship fought a desperate battle to keep from sinking.

"Well?"

"I didn't have any money and I wanted a sketchbook. I didn't think Richard would mind if I sold his wedding band."

Justin listened and waited, then saw she was finished. He could only stare, that's all, just stare at her. The explanation was so simple and yet it said so much. He was dumfounded, confused, shocked.

Did she think he would deny her a sketchbook? *Anything* for that matter? After buying her all those clothes . . . it made no sense. Unless she distinguished between what was necessary and what she felt frivolous.

Had she been that desperate these last few months with him? Did she truly imagine he would deny her a damned sketchbook?

"Christina," he began, wanting confirmation. "Did you honestly think I'd deny you a . . . ah, sketchbook?"

"I didn't know," she whispered. "You said not to bother you with my affairs and I didn't want to . . . I don't want to ever be a bother to you. I'm sorry. Truly."

Justin saw how much it took from her just to say that. Any other woman and he'd swear she had created the whole thing in some twisted ploy to manipulate his feelings. With Christina he knew the sentiments just revealed were honest and he felt as though a knife had pierced his heart.

God, how did they ever reach this sorry point?

"It's my fault," he said meaningfully. "I assumed you knew. In the future, if ever you want to purchase something—anything—you have only to sign a note to the shopkeeper. Mr. Richardson, my secretary, pays these notes. I won't even see them, yet alone," he added, "be . . . ah 'bothered' by them."

He paused and Christina felt his anger rising and thinking his anger was directed at her, she braced for the lashing.

"To assure me that you completely grasp the sad fact that I can't—even if I wanted to—deny you anything, I want Mr. Richardson to receive notes from you amounting to at least two hundred dollars a month."

This shocking punishment very nearly brought the tears she tried so desperately to stop. He couldn't mean it! Two hundred dollars a month! She could not fathom it. Most people could live happily on that for five years. Even if she had such an outrageous inclination, she could not see how this could be done.

"Please don't make me do that."

The silence had grown so deafening that her soft whisper seemed loud to him, but still managed to bring with it her struggle to maintain some small dignity she thought he intended to steal. This was not his intent. "Very well," he sighed, "but then you must promise to overcome your . . . ah, reluctance to spend my money. Hmmm?"

Relief swept through her and she nodded and

started to rise.

"Oh no. I'm not through with you yet."

She looked at him, trying to read from his expression what this was about. There was still anger but also . . . concern? She braced herself.

"You were also seen engaged in a rather long conversation with a man."

The statement was a demand for an explanation but she resisted. He kept mistresses yet she could not even be seen conversing with a man. "Do you have people watching me?" she asked nervously.

"No, though I assure you if I ever thought it was necessary I would." Which was not quite true. If he so much as thought she was even contemplating an affair, he'd lock her up. He had lived too long with the nightmarish thoughts of her in another man's arms; he'd never allow the reality. "Now, who was it?"

"Charles Paton, the artist." She pointed to the seascape.

"Paton? What did he want with you?" Justin did not understand his simple question seemed to hurt her.

"Nothing of interest," she said softly, returning her gaze to the handkerchief.

Justin sensed something of import here. "I know the man, Christina, well enough to know he does not engage in whimsical or idle conversation with pretty ladies he finds on the street. I would know what he said to you."

"It was nothing really." She shrugged. "He saw me sketching and he looked at my book, that's all."

"Did he offer comment?"

"Some, but honestly, Justin, he is as you say—not a

368

man interested in—you know, and, truly, you have nothing to fear, for I would never . . . do that."

"That's not what I asked you, is it?"

She shifted uncomfortably. "I'm sure you're not interested in something so . . . so frivolous."

"I assure you I am," he said and was suddenly beginning to enjoy himself. "Now what did the man say about your sketches?"

"He said I hold my pen too lightly," she looked at her hand and finished in a whisper, "as though I'm afraid to draw what I see."

Justin took this in and suddenly chuckled. "I'm sorry, Christina, but what is it they say? Art mirrors reality? Or is it the other way around?"

She did not see what he found so amusing.

"What else did he say to you?"

"Oh." She waved her hand, rising in marked embarrassment to leave. "Nothing. Really—"

"Sit" came the sharp command that instantly stopped her motion. "Do I have to go to Mr. Paton to find out what he said or shall you tell me?"

"No, no—don't do that."

"Then tell me. All of it."

She resumed her seat and wasted several seconds toying with the folds of her pale apricot dress, feeling nervous, so nervous. She felt her face flushing in stages, her breathing grew labored, and her pulse took flight, and none of this helped her frantic search for what to say. "Oh!" She suddenly found the safe ground she sought. "He lamented for some time on the poor quality of his art students."

"That's interesting considering how carefully he selects them. It's my understanding that art students

369

from all over the country are pounding on his door and some even from England. There's a long waiting list but apparently he won't take just anybody on." He watched her shocked reaction to this, then saw her look quickly away to hide it. "What else did he say? More specifically, what did he say about you?"

Her gaze darted around the space in front of her in search of something to rest on. "Oh, he said he knew you, that you were one of the few people with the wits to appreciate . . . his paintings."

"Yes, and about you?" he asked yet again, becoming exasperated.

"About me?"

"Yes!"

"He said it was an unfortunate mistake of nature to give a woman any . . . any—"

"Talent?"

She nodded but did not venture anymore.

"If you had just bought a sketchbook, how did he know you had talent? There couldn't have been more than one or two sketches in there."

"Two, but they weren't very good—" She stopped, realizing her mistake. "I mean—"

"What you mean is that on the basis of two 'not very good sketches' he concluded that you have talent."

"Well," she whispered, "I'm sure if he saw more—"

"Yes, just imagine what he'd think if he saw some of your good sketches."

Christina was embarrassed into silence. Justin knew only that he was discovering something buried in her profound self-effacing manner, something he would reveal, for it was a matter of her heart.

"Did he say anything else?"

"He asked if I painted."

"Yes?"

"Well, I said no, that I'd not had the chance."

"Why not?" He was curious.

"I . . . well, my father thought I wasted too much time in my sketchbooks . . . that it couldn't be serious for a girl and I suppose he was right," she finished softly but then tried to explain. "Painting is expensive and we could ill afford such expense."

"I see." And Justin did see. He saw all the condescension and arrogance of his sex to hers. Little wonder why there were no noted women artists when they were discouraged at every turn. Little wonder, too, where Christina got her profound self-effacing manner, the debilitating shyness she fought so hard to overcome. She had held her father in the highest esteem, he knew, but numerous times, like now when she spoke of him, he glimpsed a common tale. A small man in an even smaller world; authoritarian and rigid, winning the complete devotion and reverence of his young daughter with but small doses of affection.

"Once again, did Mr. Paton say anything else?" She nodded. "That I needed instruction."

"And by any chance did he offer his instruction?" Her nod came on the heels of a long painful pause.

"That's quite a compliment." He smiled, finally at the point. "Should I send for him. You do want to paint, don't you?"

Until that moment Justin had only glimpsed how much it meant to her. She could not at first speak or move and when he saw the tears filling her eyes, he was suddenly at her side. "My God, Christina," he

371

whispered, kneeling in front of her chair and smiling at the tears he wiped. "If painting meant this much to you, why didn't you just ask me for it?"

"I didn't know . . . I didn't think you . . . I—" She stopped and reached a hand to her mouth, looking at him and certain every emotion in her heart was plain to see. She was a breath away from falling into his arms, just a breath and she waited his reaction.

Justin realized it a second later and it disarmed him. Disarmed him like nothing else could. He stood up abruptly and moved to the mantel, keeping his back to her.

"I'll make arrangements with Mr. Paton as soon as possible," he said finally and evenly. "But there's another thing I have to say before you leave. Richard sent the annulment papers." Richard was actually waiting in town to surprise her with a visit after they were married, which would be tomorrow. "We're to be married tomorrow," he said softly. "I've made the arrangements. It will be an understandably small ceremony with only Jacob as witness. Make what preparations are necessary. That's all."

He heard no sound or comment or anything and he turned back around to find her staring at him. "I said that's all. You can leave now."

The harsh tone startled her into motion. She nodded, rose, and quickly took her leave. Lifting the skirts of her dress, she raced up the stairs. He heard her bedroom door open and shut and he imagined she flung herself on her bed in tears.

He imagined the reality.

Damn. He slammed his fist against the mantel. Every blessed time he saw her he came closer. Closer to forgetting. Forgetting that she had left him, forgetting the implicit statement that single act said about what he had known as love, forgetting the purgatory of agony it caused.

He had come so close to sweeping her in his arms, forcing her lips to his, all in a masochistic demand that she alter an unalterable truth. She might have plenty of gratitude, as though the glad fact that she drew breath was the result of his whim but she did not love him. So, God, when would he stop loving her? Wanting her so?

He wondered what he would find in her on the wedding night. Reluctance, no doubt. The necessity of consummation served as both an excuse and justification for taking her one last time. But after that, he'd not force her again, not as long as he drew breath.

Chapter Twelve

Due to her father's occupation, Christina had attended numerous weddings but none with as dolorous an air as her own. It might have been a funeral. Even nature reflected dismally by providing a steady downpour. Bleak gray skies that were but a shade lighter than the groom's own dark mood.

Seemingly unable to bear her company, Justin chose to ride alongside the carriage, despite the rains. Despondency shrouded her throughout the long ride to the church. A good mile from the church the carriage got stuck in a mud hole and, wordlessly, Justin helped her out of the carriage, lifted her to his saddle, and pressed the horse to gallop. Even so, the lovely off-white gown she had so carefully chosen for the auspicious occasion was soaked through her cloak, the skirt splattered with mud. She had spent over two hours painstakingly fixing her hair into a pretty style and by the time she walked through doors of the small church, it hung in miserable wet clumps. She looked almost as bad as she felt.

Jacob already waited inside. While she had not really expected Hanna to attend, there had always been a small glimmer of hope. Hope was crushed the moment she saw him standing alone with the reverend.

The small brick church was as nondescript as its caretaker. She did not think she'd be able to recall it on the morrow. Wearing the traditional black cloth, the small, serious man quickly got to the point. It was the shortest possible ceremony and throughout the duration she frantically searched the empty surroundings for one thing, something, anything—a single flower would do—that could signal there was joy in the world.

She found none.

Justin placed a thin gold band on her finger. Unlike the one she had pawned, it was not plain. The tiniest diamonds swirled in a delicate pattern around the band, so tiny it looked like fluid sparkles flowing over gold. It was the most beautiful ring she had ever seen. Had he had the ring made for her? Or was it a family treasure?

The minister concluded and she closed her eyes as Justin leaned over to kiss her. The first kiss in over a year and half again but he barely touched her lips with a quick, circumspect manner as though he found this small token taxing. She opened her eyes with but the smallest, hurt gasp and turned instantly away from his dark and watchful gaze.

Justin could not believe this. If she found such small token of affection unbearable, even painful—what then would she do with the wedding night? Reluctance seemed suddenly an understatement.

God, he had had it with her.

"Wait outside, Christina."

The anger in his command brought a quick withdrawal. The carriage waited out front and she entered, so distraught that she never wondered what business Justin had with the minister that he had not wanted her to overhear.

Justin asked that the date of their marriage as shown in the small church record book be changed to the very first night he had forced Christina to give herself to him. The minister thought such a generous sum was unnecessary for the commonly provided service but when Justin insisted he use it for one of his many charities, the reverend did not argue. The date was changed and with a warm smile and gratitude.

The carriage finally made its way around the huge circular drive shortly after nightfall. Jacob had turned off the road leading back to town without a word of congratulations. Justin dismounted and entered the house without ceremony, not even bothering to wait for her. It was Chessy who helped her descend. He apologized for ruining her dress and hair, never giving on that he had any idea what the day's proceedings were about. Justin had already warned him and Chessy had promised not to tell a soul—not even his sweet wife, who happened to be one of the few women he knew could be trusted with a secret.

Christina hardly listened, barely managed to mutter that it wasn't his fault and didn't matter anyway. She had only one thought. She wanted to see her son. He would be asleep, she knew, but didn't care. She just wanted to see him, to reassure herself it had all been worth this pain, that she had not just made the second biggest mistake of her life.

An hour or so later, she still sat in the nursery, staring at her child's sleeping face through the soft light of a single candle. How she loved him! For him she would endure anything. She would endure the pain of a loveless marriage, the indignity of his father's animosity.

A light rap on the door and Rosarn entered, and after discerning the somehow lovely and touching sight of her mistress just staring at the boy—a boy who had kept her running all day—she asked, "Is everything well? He's not ill, is he?"

"Oh no. I just missed him." She smiled. "Why is it I never tire of studying his sweet face?"

"Sweet while he sleeps, the devil when he's awake," Rosarn laughed lightly. "But I know what you mean. I used to stare at my own for hours on end, too. Enjoy it while you can; they grow so quickly."

Christina already knew this.

"I just came to tell you your bath is ready and I laid out your nightclothes. Are you sure you want to skip supper? I could still get a tray sent up."

"No, I'm fine. Thank you."

The nursery was conveniently placed between her bedroom and the master bedroom and so Christina merely passed through her dressing room into her bedchambers.

A fire danced in the hearth and a lamp was lit, the windows closed against the rain, and the plush, dark rose-colored curtains drawn against that. The heavy rose-colored quilt was turned down and a hot bath waited by the fire. The lovely room looked warm and inviting.

She removed her clothes, hung them neatly over a chair, and climbed into the hot water, careful to keep her hair over the rim to dry before the fire. The sweet scent of lavender filled the air. Rosarn or Aggie must have used half a bottle of the precious lavender oil.

The bath water cooled too quickly and before she felt the day's tension leave her, she reluctantly climbed out, suddenly cold. She dried off quickly, and discarding the frilly, lacy nightclothes laid out on the bed, she went to the chest of drawers. She opened the bottom one and lifted the neat pile of chemises and handkerchiefs to find what she kept hidden there.

Tonight she would wear it. One day shortly after she had arrived, Aggie had passed her carrying a bundle of Justin's clothes for laundry. She had caught the faintest trace of his scent as the maid passed. That was all it had taken. She waited until Aggie busied herself with another task, snuck into the pantry, and stole his shirt.

Tonight was her wedding night and while he would have no part of her, she would have some small part of him throughout what she knew would be a sleepless night.

No sooner had she climbed into bed than a knock sounded at the door.

"Yes?"

Rosarn pushed the door open just a fraction and remained outside, thinking her mistress was still in the bath. Christina was the only woman she knew who did not find it necessary to bathe in a chemise. She did not want to embarrass her, even though she—like all the house maids—had noticed her mistress's inexplicable lack of modesty despite her obvious sweet goodness and shyness of person.

"It's the master," she whispered, glad too that she wouldn't have to see her mistress's reaction to the first night he sent for her to perform her wifely duties. "He wants you to attend him. That's all. Good night."

Christina watched the door close quickly before she could read the maid's expression for information. Though Rosarn was not like Aggie. Aggie's face always told her what she should expect from Justin—indifference or anger.

Trying to guess what he might want at this hour, she climbed out of bed and swung the long rose-colored robe over the shirt. She held it tight about her and glanced quickly into the looking glass to make certain he couldn't tell what she had on beneath. Then she descended the stairs and with a pounding heart that signaled no small amount of apprehension.

The study was vacant. She looked in both the parlor and the dining room but found them vacant as well. He must have changed his mind or forgotten and then retired without waiting for her. She felt a sudden flood of relief and she quickly returned to her bedroom.

She tossed the robe to a sitting chair and flew into the bed like a child, burying herself in the warm quilts and almost immediately losing herself to the faint, ever so pleasant scent of his shirt. The small remnant of days long lost sent her swiftly to the distant shores of her memories, where she wandered restlessly for some time.

With her pulse racing, her face flushed, she sat up, as far from the peaceful state conducive to sleep as she might be. How could mere memories stir that sweet warmth through her loins? How could she want him so? Wanting him shamelessly like . . . like—

She wouldn't admit the shockingly unchaste thought even to herself.

Anxiously she looked around the quiet room in search of something innocuous to rest her gaze on. The lantern still burned; she had forgotten to extinguish it. The small brass gilt clock ticked softly on the mantel, rain fell in a soft patter against the window panes, and she listened with intense concentration to these but in a near desperate attempt to quiet her thoughts.

Justin waited in his bedchambers until her message became perfectly clear. She would not come to him; he would have to go to her. Fine. She could have it her way. He stormed from his room, slamming the door behind him.

Christina bolted up, alert and as still as a doe with the scent of a hunter. His footsteps warned of his anger even before he reached the door of her room. The door opened and she scrambled up to the bedpost, holding on with both hands for some false sense of security. Justin entered and stood with his hands on his hips, his long legs spread apart and ever so obviously furious about something.

"What game is this?" he demanded.

Game? She didn't know what he meant, but he seemed to suddenly take notice of his shirt. Now he would be angry about that too. Like all times of uncertainty, she bit her lip, looking every bit like the guilty child she felt.

Had he wanted to torment himself, he would have created the exact picture of her that he now stared at.

A light shining from behind to silhouette the slender shape covered in a man's shirt—his shirt, he realized. The long loosened hair cascaded carelessly around her and her face was shadowed in darkness. A picture of provocative innocence.

His anger simmered with desire and even he recognized the danger of such a potion. "Do I have to carry you kicking and screaming to my bed?"

"What?" She glanced at the bed. "I . . . I don't understand?"

"You don't?" He wondered if this could be true. "This is our wedding night." He stated the blunt fact. "Surely you don't expect me to make the same mistake as your first husband and leave our marriage unconsummated?"

After precious long seconds of true bewilderment, the reality crashed into her consciousness. She couldn't believe it. He could not bear to kiss her and yet he thought to consummate their marriage. She shook her head and all she could think was, "you don't mean it . . ."

Justin suddenly saw she truly had not known. Ignorant and innocent. The long wait for her had not been attended by frightened apprehension or reluctance. No, this was her fear and apprehension and reluctance staring him in the face, bare and real and unconceived, and so much worse because of it.

"I'll repeat myself," he said in a carefully controlled voice that he didn't feel. "Do I have to carry you kicking and screaming to my bed?"

She couldn't move, not a step, and she just knelt at the bedpost staring at him stupidly.

Justin wasted no more time and swept down upon

her, lifting her into his arms. He carried her the short distance to his bedchambers, pushed open the door, and set her to her feet before the fire. Wordlessly, he shut the door and then went to his bed to begin undressing.

Christina's gaze darted around the one room in the house she had never seen, seeing everything and seeing nothing. It was larger, larger than hers by thrice as much and looked at once enormous and spacious and ever so masculine. The fine furnishings—a long clothes closet and chest of drawers, sitting table and chairs, an impressive desk, and the huge four-poster bed—all were polished and hand carved, and everything—the heavy velvet curtains, the patchwork quilt and the rich tapestry rugs were dark shades of blue, greens, and gold. Lamps on either side of the bed threw soft light into the room. A fire in the wide brick hearth danced hungrily and though she felt its heat burn on her bare legs, she shivered uncontrollably.

He could not bear to kiss her and yet he thought to consummate their marriage; the thought repeated itself over and over until she imagined an ugly scene that contrasted dramatically with memories she cherished: he would hold her down, no kisses or touching, just— "Oh Justin, please." Her hand went to her mouth and she started crying as she shook her head. "I can't bear it . . ."

Justin stood slowly to his feet. She could not be this desperate and distressed by the thought of his touch that she would plead with him. Yet he was staring at her tears, a slight trembling of her bare form beneath the shirt, the way she hugged herself to stop from totally succumbing to an obviously enormous fear sweeping over her.

Where was the Christina who fell laughingly into his arms? Where was the Christina who once whispered to him that she wanted to spend all day kissing him just to see if it truly was an insatiable desire she felt? Where was the woman whose unexpected passion met his own time and again? And, God, what had he ever done to deserve such fear and loathing?

"Your . . . ah, reluctance is obvious, Christina," he first said and decided suddenly that he needed a drink. He went to a cabinet and poured brandy into a glass. "But let me explain something. You're my wife and I will have you tonight. Pleading, tears, not even a goddamned army could dissuade me from my intent. Is that understood?"

Christina swallowed and nodded, a growing numbness saving her from any more demonstrations of the extent of her desperation. Numbness that would enable her to go through with it.

Justin took the brandy whole, then poured another and brought the glass to the bed. It was set on the nightstand with an angry clink. He removed his boots and shirt and then watched her eyes quickly find the floor as he shrugged from his breeches. He almost laughed out loud. As virginal as if it truly were their first time. He suddenly didn't care, didn't care about anything except awakening her to what she had forgotten. And he would not make it easy for her.

He tossed his breeches to a nearby chair and then sat down on the bed and leaned against the headboard to watch her. He took a sip of brandy. "Do me the favor of undressing yourself."

383

Her eyes shot up at the cruelty of this but one glimpse at his brass stare, the evidence of his desire, and they lowered quickly. With pained apprehension, she glanced around for a place to hide.

"Not a chance. Stand where you are. And, Christina," his voice mocked her, "don't make me repeat myself."

He watched her hands tremble as she undid the buttons of his ridiculously large shirt. She finally freed herself from the garment but held it tight in front of her to cover what he'd have shown.

"Drop it."

The shirt fell to an unnoticed heap at her feet. She crossed her arms over her self and the red-gold hair tumbled past her hips.

Justin drew a sharp breath. Like Botticelli's Venus. He knew then his judgment was clouded. She could not really be this beautiful. He swallowed his brandy whole and gave his last order. "Come here."

She moved slowly to the bed until she stood in front of him. For a long moment she felt his gaze studying her and she waited helplessly. She expected to be lowered to the bed and for him to be done with her as fast as such a thing was possible.

A lone tear fell over her cheek, dropping onto her hair.

Justin sat up and swung his long legs over the side of the bed so that she stood between them. He reached for her hair and brushed it behind her back. Taking her hands in his, he brought her arms to her side, leaving her bare and vulnerable to his gaze.

"My God," he whispered under his breath, "you're even more beautiful than I remembered."

She stopped breathing.

He traced his hand lightly over the faint line that remained from her attack and he remembered the whispered promise they made as lovers, "Never let me go—'Never!'" Then his hand found another line on her breast, small and even fainter, the only remnant he could find of the fact that she had bore him his son. Bound together forever and at least for this one night he would make her his again.

Justin gently brought her to the bed. His gentleness brought her eyes open with a question but he only partially understood her confusion.

"No, Christina," he replied as the long length of him came partially over her. "This will not be over quickly."

She didn't understand what was happening. He rested his weight on his elbows on either side of her head, staring down at her. His thumbs lightly caressed her forehead, a small gesture but intimate and, yes, loving. She held her breath and kept her eyes closed, still braced for something worse than unpleasant.

Justin could have lost himself then and there. His senses filled with her lavender scent, the incredible softness of her slender form beneath him, all of which created a maddening battle for some control. But he would have her slow and at any cost to himself. As his hand lightly explored the contours of her face, he lifted partially from her to savor the sight of her unclad beauty waiting for him.

She felt devoured by his gaze, his gaze alone, and it was all she could do not to cover herself from him. It was becoming clear that he didn't intend the scenario she imagined but what he was intending seemed even worse. He would awaken her; he would stretch his lovemaking and force her open and vulnerable to him, just as he made her stand before him like that. He knew she could not resist his touch, not ever, not even knowing his hatred toward her. He would take possession of her—mind, body, and, soul—only to casually, cruelly discard her when he was through.

She could not let him do that.

With a knowing smile, Justin watched the beckoning lips thin to a hard line, the sudden look of determination set on the delicate features. He had expected it. "You would try to resist me, Christina?" he asked as his hand slowly followed his gaze.

She bit her lip and opened her eyes to see his expression of gentle mocking. She couldn't bear it. She closed her eyes again and turned away but he stopped her movement.

"I thought I explained it all once or twice before," he whispered against her ear as he came over her. His lips lightly brushed over the contours of her face, along the long line of her neck. She shivered, squirming slightly as though in discomfort. "You can't resist me. I won't let you." His fingers lightly traced over her lips, teasingly, waiting for them to open. "I'll never let you."

Her lips parted with a small pained gasp and then he kissed her. It was as the first. Gentle and tender, his lips barely brushing hers, but after one taste of her sweetness, he wanted more. The kiss deepened, then lingered teasingly, then deepened again. And like the first, it was her undoing.

One kiss became another and another.

The taste of her! He could not get enough, and as his lips left hers to travel along her neck and back again, he began working her body as a sculptor works clay. Gentle but not, caressing, exploring, slowly taking his time to prove his point. She cried out softly, succumbing to a sea of sensations his hands and lips brought her. He forced the whole of her body to race toward that promise of ecstasy, a promise she knew was but a momentary prize before certain defeat.

What thoughts she had of resisting were banished. He allowed her no thoughts. He pursued his pleasure with seemingly the sole purpose of possession. Complete possession. Whether an hour or two or none passed, she could not think to know. She only knew when she could not bear this exquisite peak of agony a moment longer, when she felt the first tremors of ecstasy and her arms pulled him to her as she called out his name.

His wait was over and he answered her cry, joining her to him in the timeless way of a man and a woman. The first feel of her nearly ended him but still he stretched his love, nearly dying a hundred times as he watched and felt the intensity of her response, his own in turn, and finally her ecstasy that at first seemed unwilling to stop. Then and only then did he lose himself to her, the intensity of it leaving him momentarily weak and dazed and stunned.

Justin rolled over, not for a minute willing to let her go. He brought her with him.

Just as shaken, if not more so, Christina buried herself in him. He could not hate her and make love to her like that! It was not possible she knew. She could feel his love, feel it, and even if he did not forgive her

387

now, he would do so soon. He had to, for his heart would force him.

The force of her love swept through her and left her shaking softly with tears. She fought for words to beg him to forgive her; words that would explain everything; words that would declare the truth—that she couldn't go on like this any longer, she loved him and desperately so!

Suddenly Justin tensed and shifted as though shocked, and she instantly reacted with fear.

No, he could not do that to her!

He lifted her face to him. Tears and fear. Before and after. He just stared as the reality swept through him in a wave of anguish.

When was he going to get it through his head?

With wide anxious eyes, Christina watched as he swung out of bed and quickly pulled on his breeches. The warmth left with him and she was suddenly shaking. He turned back to her and, without a word, he lifted her into his arms, through the hall, and into her bedroom, setting her onto her own bed. She stared in disbelief, as still without a word he turned to leave.

He stopped with his hand on the door handle. "I'll not bother you again, Christina," he vowed softly.

She was desperate, more desperate than she had ever been or ever would be. "Justin!" she cried through tears, "how . . . how could you do this to me?"

He looked back. She sat on the bed, her knees tucked under her and her hands clasped as though with desperate prayer. The long hair, tousled and wild looking, covered her nakedness and her eyes were wide and misty, and filled with all the pain he brought. She never looked so beautiful.

A hundred different replies came to his mind but they could all be reduced to the unfortunate fact that he loved her. Loved her so desperately at times—

He did not finish the thought. He turned away and shut the door. She collapsed to the bed and with all the tears her young heart could afford.

Christina sat on the window seat in the nursery with her legs up and staring blankly on to the front lawns. The day after the storm showed small signs of winter's final rest, though she noticed none. By all accounts the winter had been unusually mild for Boston and already it was warming by degrees. No morning frost covered the expansive green lawns. The sun shone through scattered clouds, reflecting back the sky and trees and lawn in puddles; everywhere there were puddles.

She was remembering idly how, as a young girl, and without the luxury of a looking glass, she used to stare into puddles after a rain and wonder if she was pretty or no. Her father caught her at it one day and harshly cautioned her against any such exercises in vanity. She never did it again.

Her father . . . Strange how the older she got the more he changed in her mind's eye. Ever since Justin. She wondered if any man could stand alongside Justin and be favorably compared. Probably not.

Little Justin's ball rolled to her and she absent-mindedly rolled it back. Justin laughed with delight and did it again. So the game began. Five minutes later he was bored and turned his attention back to his blocks. Christina returned to the window.

A carriage was drawing down the lane. Another in Justin's endless stream of visitors and business associates. She wondered what other people did the day after a wedding. She thought again of the warmth of his arms, the caress of his lips, and her already red, swollen eyes filled again with the sting of yet more tears . . .

No, she wouldn't cry anymore.

The carriage splashed through puddles as the two chestnut bays pulled it round the circular drive and stopped. A man alighted with great difficulty and with no help from the driver. His back was to the house and, wearing a traditional travel cloak and top hat, he struggled to keep something or someone inside the carriage.

How odd!

The man had the same build as Richard and not for the first time she wondered why Richard had yet to answer any of her two dozen letters. Why didn't he send a letter with the annulment papers? At least a simple note? How she missed him, his friendship and intimacy, his easy laughter and quick smiles. How she needed him now.

The man cursed in Richard's exact manner. She slowly stood up and holding her breath, watching for several seconds as the man, still with his back to her, gave a colorful lashing to the dispassionate driver.

Then he suddenly turned.

"Richard!" she cried out loud.

Justin sat at his desk, staring blankly at the pile of papers on top, unable to steer his thoughts from the night past. Christina's footsteps were heard racing down the stairs. A blur of pale cream muslin and red-gold hair raced past the open doors of his study. The front door opened and shut. He stood up and went to the window, where he confronted a scene that quite easily tore his heart in two.

Christina ran into Richard's open arms. Richard lifted her off her feet for the embrace and, laughing, he swung her round and round. She was laughing and crying in her gladness. He finally set her to her feet but only to plant affectionate kisses on her upturned and obviously overjoyed face.

Any other man and Justin would have had his pistol out. But Richard was another matter. What hurt, forcefully and quite suddenly, was seeing how happy another man could make her.

He watched as Christina jumped up and down, clapping her hands with excitement and asking a hundred questions in a rush, gestures that all seemed so feminine and girlish and just her. Like two young children, the two could not move a step, the immediate things to say were so very pressing.

Was any of what happened her fault? Had she asked for any of it? He had given her no choice from the start. Under the convenient guise of saving her life, he had first abducted her and then stolen her innocence. In a very real sense he forced her to fall in love with him.

She had never wanted to love him.

His mind tore swiftly over the events of the island that had caused her so much distress, culminating with Diego's death. He never had the chance to explain that to her. Did she know? Would it have made a difference?

God knows the hell she put him through had indeed been a cruel and severe punishment. But he knew suddenly that his anger had risen from the pain of it, the pain of losing her, the pain of facing the blatant fact that she had been so desperate to escape him she had risked everything from the simplest security to her own virtue, even her very life.

Christina's rush of questions would not stop. Richard tried to answer each one however briefly, until finally he held up his hand. "Please, Christina." He laughed. "We will have all day to catch up, but right now," he glanced back at the carriage, "there is someone dying to see you again."

"Darrell!" she guessed excitedly.

"No." A moment of sadness sprang in Richard's eyes. "Darrell will have naught to do with what he still refers to as 'colonial barbarians—traitors each', though," he smiled, "I did manage to convince him of a long summer visit before I left."

"Oh good." She smiled. "But who then, if not Betty or Darrell?"

"Before I let her out, I'll have you know that her very existence, the great effort and labor it took to get her here—including many close partings with my much treasured sanity—is, my dear," he kissed her, "but a small token of my undying affection for you."

"Oh! Who is it?" She laughed.

Richard went to the door of the carriage and opened it. Beauty, whose paws had been on the door, fell into a clumsy heap on the ground. Christina only stared, stared as one shocked by a visitor from another world. The huge dog scrambled back to her feet and, with pained yelps, she raced to her. Overwhelmed by

Christina's long-sought-for presence, Beauty first ran circles around her but finally, just as Christina overcame her shock and bent to reach her hands to fur, Beauty jumped up and knocked her to her back.

Justin made a quick dash out, knowing what damage a dog at least sixty pounds plus her weight could do, if even affectionately. He stopped mid-stride at the doorway. Christina lay flat on her back, laughing and crying again as the dog stood firmly over her, kissing her, its great tail wagging hard and fast enough to shake the whole of its body. Obviously as in love as loved.

The scene brought him in an instant to a resolution. He would have her love again. If it took a year or five, he didn't care. He would have her love again.

Laughing, Richard shook Justin's hand. "I assure you, I did not intend to put your wife in such a . . . ah, precarious position."

"No doubt," Justin said generously, still taken by the scene but seeing the necessity of aiding Christina's effort to rise. He knelt down and called the dog to him. Beauty responded to his voice and obeyed. She sniffed him out, seemed suddenly agitated and excited by his scent, and immediately she began looking for its source. Justin thanked the wisdom of nature for giving the beasts such short memories.

Richard had helped Christina to her feet, but Justin came to her side. "Are you all right?"

Christina failed to notice his concern, the other emotion plain in his eyes. She nodded quickly as she called the dog back and then demanded an explanation from Richard.

Richard got the worst of the wet grass off her

clothes as he explained. "The beast's recovery is actually owing less to my surgical skill than to its clumsy strength, all that fur. The bullet did a bit more than graze her chest but it missed by inches its heart. It took some doing but I managed to patch her up."

For this, Richard received another long affectionate embrace from Christina. Justin suddenly understood jealousy's irrational and violent nature, something he never before had cause to know.

Beauty discovered the arresting part of Justin's scent as Beau came lumbering up the hill. A fast friendship was established and the fun began.

"My God, there are two of them!" Richard exclaimed with great shock. "I am sorry now. Even this house is not big enough for two."

Christina hit him and giggled and then begged him to stay at least until the ball. Richard looked at Justin, who nodded.

"Good," Richard said, "and now, let me see our little fellow! I've missed him so! He must be huge by now—"

"Oh, wait till you see!" She rushed him toward the house, "He's almost walking and he talks all the time . . ."

Justin suffered a montage of conflicting emotion, witnessing the easy intimacy of the two as they disappeared into the house. Irrational and violent for sure. He would stifle it with a drink. A very large drink.

The two secretaries sat at their desks in Mr. Lowell's outer office on the famed State Street lane. Mr. Ferguson and his apprenticed son busily went about

394

their tasks, tasks comprised mostly of bookkeeping. Bookkeeping and more bookkeeping; for no single fortune multiplied faster than Mr. Lowell's.

A gentleman walked in unannounced, followed by two young men obviously acting as some sort of foot soldiers. Mr. Ferguson's warning signal went up. The man's brisk walk and determined stare fitted perfectly with his poorly tailored blue coat and worn boots. He had closely cropped burnt red hair and he sported a neat goatee, and this taken with the intensity of his cold blue eyes, reminded him—for some reason—of a religious fanatic. But this was a government man, he knew. He glanced at the appointment book. Empty till two. Mr. Lowell was in conference with his captains. He would not want to be disturbed.

"Yes?" Mr. Ferguson rose.

"I'm here to see Mr. Lowell."

"Have you an appointment?"

"No, but I insist on seeing him anyway."

"I'm afraid that's not possible. If you leave me your name and business, I'll set up an appointment as Mr. Lowell sees fit."

"We'll proceed my way," he said forcefully, knowing that this was only Mr. Lowell's secretary. If he could not get through a secretary, what hope was there of success with Mr. Lowell himself? A little intimidation should do the trick. "Either you can announce me or I shall do the honor myself."

"I see." Mr. Ferguson decided against calling the guards, not because he was intimidated; he wasn't. Only he didn't know this man's business and it seemed both pertinent and expedient to let Mr. Lowell decide for himself. "Your name?"

"Jean Petiers."

Mr. Ferguson rose and entered Mr. Lowell's elegant and certainly ostentatious office, interrupting the conference to announce Mr. Jean Petiers. "A government man, I think," he explained.

"Hmmm," and Mr. Lowell decided in a pause, "Show him in. Just who I want to see—a government man. Give him a piece of my mind!"

The eight captains all laughed at this, for each was intimately familiar with their employer's inclination for outspoken address, especially with anything having to do with politics.

"Gentlemen," Mr. Lowell addressed the assembly of eight men, "Mr. Ferguson will show you where we keep that French brandy. If you'll excuse me."

The captain arose amidst much talk and stepped through the wide hand-carved double doors into the outer office. Mr. Petiers, in turn, stepped inside. He ignored the lavish display of artifacts from around the world, the fine tapestry carpets, paintings, and drapes, the expensive French furnishings, the impressive collection of books behind glass cabinets, and turned his attention directly to Mr. Lowell.

For the first time in Mr. Lowell's forty odd years, his wealth—so carefully displayed—seemed at first unable to protect him. The man had not even spoken yet and for some reason he felt he already lost the upper hand. An upper hand he had always enjoyed. An upper hand he would get back before this man left the room.

"Yes, Mr. Petiers, is it?" Mr. Lowell said uncertainly, shifting his corpulent weight uneasily as he ran jeweled fingers over his balding head, always wishing for the time when wigs were in fashion. He then took to unconsciously fondling a solid gold paperweight as he studied the man. "What can I do for you?" He quickly changed his mind. "What is it you want?"

The cold blue eyes did not waver. He went directly to the point. "We want Mr. Justin Phillips and we want you to get him for us."

"You what? Mr. Phillips? Whatever do you mean?" came all at once. Then, "Who are you?"

"An agent acting for the government." This was not entirely true. In truth he was acting for the French government, but Mr. Lowell need never know this. "You, of course, are, ah friends with the party in question?"

"Why yes." Mr. Lowell heared the faintest hint of a French Canadian accent in the man's voice. Plenty of French Canadians around, some probably even worked for the government, but it bothered him for some reason. "Please, sir, you must explain yourself."

"As you know, the Embargo Act has outlawed all American shipping."

The very words Embargo Act triggered his famed explosive response. "I damn well do!" He slammed a closed fist to his desk. "And since you're a government agent, you can tell our Mr. Jefferson what a foolhardy act it is! I'm all for staying out of the war— any war—but to try and stop shipping! Well, I'll tell you, the city is already swinging into a severe depression. Unemployed sailors swarming the streets like packs of hungry rats, businesses failing—"

"I am not here to discuss the wisdom of the new law, though your sentiments, sir, are noted," he calmly interrupted. "We all want to end the act and as soon as possible," he said significantly. "Which leads me to the point. The act will indeed force England and France to acknowledge American rights to the seas but only if smuggling can be stopped. And we both know the most successful venturer in this enterprise is—Mr. Phillips."

Mr. Lowell did in fact know this and Justin's astounding abilities had not only earned his respect and admiration but had often nourished many profitable deals between himself and Mr. Phillips.

What he wondered and what made no sense to him was that he, too, ran one of the most successful smuggling operations in the country. Did this man know of Mr. Phillips's smuggling but not his own?

"Over four hundred American ships seized," Mr. Petiers continued, unable to read Mr. Lowell's response so far. "And only one of them Mr. Phillips's. The one in which he was captured and somehow—no doubt owing to English incompetence—escaped from. Mr. Phillips sees the Embargo Act only as yet another ripe opportunity to make a fortune. And we have already gathered the arresting information that he will be working this time with his own uncle—or father, as some say—Lord Winston Phillips. What we want you to do is to find out where and when Mr. Phillips's ships will receive the stolen goods and where and when his father will receive them in England. The shipping plans."

Mr. Lowell stoically concealed his incredulity. He was not stupid; no one reached his lofty position of wealth and power on idle brains. Presently, his mind clicked into action and quickly reached a series of startling conclusions.

"So, you want me to, ah, spy? On Mr. Phillips. And is there a reason I should do this? I mean— besides the obvious service, turning traitors in to our young republic?"

"Besides the obvious service to your country," he now lowered his bait, "we will in turn leave your own prosperous smuggling activities uninhibited. Neither the navy nor the militia will interfere with your ships."

So he did know. "Let me get this straight now." He stopped himself from laughing in this man's face outright. "You will let one smuggler go in order to catch another?"

"The lesser of two evils."

"I see. And can you guarantee that my ships will be ah, 'uninhibited'."

"Well, there are no guarantees in this world, but—"

"Just as I thought," Mr. Lowell interrupted. He leaned back, folded his hands across his stomach where he stroked a shiny gold chain. "I beg to disagree. There are a few guarantees. One is that you are not a government agent, at least American agent. I know my fellow countrymen and I know," he said with the innocent self-righteousness shared by nearly all Americans, "we do not do business by back-stabbing each other. I'll wager you're French. Yes," he said to himself, "you must be. Secondly, I'll guarantee that if you do not leave this office in two minutes, you will certainly wish you had." He then rose and calmly moved to the doors. "Good day, Mr. Petiers."

Jean Petiers's face had reddened in stages and he too quickly rose. "Not so fast, Mr. Lowell," he cautioned. "I wouldn't turn down our offer so quickly—"

"Oh? Let me guess—now you're going to blackmail me? Perhaps you've discovered my mistresses—something of that sort?"

That was exactly where he was headed.

"Well, when you tell my wife, do me the favor and also inform her I'll be late for supper tonight, will you?"

Mr. Petiers stiffly, though quickly, walked out the door into the outer office where his men followed him out. He had not expected such formidable difficulties with Mr. Lowell. No indeed. The failure would force him to take the next, more extreme measures. While he did not normally like to involve women in any spy activities, he was probably left no choice now. He would first try a house servant and in the event that failed—and he thought it might—he would have to involve Phillips's young wife.

Before he resumed the meeting with his captains, Mr. Lowell called his secretary into his office. "Ferguson, send a message to Justin Phillips. No, wait—he's not in town right now. Get me that captain of his then—Jacob Robbins. Tell him it's important that I see him. Right away."

"Yes, sir."

An invitation to the Phillips ball was a highly sought-after card by Boston's society. The ladies anxiously awaited meeting the beautiful young lady who managed to capture the notorious, infamous, and ever so wealthy Mr. Justin Phillips. And then, too, who could resist an evening of dancing and music, fine food, and new finery? The men had other reasons for looking forward to the ball. They wanted the chance to discuss Jefferson's latest outrage at length, and this with the collective wisdom of everybody who was anybody. They also wanted the chance to ascertain the truth of the rumor that Mr. Phillips planned to run the embargo. Fortunately, just about everyone who wanted a card had received one, for the ball was unquestionably the largest affair of the season.

Richard's visit successfully distracted from Christina's growing nervousness until the actual day. Justin had employed a dozen more servants for the preparation, as well as the event itself, and, unbelievably, she had almost naught to do to help. She could hardly sit still for the bath, or Aggie's elaborate hairstyling.

She tried over and over to tell herself that her fears were unfounded and probably irrational too. People would not measure her every move and judge her short. They would not wonder how Justin ever came to marry a meek, socially inept reverend's daughter. They would not sense his animosity toward her and then search for reasons.

Still every ounce of fear was etched on her face as— feeling every bit like her maid's work of labored art— she finally stood in front of the looking glass. Like staring into puddles, this always caused some small anguish and she quickly reached an unkind judgment. So frightened by it, she could almost cry.

No observer could possibly understand, much less predict her fears, for there were absolutely no visible grounds for her insecurities. No one except Justin.

Justin entered her bedroom and he silently motioned the maids out as he stepped quietly behind Christina. He took in everything at a glance, her apprehensions, the inability to see herself as beautiful, every insecurity written in her wide, anxious eyes. And the sight of her standing before the glass like that would remain forever etched in his mind.

"You're beautiful, Christina."

It was an understatement. The gown and hair both were fashioned from the French Napoleonic court, currently in love with the ancient classic Greek style. The empire dress was made of a pastel blue silk, with folds of a white transparent-type material over that and all trimmed in a delicate lace. The short puffy sleeves left her shoulders bare. Her hair was lifted into a pile of loose swirls, with the tiniest of curls left to surround her face.

Christina's gaze focused on his reflection standing next to hers in the glass and, uncertainly, she lowered her lashes, then looked back at her own reflection. She didn't expect a compliment from him and, worse, she couldn't believe it.

"This dress," she whispered because she was close to losing what small voice she had, "Richard said it was the prettiest and, and—"

"Christina, sweetheart, look at me," he said quietly, turning her around to face him. She lifted her eyes to him and with a desperate plea for help. "Are you really this afraid?"

She bit her lip and nodded.

Justin took her hand and led her to a chair. Before Christina grasped his intent, he lifted her on to his lap. "Close your eyes."

She hesitated at first, not knowing why or what he was doing.

"You remember, don't you?" he asked softly. She searched his face, remembering only too well but hardly able to believe he did. His eyes were intense, searching as well. She took the risk; she closed her eyes.

Justin paused for long minutes as he felt her tension slowly drain from the moment she shut her eyes. She was soon leaning against him, enfolded neatly in his arms, like how many times before? He could feel the slender curves beneath the layers of clothes and, teased by that lavender scent of hers, the same scent she had worn the night of their wedding, his body's response was quick and predictable. He found himself suddenly fighting for control.

"I want you to remember," he whispered, "a time not so very long ago. A time when you were very much in love." His voice, its rich male timbre and gentle coaxing, the slow caress of his hand, the inexplicable warmth emanating from him and the steady beat of his heart, all effortlessly transported her to that time.

"Just for tonight, we will remember that time—before anything happened. The time when we were bound by our love forever, before even the birth of our son. Can you remember, Christina?"

She nodded.

"Any time tonight you feel afraid, or you feel your shyness start to overwhelm you again, or anything—if someone so much as asks you an impertinent question—I want you to come stand by me. I'll be there for you, Christina," he whispered with feeling. "And together I know you won't be afraid."

Christina opened her eyes to him and he saw her unexpected hope. He could not resist; he did not try. He sealed the bargain with a kiss. So gentle and sweet, the kiss filled her with a sudden potent rush of her love, that she, too, could not think to stop desire's call. The kiss deepened and before Justin could think to warn her, he felt her arms slide around his neck.

He stood up, bringing her with him, kissing still. It was worse. Her head tilted back and she pressed her slender figure against him, arching her back, all of which were signals he could hardly resist. He could not think to wonder at her response, nor she his. The bargain effortlessly, quickly ignited something that seemed just waiting to spring to life; a something that hardly cared that people were already gathering downstairs, cared even less that it wasn't supposed to be there under the present circumstances. Mindless and potent, that something wanted only consummation and wanted it now.

Justin finally pulled her arms from his neck and broke the kiss, startling her by his laughter. "Christina, sweetheart, don't do that to me. Believe me, I'm a man with little to no willpower when it comes to such things. And you have no idea how quickly I could get your clothes off and lower you to the bed."

"I'm . . . I'm, sorry, I—"

"No." He stopped her. "Tonight there will be no apologies, remember?"

A smile suddenly lifted to her eyes. She would not question this bargain tonight. She needed him tonight and for this one night he was hers again. That was all. She would not even allow herself to hope that it was a new beginning, however fragile.

"Shall we greet our guests?"

She nodded and, with a warm smile, he led her out. While she did not dare, he did. Hope burned bright in his heart, a hope that could not be extinguished by his many doubts.

It was only three o'clock in high afternoon when the last of the first group of guests finally arrived. This party was composed of five couples, plus two unescorted gentlemen, and of course Richard. They would enjoy dinner before the other guests arrived for the ball. Introductions went smoothly, though she knew she could never keep the various names attached to each new face. Richard stood alongside her in the receiving line and Justin too, true to his word, kept firmly by her side.

Rosarn and Aggie had both drilled her on the finer details of protocol and formalities for the past long week. Her own education on these matters had not been neglected but nothing in which either her father or Madelyne had prepared her could cover an affair as large or formal as this. Any time she stumbled, or suffered a moment's confusion, Justin was there to cover, startling her each time by his natural ease in such a formal setting. It was as though his wit and charm were suddenly set free to dazzle. And this was a man who was just as comfortable, perhaps more so, among a group of hardened, ribald sailors. She thought again of his great polarities of character and could only wonder.

By four-thirty the party was comfortably seated in the dining room. Hope outdid herself. After the initial brandy drabs and fine ports, after the traditional first two courses, came among other tasty dishes, pot roasts and ham, stuffed potatoes, creamed corn, mixed vegetables, fresh wheat rolls. The table was a lovely sight too and Christina's heightened senses took in every detail. A fine lace tablecloth covered the whole. Each matching piece of crystal, china, and silverware seemed pieces of art themselves. A warm fire and elaborate candelabra threw bright light into the darkening room. The gentlemen looked handsome in their formal black coats and lace collars and their ladies pretty in a smattering of pastel-colored gowns.

A short speech by Justin convinced everyone present that Dr. Morrison was the most gifted young surgeon the New World had ever chance to lure to her shores. Richard did not argue the point. Mr. Campbell, dean of Harvard, seemed particularly interested, and inquiries into Richard's background began.

Throughout the dinner, Christina felt in a trance. She had no idea how thoroughly charming others were finding her. Always far more interested in others, her natural tendency was to defer questions back and she did so time and again. A person would politely inquire into her background, then find themselves explaining their own. This created an alluring, through somewhat incongruent, air of mystery yet accessibility. The party became even more interested.

She heard herself responding, even initiating occasionally. She heard herself laughing too. But there remained a part of herself on a warm sand beach on a distant island, wrapped in his arms before a campfire. She kept looking to him only to discover his gaze had already been upon her.

Mr. Lowell went into great detail to explain how he got his title "King of State Street," this somehow following an inquiry into Christina's initial association with Justin. He was a determined man, and while he had a number of agendas tonight: discussing the current political situation with Mr. Phillips, sharing a good laugh over the bumbling French idiots, enjoying music and dancing with his lovely wife—now he would capture the elusive Christina Phillips.

Toward this last measure, the older gent raised his glass in toast. "A toast," he announced to the group at large. "To Christina, the newest, most welcomed, and certainly loveliest addition to our society."

Christina blushed prettily but refused to share the honor alone. "And to Dr. Morrison," she added softly, "whom I'm sure will prove a far more valuable addition to society."

Glasses were raised again but Mr. Lowell chuckled. "You deferred yet again, Christina, but this time I shall not let you escape. Besides," he looked at his wife, "Muriel has cautioned me that tonight will be my last if I don't ascertain the truth of those delicious rumors about you." The group laughed good-naturedly. "Once and for all," he said, "do tell—could the fairy-tale romance with your husband possibly be true?"

"Do tell" came from all corners of the table, echoing all at once.

Christina looked first shocked, then pale. She suddenly found the napkin on her lap fascinating. She glanced quickly at Justin. He nodded slightly; his smile told her she had naught to fear, that she trespassed safe ground. She turned back to Mr. Lowell. "Dare I ask what rumors need my verification?"

"The one that has it you met on the ship that carried Justin to prison in what," he growled, "what was yet another attempt by the English to rid our young republic of its best privateers and," he added

407

with a smile, "it was love at first sight?"

She could not look at the anxious, expectant gazes of the party at large. How had anyone come across this information? Would she never adjust to the American's brass forwardness? "Yes, that's true." She fondled her crystal goblet as she softly replied. "I met Justin on a ship sailing to Australia and, yes, he was an English prisoner."

"Yes?"

She paused nervously, then looked at Justin. "I can't answer the rest. I've been taught not to answer for my husband."

Polite chuckles followed this clever evasion and all heads turned to Justin, whose own gaze rested on Christina. There might not have been anyone else in the room. "A lesson well learned, for I can indeed answer that myself. Yes," he said, remembering the young girl, that long rope of hair and the black widow's weeds, hiding in the corner. "I fell in love the moment I saw her."

Christina felt his love as a tangible force that bridged the distance between them. No, don't let him make you hope again. It was only for the night. One night to love him again . . .

"And you, Christina? Did you fall in love at first sight?" Mr. Lowell persisted.

"My wife," Justin smiled, "needed a bit more convincing." The group laughed at this. "As for the rest of our auspicious beginnings," he looked directly at Mr. Lowell, "suffice to say," he smiled, "no gentleman would inquire further."

Hearty laughter followed this obvious end to their curiosity and Christina breathed a sigh of relief. She then rose and, following the age-old tradition, she asked the ladies to join her for tea and music in the parlor before the other guests arrived for the ball while the men enjoyed brandy, tobacco, and, of course, politics.

The rest of the evening was a blur in her mind. A blur created by a whirlwind of people and laughter, music and dancing. The ball was a huge success. It was well past midnight and closer to dawn when the last of their guests took leave, and when the servants were congratulated and dismissed, when the lights were extinguished and Christina found herself alone in her room.

She sat at the dressing table in her nightclothes, brushing out her hair. Still filled with the night's excitement, she knew she could find no rest, not after all the people, dancing, and laughter. She thought over all parts of the evening, but again and again she kept returning to those times she found herself dancing in his arms.

Holding a bottle of sherry and two glasses in his hand, Justin entered her bedroom and, just as he had twelve hours ago, he stepped behind her in the mirror unnoticed. Her hair was brushed smooth, spreading like a giant gold fan over her nightclothes. The less he noticed of the nightclothes, the better, he immediately realized. A single candle lit her reflection. She had a strange, faraway look. What thoughts caused that sweet smile on those lips?

"What are you thinking of?"

"Oh!" She turned, rising all at once. "Justin . . . you startled me!"

"I didn't mean to. I came to congratulate you." He

409

held up the bottle and glasses, then after setting them on the sitting table, he returned to stand by her. "You were a wonderful success."

"My thanks to you," she replied sincerely. "You were with me the whole evening and—"

"No. I'll take no credit for your success," he interrupted with a smile, knowing well how to stop her deferment. "I don't think you realize how quickly people take to you, how much they like you." She watched him expectantly, though with obvious uncertainty. He stood so close she could feel his warmth, a pleasant scent of brandy mixed with tobacco. His hand was suddenly brushing through her hair. "I would ask again. What were you thinking of just then?"

"I . . . I was thinking of dancing."

"Oh? With anyone in particular?"

She nodded.

"Dare I inquire who?"

"I was thinking of you," she whispered but then frightened by the intimacy, she added quickly, "You're a marvelous dancer."

"So are you." He smiled. Never had any lady fitted so naturally in his arms, or danced so with such light grace. "Especially since your only dance instruction came from Richard and Darrell."

"How did you know that?"

"Richard commented as we watched you. He tried to take credit." Justin laughed and Christina smiled. "What happened anyway? Didn't your father know the importance of dance instruction to a young lady's education?" The question was asked lightly and teasingly but he immediately saw in her eyes his

410

mistake.

"No, he didn't. He thought dance instruction—"

"—Frivolous, like your sketchbooks," he finished for her. She nodded and he expected her to next excuse her father's petty tyrannies and was surprised when she didn't.

"It's such a small thing really, but sometimes I don't think men realize that, that . . ." She groped for the right words.

"That small things can be important?"

"Yes." She nodded and with a wave of her hand to dismiss what she would next say. "I remember trying to understand, even believe that dance instruction was frivolous. In my youth and idolization I tried to believe everything he did. Yet, the dance instructor would come to town and I would watch all the other young girls run off to lessons. They would each carry these special cotton, sometimes even silk slippers in their hands—to replace their boots and oh—" she smiled thinking of it, "how I wanted a pair of slippers like that. If ever I have a daughter, I'm going to get her a dozen—" She stopped abruptly realizing her reference to a daughter and she looked at Justin for his response.

He made no response at first, though his eyes were suddenly alive with amusement and, yes, fondness. He was looking at her as before, when they had been very much in love. She felt suddenly confused again, unable to understand his apparent change in attitude, still unwilling to harbor any hope.

"No," his hand lightly caressed her cheek, "don't be frightened. I'll ignore the reference to our daughter, at least for now." He smiled. He then led her to

411

the sitting table, where he poured the sherry. "At the risk of ruining our lovely evening, I want to explain something to you," he began. "I, too, was thinking of dancing. I was thinking that after all I've known you, after all we've been through together, I have not—until this very night—shared such a simple thing as dancing with you. It made me think of a hundred other things I've not done with you. The small things that are indeed important."

He struggled for several long moments. What he was trying to say was that he wanted a new beginning. He wanted to start at the beginning he had never given to her. He wanted to court her; to take her wining and dining, dancing and to the theater. He wanted to buy her things: dresses and hats and trinkets, send her flowers and cards—the whole lot of what he had never given her. He wanted to win her love back again.

Beginnings were fragile, theirs more so than most. And he was not even sure it was possible. But if it were possible, he needed to understand what had happened.

Christina had waited through his pause, not knowing what to make of it, yet alone knowing what to make of his speech. She would not hope, not matter what—she would not hope and, despite this, her best effort, a small twinge of expectancy made her pulse flutter wildly.

"I once said that I would never trust to love again; I'm not sure of that anymore."

She held her breath.

"I also realized that I've never asked you. I always assumed I knew." He looked at her intently. "Why did you leave me, Christina?"

He might have thought she hadn't heard the question, except a montage of emotions suddenly played through her eyes, as though she was reliving the event. Then she suddenly stood and turned away from him.

"I was confused," she finally began. "Terribly confused. Part of me was always afraid of you—of the way you settle matters so forcefully and with . . . violence." She told of seeing the haunting scene with Diego, of how Cajun had warned her not to pass judgment and then much later how Richard had known of Diego and how he had explained what had happened. "I only knew what I had seen and this coming after what your men did to her and oh, so many other incidents. Justin," she whispered, "I loved you very, very much but I did not think I could live your life with you."

Justin tried to consider this, the implications and all that it meant but his mind had stopped on the past tense she used with love and so the next question came without thought. "Why didn't you tell me these things?"

She swung around with a look part incredulous and part something he rarely had a chance to see from her. A brief flash of anger, quickly concealed with lowered lashes. The message was clear, however. She had told him; in a hundred different ways, she had tried to tell him. And he had paid no heed.

"I'm sorry," and indeed he was, "but, God, Christina, if you had only told me you wanted to leave—"

"Would you have let me go?"

Again he was rebuked and in his silence rest the obvious answer.

She turned back around and said softly, "Only in

retrospect did I understand my mistake. A mistake I know you can't forgive."

He came to stand behind her, turning her around to see a question in her eyes. "We both made mistakes that need forgiving. But you're my wife now, the mother of my son and nothing can change that. We have a lifetime ahead of us and, God, Christina," he said with feeling, "if we gave our love another chance, it could be a good life. I want to start over. And I want to know if it's possible."

Words that made dreams come true. Christina managed a quick nod, one she felt through every fiber of her being. Had Justin any idea of her desperate struggle not to throw her arms around him and demonstrate just how much she loved him, he would have ended the night in the way he so often imagined. But as it was, he remembered only too well her tears from their wedding night. He would not force her love. He would wait until she came to him.

"All beginnings are fragile," he said softly. "Ours more than most. We must trespass cautiously."

She nodded quickly.

"Are you going to cry again?" He was smiling.

She lied and shook her head.

"Then I want you to end the night like you started it. Seal our beginning with a kiss, my lady."

He watched her reaction carefully. A smile of pure joy lifted through her as her arms reached up and around his neck, and with no temerity whatsoever, their beginning was sealed. Sealed with a kiss so sweet he felt his firm resolve melt. The taste of lavender and sherry, the small weight pressed against him, and a passion he suddenly knew could never die. He broke the kiss and for a long moment studied the joy so plainly apparent and wanted her happiness far more than his own; he kissed her forehead and said good night.

Three days later she received a large box filled with a dozen silk dancing slippers and a note that read: "To the dances that await us." She laughed and then cried and then laughed some more.

Chapter Thirteen

Christina looked at her son, playing with a large ball on the lawn nearby. He was the problem. She turned back to Charles Paton, who was packing his things onto his mount in preparation to leave. "But it will take at least a week of work!" she pointed out. "Probably longer!"

"If you have something against work, you should not harbor pretenses of becoming a painter. Women . . ." and he muttered something thankfully unintelligible.

Christina folded her arms across her front and if he could have seen under her skirts, he would have glimpsed her small bare foot furiously tapping the green grass. "I wouldn't mind if I just understood the point of it."

"You, my dear, do not have to understand anything. You simply have to do it." He mounted his horse with surprising agility. "Until next week," and he kicked his horse forward.

Watching him leave, she suddenly called out with a

last-minute hope, "Are you sure you won't stay for supper?"

He stopped his mount. "I have more important things to do," he called back. "Things like painting! And if you could rid your mind of its trivial pursuits, you would realize the same!"

Charles Paton did not hear her uncharacteristic and very unladylike response to this as he urged his mount on. His back was to her and distance was put between them, and she did not see his smile of intense satisfaction. Satisfaction that had never before come from teaching a student.

Justin was returning home. The sun just began lowering in the clear afternoon sky. Trees rustled softly with a light wind. Long shadows fell over the road. The cool but pleasant air carried the fertile scent of growth and everything seemed to burst into green shades of spring.

The optimism in his heart found voice in a fine loud whistle. Optimism about everything. The next six months in an illustrious career as a smuggler, or, more politely, a privateer. This excitement on top of discovering love anew.

He had taken Christina for a long week in town. They had wined and dined, socialized at dinners and danced at parties. They had shared long walks, open air carriage rides, and picnics in the park. They had talked and laughed and for the first time together, they had played, teased, laughed with their son. And while he still waited for her, no matter how difficult this was and it seemed to grow more difficult each passing day—he knew they were progressing down the path of forgiveness.

Once he dealt with those bothersome French agents and saw his ships off, there would be even more time to spend with Christina and little Justin, time with her that he both needed and wanted.

Coming up from the opposite direction, Justin met Charles Paton on the road just off his property grounds. The two men reined in their mounts, exchanged greetings, and Justin first asked how the lessons were proceeding.

"I don't mind telling you, Christina is the best student I've ever had and, God knows," he looked away, stuttered slightly, "I've had too many."

"Really!" Justin was pleased.

"She has an astonishing talent, the artist's sense of what is right, as well as a good dose of perfectionism." Feeling unusually expansive, he elaborated. "I give her an assignment that all other students will take a half day to complete, at most a day. She immediately perceives that to do it right, the task will require a week of work."

Justin smiled in response. His horse wanted more rein, rolled its head and danced and, like all good horsemen, Justin responded without thought to loosen the bit. Then removing his water cask from his saddlebag, he took a long drought and handed it to Charles.

"To tell the truth," Charles said after his own long drought, "I might even be enjoying myself if she weren't so infuriating."

"Infuriating? Christina?"

"Aye. Each of my simplest statements are met with ten of her questions. Ten! She never stops and then too, I like my students to quake in the wake of my voice. A proper dose of fear and intimidation is good for any teacher-student relationship. For some reason, the more angry and insulting I get, the bolder she becomes."

"Christina?" To say the least, Justin was intrigued by this perspective of Christina. If there were any one set of characteristics that were ill-matched between them, it was her gentleness and timidity. So gentle and in that sense fragile, he had to exercise the utmost care not to frighten and intimidate her.

How had this man made her overcome it?

Charles Paton handed the cask back. He understood Justin's incredulity but knew not how to explain. Christina would overcome anything put between herself and painting simply because she had the passion. Had Rembrandt been born in a den of thieves, it is not true—as people often thought—that he would have become a talented pickpocket. No, he would have found his way to an easel sooner or later. So it was with Christina. Not only did she overcome the fact of her sex but she was beginning to overcome the very timidity that had prevented her from recognizing her talent. Talent that did not fit into the picture she had of herself. There was no place for anything as grandiose as talent. Until now.

"It's truly a shame," Charles said to himself out loud and with a shake of his head.

"What?"

"This sad fact of her sex."

Justin chuckled. "I'll have to disagree with that."

"Hmmm," he replied with a smile of understanding. Fortunately, he had rarely suffered from the effects of love over his lifetime. While he had a number of mistresses and lovers throughout his life, he regarded them with just slightly more esteem than a good book or a bottle of rum and, in the end, women fell into the category of things that stole from his passion. "Well," he sighed, returning to the subject, "she could possibly reach great heights if she just weren't so . . . so utterly female!"

Justin laughed, and after settling the matter of smuggling paints and canvases into the country—things which would not be available with the Embargo Act—the two parted with good-byes. He turned his mount toward home and resumed his whistle. Winter had indeed melted into the bright promise of spring.

The grand manor stood at the end of the long tree-lined lane and beyond that the lake glistened in the afternoon sun. Off to the side and through the trees stretched acres of expansive lawns. Beau barked and Justin turned to catch sight of Christina and his son in the distance. It was an idyllic scene: Christina stood in front of her easel, his son played on a blanket nearby, and Beau and Beauty romped together over the lawns. He moved to become a part of it.

"Oh look who's here!" Christina called as she swept her son into her arms to see.

Justin laughed as the dogs, followed by Christina and his son, all ran up to greet him. He swung off his horse and first took Justin into his arms. He tossed him into the air and swung him round and round until he heard his son's excitement burst forth in peals of uncontrolled laughter.

Christina felt that tingling excitement all young ladies feel the first time they're courted and in love.

She could not suppress the joy in her heart. Ever since the night of the ball, the long week's holiday in town, just seeing him made her feel . . . well, giddy! As though she had enjoyed one too many glasses of champagne—drunk on her happiness.

He could see her happiness; it shined through her, and as they exchanged pleasantries, a similar rush of emotions filled him. In the first few moments with her he felt much like a schoolboy—and God knows this was new to him—and today she looked the opposite part of a schoolgirl. Her hair was parted and two long braided ropes fell well past her waist. Splashed with paints, she wore a smock over a pale yellow day dress. She looked like a peasant girl, and mid-sentence she lifted her skirts to see what he knew he'd find. Two very bare feet. He smiled.

"I couldn't resist. The day was so warm," she explained. Indeed she could not; ever since the bare-foot days on the island, she could don neither boots nor even slippers without discomfort. "And neither could your son," she laughed, tickling little Justin's bare feet.

Justin was trying to reconcile the fact that this young girl was one and the same with the temptress in silk night robes, the beautiful and alluring creature at the ball.

"I saw Mr. Paton on his way out." He smiled and let Justin down to the ground. "How did it go?"

Quite suddenly and dramatically her mood changed.

"Awful! The man's impossible, just impossible! He's insolent, insulting, mean and arrogant— though," she admitted reluctantly, "his arrogance is

421

justified and I cannot fault him that. He never likes anything I do and the worst of it, the very worst of it, is it's been two lessons now and he still has not let me put a brush to the canvas! Imagine!"

Suppressing a chuckle at the rush of her words, Justin tried to imagine any other time she had become so passionate. And besides some noted exceptions, he could find none.

"And do you know what he'd have me do?" She returned her gaze from the canvas.

"What's that?"

"He instructed me to paint on paper thirty shades of each color! That's black, white, brown, green, yellow, blue, and red! It will take me a week at least and, oh!" She looked at her son on all fours trying to catch the dogs. "It's all your fault!"

"My fault?" Justin tried to reason this through.

"Yes!" she cried out and, laughing, she ran to catch little Justin. She lifted him into her arms and the picture of her laughing, holding him in the air, the sun setting behind them to silhouette the whole, would be yet another to stay forever in his mind.

"You gave me him, didn't you? And you," she talked to the younger of the two, "are such a handful! Never a moment's peace with you, is there?" Little Justin laughed with a whole body grin and she handed him safely back to his father. "Why couldn't you give me a son that at least takes naps like other children?"

Justin chuckled and shook his head. If she was in any way dissatisfied with their first child, he would be more than willing to give her another and he was about to tell her this when suddenly she was serious.

"Did you speak with Mr. Paton?" she asked in a pretense of nonchalance.

"A bit."

"Did he comment on my progress?"

"Yes."

"Oh." She looked away. "I imagine he said he'd not even bother with me if you weren't so very generous."

Justin saw that she truly expected this and, unbelievably, she was afraid to hear his response. "Christina," he reached a hand to her face, "he said—his exact words—that you were the best student he ever had."

She looked up. Marked disbelief mixed with marked fear. He might have just told her he had it on good word that the world was going to end on the morrow. Then she turned quickly away and pretended to busy herself with gathering her things. "You're just teasing me," she whispered on a frightened pause.

Justin put his son back to the ground and moved to Christina. He was about to take a drastic measure to force her to confront the happy fact that she had talent. A lot of it. He reached for her arm, but in the same instant, Beauty drew their attention with a loud yelp of pain.

Christina took in the sight at a glance and darted forward, only to find Justin's strength suddenly wrapped around her in restraint. Wide eyes watched as Beau mounted, tried to hold Beauty still with his jaws around her neck. This, however, was not Beauty's cause of pain. "What's he doing to her?" she asked in a panic.

Justin looked at the distress in her eyes and laughed, "Even you're not that innocent. They're just mating, silly. Beauty must be in season."

Beauty cried out in acute pain and tried desperately to tear away from Beau. This was not possible. Christina tried desperately to tear away from Justin. This was not possible either. "He's hurting her! Make him stop! Oh, please!"

"Not a chance." One would likely lose a hand trying to interfere. After all dogs were just animals, answering only the call of the wild while mating. He was about to explain the simple facts of life when Beauty, mindless with fear and the pain of it, screamed in a long howl.

"Oh God! Let me go! Let me—" She squirmed, prying desperately at his arms that would not loosen. Beau was killing her! Something was terribly wrong; a simple mating would not hurt so much. "Please let me—"

"Stop it. You're not going—" The sentence nearly choked him and he froze in sudden shock. The similarity of this, the very words he uttered, to a scene best forgotten crashed into his consciousness a mere second before the déjà vu experience hit her too, hit her like a stone to her head.

The dogs were forgotten. Breathing hard, she went limp, like a lifeless doll. "Let me go," she said slowly in a voice intense with the pain of her memory.

Justin instinctively released her. With neither pause nor a word, she took flight. Leaving the dogs and little Justin. Leaving him. Running as though from a world turned suddenly into a nightmare.

Justin did not move to stop her. "All beginnings are fragile," he whispered to no one but himself, hoping against hope that a beginning had not just ended.

Christina skipped dinner. She had not seen Justin since it happened. After finally seeing her son to bed, she sat in the upstairs sitting room lost to her art work. Aggie and Rosarn sat quietly with her. Aggie knitted a loose blanket for her charge, while Rosarn busied herself darning the socks.

Christina tried to keep her mind on task but her thoughts kept spinning with unpleasant memories. She kept shoving them out of her mind's eye. Unlike Justin, she refused to even consider that the afternoon's unpleasantness could ruin their new beginning. Something so grand and wonderful could not be shattered like glass. They were bound to have setbacks, and while tonight she struggled to escape the past, tomorrow would be yet another new day. She would wake early, ask Hope to fix a special morning meal, and she would greet Justin at the table and with a smile. A smile that said all was well again. A smile that asked for another chance.

Aggie and Rosarn had mutually agreed to keep their mistress company for the night. The house had been suddenly filled with happiness ever since the success of the ball. The master and mistress were on terms now and a fine lovely pair they made. Now something was amiss. They were not only curious, hoping Christina would confide in them, but they were caring as well.

A knock sounded softly at the door and Mary, the downstairs maid, popped her head inside. "The master wants to see you." She was looking at Rosarn.

Christina set her paints down to rise.

"No, ma'am. He wants to see you, Rosarn. Right off."

425

Christina watched Rosarn look at Aggie and both women looked terribly frightened of something. "What about?" Christina asked for Rosarn.

"Didn't say, ma'am, but he called Chessy in too."

Christina couldn't comprehend Rosarn's apprehension. "Do you want me to stand by you, Rosarn?"

"No, no." Rosarn shook her head. "I didn't do anything. I know he'll understand." And with that, she left.

"Understand what?" Christina asked Aggie as the door shut.

"Oh dear. 'Tisn't my place to say. You must ask Rosarn herself." Then, almost apologetically, "Do you mind if I take leave now?"

"No," Christina sighed softly. "I think I'll retire too." She looked down at her sixteen carefully created shades of black and gray and began sealing the paint. Aggie left quickly. It took half an hour just to seal the paints and put her things away. This was only because she moved so listlessly, like an aging and frail person who moved beneath the heavy weight of an unkind life—and this despite her resolve that all would be well again.

Undressed and in her bedchambers, Christina began the arduous task of brushing out her hair while sitting at the vanity. Her door was open a crack, and from the hallway, she overheard the curious conversation between Aggie and Rosarn.

"Well?" This was Aggie's hushed voice.

"You wouldn't believe!" Rosarn cried in a whisper. "He thanked me! He said it meant a lot to him to have people like me working for him and he was so sincere too! Gave me a lift just listening to him. And

426

look! Look what he gave me."

"Oh my. A twenty-dollar gold piece!" Aggie said excitedly.

"But that's not all. He told me to send my James to him."

James, Christina knew, was Rosarn's oldest son.

"Said he'd sponsor him as an apprentice either as crew on board one of his ships or as a printer. Whichever the boy wants. And all because I refused to do that man's bidding. I told Mr. Phillips what I had said to the man was all—that he could tell folks whatever he wanted about me. Everyone knows James was born well before the nine months after my wedding anyway and heavens! 'Tis such old news by now, can't think of a soul who'd care. Then, I told Mr. Phillips the rest. I said that no amount of money could convince me to turn on the good fortune of my master."

"Ohhh! And what did Mr. Phillips say to that?"

"He wanted me to tell him how much the man offered me and I did. Mr. Phillips laughed when I told him, I don't know why, and then, then—this is the best part, he promised to add the sum on to my wages spread over the next year! Chessy got the same too! Can you believe how generous he is . . ."

The voices drifted down the stairs. With her brows drawn together, Christina tried to comprehend what she had just heard. Apparently Rosarn did something to earn Justin's gratitude. His very generous gratitude. And Chessy as well. She'd have to get the details tomorrow.

Christina slipped beneath the thick covers on her bed. She would not think of those times anymore. She

427

would not think of any of it anymore, she vowed unrealistically, and with a great upheaval of pillows and covers, she turned on her side.

Perhaps because of her vow, she found herself staring at the lantern she always left on in the event of one of her awful nightmares. She had not suffered one in ever so long, not since leaving England and coming here, but just in case . . .

Don't think of that, anything but that.

The last thing she felt before dropping off to sleep was a small twinge of fear. The fear of a lizardlike alligator with unmerciful razor-sharp jaws.

Late at night, working in his bedchambers, Justin signed his name to the letter to his father. It would leave with the first of his ships that would boldly break the embargo and sail to its fortune this week. Remembering Charles Paton and Christina, he added a postscript asking for the paints and canvases to return with the ship. Then he folded it into an envelope, poured the candle wax into his gold seal and the envelope was properly sealed.

He leaned back and poured himself a brandy watching the wax dry. In the wrong hands, the letter could see him hanged. It contained the dates and places in which his father's men would meet each ship, along with rough approximations of what cargo to expect on each ship. Tomorrow he would see the letter to Jacob, the only person in the world he could trust with it, also—not coincidentally—the captain of the first run. Once dried, he rose to bring it down stairs to his study. If only he could carry the letter to England itself.

He stopped halfway down the stairs.

The letter might not be safe in his study. Rosarn and Chessy were obviously trustworthy but who knew what other servants those French idiots might approach? He cursed softly, thinking he ought to just shoot the bothersome bastards. He certainly had just cause but even that seemed more trouble than they were worth.

Abruptly Justin decided to play it safe and carry the letter as well as the final log plans into town himself. At first light.

He slipped the letter into the pocket of his loose black robe and turned back up the stairs. He stopped outside Christina's door and paused with indecision. Unable to resist, he quietly opened the door and stepped into her room.

How many other countless times had he found himself like this? Standing over her bed to watch her sleep, using every ounce of control to stop himself from waking her, but still agonized by the ever-so-pleasant fantasy that she would wake on her own, find him there, and want him just half as much as he wanted her. How many times? A dozen? Fifty? A hundred?

He chuckled lightly. How thoroughly lust took a man's sanity!

Tonight her beauty was concealed from him. Only her head showed above the covers and she slept with her face turned into the pillow. As always before bed, she had pinned her hair into a loose pile on top of her head. She must have been sleeping restlessly, for long tendrils had already fallen and covered her face.

What he did next made him think he had drunk one too many brandies. Expecting to find her in one of the nightgowns that teased him so, or perhaps one of his silk shirts, he lifted the covers from her. What he discovered was just so much worse.

He just stared. She wore not a stitch of clothing; her beauty beckoned innocently. He felt his body's quick response. He quickly enumerated every bloody reason why he should not wake her. Not tonight, after the afternoon's misfortune, especially not tonight . . .

And still he hesitated.

Sensing a sudden loss of warmth, Christina stirred in her sleep. Stretching, she arched her back and turned over, seeking to find the warmth again. No temptress could have contrived a more seductive movement and Justin half groaned, and gently lowered the covers back. He was playing with fire. The right moment to leave had long passed.

His hand touched the door handle when he heard a muted cry and he turned back unwillingly. She began tossing and turning, lost to the throes of some dream. He started to leave again, but her arms and legs started thrashing with what he suddenly knew was the desperate effort to get the creature off. She bolted up, as a scream broke through the nightmare and into the cold night.

But this time he was there. Somehow, long before the reality of where she was could break through the terror, he was already there, knowing exactly what to do. He pulled her into his arms and lay back against the bed, holding her so tight it forced the thrashing to stop. So tight he would have sworn he was hurting her if experience hadn't taught him differently.

She fell into choked gasps of relief. Then that voice, his voice and those words whispered softly against her ear. The terror melted, dissipating with his each breath, each gentle push of his hand through her hair, each swift beat of his heart. Until finally she could speak and she said what she always said: "Don't let me go."

Justin knew his part. "Never."

Time slipped into another sphere. She had no thoughts, but gradually, ever so gradually, she became aware of him. His hand still gently combed through her hair. She was enclosed in his arms, surrounded by his warmth. The ever-so-pleasant scent of him filled her—brandy, the faint aroma of candle wax, and ink, all blending with the clean masculine scent that was just him. His long length pressed against her so and—

She opened her eyes to find him staring at her. Justin had been suffering a similar, though far more maddening, assault on his senses. Either he lowered her beneath him and took those lips or he was going to meet with the ice cold water of the lake. One or the other, and soon.

"Christina," he whispered as his hand strayed behind her ear and lower, reluctantly stopping at her shoulder. He would not force her. "I can't comfort you any longer. Not without—I . . . I have to leave."

"No. Please don't leave me."

He searched her face to see if she understood what that meant. He found plenty of emotion in the soft gray eyes, none of it fear. "Say it. I want to hear you say it."

"I love you," she whispered. "I want you to love me. Please."

She did not have to ask twice.

Justin's pleasure found no limits that night. He

could not get enough of her, he wondered if he ever could. Soft morning light filled the room as—not for the first time—they lay spent in each other's arms and still he wanted her again.

His lips brushed her forehead as his hands ran lovingly over her back. She brushed her face against his chest and closed her eyes, lost to that warm feeling of not being able to get close enough. The insatiable fuel of desire. "I love you," she said simply and again.

He smiled and moved to find her lips. He would ride her again and again until she finally begged for release and then he'd let her sleep only to wake in his arms and start their love again.

A soft rap sounded at the door.

His lips left hers but briefly. "Go away."

"Sorry, sir," Rosarn called through the closed door, her voice sounding muted and nervous both. " 'Tis your man, Jacob. Says it's urgent."

Justin rose with soft curses. He found his robe on the floor beneath the headboard where it had once been flung. He lifted it and swung it over his shoulders. He was about to tell her he would be back in minutes when, just that quickly, he saw she was asleep. He smiled, kissed her lightly, and left the room.

He met Jacob in his study and immediately perceived his friend's agitation. Jacob paced the floor, muttering to himself as he did so. He was so agitated he did not at first notice Justin. "Jacob, what is it?"

Jacob stopped and looked up. "It's the entire crew of the *Independence* in the jailhouse, that's what!"

"What?" Justin pulled the servant's bell to get some coffee.

"Aye. The bloody fools got into some tither at the Boar's Inn where they were drinking last night. I've spent all night trying to get them out, but what with all the unemployed sailors since the embargo swarming the streets, fights breakin' out every hour, the magistrate decided to make an example of them."

Justin immediately perceived the problem. The *Independence* was being loaded at the very moment in a hidden cove some twenty miles down the coast. Once loaded, the ship had to set sail; it could not sit around waiting to get caught.

"Who's the magistrate?"

"Judge Claighborne."

"We're in luck." Justin smiled, remembering the man, remembering how he had been particularly enchanted by Christina at some or another dinner last week. "I'll run into town and speak with him."

"Good, 'cause I offered to pay both damages and fines and still the old goat wouldn't budge. Well." He looked at Justin, still in a robe. "Time's a wastin'. We got to have them out by nightfall."

"Yes. Right." He shook his head and chuckled, realizing he had left his thoughts upstairs. "I'll get dressed."

"A fine idea!" Jacob nearly shouted.

The two men left in haste within the half hour. They were halfway to town when Justin reached into his saddlebag for a water cask. The movement abruptly reminded him of another pocket, then his letter.

He cursed out loud. Cursing was beginning to become a habit. It was simply not like him to forget, forget anything. He did not have to search long for his excuse; she lay sound asleep in an upstairs bedroom of his house, several miles back.

"What's wrong?" Jacob asked.

"I forgot my letter."

"What letter?"

"To my father."

Jacob knew what this meant. He stopped his mount. "Want me to go back?"

"No, it's probably safe, but when we get to town, I want you to put some men on those French agents. They're beginning to make me, ah, nervous."

"Aye, probably wise," Jacob replied as he spurred his horse on. He would handle it himself. After all, the French agents had tried to get through Mr. Lowell and two house servants already. No telling who they'd try next.

"Nothing serious," Justin decided. "Just have them watched so I know what moves they're making."

A wry smile lifted on Jacob's tanned face. "You're going to set them up, aren't you?"

"Might as well let them bury themselves and save us the trouble." He discussed his plan as they rode, and after finally settling on the details, Justin saw a gray dove suddenly lift from a tree as they passed. "Another thing," he said after slowing his mount.

"Yes?"

"It's time to forgive her. I want you to speak to Hanna."

Jacob smiled and surprised Justin with "I already have. I left Hanna's note at the house."

Justin returned the next day at dawn and the first thing he did was climb the stairs to Christina's bedroom. An empty room greeted him. She was not there, nor were her things. Her closets had been emptied and her vanity cleared.

A smile lifted through his confusion. He went to his bedchambers and, sure enough, looking small in the large bed and buried in the covers, there she slept. His son fitted happily in her arms.

The sight quickened his heart and brought another smile. He placed a thick log into the fire to bite back the morning chill and then sat on the bed and, like so many times before, he contented himself to just watch them sleep.

A sound sleeper but by no means a late sleeper, dawn awakened Christina as the soft click of his heavy black boots on the polished wood floor could not. She stirred, turned, and opened her eyes.

"Justin! You're back!" and hardly expecting her reaction, he chuckled as she fell into his arms. It was predictable. He lay back against the bed, pulling her over him. Watching his gaze rake over her, she became conscious of how she must look. She arched her back to lift partially from him as she brushed a long lock of her tousled hair back, then tried to keep the thin string of her flimsy nightgown from falling off her shoulder. "Oh I look a sight," she began apologetically, but a sudden awareness of his quick arousal brought her lips to form a perfect "Oh!"

Justin chuckled as his calloused hands toyed with the silk strings of a nightgown he'd see in hell. "You look a sight all right," he agreed, pulling a pin to have the long hair spill over his arms. His hands felt over her shoulders to the thrusts of her breasts beneath the gown. She bit her lip and held her breath, her eyes shining with excitement. The feel of her small body, still warm with sleep and somehow softer than he had imagined, made him sigh in sudden inexplicable frustration. He suddenly lay back to look at the ceiling, folding his arms behind his head. "I'm tired, Christina. Do me the favor of unbuttoning my shirt."

"Oh." Understandably, confusion spread over her face. Exhaustion never stopped him before! He was hard with desire and she was acutely conscious of this. Consciousness somehow connected to her heart, its pace was racing.

Trying to conceal her disappointment, she undid the buttons of his shirt and pulled it out from his breeches, so lost to the display of chest, muscle, and bronzed skin, she failed to notice the telling laughter in his eyes.

"My belt buckle and breeches please," he said with a convincing yawn, adding, "My breeches feel suddenly tight." She sat up on him and unfastened the thick black belt but paused with the buttons that would require intimate contact with his thriving, vital parts, parts that seemed disconnected from his intent or manner.

"Would my wife deny me such small service?" he asked innocently enough.

She shook her head and giggled.

"Good. Then on with it, girl."

The task caused him no small agony and she seemed to be taking her time about it, her laughter telling him he was creating a tease. He chuckled and reached out to lift the nightdress above her waist, immediately perceiving the convenient fact she wore nothing beneath. "This is bothering me," he said and tugged once at the nightdress, freeing her breasts.

He pulled her back over his long length while her hands braced on his shoulders. The arresting position brought excited giggles, giggles interrupted by small gasps as his hands wasted no time in exploring the objects of his fascination.

"It occurs to me I've neglected your education."

"Oh?" She gasped again as his mouth teased where his hands had just left. Those hands finally wandered to her buttocks, where he began moving her back and forth.

"I've not taught you to mount or ride yet, have I?" She could not now reply, though the rosy flush told him he was on the right path, and he chuckled as he slipped his shaft into the moist recess awaiting him.

"Ah you've handled the mounting like a trouper," he told her. "Let's see about the riding. One starts slow." His hand on her hips determined the pace. Her eyes widened and a giggle escaped from the hot passion quickly overwhelming her. "Quiet," he warned in a husky whisper, "our son would ruin this lesson."

She could not stop laughing though, even as his hot length fanned heated fires through her.

"Where was I?" he asked after fighting a pleasurable battle for some control.

"The pace!" she reminded him in an excited though hushed whisper.

"Ah yes, the pace! A good rider will gradually increase his mount's pace. Should I demonstrate?"

"Please!"

The point was made as Justin, using his impressive expertise, brought the lesson to a wondrous climax for both of them. When she finally fell on top of him, dazed and exhausted, she could only wonder at him. She had laughed many times before and many times after but never during his lovemaking. The thought made her giggle again and the sound was as happy and sweet as the warm afterglow that surrounded them.

They were laughing and teasing just as before and, oddly, it was this very thought that gave Justin a moment's pause. He was loving her again—how he was loving her!—and as vulnerable as he had ever been, perhaps more so. It was a gambler's game and the stakes were high, to have loved once and lost was enough for any lifetime. The only thing worth the risk of losing again was the thought of a life with her and this love.

With laughter still in her eyes and a pretty blush, Christina sat up and tried to piece back together some semblance of her nightgown. The sleeping garment was in hopeless disarray; her attempt was futile and Justin, watching this, suddenly chuckled. "Once never seems enough with you," he said, and reached to pull her back, but just as the third party decided to wake up too.

They spent the next half hour or so as three young children—instead of one—playing on an oversized bed. While Justin could entertain his son like no one else, but a half hour was a very long time in his son's life and the little tyke finally, rather abruptly, grew tired of his parents. Oh he loved the laughter, teasing, tickling, the wild tosses in the air, but it was time for him to get on with his own life. After all, he was hungry.

Justin leaned against the bedpost to watch Christina as she attended to his son, bathing and dressing him for the day. He wondered if it was normal to experience moments of jealousy of one's own son.

Wearing his discarded shirt, Christina held back her news to inquire about his trip. Justin related the difficulties of getting forty-three men from jail. "It couldn't have been done if Judge Claighborne hadn't been so taken by you—I had to promise him a dinner. I think the lascivious bastard just wants to look at you."

"That's not true!" She pretended affront. "We two have a lot in common. Why, he's very interested in art."

"Among other things." Watching her bend over, his shirt dropping to present him with a maddening view, he was quite certain old Judge Claighborne had far more in common with him than her.

"Guess what!" she said in sudden excitement, setting little Justin to the floor to explore the fascinating space of his father's room. "You're not going to believe it, but—" She stopped to steer little Justin from the fire poker.

Justin was trying hard to believe he was restraining himself from throwing her to the bed. He thought he could believe anything else.

"Hanna wrote me a letter."

He smiled. "I know. Jacob told me. What did she say?"

"Oh so much! I must have read the letter a dozen times, over and over. I tried to write back. I started and stopped as many times, until the wastebasket was overflowing with my attempts. I have to see her. Oh please—let me go to town?"

"I can't, sweetheart. Since the embargo, the town is just bursting with idle sailors, all looking for trouble." His gaze tried to penetrate the material of his shirt. "And you," he finished meaningfully, "look like trouble."

"Oh, but with Chessy—"

"Chessy," he chuckled, shaking his head. "I can't spare the number of men I would need to see you safe." Her disappointment was plain. "Jacob will be gone in another week. Hanna can stay with us for the two or three months he's gone. You can wait a week, can't you?"

"It seems an eternity."

"Come here," he said. "I'll help you pass it. Eternity sounds almost long enough."

She giggled and just as she was about to fall into his arms again, little Justin discovered the wonders of his father's drawer. As Christina rushed to save her son's freshly donned clothes from the ink jar in his hand, Justin found a new keen appreciation of something he spent a good part of his childhood hating—governesses. But he had to laugh when his ink not only smeared across his son's face, but was also tossed on to his mother's, or rather his, shirt and this with the unmistakable grin of malicious forethought.

The time for discipline had just arrived, only Justin was laughing too hard to do anything about it.

Christina heard his laughter only too clearly. "Darling." She smiled sweetly, picking up her son who still held tight to the half-empty ink jar. "That's wonderful fun, isn't it? Let's show your father just how much fun it is to throw ink on people."

440

Little Justin giggled with anticipation. Ink did not wash off skin easily and Justin was quick to rise. He grabbed his robe from the foot of the bed and held it up to protect himself. And he found himself looking down into two empty pockets. "Wait, Christina."

His voice warned her.

He felt into each pocket. Empty. "Did you take a letter from my robe?"

"No. Was it important?"

"Christina, I—" and he began explaining, even as his eyes searched the floor. She took the jar from Justin's hands, lifted his shirt, and set him to the floor. Justin quickly explained the importance of the letter, then told of Rosarn, Chessy, and Mr. Lowell, the French agents. Christina was all concern, suddenly remembering the maid's conversation, which she had completely forgotten about. "God," he finished. "In the wrong hands, the letter could see me hanged."

She became frantic. The search was on. Three hours later, after calling in both Rosarn and Aggie, after going over every single detail of the past day of moving, after searching every conceivable place and countless inconceivable ones, the letter was still missing.

Justin faced the unpleasant reality.

He ordered every employee and servant in his hire to gather in his study within the hour. There were to be no exceptions. Anyone who could possibly have access to his house had to be there. Someone, somehow, had stolen the letter.

After discussing the situation with Chessy and determining the interesting information that no one had left since the letter was stolen, Justin knew exactly what to do. He first sent message to Jacob. Sent it by Hope's seven-year-old-grandson, one of the only people Justin thought to trust beside Chessy and Rosarn. They would have to remain at the house for Christina.

With breakfast laid before him, Justin sat in the dining room piecing together the only probable explanation. Someone had been in the house that night, intent on gathering some information for the French agents. The person had been hiding downstairs when they saw him leave his room, carrying the letter in his hand. They must have watched as he changed his mind, then slipped the letter into his pocket and went into Christina's room. Somehow, the next day, probably during the confusion of the moving of her things, they snuck into the room, found the robe and the letter.

This seemed more likely than someone just sneaking about until they came across it. Who would look in a robe pocket for something of that nature? And none of his other things had been disturbed, as far as he could tell.

Yes . . . that must be how it happened.

Holding little Justin in her arms, nervous and frightened both, Christina watched as one by one the servants and employees filed into Justin's study. It took nearly half an hour before everyone was gathered and accounted for. Finally twenty-three people waited for Justin to address them. The spacious room looked crowded. There were hardly enough chairs to accommodate everyone, though most chose to stand anyway, feeling uncomfortable in the private domain of the man who not only paid their wages, but also the man who commanded so much respect and admiration.

Justin entered the study, and after carefully searching each face, he went right to the point. "Someone, one of you here, has stolen a letter from me. This letter could see me hanged." Murmured astonishment rose from the gathering, quieting quickly as they waited for him to continue. "Undoubtedly you— whoever has stolen this letter—have been bribed by an agent of the French government. It seems these agents will do anything to stop me from trading goods to the English. While it is true that this letter could provide ample evidence to see me hanged by the French, American, and English governments, I assure you I am perfectly capable of sparing my neck and no doubt I will. However, the letter in the hands of the French agents would jeopardize the lives of each of my men on two ships that have already set sail."

He paused and said meaningfully, "Chessy has informed me that no one has left the premises since the letter was stolen and, therefore, I can be reasonably assured one of you still has it. I want that letter. I happen to know how much the agents are offering for it. I will pay ten times the figure. And to each one of you here."

Rosarn and Chessy had shared with everyone just how much the French agents had offered. Math was suddenly easy for each person; the figure was multiplied by ten, that figure multiplied by the number of people in the room. The result was astonished exclamations from nearly everyone present.

"Hear me out," Justin quieted the crowd. "You are all dismissed for the next three days to provide the opportunity for one of you to make all of you a nice sum of money. I am going to leave immediately for my townhouse. Whoever has the letter is to get it to my townhouse within the next three days. I don't care how you do it, just that you do. Needless to say, no questions will be asked of anyone's comings or goings."

Not one person could stop from examining the faces of the others in desperate effort to discern who among them could deliver such happy fortune.

"That's all," he finished. "With the exception of Rosarn and Chessy, who will stay on with Christina and Justin, you are each dismissed."

For a moment everyone remained motionless but then, as though reaching some collective decision, everyone moved at once. Justin spotted Hope in the crowd and he smiled. "Hope, you stay on too. I know you didn't do it."

The old woman flashed her famous toothless grin. "But I wish I did," she said honestly. "I'd save you the bother and turn it over now. Then I'd collect my bonus and buy me a fine new hat."

"Don't I pay you enough for a new hat?" he asked teasingly.

"Hell yes!" she declared in a breath. "I's the best paid cook in the county but you know I save all my money to see my children and now gran'chil'ren into trade school."

"A good idea, though I still think you owe yourself a hat. I think I'll buy you one next time I'm in town."

"Don't you dare. I don't take nothin' from no one for nothin' never," she said all at once, explaining what everyone had heard many times before. "That's what slavin's all about. My gran'pappy and my pappy all wore them chains too long afore my pappy had sense enough to escape the paddy rollers and follow the North Star. I remember the tales too clearly to ever give a mind to the idea of gettin' or givin' anythin' for nothin'. No sir, you save that hat for a Michaelmas gift." She wisely explained just how he should give her the new hat.

Justin laughed and Christina, watching from his side, wondered. How could he stand there bantering with Hope when their very lives seemed on the bare thread of the good will—or greed—of someone whose identity they didn't even know. If he didn't receive that letter in three days, he would have to leave and hide out, probably for years and, oh! His men's lives were in jeopardy! And— "This is just like you!"

Justin and Hope turned their attention.

"Justin! I'm so scared! What if—"

"Don't you worry now." Hope stopped her. "The good lord takes care of his own." She knew how many of her people Justin's ships had set free and she had some idea of how much Justin gave to the abolitionist paper, the *Libertine*. "It will all work out, always does. You'll see." With that she planted a warm kiss on Christina's cheek and then left.

While Justin was not at all sure if he was in the class of the "lord's people," he was equally certain all would be well. For he would see to it. Quiet amusement met her concern. He spent the next few minutes trying to reassure her but this, it seemed, was as futile as filling a bucket with the bottom rusted out.

For she had a premonition that something awful was going to happen.

"Take me with you!" she begged as he loaded the saddlebags on his waiting horse outside.

"I can't—"

"I could have Justin ready in minutes and, oh! We could stay with Hanna and—"

He stopped her by gently pressing his finger to her lips. "I won't have you in town without me and I won't be staying there very long." Planning to tackle the problem from both ends, he would be in town just long enough to get Jacob and a few others to stop the French agents himself, whether or not the letter showed up at his townhouse. He would be bothered no more. "I'll be back before you know it. You'll see." He kissed her good-bye and mounted the waiting horse.

She watched until he disappeared down the lane, shivering despite the warm midday sun. The only way she could think to shake a suddenly monstrous anxiety was to continue searching for the letter. There was still a chance that it had just been misplaced, admittedly a small chance, but existent none the less. And she would have no rest until it was returned to Justin.

Following Jacob's orders, Steffen and Miles tracked the three men they knew were the French agents. To their utter surprise they followed the men from town out to Justin's very own house. Their orders were explicit: just watch and report back any meetings with anyone.

"Pssst," Steffen called to Miles, who was hiding the horses and himself in the shade of the forest. "Come on! I found some cover where we can watch the bastards."

"Where are they?" Miles asked, bringing the horses around.

"Lurking in the woods on the edge of the lawn, like a bunch of highway cowards. And it looks like they're settin' a spell—they watered their horses and set out some grub."

Steffen and Miles soon found themselves watching the unsuspecting party from the cover of boulders at the water's edge. They left their horses about a mile down the road, hidden in the forest out of view. Their position offered a fairly good view of the lawns and the forest's edge where the French agents hid in turn.

"What the hell are they doing?" Miles asked as Steffen finally lowered the glass.

"Beats me," Steffen replied, "but I suppose we'll find out. I only know what Jacob ordered and what those fools must know."

"What's that?"

"That Justin is not home. Geez! Camping out on his front lawn." Steffen chuckled at the idea. "Nobody could be that stupid."

"Why don't we just shoot the bastards anyway and be done with it?"

"Orders."

"Well, I feel like a bloody idiot watching bloody idiots do nothing," Miles confessed. "Whatever they're going to do, I hope they do by nightfall. I sure don't take none to the idea of spending the night on a cold boulder when I got such a fine-looking lass waitin' in a nice warm bed. Did I tell you about her . . ." And the two men talked on as they watched and waited.

* * *

Christina emptied the last drawer of her vanity. A sewing box, needles and white silk thread, thimbles, scissors, a pair of lace gloves and scarf, a gold chain, and a perfumed sashay. Nothing. The futility of looking for the letter in such places hit her and hard, sweeping her with anxiety anew.

She needed a walk, a very long walk. She turned Justin over to Rosarn's care, grabbed a pretty flowered shawl, and headed down the stairs. Chessy whittled in the parlor at the fireplace but otherwise the large house was unnaturally quiet. Hope was busy out in the kitchen, fixing supper. She told Chessy of her intentions, assured him she wanted to be alone, and then left the house.

Chessy returned to his whittling. He tried to think of some reason why Christina should not be out walking alone. He could think of none. No harm in a walk.

Why then did he have a bad feelin' tickling his brain like a feather to naked skin?

Darkness began to sweep over the landscape. The muted colors of twilight shrouded everything, concealing what she saw would soon be the bright light of a rising half moon. She breathed deeply the fresh springtime air as one by one she tried to find the muted shades of twilight in each color she would paint: the dark, almost black blue of the lake; the russet color of the low rolling hills behind it, this in contrast to the patches of forest green, now washed in a golden red; the dark silver of the boulders, the black of the smoke rising from the chimney of Hope's family cabin near the lakefront. Anything to distract her from unpleasant thoughts of an uncertain future.

She made her way across the lawns, heading toward the lake, separating and studying each shade of color the land presented. Beauty and Beau romped alongside her. She would circle the lake but, just as she thought this, she stopped.

It would mean crossing the creek, she realized, and that inevitably meant soaked boots in the uncertain light. Then, too, it was already getting late and—

The shadows of three mounted men abruptly emerged from the forest edge.

Christina froze, not with a fear of the French agents or the idea that these men meant Justin harm but with the instinctual, far more primitive fear of a woman alone and unprotected being approached by three strange men. And frozen she was, for running was not even a thought yet.

Jean Petiers had waited for this opportunity for nearly a week. He and his two men—Franz and Robert—had been holed up at the roadside and in town, watching and waiting for a clue as to how to get to Phillips's wife. Speculations had been endless, especially after watching first Phillips and then half his household travel into town. This was their opportunity, their last chance.

One man came forward, while the other two held back. Barking wildly, Beauty and Beau sensed sudden fear and came immediately to her side in defensive positions. Beauty would not warn but Beau found it necessary and he barked warning as the single rider approached. This gave her courage. The wide open space of the lawn told her to stay put. There was safety in open space.

* * *

"My God, they're meeting with Christy!" Steffen said in confusion.

"Justin's wife?"

"Aye. What 'as she got to do with them?" he asked out loud. He could make out only dark shapes but Christina's thick braids caught the moonlight. It was her, he knew it was her.

"Shouldn't we do something?" Miles wondered in turn.

Steffen didn't know. Jacob never said what to do if the agents met with Christina. Watch and report— that was all. "Jesus, though, if that bastard lays a finger on her—" He didn't finish but he quickly observed that wasn't what the meeting was about. She was waiting for the man. Besides, the bastards would have to shoot the dogs first, if it ever came down to it.

Steffen couldn't figure out what was happening. He had always liked Christina, but like the others left on the island, he witnessed firsthand what she had put Justin through. While he normally never tried to fathom the workings of a woman's mind, he had— again, like everyone else on the island—spent many hours contemplating how she could possibly have left him, for Justin was one of the best men Steffen had ever known; he could generate a long list of superlatives to describe the man for whom he was proud to work. And even more to the point, Christina had loved Justin, or so everyone thought . . .

So why had she abandoned him?

This question came back to Steffen presently and while he had trouble imagining Christy capable of treachery, like a bell ringing in his head, he suddenly had reason to suspect just that.

450

"Here." He handed the glass to Miles. "I've got to hear what they're saying."

"You would ruin Dr. Morrison's reputation?" Christina asked in disbelief. Jean Petiers could not take his eyes off the two huge monstrosities of dogs, each standing alert in a chorus of low growls. "I will do what's necessary, madame, and so will you. After all, no harm to your husband."

Lying to convince her to do the treachery, the man claimed that all he wanted were the dates and location of any of Justin's ships' destinations in order to fairly bargain for the goods. He said Justin refused to give the information himself only because he wanted to keep the number of buyers low for a smooth transaction. What Christina had trouble believing was that he thought her witless enough to swallow this tale. The apparent fact that he did, though, gave her some courage. While at first her fear had produced her stumbling temerity, now she had to pretend dull wits to convince him she believed it and would do their wretched bidding. This, in order to buy Justin time to stop them before they did in fact ruin Richard.

"I . . . I don't know what you mean? L—log books?" she asked in a voice that nearly trembled with a pretense of fear.

A lovely girl but obviously dull-witted. "They're big red leather-bound books. Surely you must have seen them? There should be a master plan too."

"I . . . I don't know! Oh please, sir, I . . . I can't do this!" She grasped her hands together as though in sudden panic.

"Now, now, madame, you must try. Think of your

451

. . . ah, friend, Dr. Morrison."

"Oh! You wouldn't really hurt Richard, would you?"

Madonna but this filly might be too dull-witted. "I have a job to do, that's all," he snapped, suddenly angry. "Ah!" He thought of another way. "Search your husband's correspondence, especially any letters destined for England."

"Letters?" she questioned meaningfully.

He nodded. "You know of the old oak in the park?"

"In town?"

"Yes." This too was a lie. They wouldn't go to this length for all they would have to do would be wait by the roadside for her to pass. "A man will be waiting there for three days. Drop the letters to the ground and if the information is good, we will refrain from harming Dr. Morrison."

"Three days? Oh dear! Oh dear! I need more time!"

"Three days," he repeated. "And for God's sake, come alone."

"Alone? I'm not allowed out alone! I can't do it! Not in three short days!"

"You have your instructions, madame. Good day," and he turned his mount around and pressed the horse into a gallop, disappearing into the forest with his men.

Steffen watched as Christina turned back to the house in a run. He had not gotten close enough to hear the whole conversation, only small bits and pieces. But enough. Enough to know that he had been blindly misled about Christina. Enough to

452

briefly consider shooting her to save Justin the agony.

Christina rushed into the house calling for Chessy and Rosarn both, Hope if she was around. Chessy dashed out of the parlor and rushed up the stairs after her. "Oh my God . . . Oh, my God . . ." He knew something terrible was going to happen! He knew it!

In her excitement and haste, Christina left the front door open and Beauty and Beau seized the rare opportunity to come inside. Seeing that the excitement was upstairs, they started up, each fighting to get there first.

Rosarn was in Christina's dressing room still trying to get the ink off her charge. Hearing Christina's call, she went into the bedroom. Christina went into the nursery. Chessy followed Christina. Calling to each other, the parties switched rooms and several confused moments passed before they all found each other in Christina's bedroom.

"The French agents! They're here! They talked to me! They don't have the letter!" she cried at the exact moment two large dogs, fueled by the high excitement in the air, burst into the room. For but the briefest moment, Christina's statement took precedence over two dogs, eight muddied feet between them and in a bedroom that had just been cleaned.

"Oh my God" was still all Chessy could manage.

"Where?" cried Rosarn who, protectively clinging to little Justin, turned at once to the window, half expecting to see the charge of a French brigade. There was nothing outside. She turned back around and screamed, "Stop them before—"

It was too late. Beauty jumped onto the bed, lowered to her haunches daring Beau to chase. Beau never backed from any challenge, and just as Christina threw herself on him, he jumped onto the bed. Falling to the ground, Christina picked herself up. She and Chessy both snapped into action. Chessy went for Beau, she for Beauty.

Rosarn watched in mute horror, finding the eight muddied paws on fresh bedclothes a far greater disaster than the French had ever created for her English ancestors. Certainly more imminent. Little Justin watched with giggles of sheer delight. He squirmed and squealed, wanting to get in on what looked like the most fun since tossing ink on his mother.

Convinced that Chessy and Christina were joining their game, Beau and Beauty resisted. Beneath the weight of nearly four hundred bouncing pounds of dog, another two hundred and fifty or so pounds of persons, was the bed. A bed not made for such excess.

The bed crashed with a great clamor.

A moment of stunned silence followed.

"Oh my God," Chessy said yet again.

Justin squealed with the wonder of it.

Rosarn felt faint, decided she best set Justin to the ground before she fell.

Christina picked herself up, looked at the two dogs, and in a voice she had never used before, "Get out!"

"The bed." Rosarn fanned her face.

"Forget the bed. The French agents," and she excitedly explained what had happened. After repeating the story twice, she finished with the point, "You must take a letter to Justin to tell him to come home."

"I ain't leaving you with no French folks runnin' about. Uh, uh." Chessy shook his head.

"Chessy! There's still plenty of people about—"

"No thar ain't. They most all left for town, whether to give back the letter or no, I can't say." Though, in truth, Chessy knew each of the other servants intimately. He couldn't imagine one who would steal it, even for a pot of gold. Folks have some principles, he knew, and often thanked the stars for it.

"Mac and Tomas are gone?" she asked.

"Sure thing and knowin' the two of 'em, they be stone-cold drunk in some gutter by this point. Only ones left is Hope, Rosarn, and him—" he pointed to Justin. "And he ain't good for nothing but trouble. Ole man MacPherson still here but I wouldn't trust the man to guard a piece of penny candy from a child."

According to popular thought old man MacPherson had slipped into his second childhood. No one could remember who had hired him and for what, but about all he was good for was sitting by the fire in his rocking chair, retelling fragmented stories of battles with the Indians. Hope had even started hand-feeding him.

Christina considered this. "There's always the Johnsons and they're only two miles up the road. And Hope's family. If I need help—"

"Catch the boy, Missy," Rosarn warned, always concerned with the immediate. "He's going to get hurt in the ruins of that bed."

Instead of picking Justin up, she motioned Chessy to help her set the headboard straight. She took one side and he the other as she continued trying to talk him into it.

He lifted the headboard with a heave. "I just—" He stopped as a slight whisk sounded, like something

455

dropping. Two pairs of eyes locked on the floor and Christina gasped. She bent down to pick up the letter. A letter that had been stuck between the headboard and the wall.

Finding the letter changed everything. Chessy was convinced of the necessity of bringing Justin a message. Christina wasted no time in writing it.

Justin,

I found the letter! It is difficult to explain the particulars, for I write this in all urgency. The letter was lost behind the headboard of my bed, where it must have fallen from the pocket of your robe. The seal is *not* broken!

The French agents have found their way to our house and have accosted me on my walk. I pretended the dull wits of a silly housewife, convincing them of my willingness to do their treachery in order to stop them from ruining Richard's reputation, which he threatened to do! We have only three days to stop them.

Please hurry home! If I do not see you or hear word from you by the morrows noon, I shall borrow the Johnsons' driver, as there is no one to escort me, and take the letter to you directly.

My love,
Christina

Chessy argued over the last passage. Christina insisted. Justin needed the letter and she was just as safe carrying it into town as she was holding it at the house—empty except for three women and a boy.

"But I know the Johnsons' driver and ol' man Raymond's 'bout as good as MacPherson."

"Oh! Men make too much fuss over such things and besides, Chessy, if Justin doesn't want me to come to town with the Johnsons' driver, he'll send someone else to escort me."

"I don't know . . ."

"Oh please! You must hurry now."

"I don't know," Chessy repeated as he placed her letter in his jacket pocket. "I just don't know."

Chapter Fourteen

Chessy saddled what he knew was the fastest horse remaining in the stables, Saber. The situation demanded urgency but, even more important, he wanted to get Mr. Phillips in charge of the events that were beginning to overwhelm him. He could always handle himself, his sweet wife, the tasks of being someone's driver. But this—letters and spying and French agents—it was all beyond him. He wanted it over and as soon as possible.

Chessy turned from the estate on to the main road shortly after midnight. Abright half-moon broke the dark of night, permitting reasonable safety at a gallop. He pressed the young, spirited, and barely green broke mare for all he dared. He wore a hand-knotted scarf and hat, leather gloves, and a thick sheep-lined coat, and despite these layers of clothing, the cold night air felt like a continuous slap to his skin. Still he raced on and the dark landscape became one long blur passing at a frightening speed.

A good four miles later, Chessy discerned the sharp

bend in the road just in time. He slowed his mount. Perhaps his aging frame could take no more of the jostle, or perhaps he needed an easy breath, a moment's warmth from the bite of the wind, yet more likely, what his wife often claimed was true—he had the gift of the sixth sense.

For suddenly he felt need for caution. Feeling this, Saber pricked her ears, Chessy did the same and as he rounded the bend, he listened to the snorts of the winded horse, the click of her trot, his own heavy breathing. Just as horse and rider rounded the bend, a lantern light flashed, then out. Like apparitions emerging from fog, two dark shapes of men appeared on the road.

Highway robbers! Highway robbers, he knew, and in that instant, he kicked spurred boots into the horse's side to make a run for it.

Winded and frightened, Saber refused any more abuse and with an angry snort the young horse reared high into the air and rid himself of her rider. Chessy fell to the ground with a thud, unhurt but suffering a deadly moment of disorientation. The men quickly fell upon him.

"It's the driver!" was said in a French accent. And Chessy suddenly knew he was in far worse trouble than with any run-in with highway robbers.

A man pulled Chessy to his feet from behind and with a grip that told him to offer no resistance. Petiers stepped in front of him and looked the captive over. "Let me guess." He almost smiled. "You—*mon ami*—are carrying a message to Mr. Phillips from his

459

loving but witless wife. Only she's not so witless, is she? Madonna," he swore with low viciousness, "I suspected it. Where is it?"

"Uh un." Chessy shook his head.

Petiers's pretense of calmness exploded and he kicked a knee hard into Chessy's groin. Chessy cried out and doubled over with shocking pain as hands reached to frisk him.

The loud cock of a pistol sounded from behind them and everyone froze as a gruff male voice said, "Stop right there," and Miles explained, "I shoot first and ask questions later."

Miles held the men at gunpoint. Abruptly released, Chessy fell to the ground, still doubled over in pain, throbbing from the center of his being throughout his body. Petiers and Robert stood perfectly still. Too still if anyone had noticed, for they waited on someone.

Steffen had left Miles for town once they saw the French agents holed up by the roadside. Neither of Justin's men had been able to fathom what the French agents had been up to, waiting by the roadside again, but Steffen had told Miles to simply watch. Which he had done for a couple of hours until he saw that the time for watching was over and the time to do something had begun.

"Where's your other man?" Miles demanded.

Gasping and spitting up, Chessy struggled to lift his eyes in time to scream, "Behind you!" A boot kicked hard into Chessy's face just as a heavy branch crashed hard on to Miles's head. Miles crumpled like so much cloth to the ground. His finger pulled the trigger. Blood filled Chessy's mouth and the last thing he remembered was a pistol fired at the bright light of a half-moon.

Petiers looked down at the two fallen bodies and motioned to Franz. Franz shook his arms like a dog shakes a wet coat, aching from the blow given with all his strength. Then he picked up Miles's pistol and knowing there was one shot left; not wanting to waste the fire in his own pistol, he aimed the weapon at the fallen man's head and shot.

Petiers ordered in his flawless French, "Find his horse. And you," he said to Robert, pointing at Chessy, "search him."

"Who do you think he is?" Franz asked in charge of Miles.

"One of Phillips's men for sure."

"Only one man?" he asked as his eyes lifted to nervously search the surrounding darkness.

"Had there been another, he would have made his presence known, don't you think, *mon ami*?" Petiers replied. Though it was indeed odd to send only one man.

Robert quickly produced Christina's letter from Chessy's pocket and handed it to Petiers, for he could not read his own native French let alone English. Petiers read it, looked up, and knew. "Madonna! We're in luck!"

"It's preferable to killing them, don't you think?" Justin asked Jacob as the two men enjoyed a huge morning meal together in the dining room of Justin's townhouse. They had been up hours before dawn to see the ship loaded and off, and both had worked up a voracious appetite.

"Aye, I suppose," Jacob agreed in a tone that contradicted his statement. He watched as Justin smothered his eggs, ham, fried potatoes, his flat cakes, and his corn bread in a thick pool of maple syrup. He had to smile. The only thing Justin loved more than maple syrup, he often thought, was Christina and his little tyke.

And God knows, Jacob thought to himself as he used what was left of the syrup, Justin was suddenly a happy man again. Even the missing letter, the idea of a servant's betrayal seemed hardly to bother him. He was whole and ever so in love again, and Jacob was happy for him.

Jacob mused over Justin's intention to drop the French agents off on some deserted island rather than turn them over to the law or kill them as they probably deserved, and knew where he got the idea from. "I cannot wait till we get a ship back to the island to see how ole John is doing." He suddenly laughed. "I just hope that wench hasn't found a way to do him in yet."

"John's about the only man I'd leave with a woman like that. I daresay he can handle her." Justin swallowed his coffee and added with a chuckle in turn, "I hope."

"Women," Jacob voiced an age-old complaint. "Sometimes I think the creator made them soft and sweet just to deceive us poor bastards."

"No doubt. Though few women are capable of her

kind of chicanery; of concealing such maliciousness in their femininity." Again Justin could not help but compare Lady Knolls to Christina, the startling contrast always meaningful to him. One represented the worst in a woman, one the best.

"And thank God for that," Jacob finished and turned the conversation back to work. They fell into a heated discussion of another of Justin's captains, one whose drinking excess caused some doubt over his ability to make the run. Justin had just pushed his plate away and was weighing the decision to have the first mate assume the position when a servant announced the arrival of whom they waited.

"See him in," Justin ordered. Steffen would know the location of the French agents. Everything else was arranged: five men waited at the very moment to take the three French agents into custody. One of Mr. Lowell's ships, the only one leaving that day under the pretense of being a passenger ship, waited in port for their arrival on board. They would be brought to a small uninhabited island near Jamaica—Jamaica being the port to which the ship sailed. Mr. Lowell had thought it a wonderful idea and had been more than willing to do the business for Justin.

Steffen walked into the dining room, wearing all the evidence of something terribly amiss. He stood awkwardly before them with his head lowered, and his great shoulders sagged and his hands nervously turned his hat. He might have come to announce the death of a loved one and indeed he would have preferred that task.

"Did you lose 'em?" Jacob assumed the worst.

"No. Miles is out there now. I know where they're holed up." Stalling, he was silent, except to decline the invitation to join them at the table.

"Well, what the hell's the problem?" Jacob asked. "You're actin' like a Puritan lad on his weddin' day."

"I don't know how to tell this is all. It's bad, real bad." He finally looked at Justin. "It has to do with your Christina."

"Is she all right?" Justin rose with the question.

"Oh aye. She's fine, just fine. But well, we's—Miles and me—we followed the bastards out to your house."

"My house?" Justin did not expect this.

"Aye and we waited and watched like ye said. 'Twas your Christina that met with them. She walked right out of the house just at night fall, when 'twas all dark, and met them on the lawn. I couldn' get close enough to hear it all but I heard enough. Enough to know 'twas not good, not good a'tall."

Justin stood now, with his fists resting on the table, searching the man with incomprehension. "You saw Christina meet with the French agents?"

Steffen nodded.

"Spell it out, Steffen."

"Like I said, I couldn' hear it all. Dr. Morrison was mentioned. I didn' get that part. Logbooks were mentioned and a letter—correspondence to England. Then they planned to meet at the oak tree in town. Couldn' hear when, though. That was it." He paused and shifted nervously, signaling the worst was over. "She went back to the house. We followed the bastards down the road a few miles where they're holed up. We couldn't figure why but they seemed bent on staying, so I left Miles watching them and I came here straight up."

Justin stared hard for a long moment before his questions began. "What did she say to the man?"

"Don't know. Couldn' hear her hardly at all, not with her soft voice."

"How was Dr. Morrison mentioned?"

"Don't know. Somethin' about him being her friend is all."

"Who mentioned the letter?"

"He did. Said to bring it to him."

Several more questions were asked. Steffen repeated the story twice. Sitting mute throughout, Jacob watched Justin finally turn to face the window. The silence was deafening; the click of his cup as he set it slowly to the saucer sounded like a bang of pots. And Jacob realized quite suddenly he had not drawn a breath.

"There is a mistake here," Justin finally said, but much too slowly. His mind was blocked by emotions. He could not think through the situation, though he struggled for long minutes to do just that. All he knew was "There is a mistake here. Christina would not do that, I know—" He turned in sudden fear to Jacob. "Come on." He rushed to the door. "I want those men."

Christina waited in the parlor. She nibbled from an apple-and-cheese tray Hope had just brought her,

465

watching as the hands of the clock signaled half past one. Rosarn was taking a very long time about it.

When the noon hour struck and there was still no word from Justin, she had sent Rosarn to the Johnson's house with a note asking if she might have use of a driver to take her into town. She explained it was an emergency, that Justin had dismissed the servants for a holiday—this was not unheard of—and that she had to get to town that day.

She could not fathom why Chessy had not told Justin to send someone back to escort her. Perhaps he forgot to mention that there was no one here to bring her into town. But hadn't she mentioned it in her letter? And then, too, Chessy had been so concerned about the issue . . .

"I'll just bet Rosarn is dallying with Jane," she complained to no one, unless one counted little Justin playing on the floor. Jane was one of the Johnsons' maids and Rosarn's dearest friend, save Aggie. "She's probably telling Jane everything and Jane will tell somebody else, who will tell somebody else and so on until finally it gets back to Mrs. Johnson and by then the story will be all twisted and silly and outrageous and oh!" she said as she got up yet eager to look out the window. "Hurry! Hurry! Hurry!"

The Johnsons' carriage finally turned down the lane. Christina swung on her cloak, lifted Justin to her arms, and picked up her bag, a bag filled with a change of clothes for little Justin, an evening gown for herself, a brush, toilet water, a small present for Hanna, and the letter, and headed out the door.

466

Raymond, the driver, was a pleasant older fellow. As he swung down from the driver's seat, he told her the Johnsons were glad to lend his services, and then lied as his mistress told him to do. "No problem." He grinned magnanimously. "I was just headin' into town anyway."

"How lucky for me!" Christina smiled in turn, knowing this for what it was, a neighbor's white lie. She liked the Johnsons and thought to send one of Hope's apple pies over with a sweet note as soon as she got back. Hope loved to share her cooking, especially her apple pie, while she hoped to counterbalance the gossip with her good deed.

As Raymond helped her inside, he told her Rosarn planned to pass the afternoon, and probably the evening too, with her friend Jane. "Is that all right?"

"There's no one left here anyway and we should be gone for days."

The old man smiled, told her to knock on the side should she want to stop, and then shut the door. He climbed up onto the seat and slashed the whip on the horse's back. The carriage bolted forward and they were off.

Justin motioned silently for the other five men to turn back around and cover the three French agents from the other side then he, Jacob, and Steffen dismounted. "There they be," Steffen whispered as he looked around the thick forest for Miles, "but I don't see Miles anywhere and I left him right here— Look, there's our tracks." He pointed to the broken twigs at their feet, the imprint of horses' hooves.

"He probably left for town too," Jacob whispered into the silence of the forest. They waited for the men to circle the three French agents. Jacob would signal with his famous crow call when they should move. "It looks like they're waiting for something, all mounted, staring up the road like that, don't it?"

Justin said nothing. He was thinking ahead to the questions he would ask and the answers he would hear. He refused to confront his fear of those answers. He held the reins of his mount tight. Bursts of moist fog came from the horse's nostrils, this despite the mid-afternoon sun in the cloudless sky. A broken promise of spring, the day still held a winter's chill, and wearing a suede and sheepskin vest over a heavy cotton shirt and for one of the first times in his life, Justin was acutely conscious of the cold.

The sound of a carriage approaching was heard by all. "Ah," Petiers laughed, his voice carrying eerily through the silence of the forest, "here she comes now. A little late but . . ."

Here she comes—echoed in Justin's mind over and over. He choked back a loud "No," starting forward to stop what would happen, but Jacob caught his arm in a fierce grip and their eyes locked. "You've got to see it, Justin. You've got to know for sure."

Justin stared into Jacob's fine blue eyes, seeing only Jacob's pain, a pain he knew was for him. He wanted to yell it wasn't true, there was a mistake—somehow, someone would explain what was happening. Instead he fixed his eyes ahead.

Christina was lost to a game of teaching her son his numbers, thinking he could learn one and two as easily as mother and father. Little Justin thought the point of this game was to catch her fingers, which was boring, far too easy to be fun, and he decided instead to reach for the ropes of hair wrapped around his mother's head. He lunged for the target and fell hard against her just as the carriage came to a halt. Voices sounded from outside and he felt his mother tense.

Raymond eyed the three nicely dressed gents who stopped him on the road, at first unalarmed. He was smiling.

"We'd like to speak to your lady." One fellow smiled back pleasantly, and before Raymond could respond, two of the men went to one side while the first man brought his mount to the other. Raymond suffered a moment's uncertainty, and just to be safe, he stood up and lifted the seat to get his hands on the pistol he kept there.

Closed against the chilly air, the shutters were suddenly lifted from the outside and Christina gasped as she looked at the two unfamiliar faces on the one side and the one familiar face on the other. She pulled Justin tight against herself.

"The letter, madame" was all he said.

"What letter? What do you want? I—"

"Do not," he warned, "make me draw a pistol. Your driver has just reached for his and he will go first." He looked at little Justin, who was staring back in confusion, not liking this man's goatee, his sudden appearance, or his mother's fear of him. The little boy reached out to sock his face and Petiers, smiling, caught the small hand in his. "Your boy will be the second."

Christina stared in a moment's horror.

"Your son, madame."

She reached slowly into her bag.

No one could hear what was being said but all knew it was Christina in the carriage. Justin had caught a brief glimpse of that red-gold hair just before the man pulled his mount to the side and blocked the view. He desperately struggled to explain why Christina was using the Johnson carriage and driver rather than theirs and Chessy. There seemed only one explanation, an explanation he could not face.

She could not ask Chessy to participate in this treachery.

He could not face it until the very moment the small hand reached through the window, holding the letter out to the man. Reality crashed into his mind like a blinding white light of pain. She might have just shot him point-blank in the head, not once but a thousand times.

Jacob signaled loud and clear and, with a surprising charge, seven men with drawn pistols quickly surrounded the carriage and the three mounted agents. There was a smattering of horses' hooves, shots and cries, as the three men fought for some balance to aim their own quickly drawn pistols. A shot fired, then another and another and two men fell dead. Christina screamed and fell to the floor, covering Justin with her body. Shocked, Raymond stood like a marble monument to Lot's wife, frozen, not knowing who to shoot until he saw Justin, the last to emerge from the forest.

Petiers fell from his mount onto the lifeless body of Robert, feet away from his other man. "You killed them! You—oh, my God!" He burst into tears of rage. "My men—"

Seven pistols aimed at one man.

Overwhelmed by the sight of the two dead bodies of his men and his own crashing defeat, Petiers slowly stood up. Crazed with madness, he did not hear Jacob's demand to drop his weapon. The demand was repeated but all he saw was Justin Phillips and to this target he raised his pistol and aimed with trembling hands.

Seven shots fired in close succession and Petiers too fell dead on the road.

Christina's body jerked with the thunderous explosion. Little Justin could not grasp the point of this game. The floor of the carriage was hard, his mother's body stifling, the noise hurt, and the smell of smoke, mixed with his first scent of blood and death, all brought an unearthly wail. He wanted up! Christina could not move, would not move, not for her life, not even after the silence told her it was over. There was no thought except that her child was in danger.

"Drag the bodies to the gravedigger. The paupers' lot for them." Jacob snapped orders to the men. After staring blankly at the torn and bleeding mess that had been Petiers, Raymond found himself quite sick, and Jacob waited until the bodies were removed to ask,

"Did you have anything to do with this?"

"No sir! No sir!" Raymond was a rush of words. "My mistress just tells me to drive the lady to town and I do that. I pick her up and head down the road and then, then these three men stop me and say they want to speak to the lady. Well, I didn't know and so I drew my own pistol and—"

"All right." Jacob stopped him. He looked at the carriage, then at Justin.

A small voice came from inside.

"Jacob? Jacob! Is that you? Is it over?"

The soft voice affected Justin like a whip cracking in the air. His gaze shot to Jacob for help. No help could be given, not in heaven or on earth and Justin suddenly kicked spurs hard into his mount's side. The fine stallion leaped into the air, horse and rider swallowed by the forest.

Jacob turned back to Raymond. "Take her back to the house. You two." He pointed to the two men. "See that she gets there and stays there."

Christina could not comprehend why, if the danger was over, no one was coming to her. After hearing Jacob speak to Raymond and sensing the danger over, she had lifted Justin to her arms to quiet him. Cautiously, she raised her head through the open shutter. For a brief moment she met Jacob's eyes and that one look frightened her to the depth of her soul.

"Move it!" Jacob suddenly shouted at Raymond, and almost instantly the carriage jerked into motion. The old man brought the carriage around and then pressed the horses to a fast pace. Christina looked back to see Jacob sitting on his mount, staring after her with the same frightening look.

"Jacob! Jacob? What happened?"

Jacob couldn't hear her but would not have answered even if he had. When the carriage and its escort were out of sight, he retrieved the letter from the road, mounted again, and turned his horse to the direction Justin took. A direction that led, he knew, to a certain hell.

Christina paced in front of the mantel in her own bedchambers. Little Justin was asleep in the nursery. The servants had been called back. Yet no one had come to her to explain. No one had explained why her door was locked.

And where, oh where was Justin?

After creating a hundred and one unlikely explanations for the locked door, she plopped into a chair and forced herself to face the unimaginable. She went through the events piece by piece. Jacob and his men rescued her at the exact moment she handed the letter to that man. How did they know where to find the agents? The answer came immediately. Justin had men following them; there was no other explanation. For how long? Had they seen the French agents accost her on the walk?

No, she realized. Surely Justin's men would have come forth to save her. Wouldn't they? But if they hadn't? Her thoughts traveled over the conversation from the point of view of someone watching from a distance. Her heart started pounding and she jumped up as she began to grasp what had happened.

Chessy brought her note to Justin. But his men, Jacob included, knew nothing of it. They had witnessed the interaction between herself and the agents, one in which she pretended willingness to betray her husband. And the—

"Oh no, they couldn't have thought—" she said out loud and stopped, suddenly seeing how it might have looked when she handed the letter to that man, especially if one had not heard his threat to fire a pistol at her son.

Jacob . . . that explained everything! He thought her in compliance with the agents. Oh! How could he?

Just as she felt a burst of furious indignation, she remembered. The letter, madame. The letter, madame. The letter, madame. The French agent knew of the letter she carried and he knew because he had gotten her note from Chessy. Justin never received her note and, oh God, was Chessy killed?

He must be dead! Poor sweet Chessy! If he were still alive he would have told everyone of the mistake! The awful mistake! Someone must be sent to look for Chessy!

She rushed to the door and began pounding, calling for help.

Downstairs, lying on a sofa in darkness, Justin listened to her cries. For a while the noise drowned out his thoughts and for this he was glad. He poured the last of the brandy bottle into his glass and drained it whole.

After trying to stifle the violence of his emotions, a violence he had tried to quench by running seven miles to dive into a lake of near freezing temperature, swim for nearly an hour until the numbness in his limbs threatened to drown him, and all this finished with two bottles of potent brandy, he lay in the darkened study remembering. Remembering every detail of each of a thousand memories he had of her. He was trying to see them from a different perspective, her perspective, a perspective born of the intent to deceive.

He could not do this. He tried over and over but the memories spun clear in his mind. That shy smile, the sweet music of her laughter, the welcome of her small body to his touch. Christina laughing with his son. These could not have been a facade. Sometime, somewhere in the midst of their time together, she had loved him.

The pounding stopped abruptly upstairs.

The trouble was he had seen that smile and heard her laughter, he had even owned her passion in the last two weeks. This, when she was planning to do something that could have seen him hanged. Rationally this made no sense. How could she have done this? To do it, she could not just be malevolent and cruel, but sick of mind. Sick in a way other people named evil.

Christina and evil . . .

"No" came in a rush of emotion that brought him to his feet, throwing his emptied glass into the fireplace. The violence brought a tumble of confused thoughts. She had done this—he had seen it with his own eyes—yet she couldn't have. She couldn't have!

Richard was mentioned. Did they threaten her with exposing Richard? Would she trade Richard's reputation for his very life?

He set up suddenly and shook his head, trying to calm down just long enough to ask the one question he had to know. Nothing made sense but the violence of his emotions, a violence that was the only life force left in him and, while he knew the danger, he had to find out. He had to know! With the bottle still in hand, he left the study and climbed the stairs.

Jacob heard this and rushed out from the parlor. "No, Justin!" He called from the bottom of the stairs. "Don't go up there! Her trunks are packed and ready! I can see her on the ship—"

Justin stopped but never turned around. "I have to know" was all he said and this in a voice so calm Jacob had reason to fear for Christina's life.

"Oh lord . . ."

Near crazed with anxiety, Christina jumped up at the sound of the door being unlocked. Justin opened the door and slipped inside. Suffering a rare moment's disorientation, he leaned against the door.

"Oh, Justin!" She started for him.

"No!" He held up his hand to stop her. She took in his disheveled appearance, the nearly empty bottle of brandy, the madness in his eyes. "Don't come near me," he said simply. "Whatever you do or say, just don't come near me."

476

She froze with an incredulous moment of disbelief. He thought what Jacob thought. He thought her guilty of that horrendous crime and, "Oh Justin, you don't really believe it? You can't—"

"Oh no, Christina. No more innocence, please. No more deception or lying. No pretending that what I saw didn't happen. I just want the truth. Just tell me why. Why did you do this?"

"But I didn't do it! I can—"

He flung the bottle against the wall. "Damn you girl! Don't lie to me!" Steffen saw you meeting with them—right here on the front lawns after dark. He saw you! Just like I saw you! Saw you hand them a letter that would hang me!"

"No," she cried. "I didn't—I mean I did meet with them . . . No—they met with me . . . while I was walking. They were waiting in the forest—"

"Yes, they were waiting, waiting because my wife told them that I wasn't there!"

"No, that's not true!"

"Oh? I suppose you'll deny that you planned to meet with them—to bring the letter?"

"Yes! I mean no—I didn't even find the letter then—"

"Then why did Steffen hear it mentioned?"

"He mentioned it! That man! Oh Justin, don't you see? I was just pretending!"

"Pretending? Were you pretending when I saw you hand him the letter?"

"He threatened me! He said he'd shoot—"

"There were no pistols, Christina."

477

"But he did!" She was crying now, trembling, not knowing what to do or say to make him believe her. "I was bringing the letter to you—"

"To me?"

"Yes, I—"

"Stop it!" he shouted, coming on her in an explosion of movement. He took her by the arms, stopping just short of shaking her senseless. "I've had enough of your lies! I know you did it! I know how you did it! But I don't know why? Why?"

Fear engulfed and choked her with a silent "no" that shook her head.

"Ah, my little whore," he said in a sudden and frightening change of voice. "That's what you are, you know. Only yesterday you lay in my bed and this while planning my hanging. Your performance was very convincing too. Very convincing, sweetheart. As a matter of fact, the only thing lacking in your performance, the only thing all truly good whores have over you and the one thing I will have from you is honesty! Answer my question! Why?"

"But . . . but . . . I d—didn't do it—"

"Damn you!" and his raised arm came hard across her face. The blow threw her to the floor and she went out quickly, easily, surrounded by a sudden safety of a black void.

Justin stared at her lifeless form until his rage and pain blinded him with his own tears. The shock of what he had never imagined doing to any woman, least of all Christina, could not break through the question that remained unanswered.

Why? Why did you do this?

Richard sat by the fireplace in blissful contentment, reading the medical journals found in Harvard's impressive library. The house was quiet, save for the crackle of the fire, the clink of his spoon as he stirred his tea. The last of his patients left hours ago, his maid recently, and he used the rare midnight hour of quiet to study.

Thanks to Justin, Richard's practice was booming. He was already reputed to be the best surgeon in town; one patient led to five others until his appointment book was full to bursting. A two-week wait if it was not an emergency. He would have to hire an assistant soon. There was a meeting scheduled at the end of the week with the dean of Harvard. The New World far surpassed anything he had dared to hope for.

Hearing a carriage pull up in front of his house along with the clamor of horses' hooves, he looked to the window. An emergency, he knew. He set down his tea and rose to meet them at the door.

Justin swung open the door without knocking just as Richard ran into the hall.

"Oh my God!" he said, seeing who rested unconscious in his arms. "What happened?"

"I hit her."

"You—" Richard stumbled over the word but, trained to act in emergencies, he snapped into action. "Bring her in here." He pointed to his examining room while he moved to light the room.

A half hour later he finished examining her and saw her up to his own bed. Her vital signs were good, and he had seen worse head bumps that did no harm. She'd either wake soon or slip from unconsciousness into sleep. Justin was lucky; his blow could probably kill a lesser man, yet alone a woman.

How in heaven or rather in hell's name could he have done such a thing?

Justin leaned against the fireplace, staring into the flames. He did not look up when Richard finally joined him in the study. "Is she all right?"

"I think so," he replied solemnly. "What happened, Justin?"

"I hit her," he repeated.

"You're drunk," Richard suddenly noticed.

"Yes. Quite."

"God, Justin, did you just get so drunk that you—" He could not say it.

"Yes and no. It's not so simple." Justin started through the events in an effort to explain. Richard kept interrupting with questions and Justin answered, hoping somehow Richard could explain it, but soon seeing he could not.

Richard had only one response to the fantastic tale that finally ended. "Christina did not do that."

"I saw her. I saw her put the pistol to my head and pull the trigger."

"Think on it!" Richard demanded, coming to him. "Christina? Christina could not hurt her own worst enemy yet alone the man she loves more than life itself. And you," he suddenly accused, "you have

480

condemned her before hearing her explanation!"

"She would deny what I saw! She can give no explanation because there is none, save that she has hated me," he suddenly realized, "probably from the start."

A violence still radiated from Justin and Richard knew better than to defend Christina; he had no weapons in which to defend her anyway. He would have to wait until she woke and explained.

"My men will be waiting outside," Justin said in a voice that registered sudden exhaustion. "When she wakes and when you feel she is well enough, they will see her on board a ship that is sailing to Jamaica. She and Justin will stay with my relations there. Little Justin is already on board."

His son! He would lose his son in this as well. Lose him because he had not the strength to hurt her as much as she him. The silence filled his pain and then he resumed in a distant whisper, "Tell her though that it will not be forever. Tell her that someday and soon, I will find the strength to take him from her. Someday," he whispered passionately, "I will be able to hate her that much."

He looked up as though waking from a dream. Richard stared with unspeakable sympathy, wanting desperately to say something, anything to ease it, anything to stop him from sending her away. Justin was too torn to notice, yet alone respond to Richard's sympathy.

Until Richard found what he'd say. "When Christina lived with me she used to have a recurring dream."

Justin first thought he was going to describe the nightmare with which he was only too familiar.

"A dream where she spoke to you. Over and over again she'd cry in her sleep, 'Don't let me go, please don't let me go.'"

The whispered promise they made as lovers . . . Justin felt a dagger pierce his heart.

"Don't do it, Justin," Richard deplored. "Don't send her away before she explains."

"If only she could explain," he said after a pause, and then he would hear no more. He moved to leave. As he opened the door he realized he would probably never see Christina again. He suffered a fleeting moment in which he fought not to turn back. His hand shook as he shut the door and thereby broke the promise made to the only woman he would ever love.

Chessy woke in the middle of a cold night, having no idea what night it was. He immediately perceived a number of arresting facts. His head felt like it was split open with an ax and his jaw was broken. His pants were soiled and he smelled worse than a dead skunk. He was chilled to the bone; he might have been sitting in the fires of hell.

He spit out two teeth, the raunchy taste of old blood. Damn, but he'd be a grinnin' like old Hope afore his time! And that weren't the worst of it, no sir.

No the worst of it was he was sittin' on a bed of prickly needles with his arms and legs embracin' the trunk of a pine tree like a dog humps a bitch in heat.

'Cept that he had none of the pleasure and all of the pain. Ropes bound his wrists and ankles and this made him wolf bait.

He tensed and looked around the eerie darkness of the forest, the idea of being wolf bait choked the cry in his throat and left him in an unnerving silence. Thoughts spun quickly. He thought of Christina heading into town with the letter. And when he thought of the trap those Frenchmen would surely set for her, of her lying on the road dead or bleeding, or wishing she were dead, he started screaming. One loud, long scream that lasted for hours. Wolves or not, his vision screamed for help.

Rosarn was finally returning from having spent the night at Jane's. Waiting on the front steps for the first sight of her and bursting with the news, Aggie ran out to meet her. "Rosy! Rosy! You won't believe what happened to the missus! I swear—"

"Oh I know all about it," Rosarn informed her with a dismissing wave of her hand. "I was there, you know—why, I even saw the missus off! Then I spent the night with Jane. You should have seen us," she laughed, "sitting up in bed, clacking away like two old hens in the coop. All the way to dawn. Oh!" She clapped her hands in excitement. "Wait till I tell ye the latest—" She looked at Aggie's stricken face. "Well, what's wrong, Aggie? Ye look like ye just passed judgment day."

"You know about it? About the missus findin' the letter?"

483

"Aye! I said I was there with Chessy when she found it. I went to fetch Raymond to drive her into town to see it to the master. Don't tell me!" She suddenly realized why Aggie was so excited. "We still get the bonus! Mr. Phillips will see us get the bonus even though 'twas his missus that found it!"

"No, no!" Aggie was shaking her head. "The missus betrayed him! She was the one! She turned the letter over to the Frenchman herself! He saw it! He caught her red-handed! Can ye believe it?" Aggie still could not. "Our own sweet missus doin' such a wicked thing? And he went up there last night and, and he struck her! Knocked her out cold and then he took her to town! But, and this is it—he took her trunks! I was told to pack 'em myself."

"What?" was all Rosarn could say.

"I says . . ."

It took Rosarn a good half hour to understand that something was horribly wrong. Something that no one knew yet. Something that had to do with . . . "Chessy? Where's Chessy?" she asked in a sudden panic after Aggie and the other servants went over the incredible story yet again.

Everyone gathered in Hope's kitchen looked around.

"Chessy ain't back yet," someone realized. "His wife's out back in the garden—"

"Oh dear!" Rosarn cried, and in a rush she tried to explain.

Christina woke at dawn's light and opened her eyes

to Richard sitting by the bedside watching her sleep. Why was Richard watching her sleep . . .? "Richard?" she said in a question.

"Don't move, darling," he said in a voice all concern. "You've got a nasty bump on your head."

A bump? . . . She felt her head, and as she did so, her memory returned with a quick panic. She was afraid to move, to even look, until she knew. "Where . . . is he?"

"He left you with me."

She cautiously glanced around the room to ascertain the truth of this and, once done, ignoring all medical advice, she fell into Richard's arms. "Oh, Richard," she cried. "I didn't do it . . . I didn't do it!"

"I know . . . I know," he had to repeat a dozen times, for at first all she managed through her tears was this short denial of any guilt. Finally, with some effort, the story tumbled out, and after questions and answers and a hundred too many tears, the urgent point was grasped.

"He never received my message and they knew I was coming with the letter, so . . . Chessy! Oh, I'm afraid they . . . Oh please, someone must be sent to look for him!"

"Yes . . . yes, I see. I'll send for Justin immediately."

"No." This was whispered but firmly, as she wiped her tears.

"Christina, you have to explain to him what happened! My God, the man thinks . . . Why, right now

485

two of his men waiting outside to escort you like a common prisoner to a ship that's bound for Jamaica. He's sending you away to live with relations there."

"He would send me . . . away?" The full import of this slowly sunk into her consciousness. "Little Justin?" she cried abruptly. "Oh no, Richard, he would try to separate me—"

"No, no. Little Justin is waiting on board." Pacing the floor now, Richard would not venture more of what Justin had said about his son in the heat of his anger.

Christina stared off into space. Never! He had always promised never to let her go—and now he would break that vow, a vow more sacred than the words uttered before a minister. Love was trust and yet he did not trust her. He would send her away and she would go—that was all. She would leave him again.

"You should see him, darling. His pain, rage, and God, but he is mad with it!"

She was silent.

"You must explain how it happened—"

"No," she replied softly again.

He looked at her with incomprehension, then suddenly thought he understood. "Oh darling," he came to her, "are you afraid? Are you—after—" Damn but he would choke on the words each time.

"Yes . . . and no. I don't know. I only know that I tried to explain what he should have already known once and—" As though transfixed, her hand reached slowly to her face where he had struck her. "And I'll not do it again," she whispered in a firm resolve. "If

486

he wants to send me away, then I'll go."

"But he's going to find out sooner or later; he's going to know and then you'll be in Jamaica." He took her hands and pleaded for Justin. "He's suffering enough. Don't punish him more."

She wondered if punishment was her motivation; she couldn't dismiss the possibility completely. The only thing she knew for certain was that something horrible had happened to them. "I need time, Richard. I need to make sense of everything that has happened to us. Everything. I want to go away. I have to know if I still . . . if—" and like a physical force, the unfinished thought pushed her back into Richard's arms and she started crying again.

In his townhouse and lying on the couch, Justin was suffering the effects of two sleepless nights, enough liquor to stop an army, the rage and pain of losing two people he loved so desperately. The shades were drawn against the late morning sunshine. He held another full bottle of brandy in his hand, and no longer bothering with a glass, he systematically raised the bottle to his lips, drank, and set it down again. He thought if he drank long and hard enough, at some point he would be able to stop thinking.

He might have been successful, too, had his madness not drawn a series of starling conclusions stemming from his exact words to Richard. So startling, the conclusion brought him to his feet pacing in front of the mantel. So startling, it broke through the stupor of no less than three bottles of brandy.

Yes . . .

She had hated him from the start. Hatred from the moment she first saw him, so different from the imagination of a young girl's heart. Hatred from the day he abducted her, the day following when he stole her innocence. Only she had been so terribly afraid of him, so desperate to survive the ordeal, she concealed her hatred in love. A pretense of love as a desperate means of surviving. A pretense of love to appease a man she saw as, as—as what? A beast? A pirate? A killer of men and raper of women? Yes, a man despicably terrifying to her and this gross fear created the deception of love.

She escaped at her first opportunity only to soon find herself trapped again. Captured again. Again she escaped the only way she knew, by pretending love. There had been many clues throughout their time together; evidence of how she truly felt about him. The time she traded her wedding ring for a coin to buy a sketchbook, thinking him cruel and petty enough to deny her. The tears before and after their wedding night. And then, finally, the French agents presented her with an opportunity to free herself from him forever.

God it made sense!

He had never had her love! Never! He had owned her as a man owns a slave, possessing her will and even her passion, but never her heart. She had kept that far from his touch; he had not even been close.

The thought of how desperate she must have been in the last two years overwhelmed him. He felt suddenly quite mad. Mad as someone feels upon discovering their reality is not shared by others. Mad as though he just realized that when he saw the light of day, others saw the dark of night. He fell into a frenzied craze; his hands shook and his heart pounded and just as he might have thoroughly lost control, a single sane thought crashed into his consciousness and demanded attention.

"Don't ever let me go."

Abruptly his thoughts spun. Could she have whispered that while hating him? While wanting only the opposite could she have laughed and teased, wanting him with such fierce passion while truly hating him, trembling in fear? Could a pretense of love be so convincing?

"No!"

And with this single declaration, the world came back to him with vivid clarity. He knew. He suddenly knew there had been a terrible mistake. He knew this without a single doubt and this, seconds before Jacob burst into the room with a letter in his hand.

"Jacob, there is a mistake here—"

"Yes," and knowing no other way to tell him, Jacob handed him the note to read. Not allowing anyone to disturb Justin, Jacob had taken and read the note sent by Richard. The note insisted only that men be sent out to look for Chessy. He had not understood this but had nonetheless done so. There were still many unanswered questions.

And now another note.

Justin read the letter written in Christina's own

489

hand and could not at first speak.

"The gravedigger sent it over. It was found on Petiers's body. I already sent some men out to look for Chessy."

Justin raced to the door.

"It's too late." Jacob tried to stop him. "The men just returned. The ship set sail. She's gone."

"No . . ." was said as a desperate plea, and because he could not believe this, did not want to believe this, he started running. He ran out of his house and onto the busy street. He kept running and running and running until two miles later, he reached the dock and stopped.

Like a time before, he watched a ship slowly sailing to a distant horizon, taking Christina from him. The closed port bustled about him. Idle sailors clustered in small groups, sitting, standing, watching, waiting for something, anything to do. Crates of cargo stacked neatly in front of too many docked ships. A number of women, preening like cats, peddled their wares to the militamen on guard—the only men with money since the embargo. And everyone there pretended not to notice the handsome young man, so obviously drunk and wasted, perhaps even ruined, standing on the dock calling over and over again the name Christina.

The hot Jamaican sun seemed to stop at the meridian. Rows of tall palm trees completely isolated a mile stretch of white sand beach. At the distant horizon the boundless azure sky melted into the clear blue waters of the ocean. This surrounding tropical

490

beauty, the warm breeze and sand, the restlessness of the ocean water, all transported Christina to another island, another time and place.

She finally found her peace.

Kneeling at the water's edge, she teased and laughed with her son as she taught him the age-old skill of building sand castles.

Justin finally found her there.

Standing at the edge of the trees, he watched silently. He could not for his life move to them. He had set sail immediately and the short trip proved the longest in his life. The entire time he had not a single thought but of Christina. He phrased and rephrased the words he would say to explain a hundred times. He imagined a hundred responses of hers, not one of them pleasant.

The ship had hardly been secured at dock before he had jumped off and started running the three miles to his father's brothers' plantation, running because he could not wait long enough for a mount to be brought. Nor could he bear the social pleasantries required upon seeing his uncle for the first time in two years. He could barely get the words out. "Christina? Where is she?"

Somehow his uncle understood. "She went out for a picnic at the beach."

"What beach?"

"Why Justin, your beach. She's been going there every day since she arrived."

His beach . . . The beach where he spent the lonely hours of his childhood. Playing in the water and lying

491

in the sun, building sand castles. Wondering. Wondering why no one wanted him at the manor and why he didn't belong at the servants' quarters. Wondering, as he watched the great ships coming from distant places and going to still other distant places. Wondering if he had his own ship, if he could steer her destiny, if it then could take him to a place where he belonged. Take him to someone who wanted him.

Christina was on his beach.

And so, he had run to the beach and now stood watching her. He could not approach. After waiting for this one moment for an eternity, thinking of nothing else for as long, he could not move forward.

She was beautiful. The long gold hair fell unbound from beneath a wide straw sun hat. She wore a plain white summer day dress, the skirts of which were lifted and wrapped around her bare legs like boy's breeches. Stark naked, his son sat across from her with the sand castle between them. The sound of their laughter lifted over the ever present lure of the ocean, dreamlike and enchanting and distant.

He might never have moved forward but Christina suddenly sensed someone watching them. Tipping back her hat she looked to the trees. Their eyes met and for a moment he felt the world stand still. Her expression was unreadable, and before he had dared a breath, she turned away and back to little Justin.

"Look who's here, darling!"

Little Justin looked to where his mother pointed. "Fatter!" He cried out one of the only two decipherable words he had. He stumbled on to his legs and started running. Running as best as those little legs could carry him, stumbling every two steps, picking himself up and running again.

And Justin was running roo.

He swept his son high into the air and little Justin laughed and grinned and laughed again. Then he held his son and closed his eyes, holding as though he'd never let him go.

Christina returned to the blanket spread beneath the cool shade of the trees, content to watch the happy reunion from a distance. And a happy reunion it was. Stripped of shirt and boots, Justin chased his boy up the beach and down, wrestled and tickled him in the sand, tossed him in the air and swung him around a hundred times. After nearly an hour of such play and knowing just what would wear the little fellow out long enough for a nap, Justin brought him into the water for a bath.

Not a word had passed between them, and as Justin played with his son in the water, Christina rose and walked a short distance up the beach. She reached a spot where a small fresh water spring ran into the ocean, and sitting there on the warm sand, she began tossing pebbles into the blue ocean water, waiting. When she next looked up, Justin was standing there.

"Chessy? Is he well?"

The concern in her eyes reminded him of who she was. "Yes."

"I'm so glad. I was worried."

Justin forced his gaze from her and looked out to the ocean. A ship sailed in the distance. For a long while he could not speak. Having imagined this scene a hundred times, and as an actor memorizes his part, he knew the exact words he would say. He knew how he would deliver the words. He had rehearsed a million times. But suddenly nothing mattered but a simple question.

"Christina, can you forgive me?"

"Yes," she said without a thought of hesitation. It was all so simple really; the one thing, the only thing she knew with certainty was that— "I love you and I don't want to live without you."

Justin struggled to believe the one response he had not imagined.

Seeing this, she asked the real question. "But I wonder, though, if you can forgive yourself?"

"I don't know." And he didn't. At first, after he had understood what had happened, he had been obsessed with the vision of changing it. Starting when Steffen reported seeing her with the French agents. Instead of fear, stating with absolute certainty— Christina did not do that! Then going straight to Christina to find out what had happened.

He was not a man to live long on an "if only," and after just a few days of this fool's fantasy, he faced what he had done and why.

He had committed a series of abhorrent mistakes, the worst of which was breaking the trust that bound her love to him. All because he was afraid. The unconscionable act of striking her was but a symptom of his fear. The fear that had grown from the lonely hours of his childhood to shadow the whole of his life.

The fear that he would never reach that distant shore, that he would never find someone who loved him.

His vulnerability tore swiftly at her heart and she stood up, stepping within an inch of touching him. "I wish you would," she whispered in a voice that felt to him like the soft caresses of a gentle breeze. "I want to go home to Boston. I want to watch the spring turn to summer there and summer to fall. I want to share the joy of watching our son grow. I want to paint. I want to have Sunday tea with Hanna and Jacob. I want to eat Hope's pies and listen to Rosarn and Aggie's silly chatter. Justin," her eyes pleaded with him to do what she knew would be hardest, "I want you to forgive yourself. I want to spend the rest of my life loving you."

He reached a hand to tenderly brush her face and she took that hand in her own and brought it to her lips. He could not believe what he was hearing. He could believe the love in the wide gray eyes. "Christina," he whispered in turn, "I don't deserve this."

"But it's yours," she said as tears filled her own eyes. "Yours with the promise that you'll never let me go again."

Justin swept her into his arms, and while he could not yet manage to say it, his arms and his lips, indeed his entire being spoke for him. He would never let her go. Not for anything on earth or in heaven. Not now and not in a distant forever. Never.